THE DARK SIDE OF HAPPINESS

THE DARK SIDE OF HAPPINESS

VALRUE BOOK ONE

COLEY TAYLOR

A catalogue record for this book is available from the National Library of New Zealand:

ISBN (ebook): **978-1-7386244-0-9**
ISBN (paperback): **978-1-7386244-1-6**
ISBN (hardback): **978-1-7386244-2-3**

Contents

Preface i

Dijak's Map iii

Glossary iv

Prologue v

Chapter 1 1

Chapter 2 6

Chapter 3 13

Chapter 4 19

Chapter 5 25

Chapter 6 31

Chapter 7 38

The First Letter 40

Chapter 8 41

Chapter 9 44

Chapter 10 50

Chapter 11 57

Chapter 12 59

Chapter 13 65

Chapter 14 71

Chapter 15 77

Chapter 16 82

Chapter 17 88

Chapter 18 94

The Eighth Letter 98

Chapter 19.. 100

Chapter 20.. 107

Chapter 21.. 114

Chapter 22.. 123

Chapter 23.. 137

Chapter 24.. 148

Chapter 25.. 160

Kimjit's Map of the Deadlands.................................... 167

Chapter 26.. 168

Chapter 27.. 180

The Twenty Sixth Letter 190

Chapter 28.. 192

Chapter 29.. 199

Chapter 30.. 214

Chapter 31.. 222

Chapter 32.. 231

Chapter 33.. 236

Chapter 34.. 246

Chapter 35.. 258

The Thirty Eighth Letter 266

Chapter 36.. 267

Chapter 37.. 272

Chapter 38.. 275

Chapter 39.. 285

Chapter 40.. 289

Chapter 41.. 299

Chapter 42 303

Chapter 43 307

Chapter 44 311

Chapter 45 313

Chapter 46 317

Chapter 47 319

Chapter 48 326

Chapter 49 330

Chapter 50 335

Chapter 51 337

Chapter 52 341

Chapter 53 347

Chapter 54 354

Chapter 55 361

Chapter 56 370

Chapter 57 377

Chapter 58 383

Chapter 59 385

Chapter 60 390

Chapter 61 395

Chapter 62 398

The Final Letter 401

Chapter 63 403

Chapter 64 407

Chapter 65 414

Chapter 66 417

Chapter 67...424

Chapter 68...427

Chapter 69...431

Chapter 70...437

Chapter 71...440

Chapter 72...444

Epilogue...448

About the Author 451

Preface

As any writer will understand, writing consumes you. *The Dark Side of Happiness* has taken over my life for the past year and a half, and I started writing it well before then. It turned out nothing like I expected, but I love it even more for that.

There are so many people I wish to thank. First, to Sean, my amazing husband, who put up with endless harassment on my part to read my work and answer seemingly trivial questions that I insisted were pivotal to the story. You put my mind at ease. Thank you for supporting me not only with my writing, but with all my other passions.

A shout out to Marilyn, Shania, Brandon, Sean, Shannon, Lauren, and Dani, in the order of who read *The Dark Side of Happiness* in various states of disrepair and contributed to its editing. Marilyn, you received the very first draft and gave me permission to pull things out. Dani, not only did you rescue me when I was panicking about something that Aren said, but you drew the map and brought Valrue out of my head onto paper. Shania, you dealt with my neuroticism when it came to the cover, which I changed four times. You are a legend.

I must also give a special mention to Harry and Juls for their advice and entertaining dramatic readings, and the glorious person who will never know they inspired Chapter 36. This is one of my favourite chapters.

Now, a quick note for my readers about the world I have built, and a bit of context. As well as a writer, I am a dietitian, and a lover of science. You will see a few shades of this coming through in *The Dark Side of Happiness*, particularly with regards to the state of the impoverished people living in Rue, and in the majik system.

There are quite a few Valrue-specific words woven throughout *The Dark Side of Happiness*. For anyone who appreciates a reminder of what's going on, (especially people who may not be able to read a whole book in one day, like my brother) I have included a glossary at the front. However, you might notice there are a few majikal terms missing. I purposefully kept a lot of mystery to the majik because my wish is for you to learn about it alongside the characters. I do hope you'll bear with me until the next book. I promise all will be revealed.

Finally, thank you to you, my reader, for choosing my book. I hope you fall in love with Valrue and its people the same way I did. At the time I write this, I am halfway through the second book, and dreaming of the third. If I'm entirely honest with you, I don't really know what's going to happen next, but I am so excited to have you along for the ride.

From Yours,
Coley Taylor

Dijak's Map

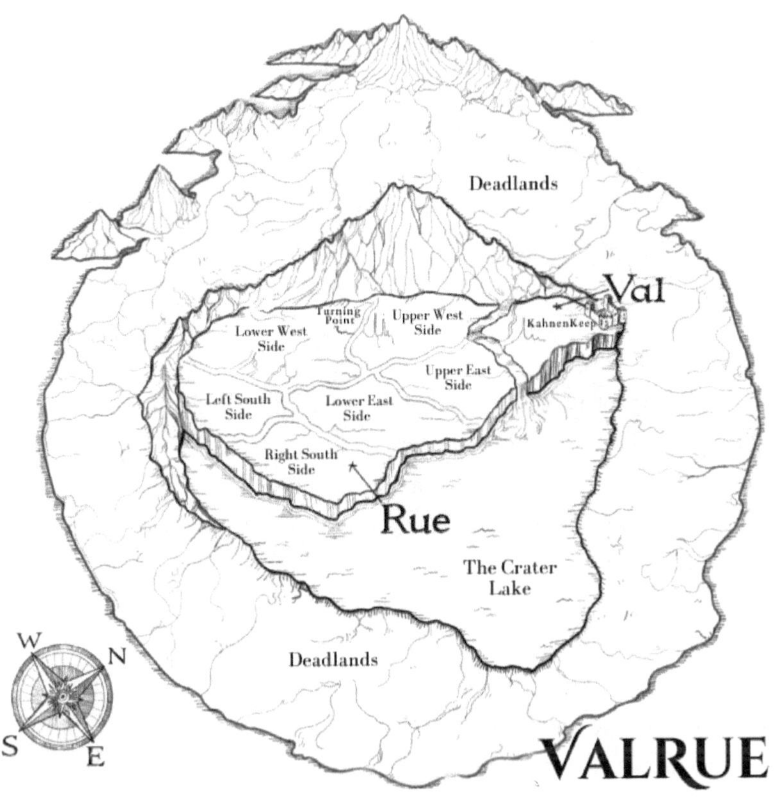

. . . A map of Valrue within her mountain crater. I imagine Rue looks different from how you remember, the streetling gangs having carved out their territories. The Deadlands continue to grow beyond the outline depicted, forming a barren expanse of such scale that no paper in my possession could hope to capture them. I do not envy the Krijen posted out there . . .

From Yours,
Dijak

Glossary

Harnessing ability – One of the two pillars of majik

Himajik – Significant majikal abilities

Kahn(en) – Minister(s) of Valrue

KahnenKeep – Government house

KahnenMayj(en) – Person(s) with majikal abilities in the employ of the Kahnen

KahnenMinder – Servants of the Kahnen

KahnenSpeaker – Voice of the Kahnen

Krijen (say Kree-jin) – Warriors of Valrue

Krije (say Kree-jay) – Ceremonial sword used by Krijen in combat

Lomajik – Limited majikal abilities

Making the Cross – Moving from Rue into Val

Mayj(en) – Person(s) with majikal abilities

Nomajik – No majikal abilities

Power – One of the two pillars of majik

Promise – Partner, typically engaged or wed

Skahk – Derogatory term for a mayj

Square(s) – Krijen in training

Squad – Group of Krijen, typically six, with a chosen leader

Streetling(s) – Homeless youth(s) living in Valrue

The People – Voting citizens of Valrue

Turned (to Turn oneself) – To die by harnessing power beyond what one has

Turning – When a mayj starts running out of power while harnessing. The sensation is highly addictive.

The Unsettlement – Crisis of majikal and natural imbalance in Valrue where, with humans as a key exception, an excess of majikal power drove almost all living things from the city

There is a character map at the back of this book.
It contains spoilers. Recommended to be viewed on book completion.

PROLOGUE

Nineteen years ago

Thunder broiled above the mouth of the mountain crater, but the rain fell quietly on the cobblestones in the city streets.

Inside the barn, it was hot and humid, the air turning heavy as the storm mounted. A dull light shone from a lamp on the floor, causing shadows to dance eerily across the scattered hay. A young woman knelt, head bowed, next to a thick wooden pillar in the centre of the barn. Her brow shimmered with sweat; hands wrapped so tightly around the pillar that the tips of her fingers had turned white.

Beneath her, her belly bulged.

The unborn babe seemed intent on taunting the young woman as she crunched forward with another contraction, having endured them for the better half of the day. She let out a low moan, echoing the heavens as thunder rumbled distantly.

The barn door snapped back on its hinges, and inside bustled an older woman. She had hollowed cheeks, and her grey hair was in disarray. She carried a wooden bucket in one hand and a dagger wrapped in clean rags and twine in the other. 'By the Great Kahn!' she cried. 'It must be nearly time!'

She set down the bucket and dipped a rag into the water, wringing it out and wiping her daughter's brow. The young woman sighed deeply before she winced and let out another moan.

'Come now,' the older woman said. 'It's time to push!' She squatted down beside her daughter and placed a steady hand on her back. 'Ready?'

The young woman clenched her jaw and heaved into her abdomen. Brilliant white light burst through the cracks in the barn walls, followed by a rumble of thunder.

'Don't forget to breathe! Breathe!'

The older woman picked up her daughter's sodden hemline and ducked her face under. 'Good, keep pushing!'

The young woman let out a faint cry and dropped her hands from the pillar, coming down to all fours on the barn floor, chest heaving.

'All right, dear, don't stop now! You're almost there!'

The patter of rain outside roared into a downpour, droplets escaping through the barn roof and plopping down into the bucket next to the two women.

Again the young woman groaned, her fingernails curling into the hay. Her mouth formed an 'o' as she pushed, and her white sleeping shirt clung to her protruding spine as it arched with the effort of her labour.

The young woman suddenly relaxed again, panting, shaking her head, tears joining the rain droplets on the floor. The older woman grabbed the remaining rags and tucked them between her daughter's legs. 'Come now, last push!'

The young woman shot her mother a venomous look before closing her eyes and gritting out a final yell, wrapping an arm around the pillar for leverage.

'That's it!' the older woman cried. Then, not a moment too soon, she reached beneath her daughter and deftly caught a stunned and bloodied baby boy.

The young woman let out a cry of triumph and collapsed weakly onto her side. 'Is it a boy? Let me see him,' she gasped. 'Is he okay? Is he healthy?' She twisted around, anxious to see her son.

The older woman glanced at her daughter before looking down at her grandson. His little body was red and swollen from the trauma of his birth, and he emitted tiny, mewling cries. The older woman bundled rags before herself and gently placed him on the ground.

'He's okay. Let me cut the cord before I give him to you.' She tied the twine tightly around the cord, knotting it close to the baby's belly before grabbing the dagger and pressing it down hard onto the cord, slicing through the tissue. She dropped the dagger next to the bucket, then pulled the rags up around the baby.

The young woman gave a cry of relief as her mother placed her son in her arms. She held him close to her face, breathing him in. 'Oh, he's beautiful! He's like his father,' she said, reaching out and brushing his tiny cheek with her thumb. Enthralled, she didn't see her mother's frown.

The older woman moved forward and stretched her arms out for the baby. 'Give him here. I'll get him cleaned up.'

The young woman shook her head. 'Not yet. You only just gave him to me. Look, look at his eyes.'

The older woman did not respond, instead looking towards the barn door as it creaked forward on its hinges, tugged by the brewing wind. She twisted her hands together, allowing her daughter as much time as she dared.

It was not long before she held her arms out once more. 'Give him here, my love. You're not done just yet. Then he'll need feeding.' She gently pulled her grandson from his mother's arms and nestled him into a cushion of hay beside her. The older woman was careful not to look at the baby this time. She shouldn't have done it before. From the corner of her eye, she saw a little fist break free from the rags, his arm curling up to his face. The older woman quickly turned away to tend to her daughter.

***

The storm had settled by the time the lamp went out. The older woman had only the moon to light her path as she crept back into the barn. She'd left her daughter to rest an hour ago, and she could see her angular figure asleep in the hay, curled around the drawer that held her baby boy. Her daughter had been too tired to move, so the older woman had provided the makeshift cot. She had tried to take the baby earlier, but her daughter would not settle unless he was close.

The hay crunched underfoot as the older woman preyed forward, cursing the Great Kahn she no longer had the storm to cover the sound of her deception. Steeling herself, she stepped over her daughter and reached down towards the dark outline of the sleeping baby, scooping the little bundle into her arms. She backed away.

The strip of moonlight coming in from the barn door lit up her frame, making her shadow stretch long in front of her, pointy at the edges. She stood still and quiet for a moment, feeling the tiny weight of her sleeping grandson in her arms. A snag of guilt taunted her, but she quashed it quickly. This was the right thing to do. The only thing she could do, to save her daughter. She had made her decision.

The older woman lifted her chin, clutched the baby to her chest, and strode out the barn door into the night.

CHAPTER 1:
AREN BHA

The dawn mist was dispersing as Aren eyed Jin across the sparring court. They'd been practising since before sunrise, and Aren was catching her breath from their latest round. Her hand smarted where Jin had rapped his dagger pommel across her knuckles.

Jin crouched across from her, a wicked grin on his handsome face. Rebelling against the brutally short Squares cut, Jin had allowed the top of his blond hair to grow out, and a few loose strands dangled over his forehead. His dark-brown eyes crinkled at the corners in amusement.

His arrogance annoyed Aren. It was her duty as his best friend to bring him down a peg or two. While Jin's tall frame would dissuade many others from duelling him, his size only stoked Aren's determination to win. Jin found this laughable, given Aren barely passed for five feet tall. But he was always happy to rise to her challenge.

Aren mimicked his exaggerated slowness as they paced around an invisible circle, not disturbing the quiet of the morning. It had been years since birdsong broke the dawn in Valrue. Aren couldn't even remember what it sounded like.

Aren's pearly-white hand hung limply next to her dagger, which was tucked into the wraps at her thigh. The sun was almost up now, and its blinding glare made her squint.

Jin moved like lightning across the space between them, removing his dagger from his wraps and plunging it down towards Aren's chest. Too late, she realised he'd waited to attack until she was staring directly into the sun.

Aren swung an arm up to meet his, but Jin's attack was so forceful it took all her strength to deflect it. She whipped her own dagger from her wraps and stabbed upwards at his exposed side.

Jin met her like a stone wall and shoved her arm back up above her head, straining her shoulder and sending a tremor down her spine. She grunted and withdrew, aware her entire torso had been exposed and Jin had ignored the opening. It was infuriating to know he was holding back.

Aren lunged, stabbing at the space where his gut should have been, but Jin had already twisted lazily away and grabbed her wrist as it soared past his waist. He tugged gently, not enough to hurt but plenty to pull her off balance. She staggered forward. Gritting her teeth, Aren spun back to face him.

Jin's grin broadened. He stood up out of his guard position and casually twirled his dagger in his hand, goading her.

Blood boiling, Aren feinted left, then changed direction and swapped her dagger into her other hand, stabbing wildly. The tip of Jin's dagger slipped under Aren's, and he grabbed the end of his own blade, trapping hers. He tugged her dagger from her grip.

Desperate, Aren reached into the folds of her thigh wraps and pulled out a second dagger, slashing viciously at him.

Jin stepped back, bringing his dagger hand to his side while flicking his empty hand up. The resulting burst of majik wrenched the second dagger from Aren's fingers and sent it sailing across the sparring court.

'You cheated!' Aren yelled as she stood, puffing and weaponless, her hands balled into fists. 'You can't win a sparring match by using *majik!*' She brought the word down to a hiss, eyes roaming the covered columns that bordered the sparring court. They were alone.

Jin slid his dagger back into the wraps at his thigh. 'You cheated first. We agreed on one dagger, not two.' He hadn't even broken a sweat.

Aren felt humiliated. Her cheeks were hot, her chest heaved, and her chin-length auburn hair stuck to her face. Her two daggers lay at either end of the sparring court, mocking reminders of her failure. 'It was a stupid agreement,' she snapped. 'A real enemy would come prepared!'

'Yes, but this is a sparring court, not the streets of Rue. You must follow the rules.' Jin folded his arms, still grinning.

Aren scowled and stalked off to collect her daggers. Jin was right, of course. There were rules of engagement, even if it wasn't a great likeness to being attacked on the streets. But there were also rules, albeit unspoken, about doing majik. Especially given the Unsettlement.

Aren tucked both daggers back inside her wraps and wandered back to Jin, who had sat down next to a nearby column. He pulled his waterskin from his satchel and took a drink before handing it to her. She took it, looking out at the sun-bleached sparring court.

The court was bordered by white stone tiles webbed with blue-grey veins. They matched the covered walkway surrounding it, the supporting columns also of the same stone. Multiple corridors branched off the walkway to different rooms of Aren's family home.

At the edge of the sparring court, there was a pond, the water within it so clear you could see the curved stone bottom. It was deep enough to swim in, which Aren had done frequently when she was younger. Shading the pond was a stone tree. The morning sun shone through its motionless leaves, speckling the water below.

Aren's family was one of the wealthiest in Valrue, having designed and produced weaponry for the Krijen since the founding of the city. To have a family name in Valrue was respectable. To have a name such as Bha was something else entirely. But Aren couldn't be bothered with all of that.

She sat down next to Jin, casting an eye over him as he pulled bread from his satchel. He tore off a piece and handed it to her before ripping off a chunk for himself, stuffing it into his mouth. 'Fuck, this is good,' he said, his voice muffled. 'Did Noel make this? A man of endless talents.' Jin leant back against the column, closing his eyes. 'You know,' he said as he chewed, 'you're getting better. When you crouch low like that? One of these days, I might actually have to put some effort in.'

Aren gazed distractedly out at the sparring court, untouched bread hanging from her hand.

'Aw, come on, Aren. I was only kidding.' Jin nudged her gently.

'Sorry. I was just thinking.' Aren made sure she had her serious face on when she spoke. 'You shouldn't use majik like that. You know better.'

Jin rolled his eyes. 'No one saw. You're not going to tell on me, are you?' He grinned and nudged her again. He was trying to lighten the mood.

'You know I wouldn't. But you really shouldn't do it.'

'You just want to win,' Jin teased.

Aren shot him her angriest look. He held his hands up. 'Fine. I won't use it. But you need to stop cheating.'

Aren threw her bread at him.

Jin snatched it from the air and stuck it in his mouth. Fifteen years as a Square had left him with the most enviable reflexes. It gave Aren a thought. 'When is your Dancing Ceremony? You're almost twenty-one. It must be soon.'

Squares trained from the age of five to become Krijen, a warrior. Their fearsome reputation was unparalleled. The ceremony determined if they would graduate as honourable Krijen or see fifteen years of their life end in disgrace, doomed to be Lost. Forever.

For the first time that morning, the smile wavered on Jin's face. 'I meant to tell you.' His hands dropped to thumb the dagger hilts at his thighs. 'It's in three days.'

'*What?*' Aren sat up straight, her mouth hanging open. 'Why didn't you say something?' Then she gasped, realising the extent of the betrayal. 'Or Bish? Or Marigold? Why didn't *they* tell me?'

Bish was Jin's closest friend in the Squares. He would also compete in the ceremony. Marigold was his promise. She was sweet and shy and mad about Bish. Aren loved that she was named after a flower. Once, Noel had shown her and Marigold a drawing of them from one of his books. They were beautiful.

Jin shrugged. 'I didn't keep it from you on purpose. It just hadn't come up. Don't blame Bish. When was the last time you saw him anyway?'

'Ages ago. But I saw Marigold yesterday, and she failed to mention it,' Aren said bitterly.

'Don't blame Marigold either,' Jin said. 'She knew I wanted to be the one to tell you.'

Aren made a face. It was true; Marigold was good like that. 'So,' Aren said, 'if your ceremony is in *three* days, explain why you're wasting your precious time sparring with me?'

Jin's grin returned. 'Are you saying you're not a worthy opponent?'

Aren wished she had more bread to throw at him. 'Leave my property, please. You're annoying me.'

Jin stood up obligingly. 'The ceremony is at noon at the arena,' he said. 'I know your father will be there, but will you come? Marigold is going, so you can sit with her.' He was still thumbing his daggers, a blatant show of nerves, which didn't surprise Aren. The Dancing Ceremony would petrify even the toughest Squares.

'Of course, I'll be there. I wouldn't miss it.'

'Thanks.'

Jin picked up his satchel and disappeared between the stone columns.

Her stomach rumbling, Aren stood up and headed to the kitchen, having thrown all her breakfast at Jin.

CHAPTER 2: THE GREAT KAHN

From his dais, the Great Kahn stared down the length of the stone slab before him. His house members sat on either side of it, three facing four. They were in a long windowless room to protect from prying eyes. Candles burned in brackets along the velvet-lined walls, causing shadows to flicker across the stern faces of the Eighth House as they murmured to one another.

Overall, the Great Kahn was quite pleased with his Kahnen this election. They were the People's choice, of course, voted in or out every two years, as was historical. A quick turnover, but if they were worthy of the role, they could stay in it for a lifetime. It was important for the Kahnen to feel a sense of empowerment to inspire them, and even more important that the People believed in a fair government. The Eighth House itself had re-elected him as the Great Kahn. It would not happen any other way, given his apotheosis over the last quarter of a century.

The Great Kahn raised his smooth brown hand ever so slightly, the murmurs dissolving into silence. The remaining KahnenMinders slipped out of the room, the heavy door closing behind them. Seven pairs of eyes turned to meet his.

'Welcome,' the Great Kahn said. He had a quiet voice, and the velvet-lined walls did little to help it resonate. The Kahnen leant towards him to hear better, as though bowing to him.

'Congratulations to our two newest members,' the Great Kahn began, nodding to a scholarly young man seated on his far left, Lord Flynn, then to an older woman on his far right, Lady Macey. The People had voted her in as a replacement for the late Lord Macey. It was obvious Lady Macey was the true strategist behind the couple's popularity and rapid rise through both social and political structures. The Great Kahn wondered how she would compare.

'We are here today to discuss the Unsettlement. For twenty years we have watched majik corrode our city. Several of you have approached me in recent times to raise new concerns and wish to present these to the house. You may do so today.' The Great Kahn directed his gaze to the balding, heavy-browed Lord Salli on his immediate left, who nodded and cleared his throat.

'We must take a more aggressive approach to quash this majikal *perversion*.' Lord Salli chewed on the last word, not bothering to temper his disgust. 'Despite the dire state of our city, there are still mayjen out there who continue to harness. We know that a mayj who harnesses their power does greater damage to the majikal and natural imbalance than a mayj who simply exists. It is clear these mayjen no longer feel an obligation, for the sake of their fellow citizens, to refrain from these selfish impulses. We must fight this wickedness. I have said it once, and I will say it again. We must. Criminalise. Majik.' Lord Salli ground out each word, as though he had something foul stuck in his throat.

His statement was met with the expected responses, with one exception. Lady Macey tilted her head to the side in supposed curiosity. The Great Kahn studied her carefully, but her face was unreadable. *How irksome*, he thought.

The full-lipped gentleman on Lord Salli's immediate left, Lord Reider, caught the Great Kahn's eye. The Great Kahn nodded.

Lord Reider took a moment to catch the gaze of each of his colleagues before he began. 'I agree with Lord Salli. The People are already familiar with the discouragement of majik. Criminalising it simply formalises this. It will be an important step in fighting for the return of balance. However, I wonder if we should consider a more discerning approach than a ban on all majik.'

The Great Kahn steepled his fingers in front of him as Lord Reider continued.

'As you are all aware, several KahnenMayjen remain in our employ for our own personal safety, and to support the Krijen with mayjen offenders. I wonder if we may be too hasty in criminalising all majik given it has its uses.'

Lord Flynn leant forward in his chair. 'The KahnenMayjen also use their majik to support several industries to improve efficiencies, do they not?'

At this, Lord Salli's brow furrowed so deeply it threw his eyes into shadow. 'To improve efficiencies?' he asked. 'Is it not counter-productive to use majik to make things easier when majik itself is the problem?' Several Kahnen nodded in agreement.

Lord Flynn tucked his chin, looking decidedly nervous under the fierce gaze of Lord Salli. But he did not back down. 'Valrue sits inside a mountain crater,' the young Kahn challenged. 'With the Deadlands stretching further around us, surely, we need to use majik, lest the city starve. How do you expect to bring resources across the Deadlands and up the mountain without majik? How do you expect to harvest crops, fell trees, and maintain the city stone, without majik?'

Lord Flynn is very fresh, the Great Kahn thought. Intelligent, perhaps, but new to this game. Not that what he said wasn't true, about Valrue. The city's location, once the envy of distant cities for its defences, now rendered it a victim of its own isolation. Valrue nestled atop a giant stone step inside the curve of the mountain crater, rolling down towards the now lifeless crater lake, the waters of which were impossibly deep.

Lord Reider shook his head in response to Lord Flynn's questions. 'It has been a long time since we relied on the KahnenMayjen, or on majik, in that way.'

Lord Salli's upper lip was curling. 'You think the People are struggling now,' he said, looking around the room once more. 'Wait until we are forced somewhere we cannot farm. We can no longer justify *any* use of majik given its impact on Valrue.'

A Kahn wearing an elegant dress and her curly hair piled on top of her head looked up at the Great Kahn.

'Yes, Lady Elira?'

'I have no qualms about criminalising majik for the People,' Lady Elira replied, 'nor for industrial purposes. It is long overdue. However, to forgo the protection of our KahnenMayjen? Surely their usefulness outweighs their influence on the balance.' Several Kahnen nodded in agreement, some looking alarmed at the thought of losing their majikal protectors.

The Great Kahn unsteepled his hands, laying them flat on the table in front of him. While the Kahnen's reliance on the KahnenMayjen galled him, he need no longer fight that battle. It was being dealt with.

'Your protection will not be compromised,' he said. 'The KahnenMayjen are already exempt from many laws. They will be exempt from this one.' Lady Elira nodded, satisfied.

The Great Kahn waited, knowing there was another objection coming. However, it was Lord Reider who spoke next.

'How will this be managed, my Great Lord? It might be possible to enforce this ban in the Deadlands and in the city streets with Krijen oversight, but we cannot monitor mayjen in their own homes.'

The Great Kahn could sense Lord Salli's excitement building. He'd been restraining himself well so far but given the way this conversation was going, it wouldn't take much to push him over the edge. The Great Kahn was happy to oblige. His expected objector clearly needed more prompting.

'It is sometimes troublesome to string up mayjen,' the Great Kahn said. 'Yet even with the Krijen cutting off their hands, it seems we have not dissuaded further offenders.'

Lord Salli's eyes lit up. 'Ah yes, my Great Lord,' he egged. 'Perhaps an additional deterrent? And if I may be so bold, I think we should be more proactive in our approach to exposing mayjen inclined to use majik.'

'You want to provoke them into harnessing?'

The Great Kahn's eyes snapped to the far end of the stone slab. Lady Macey had spoken without permission. He had expectations for the decorum of the Eighth House in these meetings. Unapproved contributions to the topics at hand could be damaging. However, the question seemed harmless, and she intrigued him. The irksome head tilt was still on his mind.

'Lady Macey, next time you will seek my approval before speaking.'

Lady Macey did not miss his threatening tone. She bowed her head in apology.

'Ask your question,' the Great Kahn commanded.

'I am sorry for speaking out of turn,' she said lifting her head. 'I merely wanted to clarify Lord Salli's intentions when he wishes to be *proactive.*'

Nothing in Lady Macey's tone or posture gave away her opinion. She was well-practised from years spent shadowing Lord Macey. It was a risk allowing her to contribute so early to the conversation, but it was necessary to learn about her. The Great Kahn did not care for puppets without strings.

'Yes, we must provoke them,' replied Lord Salli. 'Nowadays, most mayjen harness covertly, despite knowing the damage it causes. I see no issue with forcing their hand. Consider it a preventative measure.' He waited for a response from Lady Macey, but she only watched him silently, and he eventually turned his head away.

Frustration growing, the Great Kahn let his gaze settle upon Lady Hia. She was bone-white, her brown irises visible in their entirety from where the Great Kahn sat. If her jaw wasn't clamped shut, she would be wailing.

'Lady Hia,' the Great Kahn prompted, 'do you have any thoughts to share? Many of your voters are sympathetic to the mayjen.'

Lady Hia trembled in her seat. Despite her being the most weak-willed woman the Great Kahn had ever come across, the People had voted her in for a second term. While unusual, her emotional transparency had its uses.

'My-my Great Lord,' she stammered, 'I worry criminalising majik will break the trust we have worked to build with the People.' Her eyes darted wildly around the room, looking for support. None was forthcoming.

'You are naïve,' Lord Salli began, 'to think the People wish us to be merciful towards mayjen. Have you stepped foot in Rue lately? Have you seen what mayjen have done to them?'

'B-but I have worked so hard –'

Without warning, Lord Salli stood up and smacked his palms against the stone slab, sending Lady Hia cowering into her chair. 'Mayjen are scum!' he bellowed. 'We have pandered to them for too long. It is time we stood up for our city and cast out those skahks once and for all!'

Again, the Kahnen responded exactly as the Great Kahn expected, with one exception. Lord Oman clapped and banged on the stone slab in approval. Lady Elira sat back in her chair, a satisfied smirk on her face. Lady Hia scrabbled at her chest as though she'd been stabbed. Lord Flynn looked appalled, and Lord Reider frowned. But Lady Macey simply cocked her head again, watching. The Great Kahn did not like that. He raised his hand. Everyone fell abruptly into silence.

'Lady Macey,' the Great Kahn said. 'What say you?'

Her bland expression was quite intolerable as she looked up at him. 'If we have the loyalty of the Krijen and KahnenMayjen, I see no reason to protest.'

The Great Kahn waited, but she said nothing more. He stood up, and everyone rose with him. Lady Hia stumbled to her feet, looking stricken.

'We have a majority,' the Great Kahn said. 'Arrests are to be made at the discretion of the Krijen. I will enlist the KahnenMayjen for support and speak to the FaKrijen. Send a KahnenMinder for Oji.'

The Great Kahn waved his hand in dismissal and watched as everyone filed out of the room, Lady Macey leading Lady Hia gently by the elbow. At the door, she ushered Lady Hia through and turned back to look at the Great Kahn. Then she left, the heavy door slowly shutting behind her.

Almost immediately, a skinny KahnenMinder opened it again and shuffled sideways into the room, as though the Great Kahn might attack if he turned around. 'My Great Lord,' the KahnenMinder called. 'How can I serve you?' It was not customary to bow, but the KahnenMinder kept his head low as he edged closer.

The Kahnen have finally made their plans to rid the city of majik, the Great Kahn thought. And he had made his.

'I need you to do me a favour,' the Great Kahn said.

The KahnenMinder's eyebrows shot up into his hair. 'Of-of course, my Great Lord. Would you like this favour to be kept . . . between us?'

The Great Kahn nodded and smiled widely. 'You have a good instinct.' He strode towards the KahnenMinder, who shrank towards the ground as the Great Kahn bent down to whisper in his ear. 'You are familiar with the layout of the dungeons, yes?'

The KahnenMinder paled but nodded vigorously.

'You know the cell that backs onto the tunnels?'

Another nod.

'Do you know what is in this cell?'

This time the KahnenMinder shook his head.

'Good,' said the Great Kahn. 'Tonight, unlock the cell door and leave it open. *Wide* open.' He reached into his robes and pulled out a small silver key, which he dropped into the KahnenMinder's shaking palm. The Great Kahn wrapped his hands around those of the KahnenMinder, the key in the middle of their fists.

'Do not be seen. You know where my chambers are?'

The KahnenMinder nodded again, a bead of sweat threatening to break on his clammy forehead.

The Great Kahn also nodded, satisfied. 'Bring the key back to me when you are done.' He let go of the KahnenMinder's hands and stepped back. The KahnenMinder dove towards the door.

'One more thing, before you go,' the Great Kahn called.

The KahnenMinder paused in the doorway, his hand clutched on the frame.

'Do not look inside the cell.'

CHAPTER 3:
AREN BHA

Aren found Noel in the kitchen, putting together a tray of sweet preserves and freshly baked bread. He worked on a long bench that stretched down one side of the room, the wooden shutters in the wall before him flung open to let in the morning air. Cupboards, shelves, and jars of preserved food lined the other walls, and a large pot and an iron kettle hung in the fireplace next to the stone oven. A table and chairs that the maids sometimes used for meals occupied the middle of the room. Strips of dried meat hung down from the ceiling, high enough that Aren couldn't reach up to tear pieces off without a stool. She suspected Noel had done that on purpose.

Noel spoke but didn't look up as Aren entered. 'Another early morning spar with young Jin?'

Aren peered around Noel's shoulder to look at what he was doing, her hands clasped behind her back. 'He's so much better than me. I don't know why he bothers. Did you know his Dancing Ceremony is in three days?'

She moved to Noel's other side where the fresh buns beckoned, plump and still warm from the oven. They were fist-sized, made up of eight segments designed to be pulled off and smothered with preserve.

Aren's mouth watered. 'Are these going spare?'

Noel finished his tray arrangement and went to collect the steaming kettle from the fireplace. 'I don't believe any food goes spare these days,' he said as he picked the kettle up with a folded cloth and brought it back over to the tray. He placed it down carefully before finally looking at Aren.

Noel was one of those people whose age she could never tell. Aren wasn't sure if he was forty or sixty years old. He had white hair, but he wasn't balding. He had wise eyes, but very few wrinkles. He had hollowed temples, but his frame was strong and wiry. This morning he wore brown wraps with a lacy white apron tied around his waist. It made the maids giggle, but it was what he had to hand, and he insisted there was no point spoiling his wraps for the sake of masculine pride.

Aren looked forlornly at the buns. Noel sighed. 'Go on. I expect Jin ate all the ones I gave him and left none for you, did he?' Noel's eyes twinkled, but Aren shrugged. She had a tendency to throw food when Jin was around. Aren picked one up, ripped it in half, and dunked it into an open jar of preserve. She popped it in her mouth and savoured the feijoa flavour.

'I'll be right back.' Noel grabbed the tray and disappeared out the door to the main house, leaving Aren to her bun and her thoughts. A few minutes passed before Noel returned, heading to the pot on the stove.

'Noel, can I ask you something?'

Noel took a fresh spoon, dipped it in the pot, and blew on the soup. 'Mm. Yes, Aren?'

'What does it feel like, to do majik?'

Aren kept her voice low, unsure how he would react. She trusted Noel, but she'd pestered him on this topic too many times. Noel particularly disliked talking about majik.

Noel didn't answer at first. He slowly sipped his soup while Aren fidgeted with her wrist wraps. 'I've asked Jin before, but he's different,' she added nervously. 'I mean, I know you know more about majik than you say. I just wondered if maybe I *have* power, but I'm just not doing it right –' Aren caught herself before she said too much. Her cheeks reddened as Noel turned to her, a knowing look in his eye. 'Aren,' he said gently, 'you are blessed to have no majikal abilities.'

Aren's pride stung. What she wouldn't give to be a mayj, like Jin. She knew it was childish, but it was a difficult feeling to shake.

'Aren,' Noel said again, accurately reading her disappointment. 'Being a mayj is a curse, far more than a gift. You are lucky to be free of such a burden.'

'I don't understand,' Aren said quickly. 'Surely majik makes life easier? Or it used to, back when it was okay to harness?'

'I admire your curious mind, but you have a knack for picking topics you know I am reluctant to discuss.'

Aren gave him her best pleading look.

Noel sighed again. He walked to the table, pulled up a chair, and sat down. 'I cannot have you coveting majik. We will discuss this today and only today. Agreed?'

Aren nodded eagerly.

'With your own eyes, you can see what majik has done to this city,' Noel began. 'What it's done to divide the People. But what you might not know is that even before the Unsettlement, there was discontentment between the majikal and non-majikal community. It was sparked by the very jealousy you are feeling now.'

Aren felt the heat rise in her cheeks again, ashamed of herself. Noel, however, smiled at her. 'The difference is that you do not feel bitterness, unlike most people. You were born into wealth and have never wanted for anything in your life. Not everyone is so lucky. Imagine feeling inferior for being non-majikal, but also impoverished, and struggling just to survive. And then everything getting worse, because of majik.'

Noel clasped his hands in front of him. 'Being a mayj isn't to be desired, Aren. It's a condemnation. Young Jin, myself, and many others have majikal abilities, yes, but there has always been someone who hates us for it. The Unsettlement has seen us slandered worse than ever. Many mayjen stopped harnessing out of a sense of responsibility to Valrue, but also because of fear, and shame.'

Aren didn't know what to say. For once, she stayed silent.

Noel watched her for a moment. 'To answer your first question, to me, harnessing feels like moving a muscle. At first, it takes only a little effort, but if I do not stop myself and cut off the majik, I quickly tire. For other people, I imagine it might be more difficult, or easier even, depending on their power, harnessing ability, and experience.'

Aren screwed up her face in thought. 'So I could have power, but not be able to harness it?'

'Technically, yes. Harnessing ability and power are the two pillars of majik, but they have no correlation with one another.'

'So someone could also have lots of harnessing ability but no power? But wouldn't that make them nomajik?'

Noel scowled. 'A proper answer requires details I am not willing to give. But in short, no, they would still be a mayj. It would just be supremely easy to Turn oneself.'

Aren winced.

'There is much we don't know about majik,' Noel continued, 'and those with majikal knowledge are aware of the dangers of sharing it, given the Unsettlement.'

Aren could hear the warning in his tone, but he didn't get up and leave. He sat there, looking at her, clearly expecting more questions.

Hardly believing her luck, Aren hurried over to the table and pulled up the other chair to face Noel. She sat down and leant in close, propping her chin on her hands. She just had to be selective about her questions.

'How do you think the Unsettlement started?'

Noel seemed willing to answer this one. He frowned and scratched his white beard, thinking. Beards were not fashionable in Val and were even uncommon in Rue, where poverty was rife. They spoke of uncleanliness. Aren thought it peculiar that Noel kept his, neat and trimmed as it was.

'There are many theories about what led to the Unsettlement,' Noel said carefully, 'though we don't know for sure. Some think the Kahnen made a mistake with their correction planning and covered it up. Others think radical members of the mayjen community instigated it, though how or why, I do not know.'

Aren snapped her wrist wraps in thought. There was one question she'd pondered for some time. 'If an excess of majik is toxic to nature, wouldn't it hurt humans too? Aren't we considered a part of nature?'

'It's a good question,' Noel admitted. 'But you are wrong in your assumption. Humans may be created by nature, but they are the source of majik. We are the perfect example of nature and majik working in harmony. Or we were anyway.' Noel sat back in his chair, still fingering his beard. 'Despite our attempts to correct the imbalance, it has only grown worse. The forests continue to die back, and the animals are long gone. I doubt you even remember what an ant looks like.' He was right. Aren could only remember seeing drawings of them in Noel's books.

'It is a terrible shame how bad things have become,' Noel went on. 'I fear things will only grow worse as the People become more desperate, especially with tensions being what they are. But, like I said, even before the Unsettlement, it was bad. I couldn't believe what people were willing to do . . . But now . . .' Noel trailed off. He was looking into the fireplace, though Aren suspected his thoughts were elsewhere.

Aren opened her mouth, another question prancing on her tongue, when Noel cut across her. 'That's enough now,' he said tersely, a shadow falling over his face. He was still looking into the fireplace, so Aren couldn't tell if he was speaking to himself or to her. Either way, she sensed it was time to leave. She stood up and hastened towards the door.

'How many have we saved this past month?'

Aren turned back to face Noel. He was talking about the mayjen children, abandoned by their families to the mountain. Mayjen babies were often left outside the city's gates to die. It was inhuman.

What an ironic word, Aren thought. As if an association with humans made it any less cruel.

'Three,' Aren replied. She didn't understand why Noel asked about this now. 'The same as last month.'

'The Unsettlement is bringing out the worst in us,' Noel said. 'Jin's little performance this morning could get him into trouble.'

Aren shivered, despite the warmth in the kitchen. She'd thought no one had been watching.

It was a relief when Mae suddenly appeared at the kitchen door. 'Aren,' she said, spotting her daughter. 'I've been looking for you.'

Aren's mother was woven from purity with her gentle manner, rounded features, and rouge cheeks. Aren shared her freckles and light brown eyes, but other than that, Aren looked more like her father.

The weight in the air noticeably lifted as Mae swept into the room, her skirts swishing about her. Aren found her mother's love of swishy clothes rather impractical. Aren preferred to wear wraps, which fit tightly to the body. But truth be told, you could strap daggers under a skirt just as easily.

Mae looked serious. 'We've found another baby,' she said. 'The poor thing was out all night. I'm going to Mama Hidel's now. Noel, can you please wrap some food? We've got so many children there at the moment, Mama is struggling to feed everyone.'

Noel nodded and stood up, moving towards his benchtop. Aren would have loved to know what brought about his sudden change in mood. Maybe she would dare to ask him later.

Mae started collecting jars of preserves and loading them into her skirt pockets, another point of usefulness that caught Aren's interest. She entertained the idea briefly before picturing Jin, bent double, laughing his head off when she stepped into the sparring court wearing a skirt. She dismissed the idea after that.

'Let's go!' Mae had whipped around the kitchen in seconds and already had one foot out the door. Aren grabbed the satchel Noel had loaded with food and followed her mother, sparing him one last glance. He was gazing captivated out of the kitchen window, looking at something that wasn't there.

CHAPTER 4:
THE GREAT KAHN

The KahnenKeep was eerie at night. Of course, that was a byproduct of being carved into the mountain, so the moonlight became trapped before it cut too deep.

The Great Kahn did not fear being followed. No one would be so bold as that, other than perhaps the mercenary. But the Great Kahn was not going where that man would follow. He already knew these particular secrets.

At first, the Great Kahn had been reluctant to involve a mercenary. You didn't earn loyalty from men like that. You bought it. After painful deliberation, the Great Kahn decided he might not trust the man, but there was always more coin to give. It had been an enormous risk, but the Great Kahn suspected the mercenary would be worth it.

The Great Kahn was soon deep in the mountain, way beyond where the Kahnen or their Minders would ever need go. The tunnels he walked were long forgotten, and he had no intention of reminding the Kahnen of their existence. Lord Flynn, in particular, would be very interested to know what the Great Kahn kept here, given he had the dangerous persistence of a scholar. What he would find would leave him weak at the knees.

The Great Kahn stopped in the tunnel and held up his lantern. He made his way along the black wall, casting his eyes carefully. At one spot the light reflected sharply, bouncing off a palm-sized, circular plate set into the mountain rock. The plate was the darkest green, almost indistinguishable from the mountain wall in the darkness, apart from tiny webs of gold splayed across its surface.

The Great Kahn stared at it. He'd forgotten how much he hated this signature. He loathed to touch it. But he reached out anyway, grasping the plate and twisting it slowly.

With a quiet rumble, a section of the mountain wall slid open in front of the Great Kahn. He stepped through into a small room with rounded walls and a ceiling so high he couldn't see it. The lantern light licked at the walls, stacked with books. Some were in neat towers that went above his head; others were strewn about with pages torn and covers ripped off, destroyed in his many fits of frustration.

The Unsettlement. The Great Kahn had long suspected *who* had caused it. He just hadn't known *how*. He'd spent days, weeks, months of his life in this room, trying to find the answer. To save his city, he used to tell himself.

But of course, there was more to it than that.

The Great Kahn had been searching for clues in those letters for years, so when they'd stopped recently, he knew something had happened. That was when he'd sent the mercenary in. And now, thanks to that man, the Great Kahn finally knew the *how*. Unwittingly, in discovering this, the mercenary had also forced the Great Kahn to admit to himself the truth behind what drove him to desperation after all these years.

The *why*.

It ate away at him, stoked him, pained him. The Great Kahn had known the *why* from the beginning. He remembered, in chilling detail, the conversation that led to it.

The Great Kahn reached up to the wall and wrapped his hand around the twin plate that matched the one on the outside, twisting it until the door sealed shut. Using his lantern, he lit the candles in brackets spaced along the walls before setting it down on the floor.

The irony of him being in this room did not escape him. He was surrounded by every piece of literature in Valrue that had so much as a word of reference to majik, all hoarded here just after the Unsettlement began.

If only Mandavar could see him now.

The Great Kahn was not a mayj, yet he knew more of majik than anyone in the entire city. Not that it was difficult. The lack of majikal knowledge in Valrue was dumbfounding. Before the Unsettlement, there had been few mayjen, and even fewer with a commendable understanding of their own abilities. Now, with the excess of majik demanding majikal knowledge be smothered, what little remained was quickly being forgotten. Only the KahnenMayjen knew anything of consequence about majik anymore, and even they were an embarrassment now. The Great Kahn had no qualms about that. The current state of the KahnenMayjen was dire by his design.

The Great Kahn wandered past the stacks of books, searching. He had not been here since before reading that final letter the mercenary had given him, a piece of the *how* he'd waited on for two decades. Then, incredibly, the mercenary had given him that torn-out page. The game changer. Today was the beginning of the end of the Unsettlement. He could feel it in his bones.

Yet the torn-out page the mercenary had shown him niggled in the back of his mind. It stank of something he'd read over and over and eventually tossed aside. He still remembered it, likely because he'd felt it had brought him closest to the answer.

He found it.

It was a thin leather-bound black book, the corner jutting out from under a pile of scrolls. It was untitled, the author unknown, the pages filled with a hurried scrawl. When he'd first found it, the Great Kahn had grown excited, thinking it was Mandavar's personal notebook. However, after reading only a few words, he saw the letters did not have the slanting elegance of Mandavar's hand. It was not his, the disappointment of which was part of the reason the Great Kahn had discarded it quickly.

He pulled the book out from under the scrolls and walked over to the nearest lantern, flipping through it. The ink had bled through to the back of each yellowing page so the author could only write on one side. Despite the mess, it was mostly legible. The book cover was bendy with use, but the spine was intact.

The Great Kahn stopped on a page with a brief introductory paragraph, sections of which were drowned in ink.

Woven Majik X
The Weavers - X
The Spells of Weaving

While many mayjen scholars spent lifetimes in pursuit of majikal creation, only a handful were . . . let alone reproducible. This is not surprising given that a prerequisite, without exception, is to be of the Weaving expression. This section holds the descriptions of the select few creations that became known as spells. Of note, each spell is distinctive in function, though the bonds between them appear to be of the same nature, for lack of a . . . There is much debate . . . Spell, which demands further inquiry.

Beneath that were two descriptions the Great Kahn had read before, more delicately written than the rest, without any ink stains. While interesting, they held no clues as to the cause of the Unsettlement.

The Great Kahn turned the page to see another heading, a different section of notes. There was something off, though. The Great Kahn flipped back and reread the introduction. 'The select few creations that became known as spells.'

The select *few*.

There were only two descriptions. Did 'few' suggest there were more? Why not just write 'two'?

His heartbeat quickened as the Great Kahn pressed his fingers into the spine of the book, bending it backwards on itself like you are taught never to do. There, buried between the pages, right along the inside of the spine were the tiny, jagged remnants of a page that had carefully been

22

ripped out.

Oh, Mandavar.

So, the Great Kahn had never held the answer. The mercenary was worth his weight in coin, after all. How bittersweet.

23

The Thorson Spell

The Thorson Spell is the creation of a strong yet malleable bond between two or more objects. It is also called the Locking Spell, the bonded objects referred to as Lockstones.

Of great interest to the scholarly community, other objects can pass through the space between the Lockstones, leaving their connection intact. This finding gives further credence to the theory that, like Building, Weaving is the creation of bonds between matter, not of matter itself. Despite its profound contribution to our understanding of Weaving, the Thorson Spell is sadly renowned mostly for its use in majikal theatrics.

The first Weaver of the Thorson Spell is not known. The spell was named somewhat facetiously after its exploitation by the controversial vigilante Hugh Thorson. Thorson was best known as a notorious trickster who enjoyed locking criminals inside their own hideouts, before alerting the authorities. Being non-majikal, Thorson would pay for the Weaving of two objects together for his majik shows. He would convince the audience he was making objects fly, when really there was someone behind the stage moving one of the Lockstones.

The Thorson Spell became popular for the wealthy non-majikal population for the creation of easy slide doors, locks, and challenging architecture. The spell quickly became labelled as 'invasively redundant'. Given the influence of Woven majik on the delicate natural and majikal balance, its use for such mundane purposes was highly criticised.

The Thorson Spell is now thoroughly discouraged, even within the Weaving community, limiting further exploration of the spell.

A great shame, considering all its potential.

CHAPTER 5:
JIN KANJU

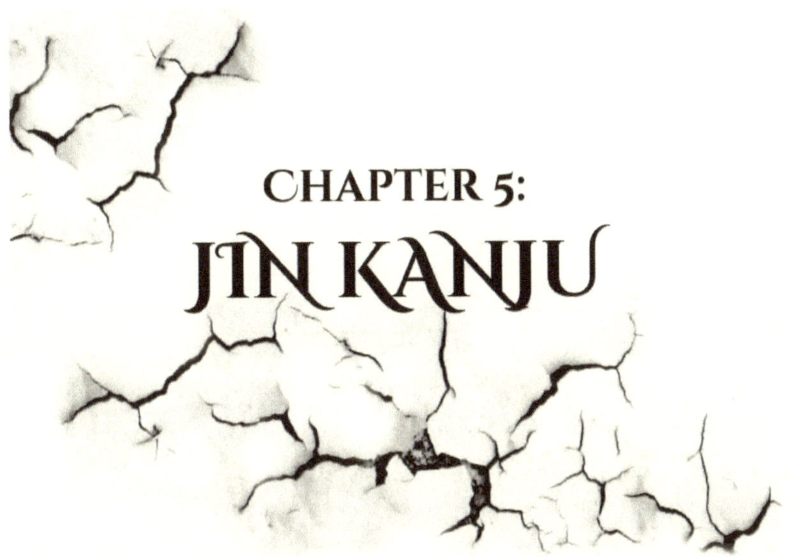

Three days went by quickly. The barracks were still dark when Jin woke on the morning of the ceremony. He lay in bed, staring at the bunk above him. Once again, one of the wooden slats hung down where the nail holding it in place had come loose. Jin reached up a hand and wiggled his fingers at the nail, releasing the tiniest flare of heat from his chest. It travelled up his arm and out through his fingertips, the slat creaking ever so quietly as the nail twisted back into place. Jin left his hand suspended there, distracted as he reminisced.

Finally, this day had come.

Fifteen years of rising with the dawn, eating the same shitty breakfast maize, getting smacked over and over and *over* by an endless onslaught of humility-inducing weapons until he learned to defend himself. He'd been beaten and inspired, torn down and pulled back up, eventually groomed into this thing he needed to be. Fifteen years of friendship and pain and determination had led him here.

Today he could become a Krijen warrior.

Today he could die.

Or worse, he could lose his dance in front of Aren and his father and Geni Igna and the Fifteenths, and he would've been better off dead anyway. Better that than being Lost.

Jin lowered his hand down onto the blankets. He heard a shuffling to his right and tilted his head towards the bunk opposite him. There, lying on his front with his bright eyes flashing in the darkness was Bish, his closest friend in the Squares.

Jin grinned at Bish. Bish frowned and inclined his head toward the door. Obliging, Jin swung his legs out of bed and began putting on his wraps, Bish doing the same. Somehow Bish had kept a small wiry figure despite a decade and a half of intense physical training. He had a thin face and pointed chin, the short Squares' cut doing nothing to flatter his thinning blond hair. Bish was kind and gentle and nothing like how Jin imagined a Krijen should be. Regardless, he was still a formidable opponent.

They both pulled on their boots and padded over to the barracks door. Jin pushed it open, leading the way out into the crisp morning air.

The Squares' training grounds were a rectangular expanse of land in the Lower East Side of Rue. The grounds contained fifteen sets of barracks, each barrack backing onto a large square of dirt used for training, hence the name. One hundred fresh-faced five-year-olds would start every year in the First Square. Each year, as they grew older, they progressed to the next barrack.

Not everyone made it to the Fifteenth Square, like Jin and Bish. It was not uncommon for the gruelling demands of combat training to get the better of the youngsters. If they made it through that, the tedious hours spent learning the Principles of War and Histories of Krijen Strategy and Command never failed to drive a few more to tantrum. In fact, Jin and Bish's barrack had particularly poor numbers, with only thirty-nine remaining. It was usually closer to fifty.

The sun had just started its steady climb into the blue as Jin and Bish headed towards the breakfast hall, even though breakfast was still an hour away. Usually they would be up already, doing their first fighting drills of the day like the rest of the Squares. For the first time in fifteen years, Geni Igna allowed them a morning reprieve. Today was the most important day of their lives, after all.

They wandered past the other barracks, watching some of the sparring techniques with vague interest turning to amusement as they neared the youngest Squares.

The Thirds had started the morning with hand-to-hand combat. One trainee had successfully flipped his much smaller opponent onto his back and was sitting proudly on his chest. His captive flailed his arms and legs uselessly.

'I remember when you used to do that to me,' Bish said to Jin as they stopped to observe.

'Not for long,' Jin replied.

They watched the little captive expectantly, but he had already given up, his arms and legs slumped in the dirt.

'Ah well,' said Jin. 'Not everyone can figure it out as fast as you.' He attempted to nudge Bish playfully in the ribs, but Bish instinctively sidestepped it. Jin groaned.

They carried on past the Seconds and Firsts, the massive groups of tiny children all sitting cross-legged and wide-eyed, facing their respective Geni. The stern-faced teachers stood at the top of each square, gesticulating about something or other. There were even a few girls sitting among the Squares. Usually, it wasn't until the Eighths or Ninths that they dropped out. Puberty was a resentful thing.

Jin pointed towards one boy at the back of the Firsts, who was curled up asleep, still not accustomed to the early mornings. Jin didn't envy the boy when his Geni spotted him. Geni were strict and laid out heavy expectations on the Squares from a young age. While this little boy may not get the smack across the shins and a month of cleaning the latrines that a Fourth might, he would still get a fairly humiliating reprimand.

Jin remembered one time as a Sixth he'd still been hungry after a meal. He'd snuck back into the line and taken a second serving for himself, leaving a comrade to go hungry. Given food was scarce in Valrue and he'd disrespected someone in his square, he'd received a noteworthy beating from his Geni and gone without an evening meal for a month. Not only did the broken ribs and hunger make training harder on top of everything else, but it was the only time he'd ever cried in front of Aren. Of course, Aren had gone straight to Noel, who'd come running with food and bandages. But Jin had quickly stiffened his upper lip and declined. He needed to see his punishments through. He regretted the tears; they hadn't been about the hurt, anyway.

The next night, Jin had sat with Bish while he ate his dinner, staring stoically at the empty spot on the table where his plate should have been. It sucked, but it felt right.

Jin and Bish reached the dining hall. It lay perpendicular to the First Square, forming an elongated T-shape with the barracks. Mealtimes were staggered and always ran smoothly as the Squares who weren't eating oversaw service. The Firsts ate first, the Fifteenths last. The Geni were Krijen, so they ate elsewhere.

Bish and Jin were far too early to start service, so they sat down on the wooden steps at the front of the building. Jin ran his hand through his new bristly hair. Bish had kindly helped him shave the top of it. Even Jin dared not flout the rules on the day of the ceremony, no matter how minor the rebellion.

'You shouldn't do it, you know,' Bish said suddenly, his voice low.

'Do what?' Jin dropped his hands from his scalp.

'You know what. You never could resist, could you?'

Jin felt a sting of annoyance. Trust Bish to sour the mood. 'That's what you're thinking about right now?' Jin asked. 'It's the morning of our fucking Dancing Ceremony and you're worried about me fixing a nail?'

'Don't act a fool,' Bish muttered.

Jin lay back on the steps and closed his eyes, letting the sun warm his eyelids. 'You're just stressed about today. Don't let my stupid antics bother you.'

The stair next to Jin creaked as Bish leant over. 'The ceremony scares me less than you doing majik,' Bish said quietly.

Jin opened one eye. 'Well, that's the most ridiculous thing I've ever heard.'

Bish looked unusually pale. Jin sat up again, glancing around to make sure no one was in earshot. 'What's got you so wound up about this now?

You've seen me use majik before.'

'Didn't you hear? The Kahnen criminalised majik. The Krijen have been ordered to purge the streets. They're to arrest anyone for majik of *any kind*.'

'Yes, but some people use majik frivolously. I'm not dumb enough to do that.'

'Oh?' Bish asked, his eyebrows raised. 'So why are you fixing bed slats in the barracks?'

Shit, he was right. Jin shrugged, unsure of what to say. Truthfully, he'd done it without thinking. He felt a little bad. When he'd told Aren the other day that he wouldn't do it anymore, he'd meant it.

But doing majik was like breathing to him. He had to try *not* to do it. He had enough control to avoid harnessing during his training, but sometimes his power just built up inside of him, and using a little here and there gave him some relief. Like scratching an itch, but better.

Bish still had that look on his face, the one that always made Jin feel guilty. 'Hey, I'm sorry,' Jin said. 'This morning with the nail, it was dumb. I promise I won't do it again.'

Bish looked imploringly at him. 'I wish I believed you. You're not taking this seriously.'

'I *am*,' Jin insisted. 'I just have other things on my mind today. So forgive me if I seem like I don't care.'

'Fine.' Bish turned his face towards the Squares again. 'How are you feeling anyway?'

'Like my insides are climbing up my throat.' Jin had actually felt okay until the smell of the breakfast maize began wafting out of the dining hall behind them. That, and his fingers were twitching slightly. It was as though the anticipation of the ceremony was stoking his power, just a little. He pressed the feeling down. Great Kahn save him if he harnessed during his dance.

'Mine too,' Bish said. 'What do we do if we end up against each other?'

Jin cringed inwardly. He should have expected Bish to ask that unspeakable question. But he turned to his friend and grinned. 'I promise not to use majik on you.'

Bish punched him hard in the shoulder. Jin could have avoided it, but he took the hit. He deserved it.

'Honestly though,' Jin said, 'the chances of that are pretty low. But we do have a smaller group than usual.'

'That's not helping.'

Jin grimaced, casting around for a different topic. 'How is Marigold?'

'Not good,' Bish replied. 'She's worried about the ceremony.' He would not be distracted from his gloom today.

The door to the dining hall behind them burst open and ricocheted off the wall, hinges rattling. Jin and Bish shot to their feet and rushed forward to help Cook, who had stumbled out of the dining room, shoving fistfuls of cutlery at them. 'Good! You're early,' she said. 'Get in here and help me. It's maize today,' she added unnecessarily, as Jin tried not to gag on the smell coming from the kitchen.

Cook stacked more mugs into Bish's already laden arms and winked at him before trotting back into the dining hall, whistling a tune. Jin laughed at Bish's wide-eyed expression. Cook always looked at Bish like he was something edible.

Balancing their stacks of kitchenware with practised ease, they followed Cook into the dining hall.

CHAPTER 6:
AREN BHA

The markets of Val were bustling on the morning of the Dancing Ceremony. Aren absentmindedly twisted her wrist wraps around her fingers. They snapped back into place loudly. Jin's upcoming dance was preoccupying her thoughts.

Snap!

He'd win, of course; he always won. He was the best at everything.

Snap!

But had she seen him spar with a krije? They'd only ever sparred with daggers.

Snap!

Of course, Jin would have trained with a krije. It was silly to think they would go to the ceremony not having used a krije before. She recalled him talking about it once and how you had to move a certain way . . .

Snap!

Aren swallowed. She was terrified of what might happen if Jin lost. She had tried to discuss the cruel fate of the Lost Squares countless times with Noel. 'It just seems wrong,' she always said. 'Wrong and wasteful.'

Noel always gave her different versions of the same answer: 'People know what they are risking. As long as they are ready to make that sacrifice, nothing will change. Let's not talk about this anymore.'

Snap!

When Aren pressed, Noel would get angry. 'Aren, you must stop this. It is an unseemly topic.' It was unfair that Noel would discuss many inane things at length, but on the Lost Squares, he refused to indulge her. However, Noel wasn't the exception. No one spoke of the Lost Squares. It bothered Aren to her core. She had brought it up once with Jin, and the horrified look on his face had been enough to ensure she never mentioned it again.

Snap!

'Aren! By the Great Lord Kahn, will you *stop* that?'

Aren looked up. Her mother was talking to a merchant peddling powdered spices. They both looked very disgruntled by Aren's wrap-snapping.

'Sorry, Ma.'

Aren dropped her hands. Her gaze settled on another pair of merchants having an animated discussion over a bucket of their pickled wares. Whatever it was, it smelled awful. Aren was about to turn back to the spice seller when a snippet of their conversation carried over to her.

'. . . Dead! Showed up floating in the lake this morning,' one of the men said, pointing in the direction of the distant crater lake.

'Never! Kian, you say?' The other man's mouth hung open. 'How'd he get there? I only saw him last night.' He rubbed his chin, looking thoughtful. 'Actually, now I think on it, I saw him on the bridge. Where did you say they found him?'

'Not far from the base of the waterfall.'

Both men were now rubbing their chins.

'Could he have fallen off the bridge into the river, then gone over the edge?'

'Nah. You'd have to be an idiot. There are a few gaps, but it would be hard to fall through.'

'He didn't . . . jump?'

'Nah, not Kian.'

'Do you think . . ? No.'

'What?'

The man's voice dropped so low Aren had to strain forward to hear.

'Did you hear about those murders? Someone's been killing mayjen.'

'Oh? Well, that's not such a bad idea. But Kian, a mayj? You've got to be joking. He's nomajik for sure. He hated mayjen. It would be lunacy for him to be one of them!'

Both men nodded in agreement. One of them spotted Aren, who had moved closer than she intended.

'Oi! You want a pickled egg?'

Ugh, Aren thought. That explained the smell. 'No, thank you,' she replied.

'Then keep your nose to yourself!'

Aren hastened back to the spice stall. Mae had heard the end of the conversation and glared after the men, affronted.

'What disgusting behaviour. And what is that *smell?*'

Mae turned back to the spice seller, who glowered at the pickled egg merchants. Pickled eggs did little to encourage business.

'Look,' Mae said, trying to draw Aren's attention. 'It's such a beautiful colour. Noel might like it to add to his bread, don't you think?'

The spice powder was golden and smelt sweet. Aren nodded enthusiastically.

'Great,' said Mae. 'I'll take one, please,' she said, pointing to the little bags of spice the seller had on her stall counter. Mae paid the required coin, and they continued through the market.

'Ma, have you heard about any murders?'

Her mother didn't answer immediately. She didn't like talking about things like this. Not with her daughter, at least.

'Only the usual.'

Aren thought over what the merchants had said. 'So nothing about mayjen killings, specifically?' Aren kept her voice low, leaning into her mother.

Mae looked very uncomfortable. 'I'm not sure.'

'Is it to do with the new ban against harnessing?'

'Let's not talk about this here.'

Aren gave up on her questions, disappointed.

Mae soon stopped at another cart selling root vegetables. People swamped it, eager to get their hands on fresh produce. The stall owners had two burly sons who stood in front of the cart, watching for sly hands.

Mae joined the queue. 'Aren, go get us some dried fruit, please.' Aren obediently headed off down the street with her satchel. 'And some limes!' her mother called after her.

The dried fruit stall was almost cleared out. Aren paid for two little bags of dried apple, then carried on towards the lime bank. The lime bank was just a grate in the wall, beyond which was a small room with a wooden desk and chair, the walls lined with large barrels of old limes. Aren had heard that half the people in Rue had no teeth for lack of limes.

Today, the grate was closed. Aren stopped and stared at it for a moment. She noticed a few other people doing the same, shaking their heads and muttering.

'Didn't open at all today,' said a voice behind her.

Aren turned to look at the speaker, a well-dressed elderly lady leaning on a walking stick. 'Didn't even get the delivery.' She pivoted on her stick and ambled away.

Aren wondered why she didn't have anyone with her. Val was safer than Rue, but Aren didn't think an elderly lady should wander about without protection. At least Aren had her daggers.

She pulled some dried apple from her satchel and nibbled on it as she headed back up the street. Over the tops of the buildings, Aren could see the black stone wall of the KahnenCull. The structure had always intrigued her, as immense as it was. She drifted down a side street, heading towards it to take a different route back to her mother.

The KahnenCull was its colloquial name, which Noel didn't like, but Aren did. It rolled off the tongue better than 'the Distribution Centre'.

All resources were routed through the KahnenCull as they came in through the Deadlands, allowing for their stocktake, sale, and distribution to the merchants of Valrue. Rumour had it the workers would take bribes to 'cull' goods from the incoming supply and reroute them to the highest bidder. And if you got caught, you'd be strung up on the bridge.

'You should not perpetuate those rumours,' Noel had said to her when Aren first repeated what she'd heard. 'I'm not saying they aren't true. Just that it's not safe to discuss such things.' Noel thought far too many things were unsafe to discuss, in Aren's opinion.

Aren rounded a corner, and the intimidating walls of the KahnenCull loomed abruptly before her. The black stone slabs predated the Unsettlement by at least three hundred years, harnessed there by a KahnenMayj. Aren had done her best to pry the story out of Noel, which he'd done with painful reluctance after weeks of pestering.

Using majik, each stone slab had been gouged from the mountain and transported to Val. Once there, they were hauled into place to form the walls of the KahnenCull and harnessed smooth, removing any possibility for it to be scaled by hand. Each stone face was so absurdly perfect that when the sun hit it, it reflected sheets of light and heat back onto the street.

Aren wondered how long it had taken. While Noel wouldn't tell her anything more and she had no frame of reference, she guessed it had been only weeks. Without majik, it would have been years, if not impossible.

Yet as Aren walked towards it, craning her neck up to see the top, it was clear that the People did not mourn the loss of such incredible majik. The walls were smeared with spit and human excrement.

Aren stopped at the base of the KahnenCull. Two black-wrapped Krijen roamed the entrance, the solid gates thrown open in deserved arrogance while they waited for the next consignment. The Krijen served as a better defence than any gate would anyway.

One of the Krijen stopped his pacing and silently regarded Aren. Aren was in awe of him. The Krijen looked so confident, so calm, his dagger hilts flashing at his thighs. It was strange to think that Jin might be one of them soon. And Bish too.

Eventually, the Krijen nodded at her and carried on.

Aren carried on as well. She followed the street as it curved back towards the market, connecting with the main thoroughfare. After about ten steps, Aren felt a crawl of paranoia up her spine, as if someone was watching her.

There was a multitude of streets intersecting the one where she stood, twisting and turning every which way. Each of them had pockets of darkness leading into doorways, down stone staircases, or to places Aren had not gone before. Having lived in Val her whole life, she knew it fairly well, though some of it was still a mystery. And Rue was over six times larger than Val. She couldn't get her head around how big it was, not that she'd really seen it. It wasn't often Aren and her family ventured over the bridge to Rue, but if they did, they never went beyond the Upper West Side. Well, at least not when Aren was with them.

Still feeling like she was being watched, Aren stopped in the street, digging through her satchel for another piece of apple while she slyly scoured her surroundings.

For some reason, her eyes were drawn down a side street to her right. Tucked away in the darkness was a small hunched figure. Aren strained to make out the detail of it. She wandered closer.

It was a beggar, a young-looking one at that. Chunks of black hair hung past his chin, framing a skeletal face. His cheeks were almost translucent under the unkempt fuzz of an immature beard and grime from the streets. His body was angular and strangely contorted beneath the filthy cloth he wore.

Aren felt a jolt as he turned his face towards her. She imagined this was what death looked like. Even his blue eyes, so rare in Valrue, lacked life. It had clearly been a long time since his last meal.

As Aren approached, she noted he acted differently from the other beggars in Val. They were not shy at all, always coming right up to you to plead for food; and when you gave them something, they would follow you down the street.

This beggar just sat there, shifting on the spot as she stopped in front of him, a blank expression on his face. She half expected him to turn and run away, but he didn't.

In fact, the beggar wasn't even looking at her anymore. His eyes darted down the street she'd walked up, then to the rooftops, then between other pockets of shadow.

Aren crouched down and gave him a gentle smile, drawing his eyes back to hers. 'Do you want something to eat?' She offered a piece of dried apple. The beggar flinched when she raised her hand but otherwise didn't respond.

Aren waved the dried apple in front of him. He didn't take it.

Aren sat back on her heels, confused. 'It's food,' she said, in case it wasn't clear. She held it out more earnestly. The beggar just stared.

Bewildered, Aren pulled the unopened bag of dried apple from her satchel and gently placed it on the ground in front of him. 'You can have this,' she said. 'We don't need it.'

Aren stood up slowly, so as not to scare him. He was looking back down the street again.

Baffled, Aren sent a final glance in his direction, then headed back to the main street in search of her mother.

CHAPTER 7:
PAKKER

It was hotter than usual today; excitement was in the air.
Pakker could smell it.

The day of the Dancing Ceremony had everyone riled up. It made it easier to do his job. People rushed about, ignoring everyone else. Ignoring him. People assumed crimes were committed at night because darkness created an illusion of secrecy, but it was just as easy to murder in broad daylight.

It wasn't even a challenge to spot the mayjen anymore. There were so many of them now, the Unsettlement causing their numbers to swell. And, of course, they were mostly children and youths, which was part of the problem. Harnessing was freshly illegal, but it would make no difference. It was hard to control a young population, especially one with streetlings. But streetlings weren't so much an issue in Val, where Pakker stood now. Rue was another story.

Pakker watched a little boy entertain himself by harnessing a stall owner's coin purse. The stall owner would pick up the purse when collecting payment from customers, then place it down on a small shelf by his knees.

The little boy sat among the contents of the neighbouring stall. With a flick of his wrist and a wicked grin, the little boy would make the purse zoom to the other side of the shelf. The stall owner became increasingly perplexed. Every time he reached for his purse, it was in a different spot.

After about ten minutes of this, bursting with suppressed glee, the little boy made the purse fly off the shelf, its contents spilling over the ground. The stall owner cried out in alarm. He scrambled around in the dirt while his bemused customers watched, questioning his sanity.

It would be effortless to draw the boy away from the stall. Bored children were supremely easy to trick.

Pakker was about to catch the little boy's attention when a petite auburn-haired girl stopped directly in front of him, blocking the boy from view. The girl wore expensive green wraps. Her head was bent, her chin-length hair obscuring her face as she dug into her satchel, surreptitiously checking her surroundings. Something had set her on edge.

The girl started towards a side street. Pakker followed, weaving between the crowd. He stopped before the mouth of the street, watching. The girl was walking towards a beggar huddled in the darkness. She crouched down in front of him, arm outstretched, holding something between her fingers.

Eventually, the girl dug into her satchel once more and dropped a little bag in front of the beggar, before wandering back towards Pakker. He turned his face away as she passed him. Then he looked back towards the beggar.

He wasn't behaving how Pakker would have expected. He didn't touch the bag; instead, he looked up at the sky. He kindled Pakker's curiosity, a rare thing. There was something off about this beggar.

There was a bang behind Pakker, and he whipped round to see a stall had collapsed, and bottles were rolling every which way. A few had shattered on the ground. The stall owner was yelling at the little boy, who burst into tears.

Pakker turned back to the beggar, only to find the street empty. He pondered the spot for a while before turning and striding past the collapsed stall, unperturbed by the broken glass and the whimpering cries of the little boy, who didn't even know what it meant to die.

The First Letter

To You

It has been only a few weeks, but there is so much I wish to tell you. Having had you as my confidant for the last five years, I feel rather disinclined to break that habit, so I have taken it upon myself to write to you, lest we grow estranged, in your absence. While it is impossible for me to forget you, I question my worthiness of remembrance in your eyes. I know you will laugh at this, but I simply cannot help it.

Let me begin by saying that while I struggle to understand the reason you left, I do not hold it against you. I am content knowing you are safe, far away from Him (you know to whom I am referring), even if it is also far away from me.

I must confess that last week, I heard a rumour about you that would have unnerved me, had I not already known it to be a lie. I must remember to not be hoodwinked by the harsh words of others. They do not know you like I do.

It may interest you to know that the docks are going well, though this has come about in a strange fashion. Fish are schooling so near the surface of the lake that sometimes they leap into the boat. Success overwhelms my fishermen. Many of them are even considering Making the Cross, once inconceivable, now a real possibility. I hope this good fortune will continue.

When you return, I will share with you my plans for expansion. So much of the lake remains unexplored. I believe if I can gather enough funds to employ a mayj of sufficient skill, we may find some real treasures in its depths. A suggestion of yours, if you recall.

I regret I must go now as the dawn calls, though I am glad my sleeplessness led me to write to you. I hope you find time to reply.

From Yours,
Dijak

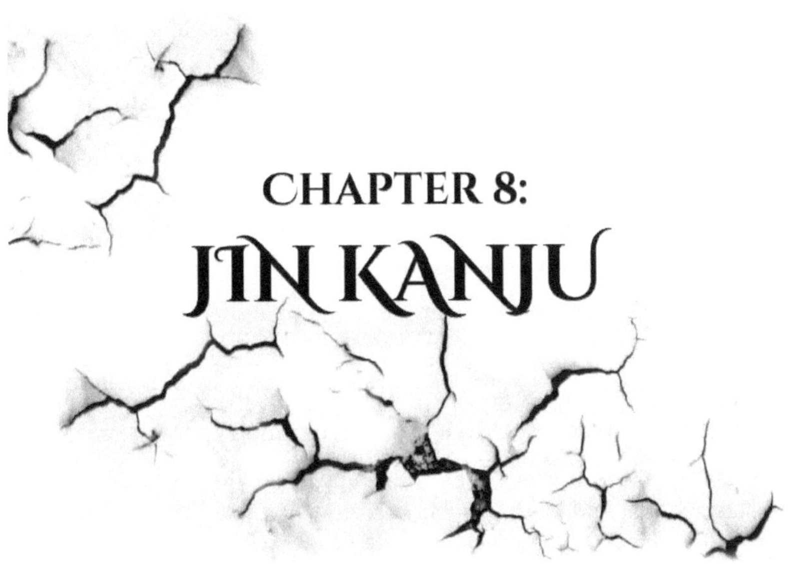

CHAPTER 8:
JIN KANJU

An hour later, Jin had finished his bowl of maize and was feeling strangely regretful it might be his last when FaKrijen Oji himself strode into the dining hall. Only years of brutal discipline kept Jin from dropping his spoon on the floor.

Immediately, the Squares rose from their benches and bowed their heads, left fists to their right clavicles. The Squares in the kitchen dropped their dirty plates and followed suit.

Jin was reeling. Other than the Geni, no Krijen ever set foot near the Squares' training grounds, let alone the FaKrijen. It was as surreal as if the Great Kahn himself had decided to take a stroll through the streets of Rue.

The FaKrijen nodded to the Squares as he stopped in the middle of the hall. Although he was not a tall man, he struck an impressive figure. He was barrel-chested with thighs like kegs, and his shock of white hair clashed with his dark-bronze skin, betraying his age. That, and the wrinkles around his eyes.

FaKrijen Oji was proof that bulk was not a barrier to speed. Jin was rattled by stories about the FaKrijen's younger days and the ferocity with which he fought.

The FaKrijen panned a solemn gaze over the Squares standing statuesque before him. 'Fifteenths, stay where you are,' he boomed, as though his body wasn't intimidating enough. 'Everyone else, you are dismissed.'

Jin's stomach dropped out beneath him. Fuck.

Squares fled neatly out the doors as FaKrijen Oji strode to the head of the long table where the Fifteenths stood. He stopped next to Jin, who suddenly felt very vulnerable, despite the weight of his weapons in his wraps.

'Congratulations,' said FaKrijen Oji. 'It is an achievement to be standing where you are. Already, you are warriors. Today, some of you will become Krijen. I know you will fight honourably. I want you to understand you will leave this day behind with my respect, whether you win or lose.'

What?

Jin felt the shock wave roll through the Fifteenths. Opposite him, Bish's eyes were as wide as he'd ever seen them.

FaKrijen Oji continued, unperturbed. 'With Geni Igna's blessing, I ask that you do me the honour of escorting you to your ceremony.' His words were met with a deafening silence. The FaKrijen looked down the two rows of Fifteenths, apparently expecting an answer.

Jin exchanged glances with Bish. Everyone knew it was beneath the FaKrijen to escort Squares anywhere, and Jin couldn't fathom why he would ask. But he was the FaKrijen. Surely they could not deny him?

The silence stretched on so long that Jin's palms tingled, power tugging on his nerves. It began to burn his fingertips. *Just do it*, he thought.

Jin cleared his throat, and he froze like a dumbstruck idiot as the FaKrijen and the Fifteenths all turned to look at him.

'It would be my honour to escort the Fifteenths,' FaKrijen Oji repeated.

Geni Igna will break my ribs again, for this, Jin winced. 'It would be our honour, FaKrijen Oji,' he said, bowing his head. The rest of the Fifteenths followed suit.

When Jin looked up again, the FaKrijen appeared satisfied. 'I expect you need time to prepare yourselves,' he said. 'I will see you at the Fifteenth Square in one hour.' With that, the FaKrijen turned and strode back out of the hall.

The Fifteenths stared after him. 'What the fuck was *that?*' Jin asked. Bish shook his head, bewildered. 'I don't know.'

Everyone began talking at once.

'Why did he come here?'

'FaKrijen *don't* escort Squares.'

'Is something happening at the ceremony that we don't know about?'

Jin leant towards Bish. 'Did we miss something?' he asked. 'Is this part of the ceremony?'

'No,' Bish said. He looked even more pale than he had this morning. 'This is completely . . . new.'

'Great,' Jin groaned.

The others began moving around them, heading back towards the barracks. 'Great Kahn help me,' Jin muttered as they walked down the steps of the dining hall. Hopefully, Geni Igna would at least save his beating until after the ceremony.

CHAPTER 9: AREN BHA

The day was rolling by slowly. Aren wondered if it was because of the impending ceremony, due to begin at noon. She wanted it to be over, but the sun had other ideas, motionless in the sky. Rather than spending the remaining hours pacing at home, Mae suggested a visit to Mama Hidel's.

The brothel was a large verandaed building on a bustling street corner. Mama Hidel kept an immaculate facade and wouldn't allow her women in through the front lest it 'ruin the illusion', in her words. It meant the building had multiple hidden back doors, which came in handy. Although Mama Hidel and the Bha family went back a long way, Mae was distressed at what people would think if they were seen visiting too frequently.

Today they used the entrance in the apothecary shop that backed onto the brothel. Noel and Mae both visited the shop regularly to pick up tonics, bandages, and other such things. People thought nothing of Mae Bha and her daughter coming and going.

While Aren gave a convincing pretence of perusing the shelves, Mae walked up to the owner, winking as she slipped a coin into his rough hands. He collected a lantern from his bench, and they followed him through to the back room, the far wall of which was dominated by a solid wooden door. The owner slipped a key from his wraps into the lock, and it opened noiselessly, worn with use. Mae and Aren nodded to him as they slipped past, Aren taking the lantern from him as they went. The door closed with a puff of air behind them.

They headed down the sloping dark tunnel, the temperature dropping. They passed other doors, marking different entrances. Many were now blocked by falling rock and debris or were permanently jammed from disuse. Eventually, they reached the end of the tunnel, marked by another door. It had no handle of any kind. Aren rapped ten times in quick succession, eager to get out of the cold.

The door swung open immediately, exposing the silhouette of a woman wearing a floor-length, bulbous skirt and a corset supporting an enormous bosom.

'Mae and Aren, my dears! Come in, come in!'

Mama Hidel stood back and let them enter a well-lit corridor with a red carpet lining the wooden floor. Staircases spiralled at both ends of the corridor, the far ones leading up, the ones next to them leading down. Mama Hidel led the way down the stairs to the bottom floor where there was a single door. She unlocked it and pushed it open, revealing a large wine cellar. It had been cleared of all its barrels years ago, but the scent of wine lingered. Wooden sleeping cots lined the walls nearest to them. In the middle of the room, children and toddlers of various ages played with a scattering of toys.

Mama Hidel bustled over to a crib and plucked a baby from it, placing it on her bosom. The tiny thing looked in danger of being consumed by her cleavage.

'Awen! Mae!'

Children crowded them as they entered. Aren picked up a little girl who threw her arms around Aren's neck. 'Hi, Piko,' Aren cooed.

A young boy ran over and began tugging on her wraps. At five, Boju was the oldest of the children and extremely precocious. 'You've been gone *ages*,' he said, pouting up at her in disapproval.

Aren stifled a laugh. It had only been three days.

'I'm sorry, Boju,' Aren said kindly, while Piko bounced on her hip.

Boju was not consoled. 'We don't get sweets anymore,' he said, 'so now I have to make my bed for nothing!' He looked utterly distraught.

'Well,' Aren said gently, 'I don't have sweets, but how about this?' She leant down and gave him a big kiss on his cheek, making him squeal in delight.

Aren put Piko down and turned back to her mother and Mama Hidel. Mae had a one-year-old girl slung across her hip, who was tugging hard on her necklace.

'*No*, Clara,' Mama Hidel tutted, leaning forward and gently tapping the little girl on the nose. 'No harnessing.' Clara looked at Mama Hidel with big eyes. The necklace slackened a touch.

'I don't know how you do it, Mama,' Mae said, massaging her neck with her free hand.

'Bah,' Mama Hidel scoffed, 'these little ones are nothing compared to that lot.' She pointed an accusatory finger towards the ceiling, though Aren could hear the endearment in her voice as she spoke about her women.

Mama Hidel glanced down at the baby on her bosom, still sleeping soundly. 'This little one was lucky to survive. Barely a month old, I think, but he's got a big set of lungs on him.'

'Are you sure he's a mayj?' Mae asked. 'He's so young.'

Mama Hidel shrugged. 'We will find out. His mama gave him up for a reason. Now.' Her face grew serious. 'I need to talk to you about my niece. You remember Maude?'

Aren nodded, thinking of the curious Bhouli girl who visited two years ago. Aren vividly remembered the white-ink patterns that crept down from under Maude's headscarf and curled across her face, stark against her deep-umber cheek. Aren thought at the time that it was cruel to tattoo a child, but Maude had giggled when Aren mentioned it and showed her the ink pot and brush that she used for the temporary patterns. She said that when she was sure of herself, she would do them permanently.

Maude had found it very amusing that Aren had no patterns on her at all. 'But you're so old!' the Bhouli girl had said. 'How can you not know anything about yourself?'

Most curious of all about Maude was that mayjen couldn't harness around her. Jin had met her only once, at Aren's house. He'd become very sweaty and pale, before staggering from the room, unable to return. Noel had looked mildly uncomfortable, managing to keep his composure, but even he excused himself after a while, apologising for not knowing what had come over him. Eventually, to spare them both further humiliation, Mama Hidel had explained the strange phenomenon of her niece. After that, Jin stayed away from Maude, which Aren thought was a shame. Although Maude was odd, she was also very sweet. Aren figured she would be around thirteen now.

'Come!' Mama Hidel said, placing the sleeping baby back in his crib.

Mae gently placed Clara on the floor with the other children before Mama Hidel ushered them back out the door and up the stairs to the next landing. The small space was crammed with a wooden table and chairs and shelves of dried and pickled food. Mama Hidel's private rooms were off to the side through an open archway.

A scantily clad woman with long dark hair was sitting at the table. Mama Hidel placed a hand on her shoulder. 'Dhuna, could you keep an eye on the children for a moment?' Dhuna stood up gracefully and started down the stairs from which they had come.

Mama Hidel was fiercely protective of her women. She trusted them without question, and they, her. Aren had gleaned only a few stories, but it seemed many of them owed Mama Hidel their lives. Aren suspected there were even a few lomajik women working here.

Aren felt her cheeks redden as she thought back to her conversation only days ago with Noel. She felt naïve in admitting her jealousy of mayjen. Being able to harness didn't necessarily get you far in a place like Valrue.

Mae and Aren sat down at the table. Mama Hidel took Aren's satchel from her and emptied it onto the table while she spoke.

'Maude is coming to stay with me from next week. My sister wants her out of Rue. She thinks she'll be safer in Val.' Mama Hidel sniffed loudly. 'I'm sure you've heard they've criminalised majik.' She slammed a jar of preserve down on the table. 'I mean, have you *heard?*' she repeated, her voice rising. 'Eliza saw the Krijen arrest the neighbouring shopkeeper yesterday. They caught him harnessing in the street.' Mama Hidel pulled a chunk of dried meat from the satchel and started tearing strips off it forcefully. 'His children, Great Kahn save their souls, saw the entire thing. Everyone is speculating whether he'll lose his hands, but I don't know why they bother because he'll be strung up anyway, and he's in no state to survive that.'

Mama Hidel had become so aggressive with her food preparations that jars of preserve were rattling on the table. Aren saw her mother glance upwards nervously. They weren't far from the main rooms of the brothel.

'Could you imagine if the Kahnen knew what Maude could do?' Mama Hidel went on. 'My sister is terrified at the thought. They'd take her away and exploit her!'

The brothel owner suddenly brought both fists down hard onto the table, making Mae and Aren jump. 'Great Kahn *save us* from those bigoted, cowardly Kahnen!' she shouted, her huge bosom rising and falling with exertion.

Mama Hidel was one of the fiercest women that Aren knew. It was a shock to realise she'd reached her breaking point.

'Mama,' Aren said, 'it'll be okay. Maude will be safe here.'

'No, she won't.' Mama Hidel looked up at Aren, whose next words died in her throat at the brothel owner's expression.

'No, Aren. This is it. The beginning of the end. They'll string up anyone now, anyone at all. Even the ones who are harnessing just to survive.' Mama Hidel leant on the table, studying its worn surface. 'We can't keep taking in new children. There's no room. There's nowhere else for them to go, either. They'll all end up as streetlings. That, or dead. I know it.'

Aren looked to her mother, but Mae was limp next to her, saying nothing. The silence was like a heartbeat, throbbing and reminiscent of their glaring mortality.

Mae was the first to break it. 'We could take some children home to the mansion,' she said. 'We have plenty of room.'

'No,' Mama Hidel said. 'You know Sid wouldn't cope.'

'He wouldn't want to think there was more we could've done.'

'No. You do too much already. *No,*' Mama said more firmly as Mae opened her mouth to protest.

'What about Maude?' Aren asked. 'We can take her.'

'That's a kind offer,' said Mama Hidel, 'but I want her here. She'll not be able to help with the children, but I promised her mother she could stay with me.' Aren nodded, though couldn't shake the dread that had settled over her.

'We have to go,' Mae said to Mama Hidel. 'The Dancing Ceremony is at noon. We want to be there to support Jin and Bish.'

Aren's heart began thumping in her chest. Mama Hidel gasped and put a hand up to her bosom. 'Oh, of course, they are both dancing today! Yes, you must leave,' she said, standing up and swatting at them. 'Jin will be looking for you, Aren.'

Aren stood up alongside her mother. 'Jin won't notice if I'm there or not. Today is the most important day of his life.'

'Whatever you say, my dear,' Mama Hidel said. 'I never could bring myself to watch a ceremony. The poor things. Jin and Bish must be terrified.'

'They'll both win,' Aren said, louder than she intended. She couldn't bear the thought if they didn't.

Mae inclined her head towards the stairs. 'Let's go. You'll be okay, Mama?' She placed her hand on Mama Hidel's arm, looking at her with concern. Mama Hidel smiled, but it didn't meet her eyes. 'You underestimate me,' she said. 'Get yourselves off now. Cheer hard for me!'

CHAPTER 10:
JIN KANJU

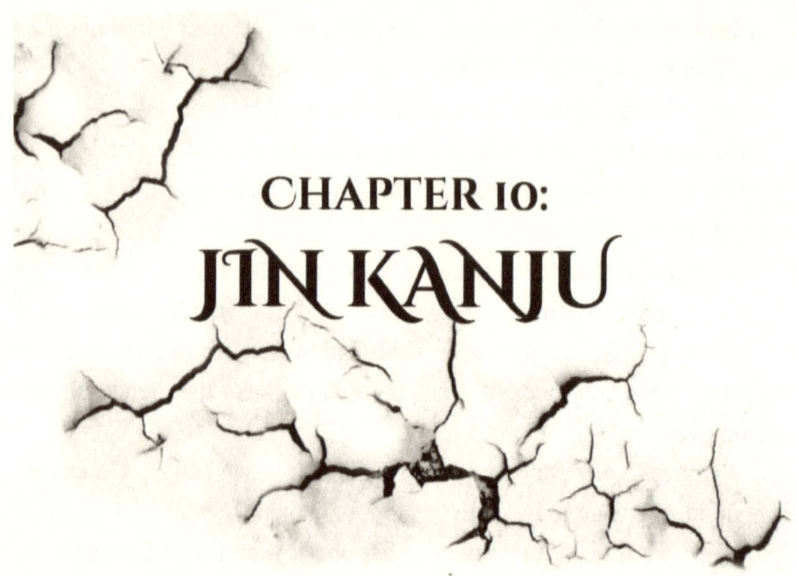

True to his word, FaKrijen Oji met the Fifteenths at their Square later that morning. The younger Squares watched from afar, jaws dropping, as the FaKrijen led the Fifteenths through the gates.

To Jin's relief, Geni Igna hadn't so much as glanced at him, instead falling into deferential step behind the FaKrijen alongside his Fifteenths.

By noon, they stood in the arena. It was a sand-covered square not dissimilar to the one from which they had come, but on an enormous scale. Tiered stone seating rose high above them on every side, making Jin feel like he was standing in the mouth of a giant beast. There were no markings on the ground, a reminder that the entire arena was open to them for the dance.

Jin could feel the weight of his krije on his back, tucked tightly into his wraps. The thin sword was the only weapon they were allowed to use, stripped of everything else. He wished he'd spent more time sparring without his daggers at his thighs. He felt too light.

But it was too late now.

The sun pounded down on them, the heat burning his shoulders beneath his black wraps.

In that moment, Jin felt a surge of admiration for the young men he stood next to. They all seemed calm and in control, but underneath the forbearance, he knew they were shitting themselves.

FaKrijen Oji courteously stepped away, allowing Geni Igna a final word with his Fifteenths.

But Geni Igna did not say anything. He passed his gaze to each of them, his expression encompassing everything he needed to say, and they to him.

For Jin, there was a surprising yet overwhelming sense of gratitude. Geni Igna had been a severe and unwavering constant in their lives. Over the years, Geni Igna had turned Jin's despise for him into a grudging respect; and only now, at the very end, did Jin understand why Geni Igna had treated them so mercilessly. He'd made them strong at the expense of kindness so that no matter what happened today, they could handle what came next.

The spectators were arriving. Throngs of people spilled into the square, climbing the stone steps, bickering over where to sit.

Jin shuddered, defenceless from the piercing, joyful screams of the crowd. His palms tingled, so he squeezed his fists tight and breathed deeply. His father was probably watching, and Jin knew it was cowardly not to look for him, but he couldn't bring himself to do it. Not today.

Aren was coming.

Soon it would all be over.

Bish was looking over the stands, searching for Marigold. The other Fifteenths already had their eyes locked on family or friends in the crowd, barred from approaching them until after the ceremony. They nodded curtly while their families waved and cheered.

Jin spotted Sid Bha, Aren's father, standing with a small group of Kahnen, not from the Eighth House. As Weapons Master – and therefore familiar with Squares' etiquette – Sid did not wave, instead giving a courteous nod. Then Sid turned to someone, and Jin saw Mae making her way towards him, jostled by the crowd. Marigold was behind her. Jin saw the relief on Bish's face as he spotted his promise. Jin still could not see Aren.

Geni Igna called an order, the actual words lost in the noise but entirely clear in meaning. *It is time to go.*

The Fifteenths circled their Geni and saluted, their heads bowed. The crowd hushed, and dawdlers rushed to their seats.

Geni Igna led them to the stands where a strip of empty stone awaited them. They sat, shoulders touching, staring down at the bare, goading earth of the arena.

A man with his dark hair pulled back and a curious upward turn of his mouth stepped forward from the stands, clearing his throat loudly. Jin recognised him as one of the KahnenSpeakers, a hand-picked voice of the Kahnen. Despite their controversial role in announcing the bidding of the Kahnen, Speakers were often well-liked, typically being former bards. They knew how to please an audience.

The crowd fell silent as the Speaker strode to the middle of the arena. 'Welcome!' he boomed impressively, considering his small frame. 'I am Teal, voice of the Eighth House. It is my honour to host this year's Dancing Ceremony. For those of you unfamiliar with the ceremony, the Fifteenths will be randomly assigned a dancing partner. Each pair will dance over the course of the afternoon, aiming to disarm one another. The undefeated Fifteenths will become Krijen, and tonight we will drink a glass to their victories!'

The crowd roared. Jin's heart pounded in time with the drums in the stands, his vision blurring across the faces in the crowd. Teal had spoken too quickly. Already Geni Igna was walking towards the Speaker to announce the first dancers.

Finally, Jin saw her. Aren was walking right next to Marigold as they made their way up into the stands. She was smiling and waving at him, as though she'd been there the whole time.

Jin let out a breath he didn't know he'd been holding and looked up to the sky. He was ready.

Geni Igna leant in towards Teal. The Fifteenths all watched his mouth move. Teal nodded and turned to face them, waiting for the rumble of the crowd to die down.

'Will the first dancers step forward,' Teal began, his voice still impossibly loud, 'Bishinrojak Lonli and Prinn To!'

Oh *fuck*. Bish was fighting first.

Bish stood up immediately, and with one smooth movement, he slid his krije out from behind his back. He walked to the centre of the arena, followed by a stone-faced Prinn.

The crowd bellowed their approval. Jin felt a pang in his gut, like someone had stabbed him with a dagger and twisted it. One of his friends was about to ruin the other. This was the price they paid to be Krijen.

Bish twirled his krije slowly and swapped it between his hands, loosening his wrists. In some ways, it was a relief that Bish was going first. Too long sitting on this stone seat was going to leave Jin stiff before his dance. That, and he'd soon be partially cooked from the sun, like a rare steak from the history books, crisp around the edges but still bloody on the inside.

Prinn had also pulled out his krije. He stood some distance from Bish, shrugging his massive shoulders. They had fought countless times before. Like brothers, they knew each other, every strength, every flaw. Prinn was not much taller than Bish, but he had a hulking form. Bish looked shockingly small next to him.

Jin sat on his hands to stop them from twitching, no longer having his daggers to thumb.

Geni Igna paced to a spot just behind the dancers where he could observe better. While there were no physical boundaries, there were rules of engagement, and Geni Igna would not hesitate to enforce them.

Teal turned to face the dancers who sank into their stances, krije tips hovering above the ground, waiting.

'You may begin!'

Instantly, Prinn crossed the distance between them, driving his krije down towards Bish's neck. With the sharp sound of metal on metal, Bish parried expertly and pushed back, krije flashing. Already Jin and the Fifteenths were out of their seats, Teal stumbling as he rushed to get out of the way.

The pair swung and parried, swung and parried, Bish backing towards the crowd. It was difficult to follow the dancers' movements from this distance, given how fast they were fighting. It took enormous effort for Jin to stay where he was and not rush forward into the arena.

Suddenly, Bish got a free hand under Prinn's wielding arm and shoved, forcing Prinn's krije from its trajectory. Prinn threw his hips to the side to avoid the tip of Bish's blade as it sliced towards him before darting away, putting distance between them again.

The arena held bated breath while the two dancers paused, before Prinn drove forward and locked them into another series of swings and parries. The pair edged closer to the lowest stone tier. The audience began to titter and shove, spilling onto the sand as they spaced a wide circle around the pair.

The dancers were not distracted by the proximity of the crowd. Bish's back was to the stands, and with Prinn's next swing, Bish's heel grazed the stone. In the split second it took Prinn to bring his krije back around, Bish grabbed the end of his own blade in his free hand and brought it up to meet Prinn's attack. The resulting clang reverberated around the arena, drawing a collective gasp from the crowd.

Prinn took the impact well, but it slowed him down as Bish twisted his krije to the side and sliced it past Prinn's exposed waist. The audience cried out as Prinn twisted, snapping his elbow down to his side, a loose length of wrap popping from his torso. He backpedalled rapidly, putting space between himself and Bish, bringing his krije down in front of him. It was obvious that Bish had cut him, though Prinn's black wraps disguised any blood blossoming on his waist.

Don't give him time to recover, Jin thought earnestly as Bish paused opposite his opponent, assessing the damage. Jin groaned in frustration, fists clenching at his sides.

No! Don't give him time –

Prinn attacked with such vehemence that Bish barely brought his krije up in time. Prinn's krije flashed and slid horrifyingly close to Bish's face. Bish missed the next parry and lurched to the side, ducking in rapid succession to avoid Prinn's blade as it swung over the back of his neck.

The force of Prinn's next downward cut sent Bish onto his backside, twisting his krije awkwardly so Prinn's blade slid down the length of his, the blade burying itself deep in the ground.

Bish rolled onto his knee and was half-way to his feet as he switched his grip on his krije and thrust it down towards Prinn's torso. Prinn let go of the hilt of his trapped krije and caught Bish's wrist, wrenching it to the side so that Bish's blade, likewise, buried itself in the ground. Prinn yanked his krije free and sent its pommel into Bish's face.

Jin cringed as he heard the crack across the arena. People in the crowd screamed.

Bish let go of his stuck krije and threw himself forward, instead grabbing Prinn's krije hilt with both hands and ripping it from his grasp. The weapon clattered across the stone steps and skidded to a stop on the edge of the crowd, far beyond the reach of either dancer.

Bish's blade was still quivering close to them, pointy end in the sand. Bish dove for the hilt, but Prinn grabbed Bish by his shoulder and flung him backwards onto the ground. Prinn straddled him and trapped Bish's arms beneath his knees, punching Bish square in the face. As Prinn readied himself for another swing, Bish pulled an arm free and seized Prinn's fist in his own. They grunted, struggling against each other.

Prinn flung out his free hand and caught – seemingly from nowhere – Bish's krije by the hilt, whipping the blade down to Bish's throat.

Bish battled against Prinn's fist for a moment longer before he realised what had happened, and he stopped fighting, allowing Prinn to punch Bish's fist into the sand.

Jin was only just drawing breath when Geni Igna's scream cascaded around the arena.

'NO!'

Immediately, Geni Igna stood above the dancers, his own weapon held up to Prinn's throat.

'NO! Despicable! You broke the rules of engagement. You used majik!'

The Geni's words sent the shocked spectators into a frenzy, shaking their fists and yelling obscenities.

Prinn was a *mayj?*

Jin could barely breathe. Heat was rising rapidly inside his chest, as though his own power was suddenly determined to suffocate him.

Two Krijen sprinted to Geni Igna's side, weapons pointed down towards the dancers. Bish was still lying in the sand, trapped under his comrade. Prinn had eyes only for Geni Igna, who had not relinquished him from the threat of his blade.

Prinn slowly stood up, allowing Bish to stagger to his feet. Geni Igna said something to Bish, and he turned, padding towards the Fifteenths. They ran to him, Jin in the lead.

Bish's face was a mess of blood, his nose and one of his eye sockets oddly misshapen.

'Bish,' Jin began, stopping in front of him. He didn't know what to say next.

'Did I win?' Bish asked, his eyes lacking focus. No one answered him. 'Did I win?' he repeated more loudly, apparently unsure if they'd heard.

Jin didn't know if Bish was in shock or concussed. Probably both.

'I don't know,' Jin answered truthfully. He looked back to where Prinn stood alone, enduring the ridicule of the crowd, the sharp edge of Geni Igna's blade still nestled against his neck.

CHAPTER II:
PRINN TO

'**D**o you understand what this means?'

Surely they know I would never cheat, Prinn thought. Squares don't cheat. Krijen don't cheat.

'They will use this. They will make an example of you.'

No. No, they wouldn't –

'Square! See me!'

Prinn focused. Geni Igna's face was right above his, twisted with rage. Of course, he was angry. One of his Squares had just dishonoured him. Outrageously so.

'You must make a choice. Do you understand?'

'A choice?' Prinn's throat was dry. His side hurt. The sun was too hot, too bright above him.

'You are going to die because of this, whether it be now or in a week when they are spent with you. I should not be giving you this choice. But I will.'

Even in his daze, Prinn understood. He had orchestrated his own inevitable execution. The Kahnen would not simply let him rot away in a cell somewhere. He would be put on display, a show of what awaited any mayj who dared to harness, no matter who they were or what they stood for. Being a Square wouldn't save him. A Lost Square, perhaps, but he'd not technically lost, and that fate was worse than this anyway. Geni Igna was offering him an undeserved mercy.

'*Choose*. There is no other way.'

It would only make it worse to resist. Prinn needed to preserve whatever dignity he had left for his family. They would be watching, now surrounded by enemies, once friends.

Prinn dropped to a knee, steadying himself with his hand in the dirt. 'Now,' he said. He curled his hand into a fist, collecting sand and crusted blood.

Prinn did not hear nor see the blade.

Everything was simply gone.

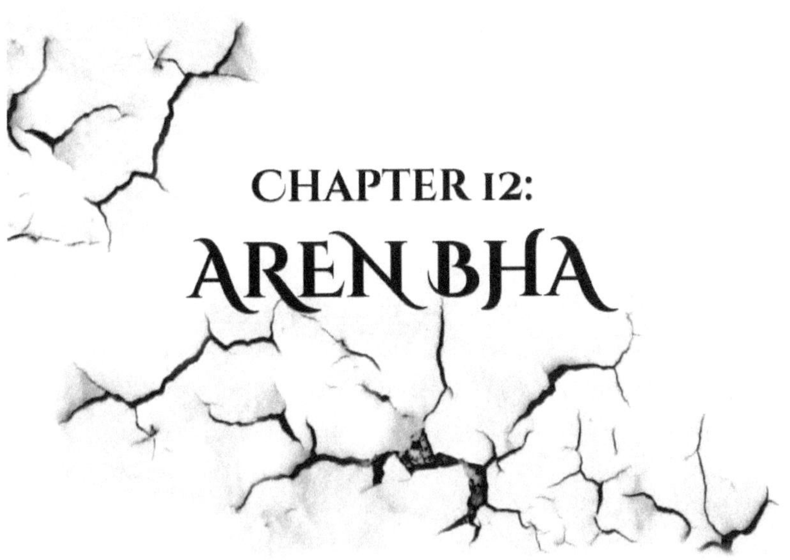

CHAPTER 12:
AREN BHA

A ren screamed as Prinn's head rolled across the ground. Unsteady on her feet, she grabbed hold of Marigold, who stood frozen beside her. They'd killed him for harnessing. Just like that.

Aren had known Prinn. Not well, but she had watched him grow up and heard stories about him over the years from Jin and Bish. He had loved music, hated one of his cousins, was a gracious loser, and had the most outrageous laugh.

Now he was dead.

Marigold clung to Aren as well, unable to tear her eyes away from the arena. Around them, people were on their feet, screaming their approval, unleashing their hatred of mayjen.

Aren began to tremble. What if Jin did the same thing? What if he harnessed during his dance and they killed him in front of her?

Aren let go of Marigold and started towards the stairs. She *would* speak to Jin. She'd barely taken a step before she felt a strong tug on the back of her wraps, and she turned to see Noel. 'Stay here, Aren,' he warned. He looked to Mae, who stood next to him, her face white. 'I'm going to find his family,' Noel said. 'They won't be safe here.'

Mae nodded. Noel slipped away into the crowd.

'Aren, come,' Mae said, holding out her hand. Numb, Aren placed her hand into her mother's, who squeezed it tightly. Marigold stood like a sentry on her other side. Together they watched as Prinn's head was bagged and his body dragged from the arena by the two Krijen who had stood by as he was beheaded.

Teal edged over to where Geni Igna stood and exchanged a few words. Geni Igna strode back towards his remaining Fifteenths.

Jin always said he was harsh, Aren thought. But that was savagery.

Teal raised his hands and the audience settled, eager to hear his announcement. 'We have a victor. Bishinrojak Lonli!'

The crowd roared, and the drums picked up a new throbbing beat to bolster the bloodlust.

'Oh, Great Kahn, thank you,' Marigold breathed next to Aren, closing her eyes.

Teal allowed the crowd a few more seconds, then raised his hands. 'Who is ready for the next dance?'

***

By mid-afternoon, Prinn's blood had dried to black and dissolved into ash, scattered across the arena. Pairs of Fifteenths came and went, no dance so vile as the first, but still horrifying to watch.

The anticipation of Jin's dance was the worst of it. When the crowd was seated, Aren could make him out in the distance, sitting ramrod straight among the row of Fifteenths. Only those victorious and those who were yet to dance remained.

The defeated Squares were gone. Once Lost, they slipped away like shadows. Aren watched them go with pity and wonder. She now understood what Mama Hidel meant when she said she couldn't bring herself to watch.

The Dancing Ceremony was obscene.

The Squares attacked one another with unbridled ferocity. One would never know they had spent the last fifteen years of their lives together, until today, forced to fight under the threat of disgrace. It was sick and bitter and twisted –

'Jin Kanju and Filip Sohn.'

Aren leapt to her feet. A cheer went up from the audience, though they remained seated, their enthusiasm wavering under the hot sun.

Aren watched anxiously as Jin rose with Filip, who sat at the end of the row. Filip was as striking as Maude, albeit in a very different way. It was especially shocking to see him without a headscarf. White patterns kissed the arches of Filip's orange brows, then disappeared up into the alabaster of his bare skull, only becoming visible again once they reached the light-gold skin of his neck.

Aren remembered her surprise when Jin first told her there was a Bhouli in the Squares. She thought they had a reputation for being peacemakers, not warriors. Especially since today seemed more about violence than anything else.

Filip's bald head was level with Jin's as they walked across the sand. He was the only other Fifteenth who rivalled Jin in height, and he was slightly broader. A guarded character, Jin had little to say about Filip other than he was unparalleled with a dagger. Aren quietly thanked the Great Kahn they were fighting with krije today.

Filip made it to the heart of the arena first. He stopped, knelt down, and swept his patterned hand across the ground in front of him. He brought his fist to his mouth, head bowed. Then he threw back his head and let out an earth-shattering roar that rattled Aren's very bones, startling the audience into silence.

'Oh my,' whispered Mae, placing her hand on her chest as the crowd murmured with vigour. Aren looked up at her mother. 'What's he doing?'

'It's a tribute, I think,' Mae said quietly. 'Intended to lead the dead up to the sky. Noel says it's an ancient Bhouli tradition. I doubt many people would recognise it.'

Marigold was shaking next to Aren. 'You meant that it's for . . . you know?' She meant Prinn. It wasn't clear if he was Lost or not, so she avoided saying his name.

'Yes,' Mae replied, her face pale.

In understanding, Aren felt a wave of affection for Filip. It was an act of love for his disgraced friend, and a very dangerous thing to do. If anyone suspected Filip was showing respect to Prinn, he risked ostracism, even if he won this dance.

Thankfully, Mae was right. The crowd didn't know what to make of Filip's behaviour, though they watched the arena with renewed interest. Perhaps there would be something different about this dancer.

Aren's attention came screaming back to Jin as he pulled out his krije, clean blade flashing. He stood a short distance from Filip, rolling his head on his shoulders, his weapon held slightly away from his body.

Aren swallowed. She had duelled Jin more times than she could count, but she had never seen him look the way he did today. Absolutely *terrifying*.

By now, Teal had learnt to start the dance from a considerable distance. He stood at the edge of the arena, waiting as Geni Igna stepped between him and the dancers. Geni Igna nodded.

Teal's now-hoarse voice rang out. 'You may begin!'

Neither Jin nor Filip attacked immediately. Instead, they paced a slow, exaggerated circle, footsteps mirroring each other akin to Aren's spar with Jin only days earlier.

The crowd was restless under the hot sun. No dance had trumped the hype of the first, and people were growing irritable. They called out violent suggestions and degrading comments, screeching their impatience at the dancers.

It was impossible to block out the sound of their cries, so all Aren could do was endure it. She twisted her loose wrist wraps around her fingers and bit her lip, waiting.

At once, Jin and Filip advanced on each other, krije coming together. They danced so fast that, at first, Aren couldn't tell what was happening. It was as though they were strung together, the distance between them never shrinking as they flowed back and forth, krije clashing.

Jin was stronger, but Filip was quicker. His blade cracked onto Jin's, knocking it down and exposing Jin's neck and shoulders. Filip whipped his blade across, forcing Jin to duck low to avoid it.

Filip had moved too close to allow Jin to get his krije between them. Instead, Jin sent a powerful kick straight into Filip's gut. Even as the Bhouli staggered back, Jin advanced on him, thrusting with his krije.

Filip grasped the end of his own blade and brought it across to parry, guiding Jin's krije to the side. Filip followed through on his twist and moved into Jin's body, his elbow thrusting up and into Jin's face. Stunned, Jin rushed back, narrowly avoiding being slashed across the face as Filip's blade came whipping back around.

Filip moved in again, gaining ground, forcing Jin backwards. The Bhouli unleashed a series of low swings, then changed tack and lashed out at Jin's head.

Aren squealed as Jin caught Filip's blade on his, allowing the tip to slide down towards his face, before flipping both blades up and over his head. He ducked beneath Filip's shoulder and thrust his elbow up into the base of Filip's skull.

Filip was too quick to feel the full force of Jin's attack. He dove over Jin's leg and rolled to his feet, twisting back around.

There was second of stillness as they faced each other, krije held at the ready over their shoulders.

Filip moved first, so fast and with such aggression that Aren screamed, but Jin grabbed the end of his own blade with his free hand and shunted it back into Filip's with enough force to send the Bhouli staggering.

Filip quickly recovered, slashing at Jin as he stepped into him. There was a burst of black material as Filip's blade sliced through Jin's wraps.

Jin leapt forward and cracked his pommel into Filip's head.

Filip brought his blade around so swiftly that Jin had to throw himself backwards to avoid it.

The pair paced around each other again.

Aren's fingers ached. She glanced down to see she'd strangled her fingertips purple in her wrist wraps. Aren dropped them and looked back to the dance. *Maybe Jin and Filip will draw*, she dared to think. Was that allowed? Perhaps this dance didn't have to end in ruin.

Both dancers drove forward again, blades flashing. They travelled to the base of the stands where Aren sat, bringing them into closer focus. She could see the sweat glistening on Filip's scalp.

Aren flinched as Filip's krije flicked across Jin's forehead, leaving a long red line. Her mother gasped and Marigold grabbed Aren's arm, her nails digging in.

Filip struck out again. Jin reached out with his free hand and wrapped it around Filip's wrist. Jin tugged hard, guiding the Bhouli's blade dangerously past his ribs to trap it beneath his arm. Jin thrust his krije upwards.

Filip slapped his free hand over Jin's fist, halting his attack, krije nicking at the spot just below Filip's ribs. Locked together, they struggled, neither giving way.

Suddenly, Jin rammed his forehead down onto Filip's nose. Filip's head snapped back, his grip on Jin's fist slipping. Jin thrust his krije deep into Filip's torso, his blade sprouting out of the Bhouli's back.

The pair shuddered where they stood before Jin sank slowly to his knees, dragged down by the weight of his dying comrade.

CHAPTER 13:
JIN KANJU

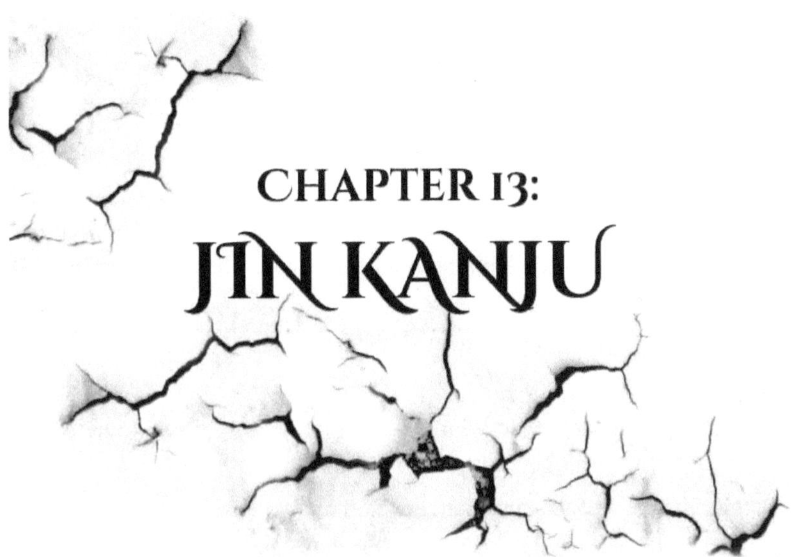

Jin's body wasn't obeying him. The hard blade of Filip's krije was still tucked under his arm. His own blade was buried so deep in Filip that Jin could feel Filip's gut pressing against his hand, still wrapped around the hilt. Jin knew he had to let go, but he couldn't figure out what to let go of first. So he sat on the ground with Filip slumped over him.

Filip was making a gurgling sound that Jin could make no sense of. He looked down at the Bhouli, unsure of what to do.

Filip lifted his head, his eyes finding Jin's.

Jin loosened his arm so Filip's krije thudded into the sand. He rolled Filip off him, easing him gently onto his side. Jin let go of his own krije, his hands fluttering over Filip uselessly.

This was something that, in Jin's fifteen years as a Square, they'd never taught him. A huge fucking *gaping* flaw in his training. What it felt like to kill someone. Or what it felt like to do it halfway.

Filip was still alive.

'Jin,' said Filip, making Jin flinch. His voice sounded wet, tarnished by the blood in his lungs. Horror crept through Jin's numbness. *No. No no no.*

How long did it take to die? How long would Jin have to wait and watch his friend drown in his arms?

'It's okay, Jin,' Filip said, his teeth red. 'I'm going to the stars now.' Filip lowered his head back down to the sand. He breathed two more bubbling breaths. Then he died.

Jin stared down at Filip's slack face. His gaze slid over the ridge of Filip's torso to the blade sticking out of his back. The entire length of it was red. There was red everywhere: red on the ground, red on Jin's hands, red soaking into his wraps –

'Get up, Jin.'

Jin looked up to see Geni Igna looming over him, his silhouette dark against the bright sun behind.

'Get up,' Geni Igna commanded again.

Jin stood up. Dazed, he placed his left hand across his clavicle, saluting his teacher. Geni Igna inclined his head towards Teal, who waited in the middle of the arena. 'Go,' Geni Igna said. 'You have won. Go claim your victory.'

Jin walked across the arena towards Teal. The Speaker jogged to meet him with a grin and grabbed his wrist, throwing it into the sky.

'We have a victor! Jin Kanju!'

Noise erupted around them. People were calling Jin's name; he could hear it in the crowd.

Teal turned to Jin, still smiling. 'Well done, son.' Teal dropped Jin's wrist, which fell loosely to his side.

This was what Jin had always wanted. Since the day he met Aren, he dreamt of becoming Krijen, the brave warriors who patrolled the streets, who could protect anyone, defeat anyone, because they were invincible; and if Jin could be one of them one day, then he would be better, stronger, like his father wanted.

Today was that day.

Jin smiled. He bowed to the audience, sending them into peals of ecstasy. Everyone was on their feet as they applauded him.

Teal laughed and clapped, and Jin strode over to the Fifteenths. They embraced him and smacked him on the back, and he noted how few of them were left. There had been thirty-nine, and now he counted twenty, including himself. Almost all of them looked beaten and bloodied and triumphant.

Bish did not.

Bish was looking at him with an expression that Jin had never seen before. He looked confused and relieved and hurt and elated all at once.

Jin held out his arms to embrace his friend. Bish hesitated. Then he smiled and pulled Jin into a hug, and they wrestled with joy.

'Well done,' Bish said. 'You're Krijen now. No going back.'

No going back.

Filip's bloodied teeth flashed into Jin's mind. He let go of Bish and whipped around, searching for where he had left Filip lying in the sand.

The Bhouli's body was gone. All that remained of him was a darkening pool of blood at the base of the stands.

***

There was one dance to go. Given there was an uneven number of Fifteenths, someone from the pool of victors was to be selected to dance against the remaining Fifteenth.

It was an honourable duty that none of them wanted.

Bish had been premature in calling Jin Krijen. All Fifteenths must be undefeated. If you lost your second dance, regardless of winning the first, you were Lost. Your victory was meaningless.

No, it was not fair. But they all knew how it worked.

Jin looked around at the victorious Fifteenths as they surrounded Geni Igna. Everyone was a little broken. Bish had recovered from his shock, but his nose was shattered, and his right eye almost entirely swollen shut.

Geni Igna strode over to Wren, the last remaining Square. Wren had black hair and was of medium height and slim build. He wasn't the fastest or the strongest Fifteenth, but he was a quick thinker. He fought in unconventional ways that had caught Jin out on multiple occasions. Jin didn't envy whoever had to dance against him.

Geni Igna held something out to Wren and dropped a small teardrop-shaped stone into his open palm. It was weighted so that it lay on its side, its sharp tip pointing directly at Wren.

'This is a spinning drop,' Geni Igna explained. 'It is the fairest way to decide who you will fight.' Wren nodded, his eyes boring into the stone in his hand.

'You have all fought bravely today,' Geni Igna said.

The victors glanced around at one another. It was the most praise they had ever heard from him.

Geni Igna stepped back. 'Close it off,' he commanded. The Fifteenths closed their circle, Geni Igna on the outside, Wren in the middle.

'Place it on the ground and spin it,' said Geni Igna to Wren.

Wren knelt and placed the drop on the ground, looking up at the Fifteenths one last time. With a flick of his wrist, he sent the drop into a spin.

It spun and spun and spun. Jin could feel the sun burning the exposed skin on his shoulders where his wraps hung off him. The heat inside him burned almost as hot, his power wrestled down deep in his chest. Thank fuck he'd been able to keep it under control.

Aeons passed.

The Fifteenths began shifting nervously. Wren let out a small moan of frustration. Jin glanced at Geni Igna who was watching the drop with the same cold expression he always wore.

Then, little by little, the drop slowed. It taunted them as its point crept from person to person, finally slowing to land on –

Before Jin could see who it was, Bish ran forward and stamped down on the drop, crushing it beneath his boot.

'I'll do it,' Bish said. 'I'll fight you, Wren.'

The Fifteenths looked at him in astonishment.

'No! Bish –' Jin started forward, but Geni Igna pushed through the circle and shoved Jin to the side. 'It is decided,' he said.

Bish picked the drop out of the sand, handing it to Geni Igna who took it wordlessly. Their teacher spun on his heels, heading towards Teal to inform him of the last pair.

'Bish, *what are you doing?*'

Jin grabbed Bish by the arm and tugged him roughly around to face him. The other Fifteenths crowded them.

Jin couldn't believe what Bish had just done. 'The drop wasn't going to land on you! Are you mad?'

Bish was looking at the ground. 'I didn't win,' he said.

'What?'

'I didn't win my dance.' Bish turned his gaze up to Jin, his one good eye tormented. 'I don't deserve to be standing here with you all.'

'That's ridiculous!' Jin wanted to shake some sense into him. 'Your opponent cheated –'

'Exactly,' Bish interrupted. 'Prinn forfeited. I didn't win.'

Jin's mouth gaped, but no words came out. The fact that Bish said Prinn's name meant he didn't believe Prinn had lost.

'He's right,' said a voice to the left.

Nommo, one of the other Fifteenths, was looking at Bish and nodding. 'If Prinn hadn't harnessed, we don't know what would have happened. Bish doesn't want to be Krijen by default. Isn't that right?'

Bish nodded.

Jin couldn't think of anything to say. He looked around at the other Fifteenths, desperate for help. Surely, someone would make Bish see sense.

Wren stepped forward, grimacing. 'They're waiting for us,' he said. Bish nodded and pulled his arm free of Jin's grip.

'No –' Jin reached out again, but Bish turned away and walked with Wren towards the centre of the arena.

'You're fucking blind!' Jin yelled at Bish's retreating back. 'I'll fight! I'll do it!' He lunged forward, but the Fifteenths grabbed him by his torn wraps and hauled him back.

'It's his choice, Jin,' someone said in his ear. But Jin kept yelling, ignoring them all. Bish was going to become Lost because of a fucking *technicality*.

The other Fifteenths shoved Jin down onto the hard stone bench. 'If you don't shut up, Geni Igna is going to have your head,' Nommo hissed at him. Jin quietened, but his heart thudded loudly in his chest. They'd lost so many friends today, and Jin accepted that. They all knew how the ceremony worked. But it hadn't crossed his mind that Bish would dance twice. That he would *volunteer* for the part.

Jin was struggling to breathe. Heat was creeping down his arms, to his twitching fingertips.

Bish and Wren reached the centre of the arena.

Teal cleared his ruined throat. 'Our final dance is upon us!' he shouted to the stands, who cheered. 'Bishinrojak Lonli is to fight again!'

The crowd cheered louder, whistling and clapping.

'He will fight Wren Yu, the final Fifteenth!'

On cue, the drums paced a new rhythm, leaning into the tension between the two dancers in the arena.

Bish stood with his krije clasped in front of him and his eyes on Wren.

Wren grasped the blade of his krije with his free hand, flipping it up and laying it across his shoulders in exaggerated relaxation. It made Jin angry. Wren never did things the way he should.

Jin remembered that Marigold was in the crowd.

'You may begin!'

Bish could not lose this dance.

Jin felt his power surging in his veins. He couldn't let Bish throw away fifteen years of his life. He had to do something. For Bish. For Marigold.

Jin would just have to make sure that no one saw, while the whole arena watched.

CHAPTER 14:
PAKKER

The dances had grown tedious. Emotions were running high, but after the first Square's beheading, no mayj would let slip their majik today. So when the final dance was announced, Pakker headed for the exit.

As he slipped onto the stone staircase between the rows, the crowd gasped. Pakker walked to the bottom of the stairs and crossed in front of the Fifteenths. Their eyes slid over him, focused on the dance.

One of the Fifteenths stood out more than the rest. He smelled like blood and his wraps hung off him in shreds. He was the one who had killed his opponent.

A wise move, Pakker thought. The People loved death, and there was nothing more important than gaining their favour. Krijen liked to think they were above all that bureaucracy, but Pakker knew otherwise. Anything under the influence of the Kahnen succumbed to their manipulations.

Pakker exited the arena and headed towards the bridge, a new plan in mind. Where there was ale, there were drunkards. Fivers, the enormous tavern in Val, would shortly be prime hunting ground. It would be busy tonight, so best to get in early.

It wasn't long before Pakker strode through its doors. Fivers was already ringing with music and laughter, the wooden tables and chairs groaning in anticipation of the evening. Empty tankards hung from hooks on the ceiling among lanterns that had yet to be lit. Darkness was still a few hours away.

Pakker bought an ale and eyed up an empty chair at a table. Rows of tankards created little walls in front of the men seated there. They were playing cards. Pakker approached. 'Do you mind?' He inclined his head towards the empty chair.

'Not if you play,' came the reply. The speaker had wiry grey hair and the beginnings of jowls. He grinned at Pakker. 'The name's Tamper,' he said. 'This is Parve, Ret, and Jija.' The other men nodded and smiled toothy smiles, apart from Parve, who had none.

'You picked the busiest night of the year for a quiet drink,' Tamper said, with a gentle slur. Pakker shrugged and sat down.

'You play jouja?' Ret asked. Ret had brown hair, brown eyes, and tan skin. He would have had no trouble blending into the wooden chair beneath him if he hadn't been wearing red wraps. *He would make a good mercenary*, Pakker thought.

'Of course.' Pakker took the hand of cards offered to him.

'Did you come from the ceremony?' Jija asked. He had the strangest intonation, glaringly obvious to Pakker. There were no outsiders in Valrue, because no one would want to get in, even if they could.

'I did,' Pakker replied. 'Where are you from?'

Jija guffawed and smacked his tankard down onto the table, spilling ale over his hands. He leant in towards Pakker and spoke in a hushed tone. 'Oh, you're a clever one, aren't you? How about this. Don't ask me where I'm from and I won't ask your name.' There was a gleam in Jija's eye. Pakker nodded. He liked this man.

The others were inspecting their cards. 'How was the ceremony?' Tamper asked Pakker. 'I didn't go,' he added. 'I can't be bothered with the crowd anymore.' Pakker wondered what had then compelled him to come to Fivers.

'It was eventful, as ceremonies go,' Pakker said. 'One Square made a fool of himself. He harnessed in the middle of the arena.'

'He never!'

'He did. The Geni took his head clean off.'

Tamper whistled. 'Bet he regretted that.'

'You know,' Ret said, 'I always wondered why it didn't happen more often.' He screwed up his face in concentration, then selected a card to play.

'What d'you mean?' Tamper asked.

'Surely there's a bunch of mayjen hiding in the Squares. Aren't we supposed to be overrun with them now, after the Unsettlement? You'd think they would try to sway the ceremony outcome, if you know what I mean.'

'It's not that simple,' Jija said, adding his own card to the table. Tamper looked up at Jija. 'How's that?'

'Harnessing can be just as tiring as swinging a krije,' Jija replied, lowering his cards and leaning forward in his chair. 'Not much of an advantage, and definitely not worth the risk. A Fifteenth is going to notice if their weapon starts moving with a mind of its own. Besides,' – he shrugged – 'no one knows how to use majik anymore. So even if they were mad enough to try, they'd just mess it up.'

Jija spoke brazenly, but Pakker was sure no one in the vicinity could hear. The noise in the tavern was making his ears bleed.

Ret pulled a face at Jija. 'How d'you figure all that?'

'It's common sense, you idiot.'

'Are there seriously no mayjen who could do it?'

'Maybe a KahnenMayj, because they are himajik,' Jija replied. 'But they have no skin in the Squares' game, and you'd have to be an imbecile to try to bribe them.'

Pakker added his card to the table. Quick as a flash, Ret slammed his card down on top of Pakker's and hooted loudly. 'That round goes to me! Thank you, sir!' He grabbed Pakker's tankard and sculled its contents. Pakker raised an eyebrow.

'Sorry,' Tamper said. 'Losers lose their drink. Get another.'

Pakker nodded. This was good. 'All right,' he said. 'Let's finish this round, then I'll buy another one.'

Jija scooped up the cards and started shuffling them. Parve, who had yet to say anything at all, grabbed Jija's sleeve and tugged on it. He began making strange gestures with his hands.

'Parve wants to know how to tell if someone is himajik,' Jija said.

Tamper laughed. 'Why's that, Parve? You working for the Kahnen now? Gonna string up some skahks for them?'

Parve made a violent motion with his hands that even Pakker could understand. Parve did not like the Kahnen. He made another series of unintelligible gestures.

'He wants to know . . . ' Jija said slowly, watching Parve's hands as he interpreted, 'so he can find one . . . and . . .'

Jija looked at Pakker, grinning. 'Parve doesn't like mayjen either,' he finished lamely. There was clearly some vulgarity left unsaid. Parve smiled wickedly, gums bared.

Tamper leant in towards Pakker. 'A few years back, Parve's brother was killed by a piece of lomajik scum. Unfortunately, the scum in question had connections. The Kahnen refused to lock him up. Parve went to do the job himself, but the Krijen caught him. They gave him some cuts, knocked out his teeth, and sliced out his tongue. So now, Parve just hates everyone.'

Jija dealt out the next round. Ret scratched his head, then picked out a card and smacked it onto the table. 'So?' Ret looked expectantly at Jija. 'How *do* you tell?'

'You boys are squeezing me dry tonight,' Jija said, though he seemed to enjoy the attention. His smile was lopsided, his ale getting the better of him. 'It's about endurance,' he explained. 'For example, let's take a mayj who throws a boulder. If he can throw the boulder just once before he's tuckered out, he is pretty lomajik. Then let's imagine a mayj who throws a boulder and can manage it a bunch of times before he's tired. He might not be himajik, but he's more powerful than the other guy.'

'So what does himajik actually mean?' Ret asked.

Jija shrugged. 'Seems an ambiguous term for someone who can do a lot of majik before they Turn themselves.' Everyone winced. Most people didn't know much about majik, but it was common knowledge that if a mayj Turned, it meant they died from using up all their power. It was as simple as that.

'Oh, I know!' The group turned to Ret.

'Well?' Tamper demanded.

Ret spoke so quietly that Pakker nearly missed what he said. 'I heard that himajik mayjen can *heal* people.'

Tamper groaned. 'No, Ret,' he said, rolling his eyes. 'Majik doesn't work on people. Everyone knows that.'

'I'm only repeating what I heard –'

'Well, there's your problem,' Tamper said. 'There's no brain between those ears to filter the muck you listen to.'

He leant forward to clap Ret around the ear. Ret had been about to take a swig of ale and jerked to the side, spilling it all over Jija. 'Ret, you menace!' Jija cried, reaching across the table and tugging the tankard from Ret's hands.

'Oi!' Ret staggered to his feet, trying to snatch his tankard back. 'Why d'you know so much about majik anyway?' This time, Ret's voice was far too loud.

Jija growled. 'What do you mean by that?'

Pakker stood up, his chair scraping on the floor. 'Time for another drink,' he said, riding over them both. 'Can I get anyone anything?'

The men yelled their preferences in Pakker's direction as he wove towards the bar, which sagged under drunk customers hollering for more ale. Pakker ducked under raised glasses and slipped through to the front.

Just then, an enormous cheer went up around him. Everyone craned their heads towards the entrance of Fivers, vying for a view of the victorious Fifteenths as they walked into the tavern. Their bloodstained wraps did nothing to dissuade throngs of admirers who crowded them as they entered.

Leading the charge was the Bhouli killer, his arm flung over the shoulders of the Fifteenth who had danced twice. Having condemned their fellow Squares to death and dismissal respectively, the two young men bore the brunt of the crowd's flirtations. Behind the pair were two young women, their heads bowed together, deep in conversation.

Pakker recognised the auburn-haired girl. Her heart-shaped face was furrowed, inexplicably sombre. The Bhouli killer kept looking over his shoulder at her, as though reassuring himself she was still there.

The other girl was blonde, with a little rouge on her cheeks and red on her lips. She smiled at their warm welcome, but the smile vanished when she turned back to her friend.

The crowd respectfully parted, allowing the new Krijen space at the bar. Pakker stepped aside, watching quietly. Within seconds, the flustered barmaids had lined up nineteen tankards on the house. The Krijen each grabbed a handle. Together, they downed their drinks.

The walls of the tavern shook as its patrons cheered. Pakker found himself crammed against the hard wooden ledge of the bar as everyone returned to their celebrations. The barmaids began their own dance as they poured more ale, spinning around one another in well-rehearsed efficiency.

Pakker held up his hand. The barmaid in front of him nodded curtly and within moments she slammed five tankards down in front of him, holding out her empty palm for payment. Pakker obliged and scooped the tankards up, carefully navigating his way back to the table.

Tamper hollered as he saw Pakker coming their way. 'By the Great Kahn's karkers, that took ages!' Pakker carefully placed the tankards down. 'There's a good man,' Jija said, pulling a tankard towards himself.

Parve was sulking, his arms folded and chin tucked. He ignored the tankard that Pakker pushed towards him. 'Cheeky git got caught cheating,' Jija explained. 'Next round's on him. So drink up, Parve!'

Ret already had his tankard between both hands and was gulping the ale down. He belched and dropped his empty tankard on the table with a thud. 'I'll have his,' Ret offered, reaching for Parve's ale. Parve snatched his tankard off the table, slopping it over himself.

'Don't waste it,' Tamper said as Pakker sat down.

Eyes skimming the tops of his cards, Pakker ran his gaze over the men in front of him. He'd found his target for the evening.

CHAPTER 15:
AREN BHA

Jin had killed Filip. *Killed* him. But no one else seemed to care. Noel said it was okay, that sometimes it happened at Dancing Ceremonies. Rarely, but it did.

Jin's victory was not what Aren expected. Had it clearly been an accident, it would have been easier to forgive. But to smile? To celebrate while Filip's blood dried on his wraps? That was the image Aren couldn't get out of her head. It did not equate with the Jin she knew and loved.

She was ripped abruptly from her thoughts when someone knocked her from behind, pitching her into the hard edge of a table.

'Sorry! Sorry –'

The culprit was already gone, shoved back by a dozen angry customers who had also borne the brunt of his clumsiness.

'Aren! What are you doing? Come help me!' Marigold was struggling towards her, four tankards clutched precariously to her chest. Aren grabbed two of them, lifting them above her head and leading the way through the chaos towards the tavern exit.

Everyone had spilled onto the street. Barrels had been rolled out the doors and set up as tables, and benches tugged out after them, now groaning under the weight of too many occupants.

A few music enthusiasts had put together some makeshift drums to complement the alto of a little golden instrument Aren had never heard before. Darkness had rolled in, but everything was so bright. She assumed it was because of the ale.

Aren had drunk a tankard and a half and found herself in a strange way. She remained determinedly sour, despite the merry atmosphere. While the other new Krijen were scattered among their admirers, Jin and Bish had tucked themselves behind a barrel outside, next to the stone wall of the tavern.

They were laughing together as Aren and Marigold approached. It was odd seeing Bish laugh like that, so deep from his belly. Even Marigold was more audacious than her typical self tonight. It all should have been dreadfully entertaining, but Aren couldn't catch her thoughts as they drifted back to the bloodstained attire that Jin still wore. Someone had thrown him a shirt as the shreds of his wraps did little for his modesty, but the shirt didn't cover all the gore. Aren did not want to stand next to him.

Marigold dropped her tankards onto the barrel and slipped happily into Bish's arms. He smiled down at her, starry-eyed. Aren placed her own tankards down as Marigold and Bish kissed. They were both so shy that it was peculiar to see them being affectionate.

The anticipation of the ceremony over, Aren envied the relief the others clearly felt. She took a sip from her tankard, feeling Jin's eyes on her. 'Aren,' he said. 'What's wrong?'

She looked over the top of her tankard at him. He cocked his head, eyebrows coming together.

'Nothing.' She shouldn't have looked at him. Her face gave everything away.

Leaving Bish and Marigold to each other, Jin took Aren gently by the arm, leading her away from the tavern. They slipped out of the brightness and into the shadows, stopping across the street in front of a closed shop.

Jin was trying to get Aren to look at him again, but she kept her face stubbornly turned away, not wanting to make the same mistake twice.

'Come on, Aren. You've been weird ever since the ceremony.' Jin's voice was soft. 'You're angry with me.'

'I'm not angry,' Aren muttered, tugging her arm out of Jin's grasp.

'All right. What's the matter then?'

Aren didn't know what to say. She *wasn't* angry with him. More confused. A little disturbed, if she admitted the truth to herself. She kept picturing Jin bowing to the crowd, smiling, basking in the glory of Filip's death. How could she explain that to him? How could she tell her best friend she felt sickened by what he'd done?

Aren finally raised her eyes to Jin's. They were full of concern. Aren just felt numb. 'You didn't have to kill him,' she said quietly.

'What?'

'You didn't have to kill him,' Aren repeated, louder this time.

'Oh,' Jin said. 'Right. *That.*'

His expression was hard to read, which was worrying, because Aren normally knew exactly what Jin was thinking. But it was the way he'd spoken that scared her the most. Like he'd expected her to say something like this. Like she was making a big deal of nothing.

'Yes, *that!*' Aren said, louder than she meant to. 'How could you?'

Jin stepped back from her and folded his arms, frowning. 'Aren, that's what Krijen *do.*'

There was definitely something off about his response. Was it patronising? Or was he struggling to rationalise what he'd done?

'You've always said Krijen value mercy,' Aren said. Her heartbeat was becoming frantic. 'Why did you do it? You didn't have to kill Filip to win. You only needed to disarm him!'

'I didn't decide to do it.' Jin's voice flat and horrible. 'It just happened. And don't say that name,' he added. 'It's Lost now.'

'Filip's not Lost – he's dead!'

'Better off then.'

Aren was shaking. 'I don't understand. I know how badly you wanted to be Krijen, but it doesn't seem right to get it this way.'

Jin looked up at the sky. Aren couldn't see his face. He was too tall. When he finally looked back down at her, his unreadable expression had cracked. 'Don't say that,' Jin pleaded. 'Don't ruin this for me.'

'That's not what I meant to do.' Aren swayed on the spot. She wished she hadn't drunk so much ale. 'Maybe we shouldn't talk about this now. Let's talk later.'

'No, now. Please. I can't have you angry with me about this.'

'I'm not angry. I'm *shocked*.' Aren bit her lip, trying to hold herself back. It didn't work. 'I mean, do you even feel badly about it?'

Jin looked horrified. 'Of course I do! How could you think otherwise?'

'You didn't act like it,' Aren said. 'You bowed and waved to the audience, like you'd just finished a performance.'

Jin groaned. 'Please don't judge me for that. The whole thing happened so fast! I wasn't really thinking. I just did what Teal told me to.'

Aren's eyes were welling up. She wanted to believe Jin when he said he didn't mean to do it; she really did. But Jin didn't make mistakes, especially not ones as big as this.

'You'll be an incredible Krijen, Jin,' Aren whispered. Before he could see her cry, Aren turned and ran back into the warmth of the crowd, to the safety of an audience. She stopped in the entranceway to the tavern, leaning on the doorframe while her world spun. People jostled her as they pushed past.

Aren closed her eyes, guilt rising in her like bile. She already regretted running. Jin had swallowed her ridicule and asked for her understanding, and she'd left him alone in the darkness. She wouldn't normally back down from a disagreement, but tonight she felt so unlike herself. She wiped her eyes and turned back to see if Jin had followed her.

He hadn't.

She hastened back out into the street, over to where they'd been standing together.

Jin wasn't there.

Panic setting in, Aren wrestled her way back to Marigold and Bish. She was so distracted looking for Jin in the crowd that she bowled straight into them, still standing by the barrel.

'Aren?' Bish caught her arm, steadying her. 'Are you okay?'

Spotting her unfinished tankard, Aren snatched it off the barrel and brought it to her lips. It was warm and flat and tasted disgusting. She downed it and wiped her mouth with the back of her hand.

'What are you doing?' Marigold's eyes were wide.

'Drinking.' Aren hoisted on a smile. 'Tonight's for celebrating, right?'

'That's right.' Bish laughed and threw an arm around Aren. 'Where is Jin?'

'He'll be back soon,' Aren said loudly. It sounded more convincing, that way. She hoped he would come back. 'I'll go get more ale, shall I?'

Before Marigold or Bish could say another word, Aren spun on her heel and headed inside to the bar.

CHAPTER 16:
LOTTIE

I t was a beautiful evening. The stars were out, the air was warm, and the soft rumble of voices carried up to the open window, a relaxing hum that Lottie could fall asleep to.

She lay on the bed, her silk robe settled across her body, a strip of porcelain skin exposed from her chin to her toes. Looking down, she could trace the curves of her figure, so richly sought after. She could not fathom why. It had only instilled jealousy in women and untempered desire in men, which had led to little else other than misery.

There was a small fire lit in the hearth, dying now. Lottie knew she should tend to it. The brothel keepers would not come into her rooms during the evening. This was a shame, because they were always interesting to talk to, and tonight had been unusually quiet. The keepers were more transient than the women (probably because Mama Hidel ran her brothel with an iron fist), but for the brief time that they worked there, Lottie did her best to get to know them.

Lottie held nothing against Mama Hidel. With her, you knew exactly what to expect. You treat her right, she'll treat you right. That was the simple way of it.

Lottie mulled over the dying embers for a moment longer, before pulling herself up off the bed. Her gown slid open, exposing her breasts and belly to the room. She padded barefoot over to the fireplace, the floor warm underfoot.

Lottie's was the strangest of all the rooms. Half of it was stone, the other half wood, as though the builders, or the mayj, or whoever had done it, couldn't decide what they wanted. Embers from the fireplace flung themselves daringly out into the open space but always fell short of the timber.

Lottie grabbed the fire poker and prodded at the ash. It released only little puffs of orange, which quickly faded away. The pile of kindling was desperately low, with barely a few splinters left. Lottie rested her hand on her hip and twirled the poker between her fingers. The keepers always stacked the firewood downstairs behind the bar.

Best get on with it then.

Lottie replaced the poker and grabbed her waist tie from the end of the bed, intending to make herself a touch more decent.

Without warning, Jin burst through her door, startling her. He looked so exceptionally flustered that she frowned at him, wondering what was wrong.

Jin paused in the doorway, spotting her on the far side of the room. He kicked the door shut and strode over. Wordlessly, he scooped her up, pulling her up onto his hips. She wrapped her legs around him and hooked her ankles together to keep herself in place until Jin slammed her gently against the warm stone wall.

Jin was rough, but in a good way. He never pressed too hard but moved with enough passion and intent that she got a little lost in it sometimes and forgot that it was actually *her* job to satisfy *him*. Jin never minded, never said he wasn't pleased. He wasn't anything like the other customers.

Jin kissed her ears, down her neck; then he angled his hips into her, allowing her weight to rest on them while he grasped her robe and ripped it out from behind her. Lottie dug her fingers into his shoulders and tilted her head back, enjoying his rough, scattered kisses, even though she knew she should do more.

It was just so *nice* to enjoy sex for a change.

Jin didn't search for her mouth with his (sometimes he did), but tonight he seemed particularly distracted. She pulled his bruised, scratched face to her chest (perhaps he would explain this later) and he obliged, nosing along her collarbone, his breath warming the tops of her breasts. She felt him wrestling with the wraps tied about his hips, and while she waited, she ran her hands through his hair. He'd cut his golden locks off, and a bristly stubble remained, which she didn't like as much. It felt different under her palms.

With a gasp, she remembered the ceremony was today. Jin must be Krijen now!

But if that were the case, he should be out celebrating. Perhaps he had come to her because he had lost his dance? Lottie shook off that thought quickly. Jin would never do that to her. But he was certainly moving differently tonight. Lottie thought he seemed distressed, or sad, or –

Jin placed his hands about her waist and lifted her up and off the wall, adjusting her until she was perfectly in place. He let her slide down onto the length of him, his hands trailing up either side of her back.

As Jin thrust into her, her spine ground into the wall for the briefest of moments before he realised and stepped back, taking her with him.

He was still wearing a shirt (which smelt rather metallic), and Lottie slid her hands up under it and dug her fingers into his flesh beneath and moaned (not out of obligation, but because it felt good, and she wanted him to know). She couldn't help but claw at him a little, hoping to pull him closer, disappointed to discover that they were already there, their bodies moving as one.

When she remembered herself, she loosened her legs from around his back to give him more freedom to do as he pleased. After all, she was a whore. She needed to act like one. But Jin demanded nothing of her other than the warmth of her body against his.

The embers in the fireplace finally faded to black; and as usual, he was silent when he came, making sure she went with him. She couldn't see his face, but she felt him tense, and she bit her lip so she wouldn't make too much noise (because it should really be about him, not her), and then it was over. He'd barely put her down before he was over by the wall where they'd started, picking up his wraps from the floor.

Lottie breathed in deeply. Concentrating, she felt for the warmth inside that wasn't hers and gently, carefully, harnessed it out of her body. With effort, she flung it into the fireplace. She made sure to get all of it; a pregnancy was much harder to get rid of once it had taken hold. It had happened once before, and she'd tried to get rid of it with majik. It had been horrific. She'd been unable to see, of course, so she'd tried to go by the feel of it. She'd nearly Turned. Luckily, Mama Hidel had found her, and they'd done it the old-fashioned way. Lottie thought she might die if she had to go through that again.

Fatigue rolled over her quickly. Harnessing was always exhausting for her. Jin had offered to do it once before, but she drew the line at that. It would be very improper for a client to take care of that side of things.

Lottie watched Jin's outline in the darkness as he swiftly tied his wraps back around himself and tugged the shirt over his head. He picked up her robe, bringing it over to her. She pulled it over her shoulders, not bothering to tie it shut. If he wanted, Jin could probably draw her body in great detail with his eyes closed.

Jin sat down on the floor and leant against the wooden bedframe. Lottie smiled and crawled over to him, sliding her legs down either side of his shoulders. She ran her hands through his hair again, annoyed that he'd cut it off. But she would get used to it.

Jin never left straight away. This was odd, for Lottie. Her clients were always one or the other (talkers or lovers); they weren't both. But this time Jin didn't talk. He sat there silently, allowing Lottie to stroke his head, rub her hands across his shoulders, trail her palms down onto his chest. She said nothing. It was not a whore's place to pry.

Whore. She knew Mama Hidel would have her head if she heard Lottie using that word. Mama Hidel said her women were better than that, but Lottie didn't really mind what she was called. Using a nicer term didn't mean the clients treated her any differently. Jin never called her that, though. He only ever called her Lottie.

A few minutes passed, Lottie's eyes growing used to the darkness.

The voices outside still carried up to the open window, and the trill of music wove between them, some singing along to the melody and others yelling over the top of it. A few joyous screams pierced through, then settled back into rolling laughter.

'She hates me.'

Jin's voice was hoarse. Although she couldn't see his face, Lottie could feel the fear in him. He seemed impossibly hot to the touch. She knew it wasn't because of her, but she dropped her hands to give him space. In response, he leant his head back into her lap and looked up at her, his eyes bright in the dark.

'I killed someone today.'

Ah. So he *had* won. The ceremony was brutal for the Squares. Lottie couldn't imagine spending fifteen years with someone, bonding over the same dream, knowing that one of you would have to take it from the other.

'Congratulations,' Lottie said with a smile. She meant it.

'Is it?'

'Don't,' Lottie replied softly. 'Whoever you killed is at peace. Leave it be.'

Jin closed his eyes and let out a long, slow breath. 'Aren doesn't believe that,' he said. 'She thinks I'm a murderer.'

Oh. That explains why he's been so off tonight, Lottie thought. This Aren girl was a problem. She was Jin's biggest torment, and she didn't even know it. Mind you, that wasn't Aren's fault. From what he'd told Lottie, Jin had never spoken to Aren about his feelings, and some girls just needed to be asked outright. Aren sounded like one of those types. Bold in her approach, she probably expected a similar display of commitment from others. Lottie suspected Aren had no idea how Jin felt about her. She would be crazy to pass up that opportunity.

Lottie's silence had clearly left Jin nervous. He was looking earnestly up at her, searching her expression.

'Aren will understand,' Lottie gently reassured him. 'Give her time to think it over. Perhaps she feels guilty because she's glad you killed someone, rather than losing your dance.' Lottie shrugged, unsure if it would be helpful to say such things.

'She says I didn't have to do it,' Jin said. 'She thinks I could have won without killing him.'

'She's wrong,' Lottie said. She knew what Jin needed to hear.

Jin leant forward, pulling away from her and rubbing his face in his hands. He was so very restless tonight. Lottie felt bad that for once, she didn't seem to be able to soothe him.

As Jin moved, Lottie noticed the metallic scent again. She ducked her head towards him and sniffed. He smelled like blood.

Jin stiffened, realising what she was doing. Suddenly he was on his feet by the door. 'I need to get out of these wraps,' he said, one hand on the door handle. He paused, then turned and looked back at her guiltily. 'I don't have any coins on me.'

Lottie shrugged again. 'Pay me double next time.' She didn't even care if he did or not. She walked over to him and stretched up onto her toes to give him a kiss on the cheek. She was in a rebellious mood this evening.

She padded back towards the bed, faintly hoping that Jin might reach for her again. Instead, she heard the door creak and close, and he moved noiselessly down the hallway.

Lottie sighed and flopped back down onto the bed, looking over at the black hearth in the corner. She pulled her silk robe around her to cover herself properly this time, which was silly, because (just like always) she was alone again.

CHAPTER 17:
THE GREAT KAHN

The ballroom looked grand this evening. Carved out by KahnenMayjen two centuries ago, it was deeper in the mountain than most of the KahnenKeep. Twisting grey columns webbed with dark blue veins supported a sky-high ceiling. Lanterns burned along the grey walls, making it look as though thunderclouds revolved above them. To the unobservant eye, the room appeared to have been harnessed directly from the webbed stone. Upon closer observation, one could see its surface was cracked in places, revealing black mountain rock beneath. Even though it once would have looked the part, it was not cardonite. It was a poor replica of such artistry, in the Great Kahn's opinion.

Previous governments had frequented the ballroom for parties, though since the Unsettlement, it was rarely used. It would be indecorous to be so lavish, so flippantly. However, the Kahnen demanded the rights of their station. To appease them, the Great Kahn allowed its use once yearly to celebrate the closing of the Dancing Ceremony. The FaKrijen was expected to attend, as well as a few city-based squad leaders. They came obediently, as always. What they thought of the evening was irrelevant.

In honour of the new Krijen, the women traded their swishing skirts for silken wraps, and men, their robes for the same. Fashion demanded that wrists dripped with bracelets and necks be adorned with golden chains that a Krijen would never wear.

Minders wove their way through the masses carrying trays of fresh fruit and wine, two delicacies where only a morsel would be worth enough coin to feed a family in Rue for a week. The Great Kahn sneered as the trays were carried by him.

Despite the reprehensible grandeur, the evening was interesting enough. The Dancing Ceremony was inconsequential to the Great Kahn, but tonight it was worth attending the celebrations purely for the intrigue of watching Oji break.

The man acted the part well. He smiled, nodded, and laughed as expected; but when everyone looked away, the change in his demeanour was striking. Oji had never seemed old until tonight. His shoulders were less square, his chin less prominent, his voice softer. His own body was surrendering, betraying him.

He knows, the Great Kahn thought. It was, of course, why Oji had been less than tame lately. He was counting down his days, trying to put right everything that he'd done wrong in his eyes. But it was too late. Oji may have some time left, but not enough to save him. The Great Kahn would make sure of that. Not because he needed the FaKrijen to die, but because the Great Kahn preferred to live.

It *was* a little tedious that Oji continued with his attempts at wiping his newfound sense of morality off onto his subordinates, though the damage would be limited. Krijen were, as a rule, rather unimpressionable.

'My Great Lord, the Weapons Master is here.'

The Great Kahn turned to see an obsequious Minder behind him, his head waist height as he bowed. The Great Kahn nodded, and the Minder hurried away, returning quickly with a short auburn-haired man who was dressed simply and neatly.

Sid Bha was clearly from wealth, though he did not flash it about, like most. He was quiet and intelligent, and it had taken the Great Kahn years to understand the man, one of the many reasons he kept him around. There was no need to be wasteful, and Sid Bha fulfilled his role flawlessly, unlike most.

'My Great Lord, you asked to see me,' Sid Bha said, nodding his head slightly. Nothing more than what was required. He looked only a little nervous.

'Congratulations on another ceremony,' the Great Kahn said. 'Your krije were forged excellently, I hear.'

'Thank you. I refine the design every year, though I would like to do it differently.' Sid Bha rarely gave an opening for further conversation. He must feel particularly passionate about this.

'How so?'

'I would prefer to create a unique weapon for each individual, rather than give the same design to all.'

'Do you not think it fair to provide each dancer with the same weapon?'

'On the contrary, my Great Lord. A single design is better suited to some than others. Every dancer deserves a weapon to complement them.'

The Great Kahn nodded. 'Let us consider it for the next ceremony. It might elevate the dances. We must keep the People engaged.'

'As you wish, my Great Lord.' Sid Bha twisted his hands together in front of him. 'This . . . this is what you wished to speak with me about?'

The Great Kahn chuckled in genuine amusement. The Weapons Master was nothing short of delightful this evening. 'No, it was not. You know Eden, yes?'

A young Krijen appeared by the Great Kahn's side in an instant. The Krijen had jet-black hair and pointed features, his chin angled sharply towards the ground while the tips of his ears stretched to the ceiling. His high cheekbones hooked his smile in place as he eyed Sid.

Sid opened his mouth, but nothing came out.

'We know each other, my Great Lord,' Eden said. He spoke fast and breathlessly. 'Sid Bha, the great Weapons Master.' It was hard to know if Eden intended to sound mocking or was simply ignorant of his tone.

'Eden is the new Reprimand Master,' the Great Kahn began. 'An important role, considering the growing number of mayjen offenders. Particularly himajik ones.' He was careful not to grimace at the word. The bastardisation of the majikal language was a good thing, even if it made everyone sound like imbeciles. But he used it to feed the ignorance.

Sid shifted, looking uncomfortable. The Great Kahn carried on.

'As you know, the Krijen have the means to capture most mayjen. Himajik mayjen provide a greater challenge. While a rarity, they are exceedingly troublesome. Given the increasing demands on the KahnenMayjen, it is imperative the Krijen can manage himajik offenders unassisted. Eden was an overwhelmingly popular choice to lead this initiative.'

Eden lifted his pointed chin proudly. 'It is an honour to serve the Kahnen and the People. I'll free Valrue from its skahk.'

Sid visibly shuddered.

'Take care with your words, Eden,' the Great Kahn chided softly. It was important to keep up appearances.

'Apologies, my Great Lord.'

The Great Kahn nodded. 'The Kahnen admire your commitment. It is an unpleasant task, albeit a necessary one.'

Eden smiled. He would enjoy the sport of it.

Sid Bha said nothing, but the Great Kahn could see the worry in the shining of his eyes. 'What do you need me for, my Great Lord?' he asked slowly, as though dragging it out would delay the inevitable answer.

'As our Weapons Master, I felt it appropriate for Eden to discuss his plans with you,' the Great Kahn replied. 'No one has a better understanding of metalwork than yourself, and exemplary designs will be needed to detain himajik individuals.'

'I do not understand, my Great Lord.'

Sid Bha was being purposefully dim-witted, his fear getting the better of him. Or perhaps he felt what was being asked of him was distasteful, and this was an uncharacteristic attempt at rebellion.

The Great Kahn turned to Eden. 'Would you care to explain?'

Eden's smile stretched thinner between his cheekbones. He cleared his throat. 'If you can imagine, it's difficult to cut off the hands of a mayjen offender when they are in full control of their majikal abilities. For starters, we need appropriate restraints.'

Sid Bha looked like he'd rather do anything but imagine it. He turned to the Great Kahn, his face pale. 'My Great Lord, my skills are in designing weapons for warriors, not to enable torture –'

'Do not fear, my dear man,' the Great Kahn cut in. 'You excel at anything you put your mind to. You want to design unique craft for exceptional individuals, do you not? This will be the perfect opportunity. You might even enjoy the challenge.'

'But I-I cannot . . .' Sid Bha stammered a few more unintelligible words before he bowed his head in surrender.

So weak, the Great Kahn thought.

Eden clapped his hands together. 'Excellent! I'll come find you tomorrow.' He gave the Great Kahn a courteous nod before striding away.

'I trust you will do your best,' the Great Kahn said quietly to the Weapon's Master. He did not look over, instead watching the other guests as they chattered and laughed together. 'It would be most unlike you to provide substandard work.'

'Yes, my Great Lord.'

'Eden will provide subjects for you to test your designs. I will not take any chances.'

'No, my Great Lord.'

'Very good.'

Done with Sid Bha, the Great Kahn strode away to the main doors of the ballroom. It would be an interesting collaboration. Eden would have innumerous perverse ideas, and Sid Bha would not have the stomach for any of them. But the Weapons Master would do as he was told, and the People would enjoy his designs. They'd become thirsty for mayjen blood.

The Great Kahn watched Oji approach Sid Bha, who was staring at the space the Great Kahn had left behind. Oji placed his hand on Sid Bha's shoulder, and the two turned together, speaking quietly. The Great Kahn could not hear what was said.

It mattered not. They would say nothing of consequence.

Satisfied, the Great Kahn turned to leave. A Minder materialised to heave open doors of the ballroom. The Great Kahn glided through, leaving the Kahnen to their deplorable decadence.

CHAPTER 18:
SID BHA

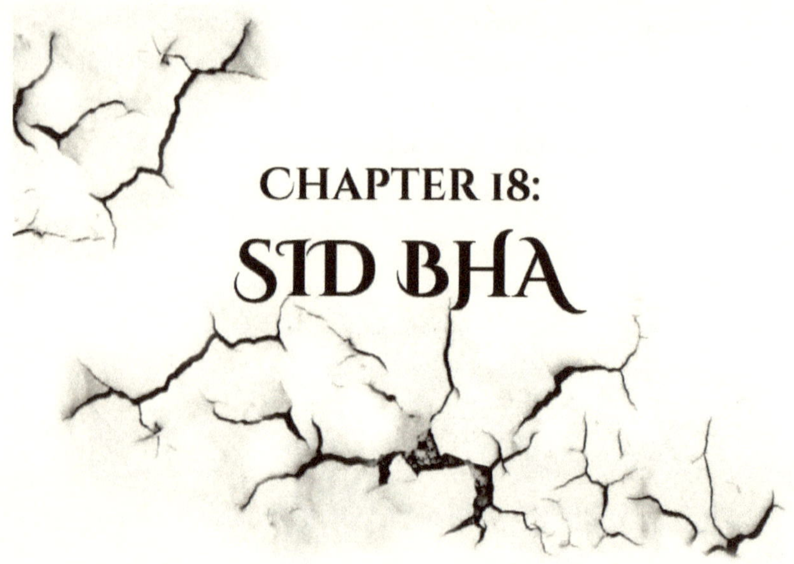

Sid did not see the Great Kahn walk away. His vision was blurry, his heart threatening to pound right out of his chest. The appointment of Eden as the Reprimand Master provided a horrifying insight into the mindset of the Eighth House. And now, Sid was condemned to weld Eden's sadistic dreams into fruition.

The People would not be repulsed by Eden like they ought to be. Most considered mayjen entirely to blame for their hardship. Sid did not believe that, not for one second. But without knowing the truth behind what had triggered the Unsettlement, there was no refuting it.

Sid doubted the Kahnen had orchestrated it. The other houses *could* have started the imbalance to destabilise the Eighth House and force the Great Kahn to step down, but it would have been an incredible gamble. One might create a majikal excess, but how to correct it? No one knew, and the other houses now conceded to the Eighth House for that very reason. They enjoyed the status and wealth of being Kahnen without the impossible expectation of resolving the Unsettlement.

Sid jumped as a hand came down onto his shoulder, and he turned to see Oji next to him. Despite his bulk, Oji moved like water, flowing quickly and quietly to where he wanted to be. Krijen had a knack for that sort of thing.

'I am sorry to startle you,' Oji said with a smile. For the first time all evening, it didn't look forced.

'You'd think I'd be used to it by now,' Sid said.

They stood together quietly, observing the room. Few guests remained respectfully behaved; most had drunk far too much. Sid wondered if the People would have much faith in their government if they could see the Kahnen now. While many of Rue's inhabitants starved, the Kahnen were spitting fresh fruit onto the floor.

'Congratulations on another year,' Sid said, searching for distraction. 'You must be proud of your new Krijen.'

'I am proud of all the Fifteenths who danced today,' Oji said firmly.

Sid stilled. Surely a slip of the tongue. 'The victors, you mean?'

Oji turned his dark eyes on Sid. 'I am proud of all the Fifteenths,' Oji repeated. 'They fought bravely, with honour.'

Sid looked around nervously. Surely the FaKrijen had not intended to be so boorish as to praise the Lost Squares. Oji had drunk too much, of course. But then Sid remembered Oji did not drink.

'Oji,' Sid began carefully, 'you have seemed off recently. Has something happened?'

Oji shook his head. 'Nothing you need to be concerned about. What did our Great Lord want with you?'

Sid noted the forced change of subject. He reluctantly obliged. Oji was worrying him. 'I am to make restraints for himajik offenders.'

'Ah.' Oji paused. 'That explains Eden's presence. I am sorry.'

'Thank you. But I'm not sure I can do it.'

Oji's expression hardened, his eyes like onyx. 'You are not a naïve man, Sid. It is an unpleasant assignment, but defying this order is not worth your life.'

Ashamed, Sid did not correct him. He had not meant that he would refuse to do it. He had meant that it scared him, perhaps too much. Sid was struggling to live in this twisted, cruel Valrue. This command was to be his undoing.

'Think of your family,' Oji said, mistaking his continued silence for defiance. 'The Kahnen will not look kindly on them if you refuse. I know you carry a prestigious name, but it will not mean much if you are thought to be mayjen sympathisers.'

Sid did not know what to say. He was thinking of the mayjen children at Mama Hidel's. Mae and Aren still frequented, despite the growing risks. It made Sid feel sick.

'You will do this, Sid. If you do not do it, they will pick someone else. Someone who is like Eden.'

Sid's eyes darted about the room. The desire to escape was suffocating. 'I-I just don't know if I c-can –' He couldn't get the words out. He was choking on them.

Oji held up his hand, and Sid stopped speaking, instead trembling violently on the spot. The Kahnen were noticing, nudging each other and whispering behind their hands.

'Be calm, Sid. You forget yourself, and this is not the place.'

Oji grabbed a drink off a passing tray and pressed it into Sid's chest. Sid clutched the goblet in both hands and looked into the deep-red liquid, which pulsed in his fingertips. It reminded him of blood.

'I am the FaKrijen,' said Oji. 'Eden is Krijen.'

Sid jerked his head up at Oji's words. 'You can stop this?'

Oji shook his head. 'I regret I cannot stop this. But I can try to make it bearable for you.'

'Are you sure?'

Flouting the wishes of the Kahnen, however minor the transgression, was an outlandish risk. And Oji had been taking a lot of risks lately.

'I've heard people talking,' Sid said. 'They noticed you arrived with the Fifteenths today. Why would you do such a thing?'

'It was important to me. I do not expect you to understand it.'

'No, I don't –'

'Do not worry about me. I have been FaKrijen for nearly thirty years. I know what I am doing.'

Sid felt like he should object further, but it was too much of a relief to know he could avoid crossing paths with Eden. Sid closed his eyes. *Thank the Great Kahn*, he thought, without thinking. The compulsion of the phrase disturbed him.

Oji smiled at Sid again, his kind eyes crinkling. 'This is a celebration. If you continue to look so sombre, I am afraid I must have my Krijen remove you.' Oji slapped Sid on the back so hard that wine spilled out of Sid's goblet.

'How is your family? Your daughter?'

Sid shook his head distractedly. 'Aren is well, thank you. She attended the Dancing Ceremony today. A close friend of hers was a Fifteenth. He won,' Sid added somewhat unnecessarily. He wouldn't have mentioned it if Jin had lost.

'A fine addition to the Krijen I am sure. What is his name?'

'Jin Kanju.'

'Ah yes. A memorable dance. Jin fought well. As did Filip.'

Sid squirmed, uncomfortable that Oji had spoken the Lost Square's name.

'Jin spoke for the Fifteenths today,' the FaKrijen continued, ignoring Sid's awkwardness. 'He seems like a natural leader.'

'Did he?' Sid took a sip of the wine, thinking it might settle his nerves. At least people had stopped looking over at them now.

'Jin is like family to us. Mae wishes Aren and Jin would become promised, though I'm not sure if Aren could be convinced on the matter.'

Oji chuckled. 'Well, if things have not changed since I was a Fifteenth, a Krijen should be an appealing match. Jin will be of a respectable station now, which I imagine you expect for your daughter. Unless I am mistaken, I do not believe I have heard of the Kanju family?'

'No, Jin doesn't come from wealth. His father lives in Val, though nearer the bridge. His father Made the Cross when Jin was young.'

Oji nodded in approval. 'Impressive. I would be interested in meeting such a man. Jin is carrying on a family tradition of great achievement.'

'I would hesitate to praise Jin's father. He is . . . unkind.'

'I am sorry to hear that. There is no doubt Jin has done well. I would hope his father would be proud.'

It was Sid's turn to remain silent, but Oji did not probe. Certain things were best left unsaid.

The Eighth Letter

To You

I am worried. I have yet to receive a reply from you. I double-checked at the Keep, and they assured me that my letters were sent in the usual fashion, down the supply routes with the Krijen. I was briefly concerned you did not reach your destination but have since remembered my sense.

Please forgive me. I am prone to over-reaction lately, given what is happening in Valrue. You may remember I recently wrote of the plentiful fishing stock? I spoke too soon.

To the city's despair, it seems the Eighth House has made an egregious error. More than anyone, you know of the efforts taken to maintain the majikal and natural harmony in Valrue. They hoped an imbalance was not the case, but the evidence is overwhelming.

They have given it a name: The Unsettlement. It seems euphemistic, considering the devastation an excess of majik could wreak upon us, though I am not so arrogant as to suggest I know more than the Kahnen. Perhaps I should consider that this name, spread by the Speakers, is reassurance that the Eighth House have a plan, and therefore it need not be considered a crisis.

You will be dismayed to know the docks have closed for the time being, the lake now devoid of life. I remember how much time we spent there, how happy you were to join me – albeit in disguise – to contemplate its crystal depths. However, I try not to feel sorry for myself, as other businesses have been devastated in much the same way.

It is not only the lake. The entire city is now empty of flora and fauna. It is so very strange to wake up and not see stray dogs waiting by the door for food scraps.

I fear the majikal community is unjustly bearing the blame. While I can understand the People's distrust of majik given the circumstances, there has been unprecedented violence towards mayjen.

Sadly, even the children are not spared. I myself found a child who had been tossed off the bridge and left to a horrendous fate. Her name is Felle. She is recovering well, though no one has come looking for her. She seems understandably traumatised, and I have yet to make a connection with her. I hope that in time she will trust again and perhaps remember some more details which may help me locate her family. However, I must take caution. I may be wrong, but it is possible it was her family who intended her harm. I do not think she is a mayj, but it is still too soon to know if she is another victim of this imbalance, or of something else.

Selfishly, I wish you would return to help me bear these burdens, though at the same time I am relieved. They would target you, given your eminence. I know you have no trouble protecting yourself. Alas, as I said before, I could not help but worry about you. In saying that, you need not worry about me. It is no secret I have no majikal talent. I am not a target.

While I was upset at the time, I am grateful now for your insistence on discretion regarding our relationship. I believed you to be ashamed of me in some way, even though you denied this. Now, I understand it was for my protection. Of course, no one could foresee this Unsettlement, but you have always said that my safety would be compromised if people were to learn of us. Once again, you were right. I feel ashamed I doubted you. Know that when you return, you will have my eternal and unwavering trust.

I must go now.

From Yours,
Dijak

CHAPTER 19: PAKKER

akker squinted into the sun, thinking about his recent conversation with the Great Kahn.

'The boy will be somewhere in Valrue,' the Great Kahn had said. 'You might assume he is a streetling, though he will look worse than most. And he will not act like one. He will not run. He will not attack. He will do anything you tell him.'

Undoubtedly, it was the beggar.

'Find him. Take him to Felle.' The Great Kahn had laughed. 'It is serendipitous, is it not?'

Pakker disliked the plan. It was full of presumption, but the weight of the coin ladening Pakker's pocket made him dismissive of that. The risk wasn't his.

Knowing Felle, she wouldn't be bothered by the precise details of how the boy ended up the way he had. She would only care that Pakker had found him. Felle was obsessed, and obsessive people were shockingly obtuse.

This would be the last thing Pakker would do for the Great Kahn. It was almost time to move on. He'd entertained the idea of the future, briefly. Perhaps he would leave Valrue. The axiom that the Deadlands were impassable was a lie. Jija had confirmed that much because somehow, he'd got *in*.

Pakker was in a strange mood this morning. He never dwelled on his kills, but today he woke up wondering if Tamper, Parve, and Ret had noticed their friend was missing. Pakker did not feel guilty, though he thought he might, this time.

Pakker's thoughts carried him through Val. The streets were quiet for now, though many people would shortly stumble outside, suffering their antics from the previous evening. Valrue had little to celebrate these days, so everyone drank to the Dancing Ceremony.

Felle's tower was simple, appearing as a small rectangular stone block from the outside with a large door at its base. From the street, the house looked much smaller than it was, artfully designed to give modesty in dissuasion of thieves.

Felle had inherited the tower from an aging man called Dijak who made a habit of rescuing children, Felle having been the last. Dijak had been a known mayjen sympathiser and had gone missing only a short while before Felle had hired Pakker.

Pakker knew she'd killed him.

Of all the people that Pakker had worked for, they'd always been the same type of person parading under a variety of different masks. But Felle was different. There was something wrong with her.

For Felle, the innate desire to be liked simply did not exist. There were some human behaviours that she expressed, namely vanity and jealousy. She was completely devoid of others, such as kindness and affection. While people lacking in those qualities would at least attempt a pretence of having them, Felle did not. However, it made her transparent, predictable. Pakker could work with predictable.

As he approached Felle's tower, Pakker pulled the hood of his cloak over his head. It was bold to use the front door, but he walked a fine line between practicality and being unrecognised.

Pakker slipped inside the tower onto the lower landing of the main staircase, which twisted and turned its way up towards the open sky. When it rained, water tumbled past each stone storey to the bottom floor, where it pooled and drained. The rooms off the staircase had arched, empty windows that looked internally to the house rather than to the street.

Pakker headed up to the third landing, where a door stood slightly ajar. He didn't bother to knock.

The room was large and airy, containing an enormous bed with a canopy against one wall. On the floor lay a giant rich-red fur from a long-dead animal for which Pakker had no name. The far wall was a mirror, the dresser centred in front of it covered with combs and coloured powders which Felle used to paint her face.

Felle was sitting in a high-backed chair she'd dragged over to face the mirror. Pakker could see her reflection. She wore nothing at all except for rouge on her lips. She had long dark hair that tumbled over both shoulders, curling as it reached her navel. She was breathtakingly beautiful, which she loved.

When Pakker entered, Felle rose and stood next to her chair, a hand resting atop the golden frame.

'What news?'

Her voice was assertive, seductive. Pakker walked to the edge of the animal fur and stopped, ignoring her body. Her preference for nakedness was born of depraved entertainment in watching other people squirm. Felle abused the social expectations of decency.

'I've found him.'

'Oh?' Felle stepped forward, eager. 'How do you know it's him?' She threw her hair back over her shoulders, exposing her bare chest.

Pakker's face did not leave hers. 'Because you paid me to know,' he said simply. 'I've observed him. He'll be obedient.'

Felle's red lips stretched into a slow smile. 'Obedient, you say? If he is so obedient, why did you not bring him to me already?'

'I'm not sure you want him,' Pakker said. 'He is deformed.'

A shadow darkened Felle's face. As Pakker suspected, her disdain of ugliness overcame other more rational hesitancies.

Felle turned and headed towards a heavy wooden trunk at the base of her bed, pulling out folds of purple material. The wraps were expensive and eye-catching, this glossy piece exceptionally so. Pakker waited while she dressed, watching the material glimmer in the light.

'Deformities can be fixed,' she said finally. 'Take me to him.' She stood in front of Pakker, hands on her hips. A temptation, in her eyes. It was true, Felle's divine figure would bring almost any man to his knees. Pakker kept his eyes on her face.

Felle smiled wickedly. 'I guess you don't approve?' She was trying to provoke him. She enjoyed toying with people.

Pakker cared little for this. 'Wear what you wish.'

Felle's smile did not falter. Her eyes trailed from Pakker's head to his boots and back again. She thought he was calling her bluff.

Felle pulled a grey cloak out of her trunk and swung it about her shoulders, snapping the clasp shut. She tugged the hood forward and tucked her long hair into it before gliding from the room. Pakker followed.

No one bothered them as they wove through Val, towards the bridge. Pakker did not know for certain where the beggar would be, though he suspected.

As they walked, Val's buildings changed. If anyone felt the urge to walk the length of Val, they would notice the slow devolution of homes spewing down the inside of the mountain crater. The sprawling webbed-stone mansions bled into the plain towers like Felle's, then became the stunted blocky homes that marked the edge of Val and the last desperate clutches of wealth.

Pakker stopped on the edge of Val, overlooking the bridge. He could only vaguely smell the stink of Rue across the river, but Felle's nose wrinkled. Pakker rather thought the smell had softened with the growing Unsettlement.

Felle was impatient. 'What's taking so long?'

Pakker did not respond. He looked to the west, down the length of the buildings, narrowing to the size of a thumbnail in the distance. At the end, tucked under the weathered side of the mountain crater, were some abandoned stables. Pakker inclined his head towards it. 'He'll be there.'

Felle took off immediately. Pakker followed, staying a few paces behind, floating through the growing crowds.

The stables were, of course, suffering from disuse. The thick wooden beam across the main entrance had fallen down. Felle stepped over its remains into the mouth of the stables, Pakker following silently. He looked down the row of empty stalls, all of which were in various states of disrepair. But it was dry and free of rot, the clutches of nature unable to take this place.

Felle looped the stables in seconds. 'There is no one here!'

Pakker had not moved from the entrance. His eyes wandered up to the loft, then above that to the roof punctured with jagged openings, through which the sky was visible. There were holes in the walls too, through which you could watch the street outside.

'He's up there,' Pakker said.

Felle swept over, hissing as her cloak snagged on exposed nails. Her eyes landed on the ladder leading up to the loft. It didn't look like it could hold any substantial weight.

'Call him down,' Pakker said. 'He will come.' Or so he had been told.

Felle's eyes narrowed suspiciously. 'You up there!' she called sharply into the quiet of the loft. 'Come down here!'

The wooden beams above them creaked. A small hunched figure appeared above them, stirring debris into the air. The figure quickly dropped over the edge to the floor in front of them, landing with a thud. Felle gave a little shriek, her hand flying to her mouth.

The boy looked, if possible, even filthier than before. His skin was covered with grime. His tunic had worn so thin that Pakker could see the knobs of his spine through the sparse threads. A white cross-hatched pattern on the boy's skin started beneath his chin and trailed down into the hollows of his chest. The scars explained the boy's obedience.

Long ago, evidence of such cruelty would have been hard for Pakker to swallow. Not anymore. Killing people was a curious thing. Each kill tore off a strip of your humanity until eventually, there was nothing left of you to feel at all. You simply existed.

The boy stayed crouched, head tucked into his shoulders, looking at their feet. Felle's upper lip curled. Pakker expected her internal dialogue was conflicted. This creature was certainly the foulest thing she had ever laid eyes on. But he was the prize she sought.

When Felle did not give further commands, the boy turned his head ever so slightly towards her. His unusual blue eyes were like that of the dead. Open, unseeing.

Felle finally stepped towards the boy, apparently overcoming her revulsion. She pulled back her hood. 'Tell me your name,' she said.

'I don't have a name,' the boy replied. Pakker had half expected him to be mute. His voice was quiet, but clear.

Felle raised her eyebrows but said nothing. Her eyes were running over his twisted form. Her upper lip was still curled. 'Can you do majik?' she asked. The boy stared at Felle, unblinking.

'Answer me!'

'Yes.'

'What can you do?'

The boy's expression did not change, though Pakker thought he seemed confused.

'What you ask me to.'

A smile spread across Felle's face, brightening her beautiful features.

The boy looked blankly back. Bewildered, perhaps.

'Tell me why you're hiding,' Felle asked, tilting her head to the side.

The boy shifted slightly. 'I'm not hiding.'

'What do you call this then?' Felle gestured around the stables, her hands sending specks of dust swirling, illuminated by strips of light creeping through the holes in the ceiling.

The boy was quiet. His eyes shifted from Felle to the stable entrance, his attention drawn to something that wasn't there.

'Look at me!'

The boy's head jerked back to Felle.

'Stand up,' Felle commanded.

The boy stood, unfurling himself. It looked painful. His legs were so curved that he was barely taller standing than when he crouched. Felle wouldn't want to be seen with him in the street.

She turned to Pakker. 'Give me your cloak.' Pakker unfastened his cloak and held it out to Felle. She snatched it and thrust it at the boy. 'Put this on.'

The boy reached out for the cloak. His hands moved strangely, his fingers curling loosely into his palms, leaving his wrists to do most of the work. He scooped them awkwardly around the material.

The boy ducked his head, dragging the cloak over his shoulders, then looked down to the clasp. Inexplicably, the boy began to shake. The whites of his eyes gave away his fear. 'Please,' he said.

Felle glanced at Pakker. She didn't know what the boy wanted.

'Please,' the boy repeated, begging for something.

It took a moment for Pakker to put it together. 'He's asking permission to harness,' Pakker said softly.

Felle seemed to like this suggestion. 'Go on then,' she said to the boy.

The clasp clicked closed with a snap. The boy fell forward onto his knees, his head bowed to the floor.

Felle was instantly angry. 'Are you tired already?' she cried.

The boy cringed into the floor but did not respond.

'Felle,' Pakker said warningly.

Felle spun around. '*What?*'

Pakker slowly shook his head at her. Not that he felt for him, but Pakker didn't know how far the boy could be pushed before he broke. He did not want to find out.

Felle flung her hair over her shoulder. 'Look at me.'

The boy looked at her with his blank stare.

'You say you don't have a name. Tell me why.'

'I don't know. I've been called things. But I don't think I have a name.'

'I will give you one.' Felle tapped her finger to her chin, thinking. 'Ah,' she said with a new cunning smile. 'Your name is Drax.'

It was meaningless to Pakker.

'You'll do what I say from now on,' Felle said.

The boy blinked. This made sense to him.

Pakker found himself reluctantly impressed. Everything had gone as perfectly as the Great Kahn said it would.

CHAPTER 20:
AREN BHA

Aren woke with a feeling of dread. It had been over a week since she'd seen Jin at Fivers. He was undoubtedly busy with important Krijen things. It was silly of her to think he would have time to spar with her.

Or so she hoped. Maybe he didn't want to see her.

Aren glowered at one of her wooden bedposts, slung with white sheets and carved all the way up its length. 'Ugh,' Aren said to it. 'I'm so angry with you, Jin!'

'I don't think he can hear you.'

Mae's head appeared above her, obscuring Aren's view of the bedpost. 'You are regressing, I think,' Mae continued. 'My twenty-year-old daughter has been replaced by her fourteen-year-old self.'

Aren scowled. Unfortunately, denying her recent sulkiness would only dig her in deeper. She sat up slowly.

Mae settled on the edge of the bed, her gentle smile dissolving Aren's frustrations.

'Ma, I feel dreadful. Was I too harsh on him?' Aren was about to add that he didn't deserve it, but she bit her lip, unsure if she meant it or not. Jin had killed Filip.

Mae reached out and tucked a lock of Aren's hair behind her ear. 'He'll forgive you,' she said gently. 'And it's never as bad as you think. I'm sure he's regretting not speaking to you before he left.'

'What do you mean "left"?'

Mae's smiled faltered. 'Did your father not tell you? Jin's squad was sent to the Deadlands. Bish went with him.'

'Oh!' That explained why he hadn't come to see her. 'When are they back?'

'In a few months, I think –'

'What?' Aren gaped at her mother. 'A few *months?* Why so long? There is nothing in the Deadlands!'

Mae looked taken aback. 'I'm sorry, I assumed you knew. I thought Marigold would have mentioned it –'

Aren groaned and threw herself back down onto her pillows. 'Oh, Ma! This is it. It's the end of our friendship. Jin will never speak to me again.'

Mae rolled her eyes. 'Stop being so dramatic. Jin adores you. A single argument won't put him off.'

Mae didn't understand. It was more than a fight between friends. It was a fundamental disagreement. Even after a week of thinking about it, Aren still wasn't sure if she could forgive Jin. At least Aren could apologise for acting the way she did, but Jin couldn't exactly extend the same courtesy to Filip.

Mae was saying something about heading into Rue. Normally, the thought of venturing over the bridge would have excited Aren, but today she barely listened as she dragged herself out of bed and over to her closet. She bent to pick up her usual green wraps, but the crusted black ones that Jin wore flashed into her mind. She decided she didn't feel like wearing wraps today. Instead, she pulled on a grey silk dress, tying the waist strap. She turned to find Mae smiling at her again.

'What?'

'You haven't worn that in a long time.'

Aren shrugged. 'I thought I'd try something different.'

'It looks lovely.'

'Thanks, Ma.'

Soon they were winding down through the streets of Val. The houses grew shorter and narrower as they approached Rue. Finally, the buildings stopped; and the mountain river separating Val and Rue came into view, Rue expanding endlessly across the other side of it, down the slope.

The bridge wasn't as impressive now as when Aren was little. *Littler*, she thought with a frown. Originally, it had been a seamless curve of black stone with shoulder-high walls, smoothed with majik. Simple and grand, like the KahnenCull.

Now it was crumbling. Several blocks had fallen into the river, so the walls looked like chipped teeth. Aren wondered what kept the KahnenMayjen so busy that they didn't repair it. It was wide enough that two carriages could have easily passed by one another. Aren wished she could remember more of the carriages. She could barely recall the horses, enormous beasts that drew back their lips and rolled their eyes at you, before the Unsettlement saw them dead in their stables.

Aren and her mother crossed the bridge in a zigzag fashion, dodging holes and people. It was so hot today, made worse by the black stone of the bridge, which reflected the heat from the sun back up at them. Aren was already sweating.

'It's busy today, isn't it?' Mae commented, as they got to the crest of the bridge. Aren knew her mother was trying to draw her attention away from the bodies strung up at the far end of it. Criminals were roped to the stone, left dangling for however long was deemed necessary as punishment for their crime. Mostly, they survived.

Aren did not need her mother's distraction; she averted her eyes anyway. She didn't like to look at them, especially when streetlings were up there. No child, however rabid, deserved that fate.

They reached the other side and entered a swell of people. Everyone wanted to move forward, but there was nowhere to go.

Aren breathed through her mouth. Few people in Rue could bathe regularly, if at all, and the smell of dirty bodies was more noticeable when they were crammed in this close. It was noisy too, the air humming with voices.

Mae wrapped her hand around Aren's and pushed forward through the crowd. It was difficult as most people were standing still, chatting to their neighbours, as though waiting for something.

The crowd grew so tight that Mae soon disappeared between the people ahead of Aren. She gave Aren's arm a particularly forceful tug, pulling Aren into a scrawny, leathery-skinned man who looked down at her in surprise.

'Sorry,' Aren said to him. 'Ma! Hold on. I'm stuck.'

The tugging ceased, and her mother's eyes peered over the man's shoulder. 'What's going on? Excuse me, I need to get my daughter through.'

The man looked down at Mae, shaking his head. 'Tough luck. You're not even close to the front. This is the best view you'll get.'

'The front of what?'

Taller than Aren, Mae stood on her toes and looked across the top of the crowd. Her eyes widened.

Aren wished she could see. 'What is it, Ma?'

Someone pushed into Aren from behind, knocking her into the scrawny man once more so that her forehead bounced off his dirty chest. He managed to twist to the side to let her through, and Aren toppled into her mother.

Mae looked frantic, pushing uselessly for a space in the crowd through which they could escape.

'Ma,' Aren said, exasperated. 'What's ha –'

'Citizens of Valrue!' a familiar voice boomed.

'Oh no,' Mae said quietly.

The crowd shushed, all heads turning towards the voice. Aren couldn't see a thing. She endured the heat of bodies pressed against her, listening intently to breathing and whispers, before the familiar voice punctured through once more.

'I am Teal, KahnenSpeaker of the Eighth House,' said Teal.

Aren remembered him from the Dancing Ceremony. Those unpleasant memories were still very raw.

'Today I present one of our finest Kahnen, his gracious Lord Salli!'

Aren wished she could have covered her ears against the thunderous roar that greeted Lord Salli. Unfortunately, her arms were pinned to her sides. The man behind her was clapping madly above her head, his elbows knocking into her repeatedly.

Another voice drifted down to Aren, one she did not recognise.

'Welcome, citizens of Valrue. I am sincerely humbled by your presence today.'

Aren could hardly breathe. The heat from the sun and the bodies pressed in on her, making her light-headed. If she didn't move quickly, she was going to faint. She spotted what looked like a space on her right and shoved desperately towards it, treading on toes and earning herself more elbows.

After a minute of furious wriggling, Aren finally broke free from the crush of people. To her horror, she realised she'd stumbled right into a sea of streetlings. It explained the gap left by the crowd.

Although the streetlings were of all different ages, skin colours, and builds, their youthful grubby faces were strikingly similar. They were dressed bizarrely, their bodies slung with leather belts and an assortment of poorly fitted clothes, many of which looked to be stolen, made of silks and satins. The youngest of them were bare-chested, their ribs protruding, whereas others had swollen tummies.

The image of the beggar from the other day floated to the front of Aren's mind, though none of them looked as contorted as he had. Aren was suddenly very conscious of her clean face and tidy clothing. She hoped they wouldn't notice her.

Two of the youths had an air about them, seemingly more important than the others. One was a tall girl with obsidian skin and patchy hair, with red ties at her wrists. The other was a shirtless, willowy boy, his chalk-white chest burnt red from the sun. As he turned to speak to the girl, something flashed at his back. Aren sucked in a breath as she saw an enormous curved sword strapped to him, secured by two strips of leather. It was a wonder the unsheathed blade didn't slice his bare skin.

Suddenly, the crowd cheered. The streetlings joined in, hooting and punching their fists into the air.

Aren looked up, realising she could now see Lord Salli above the crowd. His face was purple with exertion, probably spattering spittle over the people beneath him.

'We need to act,' Lord Salli cried, 'and we need to act now! People talk about the fate of Valrue as though we have no choice but to succumb to it. They are wrong, so very wrong. We, the People, have the means to control our future! Mayjen make us feel inferior, yes! But we have perpetuated this, allowing ourselves to be beaten down and beaten down, without realising the strength that we have, the will and vitality and the dream we share of restoring Valrue to its former glory. We have allowed mayjen to hide away, hide away and continue their majikal perversions, which are hurting all of us! They are saying it does not matter, this majik they do, to rid themselves of tiny inconveniences that are a part of life. We know they lie. Their majik is smothering us!'

The man spoke with a conviction Aren had never heard before. He was screaming at the crowd; and they screamed with him, humming with anticipation, hanging on every word while they waited for the climax.

'We must stop this! Stop this! This label of nomajik inferiority will not define us! Now is the time to take charge, make change, and rebalance Valrue. The mayjen plead false ignorance and will not stop, so *we* must stop them, for ourselves and for those we love. And if our actions seem harsh, stop and remember why we do it! We fight for goodness and justice for Valrue. This is what we do! Remember that!'

The streetlings in front of Aren were shaking their fists and stomping their feet, the hooting growing louder. The girl with the red ties curved her hands around her mouth and shouted something into the chaos. The streetlings turned to her as one, their lips moving in unison. Gradually, the streetling cries became a chant that spread across the square and down the streets, seeping like blood through arteries to every soul gathered.

'This is what we do, justice for Valrue! This is what we do, justice for Valrue!'

The streetlings grew more zealous as their chant caught on. They began shoving one another, the crowd closest to them alarmed by their jostling, thrusting back from their vigours.

Aren was swept along in a torrent of people, colliding with a wall of streetlings who had linked arms, laughing with mirth, fearless of the chaos.

The skirt of Aren's dress hooked her into the crowd, dragging her down. Stray limbs pounded against her head, between her shoulder blades, her collarbones. She lost her footing, falling awkwardly between bodies, snatching at the air.

Something heavy smashed into her face, pitching her into a blur of colours. Instinctively, she threw her hands over her head. Something flat and hard hit the whole side of her body. She felt the skin on her hip split as it took the brunt of the force. Jarring blows pounded into her skull, cracking her finger bones. People stepped on her legs and feet, grinding her ankles into the cobbles.

Aren curled into a ball, her eyes closed, tears tracking sideways down her cheeks as she shrank into the nightmare. She felt everything, it seemed, muscles, bones, brain. Even her throat grew sore. She didn't realise she was screaming until she was hauled up out of the darkness and into the blinding light.

CHAPTER 21:
SID BHA

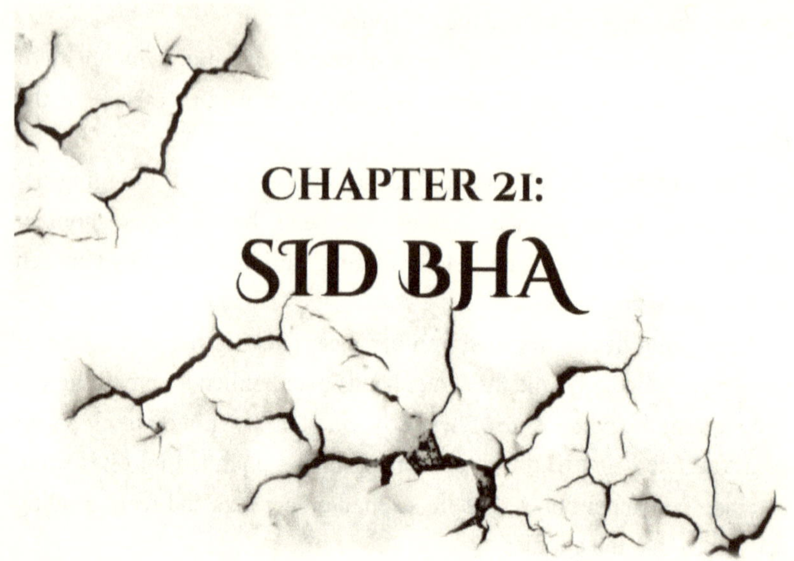

Sid stared at the cardonite armour on his benchtop. There wasn't much to work with. Three breastplates and two helms. Every piece was in impeccable condition. The orange reflection from Sid's forge danced across the dark green hue of the armour, so perfect it made Sid's eyes water. Even though he detested what these pieces would become, Sid couldn't help but appreciate their beauty, built to protect. He wished they could stay this way.

Cardonite was a mystery to Sid, which both frustrated and awed him. He doubted there was anyone left outside the KahnenMayjen who understood it or even knew of its existence. Maybe Noel.

Before he'd come across it himself, Sid knew nothing about cardonite other than what the previous Weapons Master, his uncle, had said in a passing comment. He'd died almost a decade ago now.

'Cardonite is beyond blacksmith mastery,' his uncle had said. 'Don't bother trying to recreate it.'

His uncle hadn't shared the same obsession with cardonite as Sid, dismissing further questions on the matter. Later, when Sid became the Weapons Master, he'd found the armour tucked away in the depths of Night. His uncle had kept it from him, probably to stop it being the distraction it became.

Night was where Sid's designs came to life. The room was usually pitch black, dimly lit to see when the forge was burning. The fire would cast shadows around the room, allowing him to see the heat of the metal as he worked.

Night shared a wall with Day, joined by a thick wooden door and a heavy iron knocker. Day was a rectangular white stone room with high ceilings, furnished with wooden tables scattered with his designs, and chairs with puffy cushions.

When Sid had found the cardonite, he'd been eager to see what he could do with it, so he'd placed a breastplate in his forge. To his disappointment, even when the armour had become white with heat, it refused to be worked. Sid had pounded it repeatedly, heating and reheating it, expecting that eventually it would bend or break under his hammer, or maybe under the sheer force of his will.

But Sid could not put a dent in its flawless surface.

Out of curiosity, Sid had taken the breastplate into Day. He'd prised one of the knuckle-sized diamonds from the hilt of an old sword he was restoring and drawn it across the surface of the armour. The cardonite had remained completely unblemished. The point of the diamond had been filed down.

Frustrated, Sid had tossed the cardonite back into Night for a time. There was one more thing he had yet to try, an idea his uncle wouldn't have bothered to pursue, given his distaste for majik.

Finally summoning the courage, Sid requested one of the KahnenMayjen to attend his blacksmithy. The disgruntled man had appeared in his doorway one afternoon, staring daggers at Sid as he explained what he wanted.

The KahnenMayj had turned to the breastplate with a hand outstretched, his forehead crinkled. After the longest time, his fingers curling in effort and a bead of sweat dripping down his face, the breastplate slowly bent back on itself. Sid had cried out in triumph as the KahnenMayj cut off his majik and collapsed into a chair, laughing between breaths.

Together, Sid and the KahnenMayj had discovered that with immense majikal effort, the cardonite breastplate could be moulded into any shape, including being flattened into a sheet so thin it stretched from wall to wall of the blacksmithy. It did not tarnish nor pick up debris or other matter as it was harnessed. A strong burst of majik would shear the sheet down the middle. But once split into two pieces, it could not be harnessed back together.

The KahnenMayj had tried everything. At one point, he'd poured so much power into the pieces they became a liquid mess. Still, he'd tried to force them into each other. Every time the KahnenMayj cut off his majik, the cardonite solidified seamlessly, tricking them. Sid would take to it with his hammer; and the pieces would crack apart at his touch, a perfect line right down the middle, as though the joins of it had become just another menial substance.

The KahnenMayj had not been quick to give up. Over and over again he'd melted cardonite into a ball, trying to crush it together, his face paling as his power dwindled. When it became clear that he would Turn before he succeeded, the KahnenMayj had cut off his majik, cursing as the ball thudded to the floor at his feet, breaking into taunting halves.

To Sid's dismay, he knew that unless they discovered how to create cardonite, they would never rejoin it. But the pieces were just as strong as before. They could still be manipulated.

With a pang of regret, Sid looked up from the cardonite and its many fond memories, dreading the new ones he was about to make. But he couldn't put this work off any longer.

Sid picked a helm up off the benchtop and slunk over to the heavy door to Day. He heaved it open, the light searing his corneas.

A young KahnenMinder was sitting on one of his plush cushions, waiting for him. The Minder leapt to his feet and bowed.

'Sir, how can I assist you?'

Sid couldn't remember when everything had become so formal. 'Are you here instead of Eden?' Sid asked, unable to keep the nervousness from his voice.

The Minder nodded. 'Yes, sir, though he wasn't pleased. But

FaKrijen Oji warned me of that, so I didn't let it bother me.' The Minder looked up, his mouth hanging open at the room. 'This blacksmithy is amazing. You know, I used to help my father in his shop, back when I was a boy.'

Back when he was a boy? The Minder couldn't be older than fifteen.

'Can you please send for a KahnenMayj?' Sid asked. 'I need some assistance.'

'A KahnenMayj?' The Minder wriggled on the spot. 'Really? Are you going to use majik? Can I watch?'

The questions kept coming. The Minder was, if possible, more curious than Aren at his age. Sid held up his hand. 'Please submit the request.'

'So I can watch?'

Sid didn't like the idea, but the boy looked so excited that Sid felt his resolve crumbling. 'If the KahnenMayj agrees, you may watch. But you mustn't tell anyone what you've seen.'

The Minder dashed from the room.

There weren't many KahnenMayjen now; Sid wasn't sure who would come. He half hoped that there would be no one, rendering his latest designs impossible.

Sid walked over to the nearest desk. It was laden with sketches of what looked like metal gloves joined at the wrists, each a more refined, perfected version of the previous. The gloves would trap the hands of mayjen, making them unable to direct their majik. Simple but effective. Steel might be manipulated by a himajik mayj if there was enough room inside the gloves. But cardonite would be much, *much* harder.

Although they didn't look sinister, the sketches made Sid feel sick. He'd made innumerous manacles and similar restraints before this, but Sid liked to think the people he put in chains deserved it.

The door to Day opened, and the Minder sprung into the room, unable to control his enthusiasm. 'Sir! This is KahnenMayj Stolton Ono, as requested.'

A tall man with streaks of grey in his hair and a scowl on his face followed the Minder. 'I don't appreciate being summoned,' he growled, smacking the Minder on the back of the head. The boy squealed and ducked away.

Sid swallowed. 'Mayj Ono, I am Sid Bha, the Weapons Master. I appreciate you coming at such short notice.'

The mayj eyed Sid carefully. 'Stolt will do,' he said to Sid's surprise. 'I remember hearing about you,' Stolt explained. 'A few years ago, you worked with a colleague of mine.'

Surprised again, Sid nodded. 'That's right. Though I daresay he did all the work,' Sid admitted.

Stolt swept over to Sid and peered down at his drawings. 'These designs are for cardonite?'

'Yes, though the design will need further refining.' Sid wrung his hands. 'I'm hoping you will work the cardonite for me, as your colleague did.'

Stolt eyed the cardonite helm closely. 'How did he do?'

Sid thought it was a strange question. He wasn't sure how to answer. 'Well, I think –' Sid paused, distracted by the KahnenMayj's hands. Stolt was flexing them. It came across as rather menacing.

'He-he admitted it was difficult,' Sid said uncertainly, 'but I think few mayjen could do better.'

To Sid's horror, Stolt grossly misinterpreted his comment.

'You don't think I can do it as well as him?' Stolt asked thunderously.

'I-I didn't –'

'Which design are we using?' Stolt shoved Sid aside and riffled through the drawings, knocking Sid's neat piles askew.

'This one,' Sid said quickly, thrusting the correct design into Stolt's hands.

Sid glanced at the Minder who now stood by the main door. He looked exactly like how Sid felt. 'You may leave, if you wish,' Sid called to him. The Minder fled the room.

Stolt snatched up the cardonite helm and sat down heavily in one of the chairs, the helm in one hand, the design in the other. He leant back in the chair, inspecting the design. After a minute, he placed it in his lap and ran his fingers over the helm.

'Please,' Sid said, his breath catching, 'try not to split it.'

'Yes, yes, I remember,' Stolt said dismissively. He rapped the helm with his knuckles. He tossed it in the air, spinning it around and catching it again in his hand. 'It's light,' he commented.

Holding the helm in his left hand, Stolt floated his right hand over it, fingers splayed. His brow furrowed as he concentrated. His hand shook. His jaw clenched. Beads of sweat swelled on his temples.

Eventually, regretfully, the cardonite gave under Stolt's majik, the edges of the helm softening and losing their shape.

'Ah-ha!' Stolt looked towards Sid. 'Don't you dare doubt me again,' he threatened.

Sid gulped.

'All right then,' Stolt said, looking down at the design in his lap. 'I reckon I can make this. How much cardonite do we have? Because if I'm not allowed to split this, we are going to have a problem.'

Sid flushed. 'Eventually, I think you can split the helm. But can we first trial the design from this piece? The cardonite can be worked incredibly thin. You'll have more than enough, I think.'

'It doesn't weaken when it's stretched?'

Sid shook his head.

Stolt grinned. 'The skahks won't know what hit them.'

Sid froze. Surely the meaning of that word was not lost on Stolt.

The KahnenMayj stood up again and spread the drawings out on the table, pulling out different designs from underneath the pile. 'These are all just variations on the gloves,' he complained. 'Do you have nothing else for me?'

'Just the gloves.'

Stolt must have sensed something in Sid's tone. He looked up from under his brows, as though measuring Sid up. 'Very well,' Stolt said finally. 'But you're kidding yourself if you think this is all you're going to have to design.'

Sid stiffened. 'When did Eden speak to you?'

'Who's Eden?'

Sid didn't reply.

'Look,' Stolt said. 'Half the Kahnen are out for skahk blood. They want to give the People something which will actually dissuade skahks from harnessing.'

Sid cringed. 'Why do you use that word?'

'Skahk?' Stolt laughed. 'Because that's what they are. Dirty mayjen, harnessing us into the ground.'

'Don't you see the irony in that? You are a mayj!'

Stolt shrugged. 'Sure, but I'm better than them. I use majik within reason. Take harnessing this design, for example. Imagine the mayjen we will take down, the powerful skahks that actually matter to the imbalance. Not the pathetic so-called lomajik lot.'

'And by take down, you mean torture and murder?'

Sid didn't know what made him say it. His own words made him tremble.

'Everything has a consequence,' Stolt said. 'Why does it bother you anyway? You design weapons for a living. You provide the means for people to kill each other.'

'This is different.'

'How? You think because you sneer at the Kahnen for using your designs, you're not implicated in what's done with them?'

Sid opened his mouth, but no sound came out.

'You're offended I call them skahks,' Stolt continued, 'but at least I'm not shy about where my loyalties lie. You're still in denial about which side you're on.'

Sid felt like he'd been hit over the head with the helm of cardonite.

The Cardonia Spell

The Cardonia Spell is defined as that which binds matter in an incomparably robust, lattice-like structure. Most notably, the spell is effective for creating or reinforcing structures where strength and durability against majik take precedence.

The origin of the spell is debated, though its name gives credence to the claim of Mayj Folize Cardon. However, the writings of Grakam Aam Li describe (in a disturbingly similar fashion) the same majikal creation. Regretfully, it took several years to translate Aam Li's work. The concept of dates had not yet been adopted by the Hamakan peoples, and so the spell was named after Cardon.

The Cardonia Spell was erroneously termed the 'simple' Weave by misinformed scholars. This led to the enduring belief that it is the most elementary of the Weaves and, therefore, more likely to be mastered. This is woefully incorrect. All Weaves are of the same esoteric nature, though the success of their casting depends on the power of the Weaver. Naturally, Influencers have the most success, though that is not to say others are incapable.

Although any mayj of adequate power can break cardonite bonds, once broken, they must be re-woven by a mayj of the Weaving expression. Excessive attempts by Builders to recreate the bonds will eventually lead to the denaturing of the matter itself. Thus, cardonite became quite popular for the design of weaponry and armour. If they fell damaged into enemy hands, non-Weaving attempts to harness the cardonite armour quickly rendered it unworkable.

Many Weavers incorporate their signature into their cardonite designs. This involves showcasing a particular colouring of particles from the harnessed matter, allowing others to identify their work. Likewise, non-cardonite creations can mimic the iconic webbing, which is observed in many cities where Builders have resided.

Signatures became so prevalent that some cardonite designs were mistakenly overlooked because they presented no obvious signature. For

CHAPTER 22:
AREN BHA

Aren's head broke the surface of the crowd. Her hands scrabbled at her collar, which was pulled tight about her neck. Someone held fistfuls of her dress and was dragging her backwards. No one seemed to notice she was being strangled. They were too busy running the opposite way.

Just when Aren thought she was going to black out, she was ripped into empty space and slammed, back first, against a wall. The pressure against her throat was gone in an instant.

Aren sucked in air, making undignified sounds. A shadow loomed over her, and there were arms like iron bars at her sides. As her mind cleared, fear kicked in.

'Get away from me!' Aren's voice was hoarse and raspy. Not at all how she wanted it.

'Calm down,' an unfamiliar male voice said above her. 'Just breathe.'

Aren breathed. It was painful. Her mind was like wading through mud. She squinted up at the shadow. A young man stood over her, braced against the onslaught of bodies. 'You look familiar,' he said.

When his face finally came into focus, Aren recognised him. 'You're Wren,' she gasped. 'From the Dancing Ceremony!'

Wren hissed, bringing his face down to hers. He was close enough that she could see the blood vessels around his dark irises. 'Don't say that name!'

Someone knocked into him, and he grunted, elbows buckling. 'Fuck this,' he said, shoving back against the body.

'You don't have to do that,' Aren said, still feeling a little dazed. 'I can protect myself.'

Wren snorted. 'Oh *please*.' He looked up above Aren's head, off to the right. 'Okay. I'm going to lift you up to that. Are you able to grab it?'

Aren looked up. There was a wooden canopy above her head, a strip of material slung between the planks to give shade. Not far above that was the flat stone roof of the building.

'Yes,' said Aren determinedly.

'Okay, ready? Go!'

Aren wasn't at all ready, but Wren had already tossed her into the air. She landed excruciatingly on her stomach on the wooden plank and snatched at the material, broken fingers protesting. It hurt more than she could have believed.

Snarling, she pulled herself up. Using the wall to steady herself, she wobbled to her feet, the rooftop just below shoulder height.

'Move to the roof,' Wren called up to her.

Teeth clenched, Aren hauled herself up and onto the roof, rolling onto her back. All the bony bits of her body protested, especially her hip, which throbbed painfully.

Aren lay on the rooftop looking up at the clear sky, breathing fast, shallow breaths. Everything was quieter; the noise from the crowd was muted up here. Adrenaline pulsed through her. She wondered if it was numbing the pain. It didn't feel like it.

Wren's face interrupted the perfect blue of her vision. 'You good?'

Aren rolled carefully to a seated position. 'Ow,' she said, squinting up at him. 'Yes. You?'

Wren squatted down next to her, running his eyes over her injuries. He'd just saved her life.

'Wow,' Aren rasped, her throat still sore. 'How can I thank –'

'You look like shit,' Wren said.

Aren blinked, taken aback by his noxious tone. 'I was going to say thank you,' she said. 'But maybe I won't.'

Aren made to stand up, but the movement left her dizzy. Instead, she leant on her hand to steady herself. 'You,' she breathed, trying to sort her scattered thoughts. 'You shouldn't be here.' It came out all wrong.

'I know,' Wren snapped. 'But I could say the same for you.' His monolid eyes were accusatory, running over her silk dress, her leather boots. 'You don't look like the typical Rue type.'

Aren didn't like being inspected. She scowled up at him.

A flash of recognition crossed Wren's face. 'I know who you are. You're Jin's girl.'

'I'm Aren,' Aren said, feeling annoyed.

'You're from North Val. Why the fuck were you at Lord Salli's rally?'

Aren was very aware of the way he said North Val. It was the tone people used when they spoke about snobs.

'I wasn't at the rally,' Aren said. 'We just got caught up in it.'

'We?'

Oh, by the Great Kahn. 'Mae!'

Aren tried to stand again but ended up staggering sideways and falling onto her knees.

'Stop that. Sit down!' Wren grabbed her and tugged her onto her backside. 'What's the matter?'

'My mother! I was with her, but I left to –' Aren pinched the bridge of her nose, trying to remember. 'Ow.' Her fingers hurt. In fact, everything suddenly hurt more than before. Feeling woozy, Aren lay back on the hard stone roof and closed her eyes.

'Your mother will be fine,' came Wren's curt reply. 'She would've moved out of the way.'

Tears pooled on Aren lashes. 'I can't believe I left her,' she said. 'How could I *do* that?'

Wren snorted again. 'Having you there wouldn't have made the slightest difference.'

Aren opened her eyes. 'I have to find her.'

'You aren't doing anything. I'll find her. What does she look like?'

'You can't go back in there again!' Aren sat up too fast, everything spinning.

'No, you idiot,' Wren said, pointing to the edge of the roof. 'I'll look from here. I'm not going back in unless I have to.'

Ignoring Wren's protests, Aren scrambled to the edge and stuck her head over. The screams hit her like bricks. People were drowning in the swell, spilling out from the main square into every side street and across the bridge in the distance. Aren gritted her teeth against their cries, searching for Mae. It was impossible. There were far too many people.

'This is useless!'

'Calm down,' Wren said again. 'Were you close to the stage?'

'No, we were near to the bridge.'

'If you came in from Val, your mother would have headed back that way. No one from Val would run *into* Rue in a panic.' He looked pointedly at Aren, who took a moment to register the insult.

'It wasn't like I had a choice,' Aren retorted. 'I just got pulled along by the crowd –' She narrowed her eyes at Wren. He'd settled down in the middle of the roof.

'You're not helping me look.'

Wren's jaw clenched at that. He had soft features, so it didn't suit him. 'The Krijen are here,' he said.

Aren looked down at the crowd. Black-wrapped figures had indeed arrived, moving with admirable efficiency to calm the crowd.

'How did you know? You weren't looking.'

'Because. I know how they work,' Wren said in a clipped tone. 'Why the fuck are you even talking to me?' His question was abrupt, and for some reason, he looked angry.

'Huh?' Aren had no idea what he meant. *Why wouldn't I talk to him?* she thought. He was rude, but that didn't seem a good enough reason to ignore someone. Then she remembered. Wren was Lost. An outcast, shunned, forgotten, invisible. Right. But it didn't seem right.

'Let's face it,' Aren said. 'You saved my life. I can't ignore you.'

'Yes, you can.'

'Yeah, well, I'm choosing not to.'

If possible, Wren looked even angrier. 'You shouldn't be talking to me!'

Aren leant back from him. 'Excuse me?'

'I should say I'm glad I saved you,' he said nastily, mimicking her earlier comment. 'But I'm not.' Wren got to his feet and stalked away.

Bewildered, Aren watched him disappear into the rooftops before looking out over the edge of the roof again. With the help of the Krijen, the crush had calmed a little. Bodies riddled the street, not all of them moving.

Aren wondered what had happened to Lord Salli. Should she even care? He had said some truly awful things.

Aren was throbbing with hurt. She looked down at her hands with gruesome curiosity. They were red and swollen. The skin was split across her knuckles, some of her fingers not quite straight –

'Why *are* you talking to me?'

Aren yelped. Wren was standing right behind her.

'Don't *do* that!'

Wren sat down with mocking slowness. 'Sorry,' he said, insincerely. 'Why are you talking to me?'

'You know, I have more important things to do than answer your stupid questions,' Aren snapped at him.

'Don't kid yourself. You can't go down there now,' Wren said. 'So – *why are you talking to me?*'

He was so *obnoxious*. Aren had a smart comment on the tip of her tongue, then caught herself. Something was niggling at her. Maybe Wren was being like this because he was trying to distract from something else. She thought back to the ceremony. Only a week ago, he'd lost his dance. His future. It was a lot to lose in a day.

'I'm sorry,' Aren said softly. 'You don't deserve to be Lost.'

Wren recoiled. 'Don't say that.'

'Are you okay?' She hoped it didn't sound patronising.

'What do you think?' His voice dripped with scorn. 'My whole fucking life, wasted. Do you know what that feels like?'

His reply surprised Aren. She hadn't expected he would be willing to talk about it.

'No, I don't.'

'I'll tell you then. It feels like someone cheated. Bish, you know? He must've cheated.'

Aren's pity vanished in an instant. 'No way. Not Bish.'

'Oh yeah? How do you know?'

'Because Bish has never cheated at anything in his life.'

'You would say that, wouldn't you? You couldn't spot a problem if it smacked you in the face. I bet everything in your life is just fucking perfect.'

Aren felt something snap inside. She *hated* Wren.

'Is this why you saved me?' she asked. 'So you could yell at someone who might feel obligated to sit here and take it?'

Wren reeled backwards, his eyes wide with shock, as though she'd slapped him. Aren didn't care. She turned her back on him and swung her legs over the ledge, preparing to slide onto the canopy.

'Wait!'

She shuffled herself forward –

'Aren!'

Aren looked back. Wren's hand floated down to his side, as though he'd been reaching for her.

'What?'

'Do you have to leave?'

Aren stared. She couldn't keep up with him. 'I thought you were angry at me.'

'Not *at* you. You're just . . . here.'

She scowled. That made no sense. 'I need to get home.'

'Right. Okay.'

Wren looked as though he was going to say something else. Then his shoulders drooped; his eyes dropped to his knees. He looked unbelievably wretched.

Aren felt a twinge of renewed pity. She couldn't bring herself to leave him now. Not looking like that.

'Can you help me get home?'

Wren looked up, his brow furrowed. 'Why?'

Aren screwed her face up at him. *Was he always this difficult?* 'Because,' she said, 'I'll probably drop dead on the way home without help.'

Wren shook his head. 'You don't want my help.'

'I really do.'

'People will recognise me. You don't want to be seen with me.'

Aren made a small noise in frustration. 'I don't care about that! I just want to get home. Either you help me or I try to convince some Rue stranger to take me home. Which is it?'

She glared at him. His face twisted in indecision.

'Fine. Give it a minute, though.'

'You want to wait until the Krijen have left?'

'Yes.'

Finally, something made sense.

Aren watched Wren while they waited. He mostly looked down at the rooftop, every now and then his eyes drifting up to meet hers, before dropping again.

'I meant it when I said you didn't deserve to be an outcast,' Aren said after a little while. 'It's so cruel.'

'It's an obligation. The Lost Squares shall not impose their shame upon others deemed to be worthier.' His words sounded strangely rote-learned. 'You should ignore me,' Wren repeated. 'Like everyone else.'

Aren turned her head sideways, trying to read him. It was difficult. Like trying to guess the feelings of a rock. 'I don't believe that,' she said. 'Anyway, it sounds partly self-imposed to me. I mean, if Jin had lost, I wouldn't just ignore him.'

Wren moaned, as though her words pained him. 'So naïve. Being Lost is *not* a choice.'

'What do you mean?'

'My family.'

Wren left that hanging in the air between them, as though steeling himself for what he was about to say.

'So,' he began, 'I headed to my parents' home after the dance. I couldn't see them at the ceremony. It would be an embarrassment for them.' He spoke matter-of-factly, but Aren could hear the strain in his voice.

'I waited until it got dark. I hadn't gathered my things, even though I should have been long gone. When my parents and younger brother got home, they didn't look at me, didn't speak to me. They started getting ready for bed. I followed my parents into their room. Ma was crying.' Wren shook his head, as though trying to dislodge the memory. 'They didn't say a single thing. I sat in the doorway all night, waiting. When the sun came up, I left.'

Aren almost reached out to give Wren a hug. She stopped herself. He didn't seem the hugging type. 'I'm sorry,' she said.

'You're the first person I've spoken to in a week,' Wren said. 'Actually, I should say you're the first person who has spoken to *me*. I stayed in Valrue because I thought people wouldn't know what I was, but I was wrong. People can tell, somehow. Even the ones who didn't go to the ceremony.'

Aren wasn't sure what to say. After a time, another question came to her. 'What about the other Lost Fifteenths? Where did they go?'

Wren chewed his lip, as though wondering whether to answer. 'Well,' he said, 'mostly, they left Valrue. Walked out into the Deadlands.'

'But they would die!' Aren said, shocked.

Wren shrugged. 'Doesn't matter. Your life is over anyway.'

'But what if your family changes their mind?'

'They wouldn't. Or even if they did, other people wouldn't. You'd just make your family outcasts as well. Better to leave and save them from that.'

'What about the others? The ones that didn't go to the Deadlands?'

Wren grimaced. 'I went looking. I found some of them. They just did it, you know? Dagger through the chest, or found a rope. It's the respectable thing to do, really.'

Gradually, the horror of his sentence sank in. 'That's truly awful,'

Aren said quietly. 'But you didn't.'

Wren looked down. 'No. I should have, but I missed my chance. I found the coward in me I spent the last fifteen years trying to bury.' He didn't smile, but his mouth turned up in the corners as though he was trying. It didn't match the mood at all.

'Why did you save me?' Aren asked.

Wren shot her a scathing look. 'I'm Lost, not soulless.'

Aren didn't know what to say.

They sat in silence, the sun beating down on them, its glorious warmth a harsh contradiction to Wren's reality.

Aren's head throbbed. She wanted to go home. She peered out over the edge of the roof. 'No Krijen,' she said. 'Let's go.'

Wren stood up and walked up to the ledge, running a critical eye over the scene below him. Satisfied, he leant down, placed one hand on the roof, and nimbly dropped onto the wooden canopy. He moved with the same casual grace as Jin. With a pang, Aren remembered it would be months before she would see Jin again.

Wren turned and held out a hand. Aren swung her legs back over the edge, apprehension stirring. 'I can do this bit.'

Wren shrugged and dropped quietly to the ground below. A few people standing nearby glanced over, then hurried away.

Teeth gritted against the pain, Aren twisted onto her front and eased herself down onto the wooden canopy. She clung to the ledge, dizzy again, aware she was being slow.

'Sorry,' she called down to Wren. 'My head isn't straight.'

Sucking in a few quick breaths to prepare herself, she walked her hands down the wall and entered an awkward crouch, hoping to sit down on the wooden beam and jump to the ground. Unfortunately, her foot caught in her dress and she toppled off the beam, crashing into Wren's waiting arms.

He put her down quickly, looking guilty as she gasped and leant over, clutching her side. 'Okay, no more of that,' Aren ground out. Keen to avoid further damseling, she hobbled gingerly in the direction of the bridge.

Wren walked half a pace behind. He kept his head down, ducking behind her every time they passed someone. Aren couldn't help but notice people were giving them an unnecessarily wide berth, shooting furtive looks only at her. Their eyes rolled over Wren as though he wasn't there. But maybe she was reading too deeply into it, conscious of Wren's worries.

They crossed the bridge and started up the gentle slope towards home at an aggravatingly slow pace. Wren looked up every time Aren stumbled, which was embarrassingly often. She was so, so tired. Her trembling muscles constantly threatened to send her to the ground.

'I need to sit,' she whimpered after what seemed an endless time, easing herself onto a wide stone step leading up to the next tier of streets. There were shops and towers all around them, windows filled with faces looking out at her with guarded expressions.

Suddenly, a female voice bellowed down the street. 'MOVE!'

Hands pulled Aren roughly to the side. A moment later, a woman bowled right through the spot where Aren had been, two black-wrapped figures in close pursuit.

The woman moved like the wind, blurred as she sprinted past the shopfronts. Without warning, she jerked sideways, a dagger protruding from her sleeve, pinning her to the wooden shutters of a shop. The woman flicked her wrist and the dagger shot from the wood, almost invisible with speed, her majik driving it back towards the Krijen. One of them snatched it from the air in front of his face and hurled it back, but it soared off its trajectory as the mayj gave another flick of her wrist. The dagger clattered into a side street.

The mayj slowed, her running noticeably laboured.

Just as she reached the end of the street, a third Krijen stepped out from between the narrow buildings and thrust out an arm, catching her chest and throwing her onto her back.

Aren cried out in sympathy.

The Krijen threw himself onto the mayj, pinning one of her hands beneath his knee. The mayj squeezed her free hand, and the Krijen made a horrible gurgling sound as his wraps constricted around his throat. He fell sideways, his hands to his neck, contorting in silence.

The mayj did not leap up and run, like Aren expected. Instead, she rolled herself onto her stomach and dragged herself with one hand across the ground, the other still held out towards the flailing Krijen, her nails leaving screaming white lines across the cobbles.

With a fresh spasm of pain in her gut, Aren realised the mayj was running out of power. If she wasn't careful, she'd soon Turn.

The two other Krijen arrived. One raced to his comrade, wrestling his dagger underneath the wraps about his neck and slicing through them. They burst open, the Krijen gasping as he sucked in lungfuls of air.

The other Krijen threw himself onto the mayj's back, grabbing her hands and forcing them together beneath his fists. She shrieked and twisted, trying to pull herself free, but it was futile.

Now that she was restrained, the watching spectators converged on the group, yelling profanities at the mayj. Some stood with their hands over their mouths, though whether in awe or horror, Aren couldn't tell. One of the Krijen pulled a cleaver from his wraps.

Aren's blood ran cold. 'What's he doing with that?'

She'd barely raised herself off the step before Wren grabbed her and tugged her down.

'Let me up!'

'No.'

'You arsehole, let me up!' Aren batted at him pathetically with her broken hands.

Wren grabbed the front of her dress, pulling her face to his. 'Stop it,' he hissed. 'You don't even know what she's done.'

'They're going to kill her!'

'No, they aren't. You see that weapon there? They are going to cut off her hands, stop her from harnessing.'

'They are going to *what?*'

Two of the Krijen held the mayj to the ground, impervious to her screams. A spectator leant forward and spat on her.

Aren clawed at Wren, frantic. 'We have to do something!'

'No,' Wren said. He pulled her up off the steps. 'We're leaving. Turn.

Walk. Now.'

Aren was sobbing. 'You're a coward!' she screamed at Wren. 'You're just scared of the Krijen!'

Wren didn't respond, relentlessly steering her away.

There was a sickening thud behind them and the crowd jeered. Aren choked on her tears.

'Idiot,' Wren muttered darkly. 'She should've known better.'

As they turned a corner and another thud followed, the roar of the crowd softened to a lull. Aren shoved Wren, but he was solid, and she only sent herself stumbling away from him. 'Why?' Aren cried. 'Why did no one help her?'

'They cut off her hands, that's all. She'll live.'

'How could the Krijen do that? How could you want to be one of them?'

'Fuck, you are *impossible*.' Wren shook his head at her. 'Are you always this dramatic? How does Jin deal with you?'

Aren wiped her nose on her sleeve. She didn't care about the dress. She would never wear it again after today.

Aren turned away from Wren and stormed up the hill as best she could on her wobbling legs. His comment nagged at her. It was the second time today she'd been called dramatic.

Wren fell in behind her, hiding his face once more. Aren suddenly felt guilty. Wren might talk mean, but he'd saved her life today, and probably stopped her from doing something foolish just now. And to repay him, she had called him a coward.

'I'm sorry. I'm so sorry.' Aren stopped again, swaying.

Wren's face darkened. Maybe he thought she was giving up and he'd have to carry her. He would probably do it too.

'Thank you for saving my life. You don't have to come all the way,' Aren said, feeling bad. 'I asked you to take me home to my family when you can't go home to yours. It was insensitive.'

Wren looked stunned. Then he snorted. 'You hit your head really fucking hard, didn't you?' He folded his arms. 'You're in no state to be walking alone. That, and I don't trust you won't get yourself killed trying to save some other undeserving mayj.'

What annoyed Aren the most about his response was that he hadn't accepted her apology. She stewed on that for a while before she let it go, too tired to press him on it.

They walked the rest of the way in silence. By the time the towers became stone mansions, the sun was dipping below the jagged peak of the mountain.

Aren let out a cry of relief when they turned the corner and she saw her home. She started towards it, stopping when she noticed the absence of Wren's quiet footsteps behind her. She turned to see him still on the corner, staring up at the mansion.

'I'm not going with you,' he said.

'Please come inside. You've taken me all this way. Have dinner with us. There will be plenty of food, and you can even stay if you need to –'

'I'm not going in, Aren.'

'But you must be hungry –'

'No.' Wren seemed annoyed again. 'You might be grateful for my help, but your family won't appreciate it.'

'They aren't like that. They're different –'

'You're wrong. They'll be just like everyone else, and rightly so.'

'That's not fair.'

For the first time that day, Wren laughed. It wasn't a jovial laugh, but a horrible sound that set Aren on edge. 'I wish I could be more like you,' he said.

Aren wasn't sure what he meant. She opened her mouth to ask when an anxious voice floated down from the house.

'Aren? Is that you?'

'Ma! I'm here!' Aren's voice was so hoarse the words were barely audible. She could see her mother's shape hurrying down the path from the mansion, two more figures in tow.

Aren turned back towards Wren. 'Please –' She stopped.

Wren was gone.

Aren scoured the darkening surroundings, but Wren had disappeared with more subtlety than a shadow in the night.

'Aren!'

Her father's voice quivered in the distance. Aren stalled, torn between running to them and finding Wren, to force him to stay. She was mad that he would just disappear like that, without a proper goodbye. But maybe Wren wanted that.

Mae, Sid, and Noel were suddenly at her side. Mae reached for her, then screamed, covering her mouth in horror. 'Oh, Aren! What *happened* to you?'

'What?'

Aren swayed on her feet while her mother's hands fluttered over her, as though desperate to touch her but scared she might break.

Wordlessly, Noel scooped Aren into his arms and hurried her up the path. Mae was babbling apologies to Aren for leaving her in the square, but Aren barely heard them. An enormous fatigue had settled over her.

Noel carried Aren across the threshold and settled her on one of the velvet chairs in the foyer. He dashed off, probably to get his healing kit. Mae and Sid crowded around Aren, their faces stricken.

They were talking. Aren heard the words but didn't understand their meaning. Her mind was drifting. The room seemed awfully bright, though the lanterns along the walls had only ever given off a dull glow.

'It's not your fault, Ma,' Aren mumbled. 'I got knocked down.'

Aren felt a gentle tug on her hand. Noel had returned with his little bag filled with bottles and powders of strange and wonderful scents. Someone else started dabbing at her forehead, which hadn't hurt until then. Aren's arm was too heavy to push them away. She drifted into blackness.

CHAPTER 23:
THE GREAT KAHN

The Great Kahn's fury was tremendous. KahnenMinders scattered before him, tripping over themselves in haste. It had been six months since the mercenary had taken in that insufferable creature, and Valrue was still foundering.

The Great Kahn threw open the doors to one of the innumerous stone-walled rooms, empty apart from a staircase that twisted up into the mountain. He started up the steps, his red cloak spilling out behind him like blood. He ran his hand along the cold curved stone of the wall as he spiralled upwards. There were tiny windows along the walls, too far apart to provide any decent lighting. Which spiteful predecessor had constructed this Keep? Who wanted to spend their days sitting in darkness? He was almost tempted to get Stolt to blast some holes in this prison.

Stolt, that pathetic excuse for a KahnenMayj. Even though he'd spared him on purpose, the Great Kahn wanted to scream his derision of the man. But he would not. He would not let his emotions control him. He was not so weak anymore.

The Great Kahn reached the top and stepped through a doorway onto a stone rampart, open to the mountain air. It was early in the morning. In the distance, the jagged peaks of the mountain bathed in orange light, sloping down towards the dark city. The vast surface of the crater lake was still in shadow.

Valrue looked deceptively beautiful from here, buildings rolling down the inside of the crater. The raging mountain river sliced off the very tip, separating Val from Rue, fed by a reservoir behind where the Great Kahn stood now. The river cascaded over the edge of the stone step of the city. The Great Kahn could not see it from this angle, but he knew the water fell so far that it became cloud before it hit the lake.

The bridge to Rue was barely visible, the only way to cross between the two parts of the city. Rue in its enormity spewed to the very edge of the stone step, a winding path leading from its southernmost side down to the abandoned docks of the lake. The filth that ran from its streets turned the edges of the water brown. He couldn't see that from here either.

It was not the Valrue the Great Kahn had expected. Mandavar had made sure of that.

'My Great Lord.'

The Great Kahn bared his teeth. Even the voice of the man tempted his wrath.

The mercenary was leaning on the ramparts behind him, arms folded, face calm. He had brown hair and brown eyes. No defining features about him at all. In fact, the Great Kahn had almost forgotten what the mercenary looked like. He wore the most unremarkable clothes.

The Great Kahn let his lips fold back over his teeth. His anger was simmering quietly. For now.

'I am displeased,' the Great Kahn said.

'I don't doubt it,' the mercenary replied. 'But you can hardly blame us.'

'I think you will find that I can.'

'Did you have any idea what had been done to the boy?'

'He was tamed.'

The mercenary stood up off the wall and walked towards the Great Kahn. He stopped in front of him, about a foot from his face. It was vaguely impressive. Few people would attempt to stare him down like that.

'He wasn't tamed. He was *ruined*.'

'Semantics.'

'I'm being paid to provide a service,' the mercenary said. 'I don't like it when things get in the way of that. You could have forewarned me.' His voice was soft, dangerous.

'I do not understand how the boy's obedience is a problem.'

'The boy's *obedience*, as you call it, doesn't seem to stretch as far as him harnessing.'

'Is he refusing to do majik?'

'He is cowering in a room, flinching at cracks in the walls.'

'Is he refusing to do majik?'

'No.'

'Then tell me why I should not throw you off these ramparts, for how long you have kept me waiting.' It wasn't an empty threat, but the man didn't back down.

A touch of fear flickered beneath the Great Kahn's anger. It was possible this mercenary was like Mandavar. His strings could not be pulled.

'If you want this done, we need more time,' said the mercenary. 'The boy has to *want* to harness. At the moment, it's like we've punctured a needle hole in the bottom of a bucket that he keeps jamming his finger over.'

'How eloquent,' the Great Kahn sneered. 'I have been patient. My city is drowning. I have given you the means to fix it, and you are *stalling*.'

'You've got no choice. Felle still has that final letter. You don't want it falling into the wrong hands.'

'Those letters prove nothing. They are the ramblings of a delusional man.'

'Dijak was a respectable man, in his time.'

'You dare blackmail me?'

'I dare.'

This mercenary *was* like Mandavar. Against his better judgement, the Great Kahn felt desire stirring. He despised that.

'How long?'

'As long as it takes.' The mercenary stepped back, sending his gaze over the Great Kahn's shoulder. The sun was brushing the tops of the buildings now, the slopes of the mountain the colour of the Deadlands.

'This means more blood on your hands,' the Great Kahn said, longing to provoke him.

The mercenary looked back at him, his brown eyes gentle now, his plain face unscarred. 'What do you think you're paying me for?'

***

Not long after his meeting with the mercenary, the Great Kahn was seated on his dais in the Red Room. The Eighth House members sat in silence before him, like prisoners chained to their chairs. Word of his anger had spread.

It was annoying.

Even the boldest of his Kahnen would be reluctant to speak today, which always led to a slow and boring meeting.

There was a knock at the door and a trembling KahnenMinder entered, followed by Teal, the KahnenSpeaker. Teal walked forward, looking disconcerted at the silence. The Minder quickly closed the door.

Teal bowed to the Great Kahn, a sweeping gesture that sent his nose almost entirely to the floor. He'd heard too. Good. This man was supposed to be in the know, after all.

'Speak,' the Great Kahn said.

'My lords and ladies,' Teal said with another flourish. 'I have somewhat burdensome news today, gathered by myself and my many eyes and ears on the streets. As always, I guarantee truths. My words contain no embellishment or falsehood. I will start with the topic most paramount in nature, to wit, several unprecedented public executions.'

Lord Salli leant forward, eager to speak. The Great Kahn waved his permission to the room. It did not matter who spoke today.

'What do you mean by unprecedented?'

'My lord, these executions were not conducted by Krijen, but by the People. Mayjen killed by their own relatives, to spare the honour of the family.'

Lady Hia gasped, her hand flying to her mouth.

Teal continued. 'I regret there is growing uncertainty as to whether the Eighth House will continue to act in the interests of the People. Some feel it necessary to take matters into their own hands.'

The Great Kahn stood, his chair screeching along the dais. All heads snapped around to face him.

'You promised to not speak falsehoods, Teal,' the Great Kahn threatened quietly.

Teal shook his head. 'I have excellent eyes and ears, my Great Lord.'

The Great Kahn stepped off his dais, his footfalls muted by the velvet walls.

'There is more,' Teal said reluctantly.

The Great Kahn began pacing the room. 'Go on.'

'The Krijen are compelled to interfere,' Teal said, his voice wavering. 'I was present at one such execution. The Krijen cut loose the captive mayj and made to arrest the family. Their actions were not well received.'

The Great Kahn stopped pacing.

'When the mayj was released, the crowd attacked. I am afraid the Krijen . . . overcompensated.'

'Say what you mean, Speaker.'

Teal paled. 'It was what you would call a bloodbath, my Great Lord.' His words hung in the chamber.

Lord Salli jerked to his feet, shaking with outrage. 'Are you saying that the Krijen killed innocent citizens?'

Lord Reider stood up as well. He was much calmer than Lord Salli. 'Please send for these Krijen,' he said to Teal. 'I would like to hear their account firsthand.'

'That is not possible, my lord. They are dead.'

There was a collective gasp around the room.

'Great Kahn have mercy on us,' whispered Lady Macey. Her expression drew the Great Kahn's attention, but she wasn't looking at him. She was unaware of what she'd said.

'Krijen? Killed?' Lord Reider looked shaken. 'By whose hand?'

'Like I said,' Teal said, hanging his head. 'It was a bloodbath.'

'How many citizens died?' Lady Macey asked, her eyes flashing.

'A great many, my lady,' Teal said, 'enough that I could not count.'

There was a sharp intake of breath around the room.

'Where is the FaKrijen?' Lord Salli demanded. 'This is his responsibility! Send for him at once!'

Teal strode to the door and spoke to the Minder outside, who dashed away.

Lord Salli and Lord Reider slowly sat down.

'The FaKrijen should be here already,' Lady Elira said darkly.

'He is increasingly disinterested in the running of this city,' sniffed Lord Oman. He was one of the most unpalatable Kahnen, in the Great Kahn's opinion. He did nothing but whine. But he was a good puppet.

'Please, can we withhold our judgement for now?' Lord Reider asked. 'The FaKrijen would not dismiss these meetings for something trivial.'

'I agree,' said Lord Flynn. 'FaKrijen Oji still demands our respect.'

'So why can *we* not demand *his?*' Lord Oman challenged. There was a murmur of agreement around the table.

Lady Macey turned to the Great Kahn. 'My Great Lord, what do you think about these honour killings?'

Her blunt question drew shocked stares. No one spoke to the Great Kahn that way. He had to admit her boldness surprised him.

As he strolled back to the dais, he noted the attention of his house, how their eyes followed him. He couldn't remember how long it had been like that. He used to thirst for such reverence before he became the Great Kahn. Back when he was Lord Li.

Today though, he didn't care. He was distracted by Mandavar, yet again.

The Great Kahn sat down. 'The People demand retribution for their fellow citizens who harm them. I see nothing wrong with this.'

Lord Salli looked jubilant. Lady Macey lifted her chin.

Lord Reider shuffled in his seat, uncomfortable. 'My Great Lord,' he began carefully, 'we must uphold a certain standard of justice. This is why we have the Krijen. We cannot leave this in the hands of ordinary citizens.'

The Great Kahn looked to the Speaker. 'Teal?'

'Yes, my Great Lord?'

'What do you think?'

Teal looked baffled. 'I . . . I am not sure my opinion matters –'

'Your opinion matters more than anyone in this room. You are a citizen, are you not?'

Teal paused. 'Yes, I suppose I am.'

'And you do not speak in falsehoods. I trust what you say.'

Teal chewed on his lip, eyes flickering between the Kahnen. 'Well . . . it would certainly be a strong deterrent. It would be harder to hide behind closed doors. But' – he cleared his throat nervously – '*execution* seems a steep punishment.'

'Does it?' Lord Salli piped up. 'We criminalised majik months ago. The threat of losing their hands made no difference to the mayjen; illegal harnessing remains rife. The People are clamouring for more.'

Lord Reider frowned. 'It is too extreme. We agreed with the FaKrijen that mayjen are to be executed only when they show an intention to harm others or harness purposefully to excess.'

'With *proof*,' Lord Flynn added, 'which is clearly lacking. The mayj must not have used majik, otherwise the Krijen would not have freed him. They would have cut off his hands at the very least.'

'But the mayj did harness,' Teal said quietly. All eyes turned to him.

'And the Krijen still released him?'

'Yes.'

The Great Kahn breathed through a surge of anger. The Krijen would not have done that of their own accord. This was Oji taking increasing liberties with his orders.

'What proof do you have that the mayj used majik?' Lord Flynn asked.

'He admitted to it,' Teal said. 'The mayj is still alive. He is in custody.'

Lord Flynn looked incredulous. '*How?*'

'The crowd prevented his escape. He attacked them and succumbed to Krijen arrest when the rest of the squad arrived. They were lucky to avoid the same fate as their comrades.'

Lord Salli raised an eyebrow. 'You saw all of this with your own eyes? A passive observer? Hard to believe.'

'That is true,' said Lady Elira. 'You are the Speaker of the Eighth House. Given the behaviour of the Krijen and their ties with the Kahnen, surely you would be a target.'

'I am but an instrument of the Eighth House,' Teal said. 'The People understand I act as your eyes and ears. They wanted me to see.'

The Kahnen fell into silence, pondering this statement.

'Bring forth this mayj,' Lord Salli commanded. 'I want to speak with him.'

Teal slipped back to the door and sent another Minder running. In the same moment, the other returned. He spoke briefly to Teal, who nodded.

'FaKrijen Oji cannot be found.'

Lord Reider looked worried.

Lord Salli leant back in his seat, looking smug.

'The arrogance of that man,' said Lord Oman, shaking his head.

A few minutes passed in tense silence before there was a knock on the door. Two Krijen entered, flanking a man who writhed between them. His hands were engloved in Sid Bha's latest cardonite design.

The mayj froze when he saw the Kahnen, then hoicked a projectile of saliva towards the stone slab where they sat. Lady Elira shrieked as the foaming globule landed next to her hand.

An impressive distance to spit, the Great Kahn thought, enjoying a rare stroke of amusement.

Stolt strode in behind them wearing high-collared robes that swept grandiosely about his ankles. 'Do not worry. I'm here only as a precaution,' he said to no one in particular.

The Great Kahn did not allow his lip to curl.

The mayj sneered around at them all. 'So this is where you spend your days, is it? Sitting in this cushy little room with its padded walls to keep us skahks at bay?'

Lord Oman pointed at the mayj, disgust on his face. 'This is the mayj the Krijen rescued? And the Krijen *stopped* his execution?'

The mayj lunged at Lord Oman, but the Krijen yanked him back. Their expressions were measuredly blank.

'This is it! You're all done for!' the mayj yelled at the Kahnen. 'You sent your Speaker to preach about mayjen sacrifices for the greater good, yet you don't seem to realise that half of Valrue are skahks now! So what? Are you going to slaughter us all?'

Lord Salli clicked his tongue and leant across the table towards the mayj. 'I am interested to know what you did to deserve familial execution.'

The mayj turned red. 'I did nothing,' he cried. '*You* did it. *You* poisoned them against me with your needle tongue. My own cousins came at me with knives!'

'So you admit you broke the law,' said Lord Salli.

'It's called self-defence,' the mayj spat. He looked between the Krijen holding him. 'Surely you've heard of it? The Krijen used it to justify butchering half the Lower East Side.'

Lord Reider looked disturbed. 'You would ridicule the Krijen who saved your life?'

The mayj shot him a sinister look. 'I'm just pointing out the hypocrisy.'

'We do not condone what the Krijen did. It will not happen again,' said Lady Macey.

The Great Kahn lifted his head in agreement.

Lord Reider looked saddened as he gazed upon the mayj. 'I sympathise with what was done to you,' he said. 'But we cannot excuse the use of majik under any circumstances.'

'What else would you have me do?' the mayj cried. 'They were going to kill me!'

'Our city is worth more than you not wanting to suffer inconveniences,' said Lord Salli.

'Inconveniences?' The mayj twisted in the grip of the Krijen, more spit collecting on his lips. 'You know *nothing* about what it means to live like I do! You have no idea what a difference it makes to be able to use majik, to keep my daughter safe at night. You've got servants falling over themselves to wipe up your shit, yet you expect me to deprive myself of something that makes life bearable?'

Lord Reider frowned, a sign of his sympathy brewing. He turned towards the dais. 'My Great Lord, perhaps an exception –'

The Great Kahn stood up abruptly. Lord Reider fell silent.

'You think what we have done is not fair,' the Great Kahn said quietly. He stepped down from his dais and slowly walked the length of the stone slab. 'You are right. It is not fair.'

He stopped before the mayj, who ceased wrestling against his Krijen guards to look up at him, a delightful touch of fear in his eyes.

'If I had only a single daughter to feed,' the Great Kahn continued, 'life would be so much easier. But I have a city of thousands. And *you* are the reason they are starving.'

The Great Kahn looked down at the mayj's hands, clamped in cardonite. He could picture the fingers twitching uselessly in their prison. 'Powerful then,' the Great Kahn said under his breath.

One of the Krijen frowned. 'Himajik, my Great Lord,' he said.

The Great Kahn ignored him. 'Tell me,' he said to the mayj. 'Would you kill the man who hurt your daughter?'

The mayj's eyes widened. 'You wouldn't dare –'

'So you would. Your daughter will not be harmed. But I see you understand me.'

The Great Kahn reached inside his robes and pulled out a sword. The blade was dark green with gold webbing across its surface. The Great Kahn flung it out in an arc, the tip brushing the mayj's throat. The red line it left burst into a river, and the mayj jolted, his metal hands rising to the blood.

The Krijen staggered under his weight as the mayj collapsed between them. He stilled quickly. The Krijen wordlessly dragged the body towards the door.

The Great Kahn turned and placed the sword on the table in front of Lady Hia. She strained away from it, her jaw clenched.

'It is decided,' said the Great Kahn. 'The Krijen will stand down from these honour killings. I will not have any more blood spilled in the name of protecting mayjen.'

Lord Flynn stood up, trembling. 'My Great Lord, please reconsider. What about the burden of proof?'

The Great Kahn turned his eyes on Lord Flynn. The scholar, persistent as ever.

'You would rather the People wage war with the Krijen? We have denied them vengeance long enough.'

'But . . . can you not see where this might lead?'

'You vex me, Lord Flynn. *Desist.*'

'But the city will turn on itself! You give the People permission to murder their neighbours without consequence –'

'ENOUGH!'

Lord Flynn's face drained of colour, and he slowly sat back in his chair.

The Great Kahn looked around at the Kahnen, his eyes studying every face, every bead of sweat, every corner of every smile.

How he hated Mandavar for doing this to him.

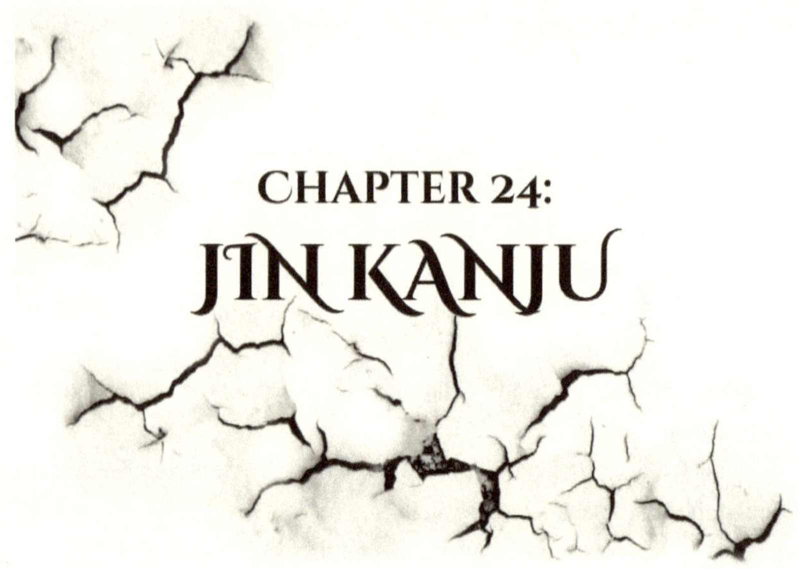

CHAPTER 24:
JIN KANJU

Nine years ago

Jin slammed Wren into the ground. The boy squirmed beneath him, one arm twisted behind his back, his cheek to the dirt. Jin pressed his knee between Wren's shoulder blades, counting under his breath.

Wren was persistent, more so than the other Squares. He often refused to tap out, and Geni Igna had to step in. Wren threw his legs around, trying to dislodge Jin. He was strong for his age; they all were. But Jin was stronger.

Five seconds.

Wren's free hand scrabbled at the air, trying to get hold of his captor. He must be in pain; he was moving so much. Jin was tempted to loosen his grip just a little. He glanced at Geni Igna, who watched with his usual iron-like expression. Geni Igna shook his head ever so slightly from side to side. *No. Hold.*

Ten seconds.

Wren still didn't tap the ground. He was turning red, little beads of sweat forming at his hairline.

Come on, Wren, Jin thought. *Tap out. Please.*

Jin glanced up at his father. He couldn't believe his father had come, even though it was customary for all the parents to observe training like this. An afternoon was set aside every few months for the purpose. Parents could see their children compete against the other Squares, shower them with praise and encouragement, whether they won or lost.

Fifteen seconds.

Jin's father watched him coldly, not a shred of pride in his face. He was a difficult man to please. Jin wished he hadn't looked. But he just couldn't believe he had *come*.

Twenty seconds.

'Enough,' said Geni Igna. Jin released Wren immediately, standing up and holding out his hand to help him up. Wren grasped it, allowing Jin to pull him to his feet.

Geni Igna nodded his approval. 'Well done.'

The watching parents clapped politely, but Jin could see them whispering to each other.

Wren walked over to sit cross-legged on the ground at the end of a line of bruised, sweaty Sevenths. Jin had been undefeated today.

Jin looked at his father. His father looked back at him. Then his father lunged through the crowd of parents and grabbed Jin by the arm, tugging him from the square. The other parents gaped.

Jin saw Bish briefly, his eyes wide with fear, before Jin was pulled away.

His father marched him down the row of barracks, past the squares marked on the ground and their occupants. Heads turned to watch, the Squares all recognising Jin.

They were almost at the exit when Geni Igna spoke behind them. He must've been following.

'Stop. Please.'

Jin's father spun around, dragging Jin with him. '*What?*'

Jin wouldn't dare to speak to Geni Igna that way.

Geni Igna looked calm, but his hands rested near his daggers. 'Training is not yet finished for today,' he said quietly. 'If you take him, he will be required to make it up.'

'So be it,' Jin's father said, turning back to the exit.

Geni Igna stepped around him, getting in his way. 'You are compromising your son's training.'

Instead of stepping back, Jin's father pressed forward, his chest almost colliding with Geni Igna's.

'This is *my* son! He does what *I* say!'

Jin waited with bated breath. Geni Igna had never once been denied. But neither had his father. They stared each other down, Jin's father face twisted with fury, Geni Igna's a mask of composure.

Jin started counting again. Five seconds went by. Then Geni Igna turned and strode back towards the Squares. Jin watched him go, a sinking feeling in the pit of his stomach.

Jin's father snatched him by the wraps on his chest and pulled Jin's face up to his. 'You don't look at him – you look at me! You think you're a man now that he's taught you how to fight? You're not a man yet.' He shoved Jin ahead of him, out onto the main street of Rue.

Jin wished he had pockets to hide his shaking hands. Instead, he clasped them into fists, held tightly at his thighs. He could feel his daggers there, their hard edges digging into his skin. Geni Igna insisted they wear them at all times. The Squares had not even removed them during their wrestling match.

They crossed the bridge, Jin making to turn right; but his father continued straight, towards the belly of Val. 'We're not going home, boy.'

Jin nervously followed his father up the gentle slope. They had Made the Cross from Rue into Val five years ago now. A few people recognised Jin and waved at him, their smiles faltering at his father's cold stare.

They halted at one of the busy intersections of Val. Jin looked around, unsure why his father had stopped here. Aren's house was further up the slope, but he doubted they were going there. Jin would never catch his father strolling around the mansions of North Val. He hated the rich too much.

On the street corner was a large verandaed building, the wooden facade erected onto the stone underbelly. Jin recognised it. His knees grew weak.

'You want to be a real man? Here you go.' Jin's father grabbed his shoulders and steered him in the direction of the brothel.

Jin dug in his feet, horrified. He'd rather be beaten than enter that building. 'N-no, Father,' Jin stammered. 'I'd like to go back –'

'Did you not hear me? You're not done, boy.' He shoved Jin towards the brothel again.

Panicking, Jin tried to run, but his father grabbed him by the back of his wraps and wrenched him back.

'You want to make a scene, do you? You want everyone to see you for the little skahk that you are?'

'Please, Father –'

'Begging is a filthy habit. I didn't teach you that! Did your Geni teach you how to beg? Ruining my son, he is –' Jin's father dragged him up the steps and through the swinging doors.

The lounge of the brothel was airy and well lit, the windows thrown open in a blatant contradiction of the private nature of the establishment. A bar stretched down one side of the room; a collection of chairs and recliners filled the other. Wooden stairs twisted up the far wall to land on each of the three floors above them. Some doors were slightly ajar, the rooms beyond blocked by curvaceous feminine shapes peeking at the late-afternoon visitors.

Jin's father dragged him to the bar. Behind it stood a sultry woman, her hands on her ample hips. She sucked on her lip, apparently lost in thought. It made her look frighteningly erotic. She spotted Jin's father and smiled widely as she walked out from behind the bar, hips swinging. She smiled at Jin too, no hint of surprise on her face. Nothing surprised Mama Hidel. Jin knew her name because everyone in Valrue knew her name.

'My favourite customer,' Mama Hidel said to Jin's father. Her voice was smooth and rehearsed. It made Jin feel nauseous.

His father thrust him forward. Jin noticed Mama Hidel wore very tall black boots, which laced all the way up her thighs. He turned red and looked back down at his feet.

'Ah,' Mama Hidel said. 'This is your son?' Jin could feel her eyes on him. 'I've heard much about you from young Aren.'

Jin looked up. 'You know Aren?' Why would a woman who runs a brothel know Aren?

His father smacked him upside the head so hard his neck cracked. He staggered backwards, ears ringing.

'You're obsessed with that little rich girl! Don't ask stupid questions.'

Jin returned his eyes to the floor.

'This boy needs breaking in,' Jin's father said.

'Of course,' Mama Hidel replied, still in her smooth tone. 'Eliza is available. She will be happy to oblige.'

'Not Aubrey?'

'Aubrey is currently with a client, though if the boy would be willing to wait –'

'No,' Jin's father said, his eyes flashing towards the open windows. 'He's a coward. He'll run. Eliza will do.'

'I won't have you underselling my women now,' Mama Hidel said, a hint of indignation spoiling her tone. 'Eliza will more than *do*. She will be an absolute pleasure.'

Jin's father did not reply. Jin dared to look up again, bemused that his father had held his tongue. His father did not like being corrected.

Mama Hidel held out her hand, expectant. She wanted payment.

Jin held his breath, hoping his father would refuse. His father hated spending coin on him. Or maybe he wouldn't have enough, or maybe –

Jin's father dug into his pockets, pulling out coin. He dropped a small collection into Mama Hidel's open palm before striding back out the door.

Jin watched him go, a battle raging in his head. As much as his father scared him, he was possibly more terrified of this 'Eliza'.

'Well now,' Mama Hidel said, looking down at Jin with a smile he supposed she thought was warm and reassuring. Instead, he felt like prey. He'd seen cats catch mice, back when they used to roam the streets. The cats would play with their prey, ripping them limb from limb. Mama

Hidel was definitely a cat.

Which made Jin the mouse.

He gulped, resting his thumbs gently on the curved hilts of his daggers. He wouldn't use them. Geni Igna would never allow that. But he'd learned to reach for them when threatened. It was a tough habit to break.

'What's your name, child?'

'Jin,' he said quietly. He wondered if he might still be able to run. What was stopping him? He had daggers. If he needed to, he had majik, though he would no doubt face his father's fist for that. Was it worth it? Yes. What was one more beating?

Jin took a step towards the doors of the brothel, which were still swinging from his father's exit. He stopped.

His father had called him a coward. Was that the problem? He could choose not to be a coward. Would his father hate him a little less, if he weren't? His father had not been impressed enough today, when he won his wrestling matches. Maybe his father needed a different type of proof that he wasn't a coward. That's why he'd brought him here.

Jin turned back to Mama Hidel, looking her directly in the eye. He pulled his shoulders back and square. Mama Hidel opened her mouth, but Jin interrupted, 'Please, don't tell Aren.'

Mama Hidel looked mildly offended. 'My dear, I uphold my women to the highest standard of discretion.'

Jin had no idea what that meant. 'So you won't tell her?'

'No, child, I won't. You have my word.'

Jin relaxed ever so slightly. *Okay*, he thought. He could do this. Though he wished she wouldn't call him 'child'.

'Where do I go?'

His eyes scanned the many doors behind them. If Mama Hidel was surprised by his apparent change of heart, she didn't show it.

'Eliza is on the second floor. Fourth door on the right. Oh, and one more thing.'

Mama Hidel slipped back behind the bar and pulled out an empty glass. She filled it with a golden liquid she poured from a jug and pushed it towards him. 'Please take this to Eliza,' she said. 'She'll be in need of refreshment.'

Slightly bewildered, Jin took the glass and wandered over to the staircase. He felt very out of place. He looked behind him, savouring one last glance at the door. Mama Hidel had already turned her back to him, busying herself behind the bar.

Jin stopped at the base of the stairs and sniffed the drink. It didn't smell like ale. In fact, it smelled sweet. He considered taking a sip, then thought better of it. He had no idea what this strange concoction was. Better not. And that wasn't cowardly, he told himself as he started up the stairs. That was just being sensible.

He reached the second floor and counted four doors to the right. The door was slightly ajar, as though to entice him in. Instead, he broke into a cold sweat. He itched to reach for his daggers.

Jin walked to the door and peered into the room. It seemed basic, dimly lit by candles. He supposed it was meant to seem romantic or something like that. He could only see half the bed, so absurdly large it dominated the room. He pressed the door open.

A woman stood up off the bed. She had strong features, a wide mouth and very arched eyebrows which must have been drawn on because they were several shades darker than her long red hair.

Jin wasn't sure where to look. She wasn't wearing much at all, just a loose robe. She eyed him with a small smile, unfazed by her young client.

Panicking, Jin held out the glass to her, slopping a bit onto the floor. It was unlike him to be so clumsy. 'Mama Hidel said this is for you,' he said, unsure how to start.

'Thank you,' Eliza said, smiling wider. 'Please put it down here for me,' she said, nodding towards a small table to the right of the bed. 'I don't have hands,' she explained. She held up two stumps, which poked out of the end of her robe.

Jin stared. 'But how do you . . . you know?' He blushed at his own rudeness. He hadn't meant to say it.

Eliza laughed a strange, genuine trill that echoed in the little room. 'Don't worry, I often get that,' she said. 'Please, come in. Close the door behind you.'

Jin did as she said, then stood there awkwardly, not knowing what to do.

Eliza sat down on the bed. She leant down and sniffed the drink delicately. 'Not surprising,' she said, turning back to Jin. 'So, your father wants me to make you a man? I was listening at the door,' she explained in response to his wide-eyed expression. 'How old are you, child?'

Jin thumbed the tops of his daggers. 'Twelve.'

Eliza raised her eyebrows. 'Hm. You seem older. You are a Square,' she added, eyeing his black wraps. Her gaze drifted down to his thumbs. 'I have no doubt you know how to use those,' she said, nodding at the daggers. 'If you would please remove them? I prefer my clients not to have weapons on them. Most of the time,' she trilled again.

Jin slowly pulled the daggers from his wraps. There was nowhere to put them other than on the table next to the bed. He was reluctant to move closer to Eliza.

'Come, child. I only bite when I'm told to,' Eliza said dryly.

Jin stepped forward and placed the daggers down on the table before turning to face her, hands still fisted at his sides.

'Is that all of them?'

Jin nodded.

'Very well. Let me see.' She leant back, running her eyes over him once more. He couldn't help it – he blushed again.

Eliza did not laugh at him. Instead, her smile turned down. 'Your father is a scary man.'

Jin froze. What did she know?

'He isn't so scary,' Jin replied, trying to sound indifferent. Unfortunately, his voice cracked on the words.

'Child, you are a terrible liar. And yes. Your father is scary. The women dislike him. But he does not hurt us, like he hurts you, and so we must put up with him.'

'He doesn't hurt me,' Jin replied, too quickly.

'My dear.' Eliza looked at him with that awful, knowing expression that all adults seemed to have when they looked at him. 'I don't know much, but I know gossip. Even before you were a Square, you had bruises. A child should not get so many bruises.'

Jin said nothing.

'Your father called you a coward,' she said, jerking her head towards the door. 'Do you think you are a coward?'

The question caught Jin off guard. 'I-I don't think so,' he said, unsure. He might be though. His father said he was, which was why he was here.

'Well,' Eliza said, 'I don't think you are. In fact, you seem very brave. One of the bravest people I have met.'

Jin eyed her suspiciously. 'You only just met me.'

'You are not the first boy whose father has dragged him here and demanded we make him a man. But you are one of the few who did it without a fuss.' Eliza stood, stepping closer. She seemed to be unnaturally tall, for a woman.

'It is quite vulgar, being asked to seduce a crying child,' Eliza said. 'It makes me feel icky. I wish people wouldn't think so lowly of me and the other women, you know? But then again, we don't give them reason to think otherwise.'

Jin had no idea what she meant. Now that she was standing, he was almost face-to-face with her breasts. They sat just below his chin. Up this close, he could see she had quite a few freckles, dotting her pale skin. He said nothing, feeling his heart beating in his chest.

Eliza sighed. 'Okay, let's get started.'

She shrugged off her robe, dropped it onto the floor, and lay down on the bed. 'Now, the first thing you'll need to know is – what are you doing, child?'

Jin froze, his hands on the ties of his wraps. Wasn't this exactly what he was supposed to be doing? Flustered, he dropped his hands, going red again.

'Keep your clothes on, please.'

That didn't seem right. Jin was pretty sure he knew how sex worked. He'd walked in on his father many times, and he'd talked to the other Squares about it after Geni Igna had first introduced the concept in one of their classes. You had to take your clothes off.

Then again, he'd also assumed a working woman would require hands. He waited for instruction from Eliza, scared to move.

'Tell me, child,' Eliza began, 'when you started training as a Square, did they give you a krije on your first day?'

'No,' Jin said hesitantly.

'And why not?'

Jin frowned. The answer was obvious. 'We had to learn how to use other weapons first.'

'Exactly. So why are you expecting this to be any different?'

Oh.

Eliza smiled again. 'Don't be nervous. Nothing we talk about today will be in the least bit scary.'

'We are just going to talk?' Jin asked.

'We are just going to talk,' Eliza confirmed.

'But . . . my father –' Jin could feel a tightening in his chest, each breath becoming shallower, sharper. His face still hurt where his father had hit him, and his palms burned a little. They did that when he grew anxious.

'Your father will get exactly what he asked for. Just not what he expected,' Eliza said. 'He will not know what we do.'

Jin was relieved. He worked to calm himself. He felt so self-conscious standing in front of Eliza, who seemed ludicrously at ease.

'Sit down,' Eliza said, patting the bed.

Jin sat down next to her. He wasn't sure where to look. She had so much *skin*.

'Is there anything you need?' Eliza asked gently.

'No,' he said. His eyes wandered over the room again, which was less terrifying than looking at Eliza. There was a trunk near the door that he hadn't noticed before. Other than that, the bed, and the table with the glass of golden liquid, the room was empty.

His curiosity got the better of him. 'What's in your drink?'

'It's java juice.'

'Why didn't you drink it?'

'I will, later.'

Jin stared at the stumps where her hands should have been. Eliza noticed his gaze. 'They were cut off two years ago,' she said. 'I was a mayj. Not a good one, mind you. But I got into a bad spot, and I used my majik to do some bad things. The Krijen caught me and cut them off.'

Jin was shocked by her honesty. 'Do you hate them?' He meant the Krijen.

Eliza understood. 'No, I don't. I used to. But not anymore. I think I deserved my punishment. And believe it or not, I have a good life here, with Mama Hidel. Better than I had before.'

'Even without hands?' Jin asked, in disbelief.

'Even without hands,' Eliza said.

Jin couldn't imagine life without hands. He used them for everything: to fight, to eat, to wipe his arse – he wouldn't like not being able to do that himself. He would definitely not ask Eliza about that. He also used them to harness, but he only did it sometimes, when it got a bit much. He didn't tell people about that though.

'Do you miss being a mayj?' Jin asked. He'd never really spoken about majik with anyone. It wasn't good to talk about, not even with Aren, or Bish, even though they knew. But Eliza seemed okay.

'I do, sometimes,' Eliza said. 'But I was lomajik. I got tired easily and had to be careful not to Turn. I felt safer as a mayj, but I used majik when I should have used my head. I grew up in Rue, you know.' She continued to chatter away.

Eliza was fascinating, Jin decided. He quickly forgot that she was a complete stranger. He even got used to her nakedness. The best thing was that she didn't ask him too many questions about himself. It was hard to keep things from the Sevenths; he wished they didn't know so much. He was pretty sure they didn't know he was a mayj, though. Bish said they didn't.

After a while, Eliza informed him that their time was up. Jin collected his daggers and stopped on his way out, his hand on the door. He turned back to Eliza.

'Can I come back?'

'Of course you can, child,' Eliza said, smiling.

'Can you call me Jin?'

Eliza laughed that lovely, genuine trill. 'Of course, Jin. I look forward to seeing you again.'

Jin left, feeling oddly pleased with himself.

The lounge downstairs was filling up with clientele lazing on the couches with drinks. The soft buzz of their voices faded as Jin walked down the stairs. He could feel curious eyes on him, no doubt wondering what a Square was doing here, a young one at that. He did his best to ignore them.

As he passed, Mama Hidel smiled and nodded to him from behind the bar. He smiled back and stepped through the swinging doors into the tired bustle of the street.

That had not been so bad, after all.

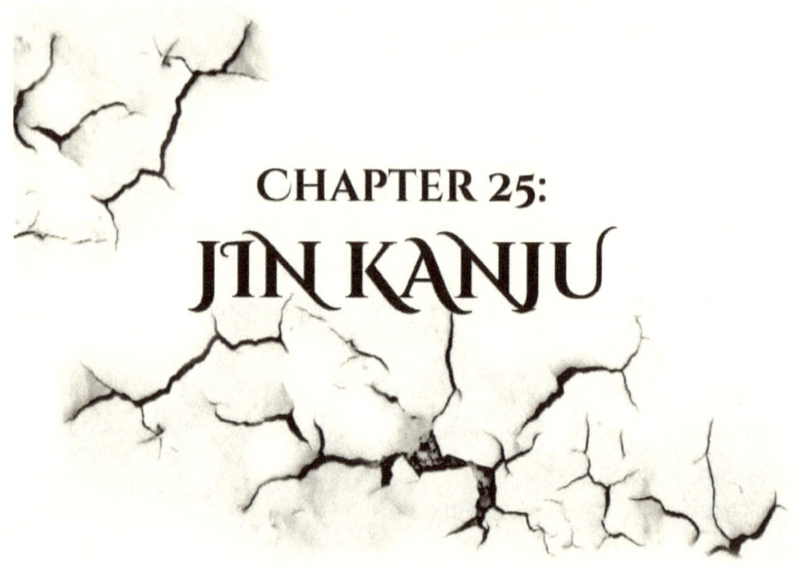

CHAPTER 25:
JIN KANJU

Being Krijen was not as Jin expected. It was so much better. For six months, he'd woken up with his eyes squeezed shut, waiting for something to crash through the dream he'd been living. It would be Geni Igna bellowing at them or the unmistakable hum of Rue in the distance. But today he woke up and opened his eyes straight away. He was here, and this was happening. Jin could breathe now.

That's why he was so fucking *pissed off* that he hadn't gone to Aren before he'd left and demanded she hear him out, so he could make it better. The guilt nagged at him like gravity. Aren was the only thing wrecking this victory for him now.

Well, that, and seeing the dead. But he buried that down, *deep*, out of the way. The dead could wait.

The Deadlands were more alive in some ways than Valrue. The days were busy, full of planning, packing, running, and reporting. It was so liberating to be out here, away from the city. They were stationed at Second Base East, two weeks from Valrue and halfway to the nearest forest. Jin knew trees were brown with green leaves, but he still couldn't picture them. There was some shrubbery this far out of Valrue, but it was starved and spindly, and it tore at you when you walked through it.

Nothing like the forest the Krijen spoke about. Jin couldn't wait to see it.

His anger subsided quickly. Bish was laughing at him, waving that pursuant, shitty slop under his nose. Jin had been stupid to think that breakfast maize was a special torment set aside for the Squares. By the Great Kahn, he was wrong. But at least they had half-decent toppings out here.

The farther they got from Valrue, the better the supplies were. This morning there was some sticky brown stuff laid out in jars called honey. It was made by bees, little creatures that buzzed and stung you. Ludicrous enough that if Jin hadn't heard Noel talk about them before he would have insisted they were someone's idea of a joke.

Jin snatched the bowl of maize from Bish and drowned it with honey. They were in the main hall at the base, seated on a long wooden bench before a long wooden table. Jin sat between Bish and Kimjit. Kimjit was the Second Base East Master. She had wide-set eyes and a tiny nose. Her black hair was shaved short around her ears in the Krijen style, blending into longer locks at the back. Like many of the Krijen in the Deadlands, she kept it pulled back in a thick braid that fell to her waist.

Next to Jin, Bish had finished his maize and was sucking honey off his spoon. He'd taken a long time to heal from his dance, one of his eye sockets now permanently warped. But he was here and breathing, and for that Jin was grateful.

'Ugh, by the Great Kahn's karkers,' Kimjit said, gesturing to Bish's empty bowl. 'You lot haven't finished growing. They need to stop sending me the freshest Krijen. We'll have no food left soon!'

Bish looked so guilty that Kimjit burst out laughing. 'For fuck's sake, get another,' she said, shoving Bish towards the maize. 'You too,' Kimjit said, prodding Jin with a finger.

'No thanks,' Jin said honestly. The honey didn't quite smother the odious flavour of the maize.

Kimjit shrugged. 'I know it tastes like arse, but it's all you're getting until teatime.'

Jin shrugged back. He'd manage.

'Your call.' With that, Kimjit unrolled an enormous map onto the table, taming the corners with paper weights. The map depicted the entirety of the Deadlands, Valrue in the middle with the sixteen bases surrounding it, a row of four circles in each of north, east, south, and west directions.

'I received the most recent detailing of the supplies, delivered fresh to me this morning,' Kimjit said. 'As you know, these are sent in advance so we know how many Krijen to send. As squad leader, you'll –'

'I'm not squad leader,' Jin interrupted.

Kimjit flapped her hand at him to be quiet. 'Let me know what you expect your movements to be, and I'll work up rations for the mission. It'll likely take three days given you're only going to First Base East –'

'Kimjit, I'm not squad leader. Can this wait until the others get here?' Jin was, however, mildly alarmed at her suggestion it would take only three days to reach First Base East. It was usually seven days between bases.

Kimjit looked at Jin as though he were a half-wit. 'I've been Krijen for over twenty years, boy. If you're not elected as squad leader today, I'll give you my meat allowance for the week.'

Just then, Bish returned with a fresh bowl of maize, the remaining four members of their squad in tow. They bowed their heads to Jin, fists on their clavicles. Kimjit folded her arms, looking smug.

Jin nodded in respectful acknowledgement, hiding his frown.

Everyone sat around the table eyeing Kimjit's map. Aside from Jin and Bish, their squad of six consisted of Pago, Jokah, Vulmin, and Meek, the last of whom Jin assumed was nicknamed in jest, because he was one of the loudest people Jin had ever met.

'Right,' Kimjit said, starting again. 'It's a straightforward mission. Get the supplies safely from here' – she pointed to Second Base East, one of the circles on the map – 'to here.' She pointed to First Base East, another circle in the same row, closer to the triangle depicting the mountain containing Valrue. 'This time, we've got a swiftrun for you.'

Everyone perked up at the word.

Swiftruns were exactly as they sounded, supply runs designed to get into Valrue as fast as possible. They were loaded with the most precious cargo and were more likely to be targeted by bandits.

As it turned out, dealing with bandits was a part of life for the Krijen. They were a nuisance, more than anything else. They came from Valrue and would set up small camps along the suspected supply routes and attempt to steal from the wagons. The usual targets were the standard, slow-moving runs typically escorted by only a single pair of Krijen.

Even this, Kimjit found laughable.

'You'd think the bandits would give up,' she'd said when Jin's squad had first arrived at Second Base East. 'I've been Base Master here for a decade, and I can count on one hand the number of times I've known the bandits to be successful. You'd think they'd learn not to fuck with Krijen.'

Bish had found the bandits fascinating. 'Why do they keep at it then?'

'The Unsettlement,' Jokah had replied.

Jokah was the oldest of the squad, probably in his late fifties. He was short and wiry, his long white hair braided like Kimjit's.

'As it gets worse, people grow more desperate. They'll try anything.'

'What will they do with the stolen supplies?'

'Take them back to Valrue to sell on the black market,' Meek had said. 'Though being a bandit seems a rather unforgiving lifestyle,' he'd added with a nasty grin, making Kimjit laugh.

It wasn't uncommon for roaming squads from the First and Second Bases to come across the dried-up bodies of bandits who'd died trying to navigate the Deadlands.

'No one makes it as far as the Third and Fourth Bases,' Kimjit had said. 'Ever.'

Kimjit suddenly smacked her hand down on the table before Jin, pulling him from the memory.

'Now, swiftruns are important. So you lot better do a good job,' she threatened. 'Some wagons will end up ahead of the others. We must accommodate this. I don't want the tail end of the pack dictating the speed while the supplies deteriorate. Some of the first swiftrunners arrived last night, so they are already staggered.'

Pago, only a year older than Jin and Bish, looked up in surprise. 'They've already come in from Fourth?'

Kimjit nodded. Pago whistled, impressed.

'That's right,' Kimjit said. 'The front-runners did a fourteen-day journey in six days. Swiftrunners have stamina that put you lot to shame.'

Jin caught Bish's eye, who nodded at him, also keen on the challenge. After six months of sprinting back and forth across the endless nothing of the Deadlands, they'd reached ridiculous new heights of fitness. Jin wasn't sure if he could get tired anymore.

'The swiftrunners all get twelve hours at Second to eat, sleep, shit, you know the drill,' Kimjit said. 'Then I'll load them up with food and water and send them on their way with you.'

Jin peered at the map, counting seven little wooden blocks placed next to Second Base East. 'This can't be right,' he said. 'There is no way six of us can cover seven wagons, especially if they are staggered.'

'Right you are, Jin,' Kimjit replied. 'I've got three more squads coming in. They'll be here by midday. You'll get three or four Krijen per wagon and its running crew of eight, double the usual allocation.'

Jin looked thoughtfully over the map. 'Are there any roaming parties doing sweeps nearby? If they can cover some of the planned route between Second and First, their presence might deter bandits.'

Kimjit nodded. 'I sent off a roaming squad about a week ago. They'll be on their way back now. I'll get them to alter their return route accordingly.'

'Anything of note in their reports?'

'She's as dead as a dormouse out there.'

Jin frowned. He didn't know what a dormouse was. 'How many wagons have arrived so far?'

'Three. The fourth is about an hour away.'

'What sort of supplies do we have? I get that it's all important, but is anything more valuable than the rest?'

Kimjit strummed her fingers on the table. 'Off the top of my head? Limes, meat, medicines. Paperwork is loaded with the slowest wagon, as usual.'

Jin looked around at his squad. 'Pago, Meek, when we wrap up here, do a quick inventory and distribute the most valuable supplies amongst the wagons as best you can.' They nodded.

Jin noticed Jokah looking at him with a wry smile. 'What is it?'

'Nothing, sir.' Jokah bowed his head. 'I am simply impressed by your thoroughness.'

'It's basic sense.'

'Right you are.'

Jin felt slightly unnerved. It was hard not to be intimidated by his squad. Everyone but Bish was more experienced than him. He didn't understand why they kept electing him as leader.

'Who has scouted this area before?' Jin asked.

Kimjit raised her hand – not that she was joining them on the swiftrun – as did Jokah and Vulmin. The brooding red-haired Vulmin had spent the last five years roaming out of the Bases East and South. Jokah had spent his whole career in the Deadlands, as had Kimjit.

'I need your help planning the route and marking rally positions,' Jin said. 'I'm thinking we hug the Crevasse for the first night. But how to get there?'

Vulmin leant in, tracing a path on the map with his finger. Mostly Vulmin said nothing at all, unless you caught him on a topic about which he was particularly passionate.

'This way,' Vulmin said in his gruff voice. 'It will take longer, but we will avoid the plains. Too exposed.'

'Good,' Jin said. 'From the Ridgeback, let's follow the Crevasse.'

Jokah nodded in approval. 'It'll be a long night, but if we move quickly, we can get to the Split by daybreak.'

It was much quicker to pass through the Split than traverse the extensive graveyard of jagged shards on either side. Jin knew this, but for some unknown reason, every instinct screamed at him to steer clear of the structure. Jin recalled the first time he saw it, mouth agape like an awestruck child. He likened it to a monstrous pair of stone hands, palms resting apart on the ground, with the tips of the fingers interlaced, forming a triangular shape rising above them. The stone was coloured by veins of black, brown, and red, which bled into the surrounding ground.

It *had* to be mayj-made, apart from the fact that mayjen designs were usually sleek and sharp, crafted with great care.

The Split wasn't. The fingers were irregular and blocky, the arms of it asymmetrical with smooth facets where giant stone shards had broken off and littered the surrounding ground.

More logically, Jin worried it might come down on them, but Kimjit insisted it hadn't eroded. It just *looked* like it was falling apart.

After a lengthy time spent planning their route, Pago and Meek headed off to check the wagons while Kimjit loaded the rest of them with rations, which they took to the barracks to pack. Jin had just waved the others off when Meek jogged into the barracks, perspiring from the heat outside.

'Sir, the fourth wagon is in. We redistributed the supplies as you asked.'

'Thanks, Meek. Everything is ready here.'

Meek leant over and picked a pack off the ground. He laughed. 'You're kidding! It's so light!'

Jin grinned at him. Even after six months, he didn't know Meek as well as he would like. 'You've never done a swiftrun before?' Jin asked.

'Nah, never!' Meek replied. 'I've mostly been doing roaming missions from First Base East. Should've known that the farther away from Valrue we are, the better it gets, aye? Base Masters and all, apparently. You know what? When I was with my old squad, before we got reassigned –'

Meek was off, launching into a story about a Krijen who got lost on a roaming mission and suffered a humiliating rescue by the formidable First Base East Master.

Jin had heard about him. Durini was over seventy years old, and in Meek's opinion, he ran his base 'tighter than a prude's arsehole'. Bish didn't approve of Meek's vocabulary, but Jin found it rather amusing.

'What brought you to the Deadlands?' Jin asked.

'Ah,' Meek said, his perpetual smile wavering. 'I –'

'Jin, sir!' Jokah's head appeared at the door. 'We need you.'

Kimjit's Map of the Deadlands

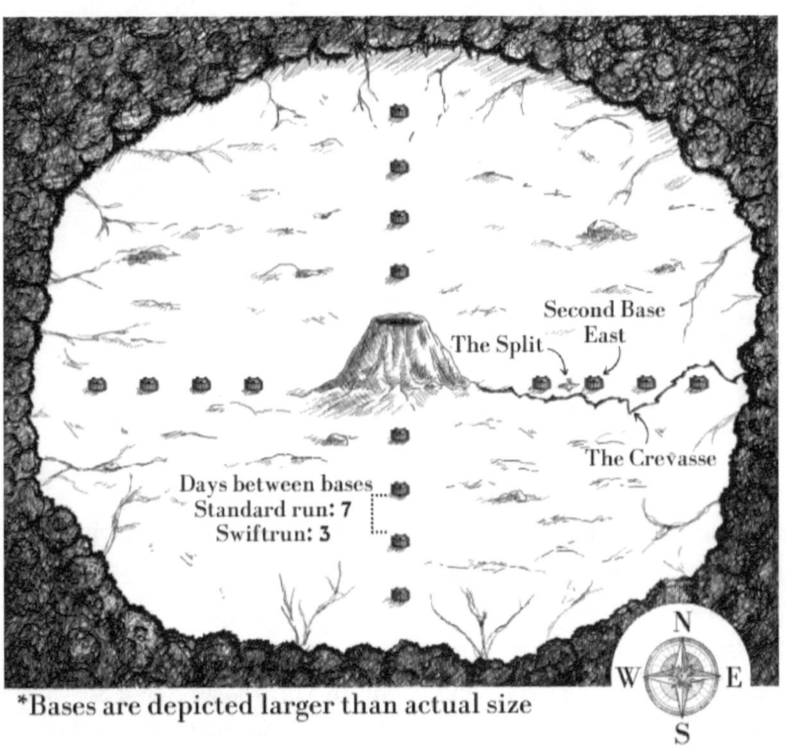

*Bases are depicted larger than actual size

CHAPTER 26:
AREN BHA

Thwack!

Aren ducked. An arm of the wooden training post spun over her head. She jumped as another one came at her knees, just as another arm smacked her across the cheek, knocking her head to the side. She leapt back, her face smarting. The many arms kept spinning, the training post taunting her. Aren eyed it up carefully, looking for an opening, then leapt back at it, incensed.

Thwack!

By Noel's reckoning, Aren had suffered a concussion, three broken fingers, two cracked ribs, and a broken collarbone. She'd sustained enough scrapes and bruises that she'd been black and blue, then green and yellow, for almost a month. Mae had been more overbearing than ever, blaming herself for what had happened. Aren had taken to sneaking around the mansion, staying clear of her mother's relentless coddling.

Thwack!

This time Aren ducked, jumped, ducked again. She brought her arm up to deflect another attack, her forearm jarred by her wooden assailant. She thrust it back with force, the training post whirling around in response. A rogue arm caught her on the back of the knees, knocking her legs out from under her. She landed flat on her back, puffing. Determined, she waited as another wooden arm whizzed over her head, before leaping back up.

Thwack!

Noel did not temper her mother's worries, and Sid had nothing to add, as usual. Aren felt that they all banded together, encouraging her to stay at home, agreeing that the city had become far too perilous for her to venture into, without good cause. Aren humoured them, feeling guilty about what she'd already put them through, and especially so for what she was planning.

To pass the time not spent sparring, Aren wandered the hallways of her home, thinking about Jin out in the Deadlands. Who was probably not thinking about *her*.

She also thought about Wren, hating that her concussion made his face blur in her mind. She hadn't mentioned him to anyone, glad her stiff fingers were a reminder of the day he'd saved her life. The rest of Valrue might forget him, but Aren was determined not to. He deserved better than that. Especially because he'd dragged her head above the waves of the suffocating, rich girl rut she'd been drowning in. She wasn't completely saved, but at least she could breathe.

Once her body had recovered from its injuries, she'd begun training daily, though now she was adding new bruises. She was getting better, but it was an infuriatingly slow process. Her wooden training post still beat her most days. Her small stature had always been a personal frustration. Maybe that's why she'd craved majikal abilities so much. If she could harness, being small wouldn't be such a problem.

But she didn't wish for majik now.

To be strong and independent, she needed to earn it properly. Bish was slight too, but he was tough and quick and good enough to be Krijen. She would be like Bish. She'd never be as good as Jin, but then again, no one was.

Thwack!

Aren cried out as a wooden arm collided with her kneecap. Another wooden arm caught her between the shoulder blades and flung her face forward into the dirt. Coughing, she rolled onto her back.

Aren missed the children at the orphanage. Mama Hidel had all but banned them from visiting now, worried it would draw too much attention.

The violence in the city had reached new heights. The People had begun honour killings of mayjen, dragging family members into the streets and butchering them for the world to see. They wouldn't allow their majik to slander them any longer, they said. They would not be responsible for the death of Valrue.

The Krijen did nothing to stop this. They looked on silently as blood stained the streets, mayjen screams echoing between the buildings. They were probably commanded against it. Aren wrestled with her thoughts on the matter. It made her sick to think that Jin would be ordered to stand there, ignoring the sounds of people dying. Though perhaps it wouldn't bother him as much as she hoped. Aren screwed up her face at the thought.

So Aren had a plan. For now, she would stay and train, until she was ready. Maybe the Krijen couldn't do anything, but she wasn't bound like they were. She could help. She could get better at fighting, get better at protecting people. Then she could go out into the streets and *do* something, rather than sitting at home, purposeless.

Mae, Noel, Mama Hidel, they all put their lives on the line to do good. Aren would too. She just wasn't sure she was ready. She needed more time to prepare.

Aren glared up at the wooden training post, towering above her. 'You won't beat me,' she said to it stubbornly. It didn't move, oblivious to her challenge.

Aren sighed and picked herself up off the ground, staggering slightly as her knee buckled beneath her. Perhaps that was enough sparring for this morning. She would come back after lunch.

Besides, Maude was coming today. Maude wasn't allowed to help with the children, so Mama Hidel sent her off to the Bha mansion, relieved to stop her moping around the brothel and bothering the clients.

Aren was dusting herself off when she heard a bloodcurdling shriek coming from the kitchen. Heart pounding, Aren snatched a dagger from her thigh wraps and sprinted towards the sound. She could hear pots clanging as she rounded the corner. She burst through into the kitchen at full speed, then skidded to a stop, backpedalling with her arms.

The two maids, Lana and Tilina, were standing on the table in the kitchen, Lana with a broom in hand. Beneath the table was Maude, crawling around on her hands and knees. 'No, please! Stop screaming!' Maude pleaded. 'You're scaring her!'

Lana hefted her broom higher, looking down at Maude with incredulity. 'What is that *thing?*'

Maude suddenly dashed out from under the table. A tiny brown blur zipped in front of her, Maude's outstretched hands scooping it up as it passed.

'What is going on?'

Aren jumped and spun on the spot, and Noel caught her hand, her dagger tip coming to an abrupt stop just short of his stomach. 'Aren!' he cried. 'What are you *doing?*'

Mortified, Aren let go of her dagger, relinquishing it to Noel. 'I'm sorry!' she said, cringing away from Noel's furious expression.

Noel looked up at the women on the table. 'Lana? Tilina? What in the world –' He stopped mid-sentence, astonished, as Maude stood up. 'Maude, is that a *mouse?*'

Sticking out of Maude's clasped hands was a little furry head, sporting an enormous pair of round ears and a tiny whiskered nose. A thin black tail curled around Maude's wrist.

The creature was trembling. Maude hugged it to her chest, stroking its head. 'Shh, it's okay, Mika.' The Bhouli girl tucked the quivering lump into the folds of her wraps. Then she looked up, appearing surprised that everyone was gaping at her.

'Please get down from the table,' said Noel calmly to the maids, rubbing his temples. 'Maude? Can you . . . ?' Words failing him, Noel pointed at the quivering lump.

The maids hastened down from the table and over to Noel.

Maude eyed the broom in Lana's hand suspiciously. Despite being barely fourteen, Maude was already much taller than Aren. She wore her usual white headscarf and sleeveless dark blue wraps, highlighting her youthful gangly figure.

Aren had always thought it odd that Bhouli covered their heads yet had no qualms about showing off their bodies. Maude had explained it to her once, saying that their scarves protected the head from the temptations of the sky, because that was where you go when you die. Aren had no idea why it would be tempting to go where dead people were. She had long since given up trying to make sense of the Bhouli.

Maude's skin was a mess of smeared white patterns. They ran from her fingers all the way up her arms and wrapped about her neck, poking above the dark blue material. Aren could see why having Maude around the brothel made Mama Hidel nervous. She stood out worse than a mouse in Valrue.

The mouse stuck its head out of Maude's wraps to peer at the people in the kitchen. It had dark-brown fur, but the skin inside of its moon-like ears was white and hairless, showing off delicate blue veins. Aren had never seen a mouse in real life before, only drawings in Noel's books.

'Maude, please,' Noel said, sounding exasperated. 'How did you find it?'

'I didn't find Mika. She found me. Honestly! I woke up one day, and she was on my pillow.'

'When?'

'I don't know. A few months ago. Before I came to Val.'

Noel rubbed his head, looking unusually haggard. 'All right.' He turned to Lana and Tilina. 'Please, carry on with your duties,' he said. 'Don't mention this to anyone. I have both your words?'

The two women nodded, then quickly left. Noel closed the kitchen door and took his usual seat by the fireplace. 'A mouse,' he said, his eyes unfocused. 'I don't understand. Is this a sign that the balance is changing? Or it is because of Maude?' Like the others, Noel had no explanation for Maude's abilities. To this day, it frustrated him.

'Have any other animals come to you?' Noel asked.

'No, just Mika.' Maude scratched the little mouse on the head.

Noel frowned. 'I would like to try something, if you don't mind.'

Maude rocked slightly from side to side, looking down at the mouse. 'Try what?'

'Could you please give the mouse to Aren, for just a moment?'

Unsure of what Noel was doing, Aren tentatively stretched out her hands. Maude scooped Mika out of her wraps and plopped her into Aren's palms. The mouse was heavier than she looked. Mika sniffed at Aren's fingers, her little claws digging into Aren's skin to hold herself steady. It was the strangest sensation.

'Aren, can you please walk towards the doorway?'

Aren walked slowly towards the door with her little passenger. The mouse soon squeaked and bobbed her head frantically towards Maude. Feeling bad, Aren moved back to Maude. Mika settled down again, sitting back on her haunches and sniffing at the air, one tiny paw braced against Aren's hand.

'Hmm,' Noel said. He stood up from his chair and walked towards Aren, reaching out his hand to Mika. The mouse squealed and charged up Aren's arm, claws digging into her flesh.

'Ow,' Aren cried. 'Stop!'

Mika reached Aren's shoulder and flung herself into the air. Maude dashed forward and caught her, swiftly folding Mika into her wraps again, giving Noel an angry look.

Noel returned to his chair, wiping sweat from his brow. Aren often forgot that Noel was affected by Maude's strange ability too. Nothing like Jin was, but enough to make him feel out of sorts in Maude's presence.

'Well, it wasn't a perfect test, but I'm fairly certain the mouse is responding to Maude's abilities to suppress majik.' Noel looked at Aren. 'She grew distressed when you took her away from Maude. We already know that Maude's ability grows weaker with distance, so it makes sense.' He looked down at his own hands. 'Then she grew significantly more distressed when I approached. As a mayj, I am a source of power, something that nature disagrees with. Granted, I am a stranger too, but the mouse was fine with Aren. How fascinating.'

Maude did not look so impressed. She glared at Noel again before looking down at the quivering lump in her wraps. 'It's okay, Mika, no more of that now,' she said, cooing at the creature.

'Maude, I'm sorry. It's not safe for you to carry Mika around,' Noel said gently.

'It's fine. I've been carrying her around for months, and you've never noticed,' Maude replied sharply.

'True,' Noel muttered, looking rather annoyed, 'but we did eventually find out. Carrying a live animal around in Valrue could bring about very unwanted attention.'

Maude was quiet.

'Maude?' Aren moved towards her and placed a hand on her arm.

'No, you can't take her,' snapped Maude. 'I'll keep her with me.'

Noel sighed. 'Maude –'

'If I leave her, she'll be scared. And you wouldn't take her, would you? That would be so cruel.'

Noel looked pained. 'It's about keeping you safe. Your life is more important than that of a mouse.'

'But Mika is just like the mayjen children!'

Noel looked baffled. 'How?'

'Auntie Hidel and Mae take in those children even though it's dangerous, because no one else will care for them,' Maude said, staring unwaveringly at Noel. 'I'm the only person who can protect Mika from majik. So I will. It's the right thing to do.'

Noel seemed at a loss for words. Aren remembered being a fourteen-year-old girl. Noel was probably having flashbacks of their standoffs. There was no way Maude was going to budge on this.

'Very well,' Noel said, his face becoming serious. 'I trust you will keep that creature hidden?'

'Yes, I will.'

'And I'll have to tell your aunt about this.'

'Fine.'

Noel nodded grimly, his jaw locked. But there was something in his expression that was off. With a jolt, Aren realised that Noel was lying.

He had no intention of letting the mouse live. A mouse was not worth dying for, and he knew it.

Aren knew it too. She felt a pang of guilt as she watched Maude pet the little lump. It was a shame the maids had seen. Lana and Tilina had been part of the household for years, but Noel would still worry. He'd say that people could be bought, and he was right.

Aren frowned to herself. When had she become so cynical?

Noel stood up to leave. Aren held out her hand for her dagger, but Noel did not give it to her. 'I don't know why you've been training so hard,' he said, 'but it worries me. I'm sorry, Aren. I can't give this back to you.'

He walked off with her dagger.

Aren watched him go, seething. How dare he? How could Noel and her mother flaunt their rebellions in front of her for the best of reasons but stop her from doing the same? Did they not think she could do it? Even Maude had found her own way to make a difference, insignificant as it was.

That was when Aren set her resolve.

She could spend many more months allowing herself to be cooped up, enduring the coddling, letting the days slip by as she clung to excuses about not being ready. But the truth was that she wouldn't know until she tried.

'Come on, Aren!'

Maude grabbed Aren's hand and tugged her out the door, across the sun-drenched sparring court to the base of the stone tree. She sat down and pulled a little pot and a brush out of her boot. 'Sit,' she commanded.

Aren settled next to her. Maude licked the back of her hand and rubbed it furiously against her wraps, wiping off old smeared-ink patterns. Maude unscrewed the pot, revealing white ink. She dabbed the paintbrush on the end of her tongue, then into the ink.

Tongue between her teeth, Maude began painting the back of her hand with delicate strokes. In less than a minute, she had created a beautiful curling pattern that spiralled as Aren looked at it. Maude held up her hand, admiring her work.

'What does it mean?' Aren was fascinated by the detail of it, the fine lines.

'It means "saviour".' Maude twisted her hand, looking at the pattern from different angles.

'Because of Mika?'

'This word speaks to me,' Maude said, turning her head to the side. 'You cannot pick a pattern on a whim, you know? But saviour feels right.'

Aren didn't know what Maude meant. Words had never spoken to her, that she knew of.

Maude looked up at Aren and dropped her hand. 'Do you want one?'

Aren raised an eyebrow. 'Am I allowed?'

Maude laughed. 'Of course you are! Why wouldn't you be?'

Aren had assumed the answer was obvious. 'Because I'm not Bhouli.'

Maude shook her head. 'That's silly. Ink patterns don't belong to Bhouli. Most people just don't know how to draw them. Do you want one?' she repeated, picking up the brush and looking at Aren expectantly.

'Ah, sure. But could I have one without all the licking?'

Maude giggled. 'You're so funny sometimes, Aren! No licking, I promise. What do you want?'

'Um . . .' Aren had absolutely no idea. She didn't know what the patterns looked like, nor an inkling of how to pick one. She remembered Maude explaining a few that she'd worn sometimes. Individually, they meant something, but when combined with other patterns, that meaning could change. They were supposed to speak of the wearer's sense of identity or something like that. It was terribly confusing.

'Saviour', however, made some sense, given that Maude was caring for the mouse. Aren quite liked the idea of something that represented who she wanted to be.

'What about "warrior"?'

'Oh no, I can't do that,' said Maude, shaking her head.

'Why not?' Aren felt more disappointed than she expected.

'Because the pattern for warrior is the same as the pattern for Krijen.'

'So I can't have it because I'm not Krijen.' That made sense.

'No, that's not why,' Maude said. 'You can't have the pattern for Krijen because it also represents violence.'

'Huh.' Aren wondered what Jin and Bish would have to say about that. 'So,' she said, thinking out loud, 'a Bhouli becoming Krijen would be bad, because Bhouli make a pledge against violence, right? So does that mean when Filip became a Square, the Bhouli cast him out?' Something clicked in Aren's memory, and she gasped. 'That's why he didn't wear his headscarf for his dance! But . . .' She frowned. 'He still had ink patterns on his skin . . .'

Distracted, Aren only just noticed that Maude's jaw had dropped. She held her brush suspended in the air, oblivious to the ink dripping onto her leg.

'Aren,' Maude said. 'You just said a very bad thing.'

Aren rolled her eyes. 'Ugh, everyone is so *weird* about saying the names of the Lost Squares –'

'No, that's not what I meant.'

Aren shut her mouth, waiting for Maude to explain. She would never understand this girl. Or maybe she just needed to listen more.

Maude looked sad. She lowered the paintbrush slowly. 'Is that actually what people think about us?'

'What?'

'That we "cast people out"?'

Aren shrugged. 'Well yeah. I mean if you make a pledge –'

'The Bhouli would be horrified to hear this!'

This conversation was like wading through stone. 'Maude. Please explain. I don't know what you mean.'

Maude leant back against the stone tree. 'Bhouli don't force people against their will. We would not stop someone from being Bhouli. It's who they are.'

'What's the point of having a pledge if you don't enforce it?'

'It's not about enforcing anything. The pledge is for ourselves, not for others. Bhouli who seek violence *choose* to no longer be the same as us – they *choose* not to go to the stars. There is a difference.'

Aren screwed up her face, struggling. 'But it's the same, right? Even if it's a choice, if they are no longer the same as you, surely, they aren't real Bhouli anymore?'

'They are always Bhouli. This is not like the Lost Squares who stop being people.'

That pulled Aren up short. It made her think of Wren, and how he'd seemed invisible to others on the day he'd saved her.

'You don't have to change what you look like, or what you call yourself, to change who you are,' Maude said. 'Anyway, Filip didn't seek violence. He was the same as us. And not wearing his headscarf had nothing to do with being "cast out". He just wanted the sky to tempt him.'

'What does that mean?'

'He wanted to die.'

Aren reeled. 'What? *Why?*'

Maude shrugged. She was always so relaxed about death. 'He probably couldn't find his purpose in life.'

As awful as it was, Aren felt relieved. It sounded like Filip's death could have been a mercy for him. Aren clung to that thought in hope, for Jin's sake.

The conversation had exhausted her, yet she still didn't feel like she understood everything the way Maude had intended. Aren leant back on her hands and allowed her head to loll on her shoulders, face to the sky. The sun warmed her cheeks. It felt nice.

'Oh! I have the perfect pattern for you!' Maude dipped her paintbrush into the inkpot and grabbed Aren's arm. 'Normally, I would put your first one on your chest, but you're probably going to want to show people, and they can be weird about that.'

Aren laughed. 'Yes, on my arm, please.'

Maude pulled Aren's wraps up and began a pattern on the inside of her wrist. 'I'll put it here so it lasts longer,' Maude said. 'The only problem is the ink is almost the same colour as your skin, so I don't think it's going to be all that visible.' The comment made Aren think of Filip again, of how his fair complexion had rebelled with the long days as a Square under the sun, leaving a light-gold tan on his hands and neck to contrast his patterns. Aren's skin was stubbornly pearly-white.

As Maude worked, Aren found a strange warmth spreading from the spot where the brush touched, an odd sensation that soothed and tingled at the same time. Her pattern took a little longer than Maude's, and Maude had to dip the ink back in the pot twice more to complete it. It was a rather cathartic experience.

'What does it mean?'

The pattern was circular, with a thick outline, and looked as though someone had pinched the two opposite ends into curling points. Tendrils filled the circle, playing around one another, all of different weights and lengths.

'Happiness,' Maude said simply.

Aren felt disappointed. She peered at the pattern closely. It was certainly beautiful. But its meaning was rather boring.

'You don't like it?'

'No, I do,' Aren said. 'I don't mean to sound ungrateful, but I was hoping for something more . . . exciting.'

'Never underestimate happiness. Few people have the privilege of wearing that on their skin.'

The hair on the back of Aren's neck stood up.

'It means you are lucky too,' Maude added.

'Okay.' Aren smiled, trying to hide her discomfort. She'd rather not get by on luck.

Maude blew gently on Aren's wrist to dry the ink. It tickled.

Aren pulled her wrist back, not sure why she felt strange. She wouldn't let the pattern get to her. And like Maude always said, the ink wasn't permanent until they put it under your skin.

CHAPTER 27:
JIN KANJU

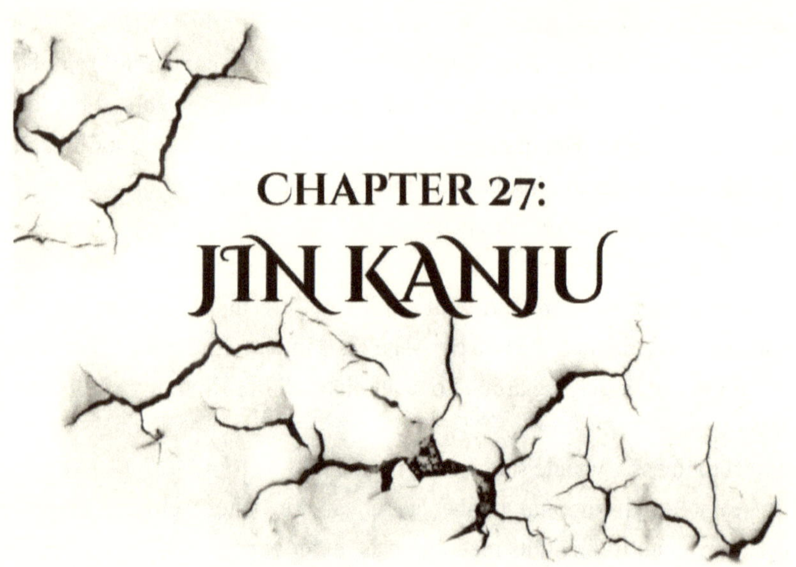

Jin and Meek followed Jokah out into the hot sun, trailing dust as they crossed back to the main hall. The sudden heat made Jin feel vaguely breathless, as though he was back in Valrue again. It was dry, for sure, but it shouldn't affect him this much. At least they were allowed to swap their black wraps for something more comfortable. Each of them wore a loose grey shirt and trousers, though they kept their thighs and forearms wrapped beneath the lighter cloth. They needed their weapons in reach.

Kimjit was waiting for them in the doorway, looking unusually shaken. She pointed to six unfamiliar Krijen sitting around one of the long tables. They were a sorry sight. One Krijen was leaning against the wall, his head rolling to the side, while a squad member tended to him, blocking his torso from view. Another Krijen sported a deep gash on his arm, the neatly puckered skin unmistakably the work of a blade. They all looked exhausted. Tonics and bandages were strewn across the table in front of them.

'These are the roamers I mentioned,' Kimjit said. 'They aren't supposed to be back yet.' Jin looked around at them all, unable to hide his shock. It was so rare for Krijen to get injured like this. 'What the fuck happened?'

'We are about to find out.'

Jin heard an awful, rasping sound. It was coming from the Krijen leaning against the wall. The squad member tending to him had shifted so Jin could see the Krijen's shirt had been removed, and he struggled for breath, which was no surprise given the fist-sized *dent* in his chest. The flesh was intact, but the bones underneath crunched inwards in a vaguely circular shape. The skin was black, the bruise spreading.

'I'm not sure how to treat this,' said the Krijen tending to him, looking back at the room. 'I think the swelling is making it hard for him to breathe. But if he's punctured a lung . . .' His voice trailed off, his face full of worry.

Jin couldn't take his eyes off the dent. 'What caused that?'

The Krijen with the gash in his arm stood up. He had a weather-beaten brown face, but his dark hair carried no shades of grey. 'I'm Squad Leader Myles,' he said in a gravelly voice. He nodded to Kimjit, Jokah, and Vulmin. He knew them.

'Squad Leader Jin,' Jin replied, stepping forward. Myles raised an eyebrow. He clearly thought Jin was a strange choice too.

'You need that stitched up,' Jin said, nodding to Myles' arm just as Bish appeared in the doorway with a needle and thread. Bish went to Myles and saluted respectfully. 'Sir, sit, please.' Myles slowly sat down, his eyes on the needle in Bish's hand. Bish straddled the bench and selected an antiseptic from the table, peering into the wound as he unscrewed the lid.

'Bandits,' Myles said, finally answering Jin's question.

Kimjit looked up in surprise.

'I know,' Myles said, noticing her expression. 'But they had a fucking mayj with them –' Myles hissed, his head whipping to the side. Bish had dumped the entire bottle of antiseptic into his wound. Infections were more likely in the Deadlands than in Valrue, and Bish clearly wasn't taking any chances. Myles didn't pull away, but he glowered at Bish.

'They'd been following us for a while,' Myles began, turning his head back to the group. 'A few hours at least. I decided not to send up a flare.

I wanted to figure out what they were doing.'

Myles sucked in a breath as Bish took to his arm with the sewing hook, before continuing with his story.

'So we camped up as usual, tucked underneath the Ridgeback. Myself and Shahn here' – Myles indicated to the Krijen with the hole in his chest – 'left Arji on lookout.' A coal-skinned man with a Deadlands braid put up his hand at the back of the group.

'We settled down some distance away, watching to see if the bandits would come. We didn't know they had a mayj at first. And if I'm being honest with you, I didn't expect them to approach in broad daylight, especially when we had our backs to the Ridgeback and so near Second Base East. They proved me wrong.' Myles grimaced.

'Stop that, Myles,' Kimjit said, rolling her eyes. 'This lot will think you don't know what you're doing. Myles is one of our veteran Base East roamers,' she explained. 'His squads have caught more bandits than the whole of Base North put together.'

Myles gave Kimjit a flat look. 'No, Kim. I was a fool.'

Kimjit folded her arms and fell quiet, a frown on her face.

Jin looked between them. Something was being left unsaid. He didn't know what.

'I assumed the bandits were new to the game,' Myles continued. 'It was odd that they were following roamers. Anyway, Shahn spotted the first pair, clear as day from where we were hiding. I signalled their position to Arji. Another pair stuck up their heads on his other side, so I moved in to shadow them. When I got closer, I saw they were carrying swords.'

'Hm,' Jokah said. 'Strange.'

'Right? Bandits can't fight for shit. They prefer to pick off Krijen from a distance with bows or spears. They won't come within arm's reach unless forced to. So yeah, the swords threw me a little.

'I signalled to Shahn, and we took one pair down quietly. Meanwhile, one of the other bandits stuck his head out to get a better look. Earned Arji's knife, straight between his eyes. Now I was expecting the remaining bandit to turn tail and run. Instead, he opened his mouth when he saw we'd killed his friends and started screaming.' Myles' face darkened. 'That's when the mayj showed up.'

'The screaming woke us up, of course,' said another Krijen. The man was leaning back against the table, arms by his sides. 'Ivan,' he said, introducing himself. 'We barely got out from under the Ridgeback when the mayj brought the whole cliff down. It completely buried our packs. Myles yelled at us to move, to put some distance between us and the mayj. The mayj started ripping chunks off the cliff and hurling them our way, like they weighed nothing.'

Myles spoke up again. 'For a moment I had a clear view of the mayj. I was about to throw my dagger his way when three more bandits arrived.' Myles shifted his gaze to Shahn, who was still rasping. 'These three bandits were not like the others. They knew how to fight. I was distracted. We hadn't moved far enough away. I left us exposed.' Myles' voice dripped with regret.

'A rock hit Shahn, square in the chest. That *skahk*,' Ivan spat, his hands balled into fists.

Jin flinched at the word, and a sudden spark of pain shot down his arm. He frowned and grabbed his wrist, hoping to disguise the movement.

'It was my fucking fault,' Myles said. 'I underestimated them.' Jin thought it strange that his squad did not defend him. They just looked on in silence, their faces grim.

'I know it wasn't good enough,' Myles said again, even though no one had spoken. 'I should've known better.'

Beneath the bristling exterior, Jin thought he could sense the squad leader's shame. The silence was long and awkward, and Jin's eyes flickered between the faces of the Krijen, waiting. With a shock, Jin recognised the tension in the squad for what it was. They *blamed* Myles.

Kimjit shifted on the spot, clearly uncomfortable. 'What happened next?'

'Shahn hit the ground,' Myles continued through gritted teeth. 'The bandits sliced me good before the others reached us. We grabbed Shahn and ran.'

Jin frowned. The tension in the room aside, something didn't feel right. 'Did the bandits dig out your packs?' he asked.

Arji shook his head. 'Why would they? Bandits know roamers don't carry valuables. That's why we thought it odd they were following us in the first place.' Arji looked back at Myles. Jin couldn't tell what he was thinking.

'It was a planned attack. They were after something,' Myles said. He looked ready to punch something, his balled fists shaking.

'Perhaps they weren't after supplies,' Jokah suggested. All eyes turned to him.

Kimjit scowled. 'What else would they be after?'

Jokah stroked his chin thoughtfully. 'Krijen.'

A stunned silence followed.

'Um . . . Has that ever happened before?' Meek asked.

Kimjit, Vulmin, and Jokah all exchanged looks. 'Not that I know of,' Kimjit said. 'And for what? For fun? It's too risky a game. Even with a mayj, it should have been a death sentence for them.'

'Yes,' Ivan said bitterly. 'It should have been.'

Myles was still looking at Shahn.

'You were lucky,' Jokah said. 'They could have buried you alive. With the mayj, it seemed the bandits stood a chance, this time.'

There was a frightening truth to these words. Jin was concerned by how easily Myles could have lost his squad today, after a series of seemingly benign decisions that turned out to be the wrong ones. He could feel adrenaline knocking at his chest as he scanned the angry faces of Myles' squad. Is this what he could expect too, if he were to make a mistake?

Myles suddenly slammed his fist onto the table, jolting everyone from their thoughts. He pushed himself up from his seat and walked outside.

'Right,' Kimjit said, drawing attention back to her. 'We've still got a swiftrun to do.'

There were crashes in the courtyard outside. Jin could hear Myles yelling obscenities.

'Hold on,' Pago said, 'it sounds like we are almost certainly expecting an attack. Do we still go?'

Everyone turned to Jin. *Ah fuck*, he thought. It was his decision.

'We have to,' Vulmin replied, before Jin could speak. 'This isn't the first setback we've had in the Deadlands. We will not allow some overly zealous bandits to frighten us.'

Jin hesitated, unsure if he could disagree with Vulmin.

Jokah glared at Vulmin. 'Hold your tongue. This is not your call.'

Vulmin said nothing, turning his eyes towards Jin. Jin felt hot, as if someone had lit a fire in his chest. There was a bead of sweat itching down his forehead. He took a breath, trying to calm himself.

Vulmin had a point. This had been the one and only setback in the six months that Jin had been in the Deadlands. But having a mayj out there scared the shit out of him. It wasn't like he could protect them using his own majik.

'Is there anything we can do about the mayj?' Jin asked.

'Increase the perimeter around the wagons to keep the bandits distant and run him out,' Vulmin growled. 'Mayjen have limited accuracy if they are too far away. We can attack when he's exhausted his majik.' Vulmin spoke confidently. Of course, he must have dealt with mayjen before. As would have all the experienced Krijen, Jin realised.

His fingers twitched as a memory of the Dancing Ceremony flashed in his mind. The krije Bish wielded had been barely the size of a pin, from where Jin had stood watching the dance. So how far was far enough? Vulmin could be wrong, if this mayj was like Jin. But Jin shouldn't know that. He needed another reason to stop this run.

'If we increase the perimeter around the wagons, we will be spread too thin,' Jin challenged. 'We need more Krijen.'

'Done,' Arji said. Jin looked around at Myles' squad. Apart from Shahn, they all nodded eagerly.

Kimjit was displeased. 'You sure? You've just come off a week's roaming. And you're two Krijen down.' Myles wouldn't be allowed to roam until it was clear he wouldn't get an infection. Shahn was going nowhere for a while, obviously.

'We're sure,' Ivan said. 'I can't wait to meet those bandits again.' His lips pulled back from his teeth. 'We'll get them for you, Shahn.'

Jin felt his panic rising. 'An additional four Krijen will help, but it's still too few.'

'Jin, sir,' Kimjit said, clearing her throat. 'I know it's your choice, but people in Valrue are relying on these supplies. There will be twenty-eight Krijen across seven wagons. That is the most Krijen I've ever heard of being sent on a seven-wagon swiftrun. Even if the bandits have a mayj, it's enough.'

No, Jin thought, it wasn't enough.

Jin looked at Bish, who had yet to say anything. Bish was the cautious one. He would back Jin up. Bish turned red under the eyes of the room, then looked apologetically at Jin. 'It sounds like we are as prepared as we can be,' he said. 'We can't delay the run or the supplies will deteriorate.'

Jin's heart sank. He couldn't press the issue any further. It would be too suspicious. 'All right,' he conceded, cringing as his father's voice rang out in his head. *Coward*, it said. The thud of Jin's heart was deafening him now. Fuck, he was even getting *dizzy*.

'I'll coordinate with the squads coming in. You four –' He focused carefully on the remaining Krijen of Myles' squad. 'If you want, we can spread you among the other squads?'

'With all due respect, sir,' Arji piped up, 'we work better together. Happy to come under your leadership, if you'll have us?'

Jin opened his mouth to decline. Surely he couldn't be responsible for that many Krijen.

'We'd be happy to have you with us,' Jokah said, smiling at them and turning to Jin to get his approval.

Everything was starting to spin. Jin needed to get out of here. 'Fine,' he said quickly. 'Let's reconvene at midday when the other squads come in.'

Everyone saluted as Jin moved past them, heading for the door, trying not to run. He burst out into the sunlight, treading over splintered wood, remnants of Myles' outrage. His heart was up in his throat, making him gag. Something was wrong. Was he having a panic attack? No, this felt different –

He bent over in the middle of the empty courtyard, sucking in deep breaths of dry air, a weight in his chest crushing him, burning him. There wasn't even a wisp of a breeze, nothing to cool him. He wanted to run. Not *away*, but he just needed to *move*, like he was full of an energy threatening to explode through his chest, just like Shahn –

Oh.

Jin sprinted to the barracks and dove not for the doorway, but for the dark gap between the barracks and the perimeter wall. There was no time to sweep for an audience.

Desperate, he dropped to his knees and let loose the fire within as he threw his hands down towards the earth, grabbing at it with majik. The ground ruptured beneath him as he tore it, and he reached down blindly with his power as best he could as the pressure and the heat and the pain drained from his chest, searing out through his wrists and fingertips. The earth shuddered beneath him as he ripped into its belly. Moments later, it was done.

Trying not to laugh, Jin collapsed against the wall of the barracks, feeling incredible.

He'd been so foolish. He'd not harnessed since they arrived in the Deadlands. He'd never suppressed it for that long before, not realising how bad it would get. Jin felt lighter now, like a weight had been lifted. Perhaps this was what he was supposed to feel like. He'd clearly lost track of normal.

Jin looked between his feet at the damage. There was a jagged black crack in the earth before him, about three feet in length, two inches wide, with a scattering of little other cracks coming off it. It must go deep because he'd felt the weight of the earth as he'd pulled at it. It was hard to use majik on things he couldn't see, but he'd not been able to think of a better way to harness his pent-up power discretely, with such little time.

Slowly, Jin stood up and kicked some sand into the crack. It was pointless; it gaped as wide as ever. If someone ever bothered to walk around behind the barracks, they would definitely see it.

Oh no, Jin thought suddenly. Did anyone *feel* it?

He jumped to his feet and ran back down the side of the barracks before peering around the corner at the courtyard. It was quiet. He stepped out into the sun just as the others began to file out of the main hall. Bish came out and spotted him immediately. He left the others and jogged over.

'Jin? Are you okay?'

Jin shrugged, hoping he looked nonchalant. 'Yeah, why?'

'You just looked a little . . . I don't know . . .'

'What?'

'Freaked out. In there.' Bish nudged his head towards the hall.

Jin opened his mouth to deny it, but closed it again. He'd never once got away with lying to Bish. Or anyone, really.

'I'm fine now,' Jin said quietly. 'I just left it a bit long, that's all.'

'What do you mean?'

'You know.' Jin didn't know how to say it without sounding awkward. 'I get fidgety if I don't harness for a while.'

'Wait. What?' Bish's expression turned from confusion to horror. 'You ran out here to do *majik?*'

'So you didn't notice? That's good –'

'No, Jin, that's not good!' Bish twisted around, looking to see where the other Krijen were.

'I don't think anyone saw,' Jin said.

Bish looked furious.

'Look,' Jin said, 'I don't know what you expect me to do about it –'

'Is this why you always did those stupid little things? Like with the nail in the bunk slat?'

It took a moment for Jin to understand what Bish meant. 'Oh, right. Yeah, I guess so.'

'Next time, let me know,' said Bish. 'I'll keep a lookout.'

'Oh no, you don't. I'm not getting you sucked into this –'

'Don't be a fool. Next time, *tell me.*' Bish turned on his heel and stalked off.

Jin watched him go, shoulders sagging. Bish was always angry at him. But at least Jin knew he shouldn't wait so long next time.

By the Great Kahn, this swiftrun could go wrong. And if it did, it would be Jin's fault, because he'd known the mayj was possibly more dangerous than everyone realised. There were so many Krijen going, putting their lives on the line, trusting Jin when he didn't deserve it –

Kimjit stuck her head out of the main hall, making Jin jump.

'Oi! Get your arse over there, they're waiting for you!'

Jin waved a hand at her and jogged off towards the yard, feeling as though a weight was already settling back over his chest.

The Twenty Sixth Letter

To You

I am sad today. I got it in my head that I would see you again soon, but as the days and weeks pass, I fear it is nothing more than wishful thinking. If I am being honest, aside from missing you, I hoped you would return given the mounting concerns of which I have been writing. You would know what to do.

The Unsettlement is worsening. Life in Valrue has become more dire than anyone could have possibly imagined. Where forest once encircled the mountain, there is now a ring of barrenness. The Krijen have even begun referring to it as the Deadlands. I have not seen it, but I hear it is well-named, there being little else other than sand and dirt and empty hills. It seems nothing of nature, other than us humans, can survive near Valrue.

The Unsettlement is putting unprecedented strain on our resources. The farmers are up in arms; the crops are pushed out farther than ever before to maintain the food supply for the city. If they are too close, they do not survive.

I suspect the Krijen are struggling. Their exclusive numbers stretch across such vast distances now, and despite the food scarcity and the lack of resources, the city's population continues to grow. I imagine the Krijen wish to increase their intake of Squares, but I doubt there are enough Geni for that. The Kahnen may also be reluctant to allow such a thing, given they have always been wary of giving the Krijen too much power. I know it is bold to write this, but I find I care less these days.

On a similar note, of which I am sure you will be more interested, the KahnenMayjen numbers are dwindling. It is but a guess, though an educated one. I can tell because of the way the city is crumbling, the way the Kahnen visit less often, with fewer KahnenMayjen at their sides. I have yet to see the lake level drop, but perhaps it will soon, without sufficient majik to draw water into the crater.

Naturally, the KahnenMayjen would have been the first to know what the Unsettlement might mean. I suspect they began to leave, early on. Nowadays, the sentiment towards mayjen would be enough to drive away even the most resilient of them. I do not blame them. No one could.

I feel obligated to tell you these things because of what I am about to ask of you. If you have not already made up your mind since you started reading this letter, please, you must come back. Of course, I wish to see you, but this is bigger than you and I. Your disagreements with the Kahnen will surely be overlooked if you can help us save Valrue. I have thought long and hard about this, and I would not ask this of you if I thought there was any other way.

Alas, again, I must go. I can hear Felle calling. She is doing well, though I believe she thinks me a bit old and dreary. I am worried she grows bored on her own, but despite my fretting, she seems to have no concerns about not having any friends. Perhaps this is one worry that I should let slide. I have many other more pressing things to occupy my mind and Felle, despite everything, seems happy.

From Yours,
Dijak

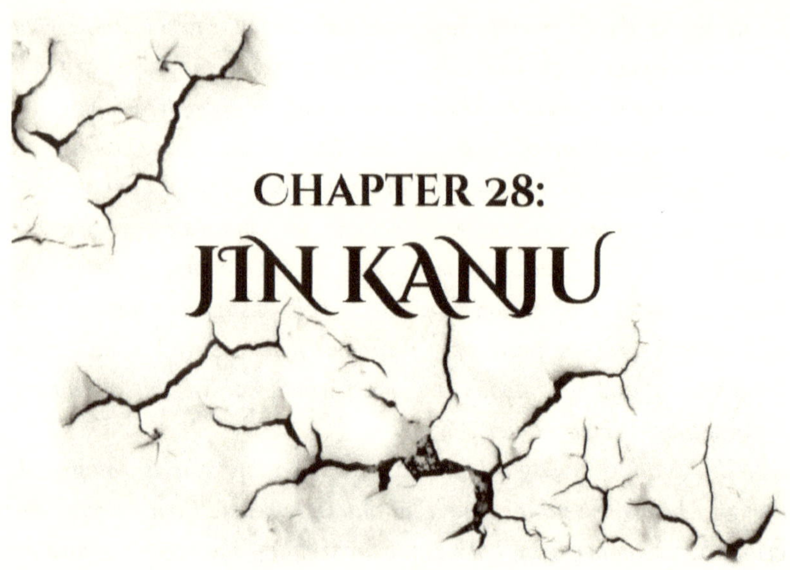

CHAPTER 28:
JIN KANJU

Nine years ago

Standing in the dusk light outside the brothel after meeting Eliza for the first time, Jin felt different, somehow. He was excited to go back and see her. Best of all, it was what his father wanted. The day turned out better than he could have dreamed.

So far.

He still had to deal with Geni Igna's displeasure from missing a whole afternoon of training. He still had to face the Sevenths with another fresh bruise that none of them put there. But that was nothing new.

He squinted at the cloudless purple sky. He could still make it back in time for the evening meal. It was quite a distance back to the training grounds, but Jin didn't mind. He felt a thrill at being out in the city by himself. They were allowed evenings off once all their duties had been done, but not for long; and unless he was going home, he never went alone. Not that he couldn't look after himself, but there was always someone to go with. He went with Bish and the other Sevenths, or Aren met him with her mother or Noel, and they wandered through the streets and did mundane things like shopping or went back to her house for a meal.

Jin loved eating at Aren's. They served all sorts of amazing things that Jin had never tried before. Lots of foods that oozed. There was fresh plump fruit that dripped all over you and chunks of meat that left little rivers of juice running down the corners of your mouth. Who knew that fancy food would be so messy? In the Squares, everything was dried and tough, and there was barely enough of it.

Mind you, that might change. The Squares were starting to drop out fast now, particularly the girls. There were only a few girls left in the Sevenths. Linija was probably the toughest. Jin had beaten her at wrestling today, but it wasn't easy. She was better than most of the boys, but Jin wasn't sure how long it would stay that way. He thought about things Eliza said today. No wonder girls didn't stick around long in the Squares when puberty started. Imagine having to manage growing breasts and dealing with those monthly bleeds. It sounded awful. Did girls really have to put up with all that? All the while being surrounded by boys who grew bigger and stronger just because they were boys. It didn't seem fair.

Then again, Jin had met lots of women who were just as impressive as men, though in a different way, like Eliza and Aren. *Well, Aren is still a girl,* he thought, frowning. And maybe his mother would've been impressive too, if she'd had the chance. *But that's your fault, isn't it?* Jin reminded himself.

His mood soured again, annoyed he'd allowed his thoughts to wander the way they had.

He stepped inside the gates and walked past the empty squares. It was quiet. Everyone was washing or resting prior to dinner. As he approached the Seventh barracks, he saw faces bobbing in the window. They disappeared as he dragged his feet up the steps. The door swung open before he reached it.

'Jin!' Bish stood there, looking relieved. A few other Sevenths were standing behind him, the usual greeting after a jaunt with his father. Bish was searching Jin's face for damage. He must have noticed the bruise because he pursed his lips. Jin didn't know how bad it looked. It hadn't felt bad. Jin smiled at Bish, letting him know he was okay. Bish did not smile back.

Bish had never really been a child. He always acted like an adult, even though his body didn't get the message. Bish was scrawnier than ever, and he had lost all his wrestling matches today. But Bish didn't seem to care. Geni Igna always told him that size didn't mean you would win. It helped, but it was more important to have smarts. Bish had plenty of those.

'Jin, are you okay? What happened?'

The other Sevenths watched Jin step inside. Filip stood at the front, next to Nommo. Prinn's head bobbed behind them. Everyone looked so serious. Not at all what a bunch of twelve-year-olds should look like.

'I'm fine,' Jin said, grinning around at them all. 'I'm okay.'

Nobody looked convinced, though their frowns lessened. He hadn't returned to them a bloodied pulp this time.

'Where did he take you?' Nommo asked, forthright as usual.

'I-he . . . we went home,' Jin said, not meeting Nommo's eyes. He closed the door behind him. There were a few titters from the Sevenths.

'You're lying!'

'You're such a bad liar, Jin.'

'Seriously, where did he take you?' Nommo pestered. 'You were gone for ages.'

'Geni Igna was really angry after you left', said Linija, who had pressed forward to the front. 'I know he is always mad, but he was even more mad than usual.'

'Yeah, we thought your father had done something,' Nommo said. Bish threw Nommo an irritated look.

They all started chattering at once.

Jin sidestepped them and headed towards the wooden cubicle which housed his bunk. They followed him. They always did this, when he came back. It was mostly annoying, and sometimes embarrassing, especially if he looked really bad. But in a way, it was also nice. They looked out for one another, like Jin imagined a family would.

'Come on, Jin, where did you go?'

More Squares gathered around, lying on the bunks or sitting on the floor in the little cubicle. It was far too crowded.

Jin sat down on his bunk. He could try another lie, but they would see through it. What would they think of him? Jin couldn't decide if they would be disgusted or impressed. He bit his lip, unsure.

'Go away, everyone,' Bish said. He moved to stand in front of Jin, arms folded. 'Geni Igna will be mad if we aren't ready for the evening meal.' Everyone grumbled, but most got up and skulked away. Filip stayed, only because his bunk was right above Bish's, opposite Jin's.

Filip climbed onto the bunk and lay down, propping himself up on his elbows, looking down at them. Nommo and Prinn stayed too. Both had washed and changed into fresh wraps for dinner. Nommo was very nosy, but fun to have around. He was usually careful not to press Jin too much, but apparently, he was trying his luck tonight. To Jin's relief, Linija had left. He wasn't sure he wanted her there, if he were to tell them the truth.

'So?' Nommo sat himself down on Bish's bunk, Prinn joining him. 'Are you going to tell us?'

Bish grabbed a washcloth and a bowl of soapy water from his nightstand and started wiping the dirt from his face. He said nothing, but Jin could tell he was listening intently.

Jin shoved his hands under his thighs to stop himself from thumbing his daggers. 'My father took me to a brothel,' he said quietly.

Prinn's and Nommo's jaws dropped. Filip sat bolt upright on his bed. Bish slopped water down himself, twisting to face Jin with a startled expression. 'What? You're –' Bish's eyes grew wide. 'You're *not lying.*'

'Nope,' Jin said. He wondered if they could hear his heart thudding. Everyone just stared at him, dumbfounded, until –

'Out with it!' Nommo yelled, delighted. 'Did you . . . you know?' He made a crude gesture with his hands, the meaning very clear.

Jin opened his mouth to speak, but Bish interrupted. 'That's not right, Jin,' he said. 'Your father shouldn't have done that.'

'No, it was okay,' Jin said. 'The women were great –'

'Oh, I'm *sure* they were,' Prinn said, laughing. 'So? What was it like?'

All the boys leant in, ears pricked. Even Bish was waiting, the washcloth limp in his hand. Jin wasn't exactly sure how to start.

'Well, the woman I was with, her name was Eliza. She didn't have any hands,' he added absentmindedly, which he regretted when the boys made a variety of noises, making him blush again. His obvious embarrassment spurred them on, and they berated him with so many questions he didn't know whose to answer first.

The barracks door creaked on its hinges. Within moments, the raucous in the room fell to a hush. Geni Igna stepped into the cubicle. He did indeed look angry.

'Sevenths, report to the dining hall. Immediately!'

Prinn and Nommo leapt to their feet, scurrying towards the door.

Legs swung down in front of Jin's face, and to his horror, Linija dropped lightly to the floor in front of him. She'd been listening on the bed above. She glanced back at him, then headed after the others. Filip climbed down from his bunk and followed her.

'You are not ready,' Geni Igna said, frowning down at Bish. It was certainly out of character. Bish raised his fist to his clavicle, head down. 'I'm sorry, Geni, I was distracted.'

Geni Igna nodded. 'I understand.'

Jin scowled. If he'd said that to Geni Igna, he would've earned latrine duty.

'Clean up and get yourself to the hall.'

Bish nodded and continued to wipe his face, taking as long as he dared while he waited for Jin.

Geni Igna turned to Jin, who got off the bed and raised his fist in respect, before clasping his hands behind his back. Geni Igna did not like fidgeting. He eyed something on Jin's cheek. Probably his new bruise.

'I'm sorry to miss training, Geni,' Jin said. 'I'll make it up tomorrow.'

Geni Igna nodded. Then to Jin's surprise, Geni Igna turned and strode back out of the barracks.

Bish looked up from behind his washcloth, staring after their Geni.

'Is that all?'

Jin shrugged. 'I guess so. He probably thought Father was going to kill me this time.'

'Don't say things like that.'

Jin shrugged again. He held his hand out for the washcloth. Bish passed it over. Jin dipped the cloth in the soapy water, wrung it out, and wiped it across his brow.

'Jin?'

Here we go. Jin hated this part. Bish was upset, and it was his fault. Jin let the washcloth slide off his face into the bowl, slowly turning to look at his friend. But Bish looked . . . odd. His cheeks were flushed.

'Bish? What's up?'

Bish hesitated, then leant in and whispered so quietly that Jin could barely hear him. 'Did you actually have sex?'

Jin burst out laughing. 'Nah,' he said, shaking his head. 'But I did go to a brothel. And I learned a lot,' he admitted. 'I've got so much to tell you. You won't believe it.'

'Okay,' Bish said, smiling weakly at him. 'Tell me then.'

Grinning, Jin launched into his story, relishing Bish's look of awe. Cleaned and changed, they made their way to the dining hall. Light streamed out of its windows in the darkness ahead, the rumble of young voices leaking out of the main door.

'You're going to go back,' Bish said as they came up to the front steps. Bish always knew things he shouldn't.

'Yeah, I guess so,' Jin said, sounding unsure, even though he'd made up his mind. He was definitely going back.

'Okay,' Bish said. 'You'll tell me about it, won't you?'

Jin punched Bish playfully on the arm. 'Of course!'

Bish nodded. Jin started up the steps, then turned back when he realised Bish wasn't beside him. He'd stopped at the bottom of the steps.

'Just be careful, okay? When you . . . you know . . .' Bish trailed off, uncomfortable.

Jin made a face. 'I don't think we'll be doing that for a while,' he said, though he wasn't sure if he believed it. He wasn't given a krije when he first started in the Squares, but he was given a dagger after about a month. It was a thrilling thought.

'I don't know, Jin,' Bish said, a rare smirk on his face. 'It's a brothel, after all.'

Delighted at his friend's amusement, Jin scrabbled dramatically at his own chest, feigning shock. 'What? Is it possible? Did you just make a *joke?*'

Bish swatted at him, but Jin leapt out of the way. Laughing, they entered the dining hall together, the warm, friendly atmosphere swallowing them whole.

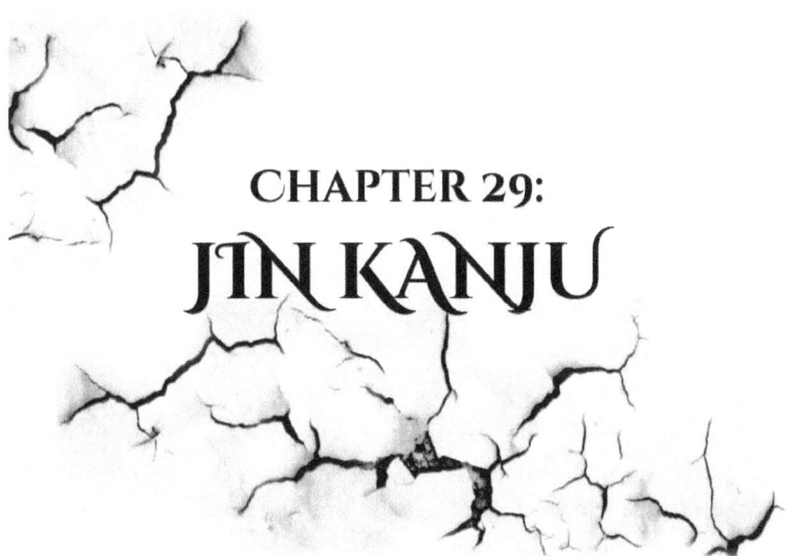

CHAPTER 29:
JIN KANJU

Jin stifled his whoop of joy as they tore down the mountainside. He did not want to give away their position. Despite the sheer number of them moving through the darkness, the only sound was the soft grind of wheels on rock. They couldn't always travel down the hills using the wheels, but this stretch of earth was rubbed raw from the winds and rain.

Jin crouched on the back of the wagon, the wind whipping at him. The buckles around the cargo were so slick with oil that it was hard to hang on. Jokah's dark outline mirrored Jin's at the front, the older Krijen plunging face-first into the night. The heads of the swiftrunners bobbed out of the wagon floor by Jin's feet.

'Wagon' wasn't really the right name. It was a large wooden rectangle with six retractable wheels. There were eight holes, two rows of four, with thick leather straps suspended from each. The straps fit over the shoulders and chest of each swiftrunner, thickly padded to protect from hours of pressure and rubbing. Two sturdy rods hung down from each hole, attached to another wide leather strap that sat snuggly on the hips of the swiftrunners. It distributed the weight across their torsos, keeping their legs free. They never ran with the wheels down. It was far too slow. There was no cover either. It was really a wooden skeleton on their backs, allowing them to cross terrain on foot that would have bested a true wagon. When they ran, it was as if the swiftrunners were a single pair of legs pounding smoothly across the Deadlands.

And by the Great Kahn, Jin had never seen such legs. Usually sprinters were long-legged and wiry, built perfectly for speed. Instead, these men were compact muscle, carrying enormous loads at ridiculous speeds. Their legs were each a mountain unto themselves. Jin had grown accustomed to Krijen strength, but this was something else. His squad wasn't carrying the load, and they were barely keeping up.

Jin had been dubious about staying with the wagons. He didn't like that Bish and the others roamed so distantly, while he coasted down the hills. But squad leaders had to stay close to call the commands and coordinate with the other squad leaders.

As Kimjit promised, three support squads had arrived that same afternoon. The four front-running wagons left yesterday evening from Second Base East, escorted by Jin's squad of ten and another squad of six. The trailing three wagons would be a whole day behind. Kimjit would not allow the swiftrunners to set off without a break.

Jin looked behind him at the shrinking black outline of the following wagon, the wheels flashing as it see-sawed over the crest of the hill. The others wouldn't be far behind.

He hadn't told Bish his reservations about the mayj. Bish would want to know why Jin was so worried, which would require Jin to either lie or tell the truth. He wasn't capable of either. So he shut his mouth and swallowed his fears, setting his already spent nerves on edge. Just in case, he'd harnessed a little before they'd set off by pulverising several stones silently to dust. He swore he'd never been this restless before. Even during the Dancing Ceremony with his adrenaline threatening to lead him astray, he'd managed to avoid doing majik. He wondered how everyone else coped. Was that why there were so many reports of illegal harnessing in Valrue? Maybe everyone was struggling to keep it under wraps after all these years. It wasn't like he could ask around, to find out if this was normal or not.

The wagon soared down into the bowl of the hills, then shot up the other side, slowing as it lost momentum on the incline. Jin and Jokah leapt off the wagon to run alongside the swiftrunners. The swiftrunners untucked their legs as the lever was pulled by the front pair, the wheels retracting slowly to allow the swiftrunners to adjust to the weight. The rhythmic thud of the runners' feet returned, clean and precise, as they continued up the hill at an impressive pace.

This hill was not as steep as the last. Jin looked to the eerie blackness of the Crevasse on their left. Beyond it stretched the turbulent body of the Deadlands, haunched peaks casting shadows that crowded around plains reflecting the moonlight. The Crevasse had torn directly through the land, sparing no hill in its path. Jin made sure they kept the Crevasse close, but not too close. He didn't trust the rock wouldn't break off under their feet and send them all tumbling into the belly of the earth.

He scanned the skyline, searching for flares or any signs of disturbance. Nothing. Nothing but the sounds of the swiftrunners breathing and their pounding feet.

Eventually, daybreak came; and the black, brown, and red veins of the Split loomed over them. The wheels of the wagon descended, and the swiftrunners let up a weak cheer, unstrapping themselves and ducking out of their holes. Jin's legs wobbled furiously as he slowed to a walk. So much for never getting tired anymore. His shoulders and hips ached where his pack had rubbed against them, and his throat was raw.

As though reading his mind, Jokah staggered over to him and helped him unhook his waterskin hose from his pack. Jin nodded his thanks and desperately sucked down water, stopping occasionally to gasp for more air.

Jokah flopped onto the ground without taking his pack off, his head propped up against a rock, hose hanging out of his mouth. 'How do they do it?' he groaned, inclining his head towards the swiftrunners, who were laughing and stretching their limbs out.

Jin unstrapped his pack and let it thump to the ground beside him. Although it was even lighter than when they'd left, it had never felt heavier.

He walked over to the swiftrunners, thanking them for their run with much backslapping and fist-bumping. The other wagons were rolling up, bringing with them more staggering Krijen and laughing swiftrunners. Everyone set about gathering their bedrolls and tucking under low-hanging rocks of the Split where it would be coolest to sleep during the day.

Given how the mayj had brought part of the Ridgeback down on Myles' squad, they had debated at length whether to stop under the Split. Personally, Jin thought lying underneath it was like standing in front of the target during training. It was the perfect place to get shot. But he knew that his aversion to the Split was not necessarily logical, so he'd mostly stayed out of the discussion, letting Flit field the debate. Flit was the other squad leader. The consensus was that rock surrounded them no matter where they lay, so what difference would it make? Jin was disappointed with the decision.

He walked away from the others and ducked behind a shard that lay some distance away. The glassy surface made it stand out from the surrounding ground. Legs protesting, Jin knelt down and looked at the trails of coloured veins. It seemed harmless. Like a pretty rock, really. Apprehensive, he pressed a hand against its cool surface. He was half expecting pain, or some sort of shock, or for it to burst out and trap his hand.

Nothing happened. Jin pulled his hand back a touch and tugged at the surface of it with just a nudge of power, intending to break a piece away from the rest. He was met with an unexpected, stubborn resistance.

Jin tugged harder, with more power. It tingled as it moved from somewhere in his core, down his arms and into his hands. The glassy surface of the shard did not give in the slightest.

Frowning, Jin cut off his flow of power and peered closer at the shard. He'd never had any trouble breaking apart stone before. Assuming that's what it was.

Jin peered up over the top of the shard, making sure he was still alone. Krijen were good at creeping. He wasn't sure he would hear them if someone came to see where he went.

Reassured, he crouched back down and held his hand out above the shard once more. He channelled power towards it again, more than he thought he would need. Then he dragged on it, digging his fingers into the air as power burned down his arms, pulling back against the resistance. Finally, he felt a slight give and a little circle of shard popped out, cracks around its edges.

Satisfied, Jin let his stream of power fade and the circle dropped to the ground. He looked down at it between his feet. It hadn't been *difficult* to harness off, but the amount of power it took surprised him. Maybe Kimjit and Vulmin were right. The Split might just be harder to break than any other rock out here. It seemed it was mayj-made, after all. Maybe that had something to do with why he didn't like it.

Jin thumbed the small crater he'd left on the surface of the shard, lost in thought. The feeling the Split gave him vaguely reminded him of Maude, Mama Hidel's strange niece. But even that was different. Being around her was a vile sensation, as if someone was yanking his insides from within him. The Split was more of a foreboding, as if he shouldn't be near it.

Eventually, Jin headed back to the wagons, walking on stiff legs. Flit was sharing food with one of her squad members whose name Jin hadn't yet learned. Arji and another Krijen from Myles' squad sat with them. Jin thought his name was Yosef, but it was getting difficult to keep track.

Jin sat down opposite Flit with Arji and Yosef and took a chunk of the dense bread offered to him. He put it in his mouth, but it was dry and tasteless and took an effort to swallow. As he forced it down, Jin could see Flit eyeing him up from across the circle. He'd seen looks like that from women before. He'd come a long way since meeting Eliza and the women of the brothel, but what had happened with Linija still bothered him. He would be careful.

Their numbers dwindled as people left to the discomfort of their bedrolls on the hard ground. Jin felt no desire to sleep, despite how exhausted he felt. His roamers had yet to return.

Flit seemed to have a similar train of thought. Soon, it was just the two of them. She looked tired, with rings around her eyes and her long brown hair falling out of its braid. Even under her loose grey clothes, Jin could see she was well-built, with strong shoulders. Not unattractive by any means, but definitely not a woman to mess with. She had a speckling of freckles across her nose, just like Aren.

Aren felt a world away. Fuck, Jin missed her. He missed their spars in the morning, her relentless efforts to beat him though she knew she never would. He missed her laughing at his terrible jokes and how she could never sit still but was always moving, fidgeting, leaping to her feet to embrace him when he visited even if she'd only seen him the day before.

'Do you want more?'

Jolted from his thoughts, Jin stared down at another chunk of bread Flit held out to him. More out of politeness than anything else, he took it. He knew he should eat more but their proximity to the Split was spoiling his hunger. But you never turned down food in Valrue. Not unless you'd stolen some already. He grimaced, thinking of his younger self.

'Thank you,' Jin said, preparing himself. He needed to be polite but firm. 'I can wait here for your roamers if you want to get some rest. I'll wake you if there is any trouble.'

Flit raised her eyebrows. 'I think you need the rest more than me, Jin.' She said his name with a small smile, as though she liked the sound of it. She leant back, watching him with a slightly different look than before. 'You look tense.'

Jin hadn't realised he was sitting rod-like on the edge of the rock, as though prepared to bolt. He stooped a bit, hoping she didn't think his tension was because of her. Well, maybe it was, in part.

'I'm fine,' Jin said, but it didn't sound genuine. He really needed to practise lying. 'I just don't enjoy being near the Split, that's all.'

'Why not? I think it's marvellous.' Flit turned her gaze up at the Split behind him.

Jin began picking at the bread. 'So,' he said, trying to think of an overtly platonic conversation topic. 'Where were you based before East?'

'I was stationed at the KahnenKeep. I helped guard the prisoners, protect the Kahnen, whatever was needed.'

'For how long?'

'Five years. But when they made Eden the Reprimand Master, I left.' Disgust dominated her face, her lip pulling up at the side.

'Who's Eden?'

Flit actually growled. 'He's a Krijen. A horrid one. I've never met a man who deserves to die more than he does.'

Jin wasn't sure how to respond. He'd never heard a Krijen be so critical of another before. He'd never met a Krijen who deserved it, though.

Flit was looking at the ground through slitted eyes. 'We have a duty to the People,' she said, 'including the mayjen. The ones in the dungeons, some deserve to be there, sure. But Eden treats them all like . . . like they aren't human.'

Jin stared. It was shocking to hear talk of mayjen without heavy derision, especially so openly. He glanced around. They were alone. Jin guessed they didn't have to be so careful, not this far out of Valrue.

'I just don't understand why Oji hasn't removed him,' Flit carried on. 'Or how Oji could let him have the position in the first place. It must be some political nonsense. I never had the stomach for all that.'

Was she criticising the FaKrijen? Jin frowned. Mayjen aside, it was dangerous to talk like this. Then again, Flit had called the FaKrijen by his first name, and he was certain no Krijen would be that disrespectful, unless there was another reason for it.

'You know the FaKrijen personally?' Jin asked tentatively.

'Yes, I do, but –' Flit stopped and looked at Jin, apparently confused. 'Wait. When was your Dancing Ceremony?'

'The one just gone,' said Jin, feeling self-conscious. Flit didn't look much older than him, but she had an air of experience about her.

'Wow, you *are* fresh. Fresher than you look,' she said, her eyes running over him again, reassessing. 'You lead well,' she added.

'Thanks,' Jin said, meeting her eyes. He looked away quickly. Those freckles.

'Oji doesn't care much for titles and propriety,' Flit explained. 'He's been able to wade through the bureaucratic nonsense in spite of that. He's been FaKrijen since before I was a Square, you know. Well, since before I was born. He's good.'

Jin nodded, feeling a twinge of jealousy. That Flit was on a first-name basis with the FaKrijen impressed him.

Suddenly, Flit sat up straight, looking over Jin's shoulder. 'They're here,' she said.

Towards them jogged six Krijen, barely a thumbnail high. Flit smiled, recognising her four other squad members up front, two from Myles' squad behind them. Soon they arrived, sweating and swearing.

Everyone plopped down onto the ground, panting and dragging on their water hoses. One of the Krijen landed next to Jin with an ungainly crash, sprawling his arms and legs out around him. 'By the Great Kahn, that was the longest twelve hours of my life,' he puffed. He lifted his head and glowered at Flit. 'How come we got the raw deal, eh? You spoiled sadists getting to ride on the wagons while we run ourselves bloody?'

Jin held his breath, but all Flit did was give the Krijen a droll look.

'Darson, may I remind you that you voted yourself as plebeian and I, the leader. You've only got yourself to blame.'

Darson grunted and lay his head back down on the ground, closing his eyes. In a way, it was nice that the Krijen didn't take each other too seriously. As a Square, Jin had expected the Krijen squad leader would be like the Geni was to the Squares, but that wasn't the case. Maybe it came from having revolving leadership. Or maybe it was Oji's influence, from what Flit had said. Jin's own squad were still quite formal with one another, though he figured they just needed more time. It was also hard to relax around a man as severe as Vulmin.

Jin stared at the spot on the horizon where the returned Krijen had appeared. Where were Bish and Vulmin? They should have been the same distance from the wagons as the other roamers. Jin thumbed his daggers, his eyes running across the landscape. He could see Flit watching him again out of the corner of his eye. She didn't say anything reassuring, not taking Jin for a fool. The Deadlands were treacherous; it was entirely possible that something had happened to them.

The other Krijen were quick to retire and slipped off one by one to their bedrolls. Flit had turned her gaze to the horizon too, her eyes glassy, unblinking. Perhaps she worried that if she closed them, she would drift off to sleep.

'Go rest,' Jin said to her as she tried to hide a yawn behind her hand.

'No, I won't,' she said, shaking her head. 'We must have two Krijen on duty when at rally position.' She was right. Jin shouldn't argue with that.

They sat in silence for a bit.

'You wasted my bread,' Flit said eventually, pointing at Jin's feet. He hadn't realised that he'd crumbled the entire piece onto the ground in front of him. 'Oh, sorry.' Fuck, he needed to pull himself together.

He couldn't think of anything more to say to her, even though she seemed eager to talk. His mind kept drifting to Vulmin and Bish, concocting all sorts of horrible things that might have happened to them, out in the Deadlands. What if they'd been attacked by bandits and hadn't been able to send up their flares? What if the mayj had found them? Jin felt a tightening in his chest again, his heart picking up its pace. His palms weren't burning yet, but maybe that was because he'd harnessed earlier and his power still needed time –

'I can't sleep,' said a voice behind them.

Jin was wrung so tight he almost jumped out of his skin. He spun on his rock to see Jokah standing behind him, groaning and rubbing his eyes. 'Who would have thought rocks would be that uncomfortable?' the older Krijen complained. He sat down next to Jin with a grunt.

Flit immediately stood. 'You good here?'

'Yes, go rest,' Jin replied, relieved she was leaving. Jokah groaned again and stretched his arms above his head. When he was standing, he barely made it to Jin's chin. He did well to keep up with men half his age.

Less than half.

Jin suddenly felt like a Square again. Back then, people told him he was good at what he did, though he didn't dare to believe it. He felt the same fear of disillusionment now. He'd fallen on his face too many times as a Square to expect it wouldn't happen as a Krijen.

'Jokah?'

'Yes, sir?'

'I-You don't need to call me "sir",' said Jin, immediately distracted.

'You are my squad leader,' said Jokah, matter-of-factly.

'I'd still rather you didn't.'

Jokah frowned. 'You don't want to be leader?'

His directness made Jin blush. 'That's not what I meant. I just thought you or Vulmin would have been a better choice.'

Jokah smiled gently, eyes twinkling as he looked up at Jin. 'Age and experience don't necessarily make someone a good leader. Don't underestimate yourself.'

Jin mused on that. 'So why *did* you pick me?'

Jokah chuckled. 'Like I said before, I am rather impressed by you. I think the others feel the same way.'

'But why?'

Jin bit his tongue, immediately regretting the questions. He hoped Jokah wouldn't find it childish, or invasive.

Jokah sat back, a thoughtful expression on his face. 'Let's see then. You think logically, even when under pressure. You command with assertion on matters you understand and admit to the gaps in your knowledge. But what I find most refreshing is your healthy level of scepticism. Krijen aren't trained to think – they are trained to *do*. But you aren't afraid to question what is asked of you.'

Jin was horrified. 'You think I'm insubordinate?'

'By the Great Kahn, son, you think I'm criticising you? No. You have integrity. Something which is considerably lacking in the Krijen. I saw how reluctant you were to send us into the Deadlands with a mayj out there. You were contemplating defying an order to spare your squad. I'm not saying we should ignore commands, not at all. But it's good to have a Krijen willing to think for him – or herself – rather than just blindly following orders.'

Jin swallowed. Jokah didn't know that Jin had failed to mention the extent of the danger to save his own skin. It wasn't a moral compass guiding him; it was cowardice.

'But the others have integrity,' Jin blurted out. 'Bish is one of the best people I know, yet none of you will re-elect him as leader.'

'Have you ever considered that Bish and the others don't want to lead?'

'Vulmin seems to want it,' Jin said softly.

'I think you would be surprised. I know Vulmin well. He is opinionated, but don't let that fool you. He doesn't want responsibility. Squad leader is not a coveted position. Squares are trained for fifteen years to follow commands. Once we become Krijen, making decisions doesn't come naturally. With very few exceptions.'

The comment made Jin think of Myles today. Maybe *that's* why the others wanted Jin to lead. To keep their own heads off the chopping block.

Jokah studied Jin, watching his expression. 'You're still fighting me on this, aren't you? What am I missing?'

'Nothing.' Jin shook his head, but Jokah wouldn't be dissuaded. 'I understand you and Bish were Squares together. Do you feel guilty about being chosen over him?'

Jin shifted, uncomfortable. It was definitely true, if not the truth that Jokah was after. But it was a decent enough explanation for his apparent lack of self-conviction, so Jin ran with it. 'Well, yes.'

'He seems like a very loyal friend, not the jealous type. On the contrary, I think he is proud of your accomplishments.'

'I don't want him to resent me.'

'Has he ever given you the impression he would?'

In fifteen years, Bish may have been critical or demanding of him, but never resentful. He'd lost – graciously – to Jin at every turn.

'No, never.'

'Then don't let such thoughts bother you.'

Jin nodded, catching himself before he thumbed his daggers. There was still no sign of Bish and Vulmin. Jokah looked calm, but his eyes darted towards the skyline. He was getting worried too.

'You had a question?' Jokah asked, a welcome distraction. Jin had forgotten what his first question had been. He had a new one now. His palms began tingling.

'What happens if I make a mistake?'

'Ah. You are referring to what happened with Myles and his squad?'

Jin nodded, looking to the ground and squeezing his hands into fists in case his fingers started twitching.

'Tell me, Jin. When was the last time you made a mistake?'

It was a strange question, but Jin immediately had an answer. Even though he didn't look up, he sensed that Filip was back again. The dead Square wasn't real, but he still terrified Jin, making him shiver despite the heat of the day.

'Jin?' Jokah sounded distant.

Jin realised he hadn't answered him. 'I-I can't think of one,' Jin said, but his voice shook. 'Why would you ask me that?'

Reluctantly, Jin looked up. As expected, there was Filip, right behind Jokah, his eyes on Jin. He wasn't wearing his white headscarf, like he usually did. Filip had taken it off just before their dance. Jin had assumed it had been to disconcert him. It had.

Why Filip appeared whole and uninjured, Jin wasn't sure. Perhaps Filip thought it was the best way to taunt him. *This is how I* should *be*, the figure said. *But you killed me.*

Jin tore his gaze away from the dead Bhouli.

Joka's face was loaded with concern. 'I understand why you're worried. Krijen are quintessential warriors, instructed in perfection, to a fault. It is one of our many failings that we ignore. But mistakes are part of life, part of learning. We have forgotten that and punish each other for it.'

Jin didn't like where this was going. What Jokah was saying confirmed his earlier suspicion. 'So I *should* be scared,' he said. 'You only chose me as leader so that I make the mistakes, and you can blame me for them.' Jin stood up, suddenly angry. Pain sparked down his wrists, his power stirring.

Jokah stood up as well, alarmed. 'No! That is not what I meant. I am only trying to prepare you for how hard this is going to be. No one wants you to fail. We trust you to lead us well. More than we do ourselves. Please, believe me.' Jokah reached out and placed his hand on Jin's arm. Jin pulled back from him, but Jokah's humility had struck soundly.

Jin sat down hard on the rock again, running his hands through his hair. 'Sorry,' he said. 'I overreacted. You can sit. I don't mind.'

Jokah nodded and slowly sat down, seeming relieved.

Jin knew Jokah wouldn't lie. Even so, Jin found it hard to look at him. Instead he looked towards Filip, regretting it immediately. Filip folded his arms and shook his ink-smudged head, as though disappointed with Jin.

Still agitated, Jin bounced his legs on the balls of his feet to distract himself from his burning hands. Another question soon found its way to his lips, now that he'd likened his own fate to that of Myles.

'What will Myles do? I mean, he's still Krijen, right? It's not like he's Lost, is it?' The thought was inconceivable. Jin had assumed that once he was Krijen, he would be safe. He'd killed to be here. The proof was standing next to him.

'No,' Jokah said. 'Myles is not Lost in the way the Lost Squares are. He will need a new squad, and he will have to earn their respect. But he will be okay if he allows himself to be.'

Jin nodded, relieved to hear it. Then he leapt to his feet.

In the distance, running towards them, were two grey pinpricks. Jin grinned at Jokah, the tension forgotten for now.

Five minutes later, Bish and Vulmin were standing in front of them, red-faced and shrugging eagerly out of their packs. 'You fuckers,' Jin said to them, laughing. 'You had us going for a minute.'

'Here –' Bish slammed his sweaty pack into Jin's chest, shoving him backwards. 'Never again –' Bish hunched over, coughing.

Vulmin had tossed his own pack at Jokah and stood with his hands on his hips, his chest heaving.

'It was about time you showed up,' Jin said, holding out Bish's water hose for him. Bish took a weak swipe at him, his heart not in it. He grabbed the hose and took a few long drags on the end.

'What delayed you?'

Vulmin held up his hand, indicating he was going to answer. He took a few more heavy breaths, then wiped the sweat off his brow with his sleeve. 'We thought we spotted the bandits,' he said. 'There were some footprints and markings that we followed for a while, but they came to nothing.'

Bish spat out the end of his hose. 'It took us off course,' Bish puffed. 'Had to backtrack.'

Jin was still smiling as he hefted Bish's pack over his shoulder and led the way back towards the wagons. Filip had disappeared.

***

Jin reluctantly agreed to a few hours' rest that day. Meek and Pago dragged him off his rock and sent him into the mouth of the Split. He managed a short, fitful sleep, at the mercy of the rugged ground and the tauntings of the black and red veins that webbed into his dreams, latching onto his body and dragging him into the deep.

The sun was setting as Flit nudged him awake. He was on his feet in an instant. 'Woah. Breathe,' she said, handing him another chunk of bread. 'You better eat this one. You ate almost nothing this morning.'

Jin took it from her, grateful. He was actually quite hungry now. He ate quickly while she ran over the route with him. They were to journey through the Split, sending half the roaming team in first, then they'd send in wagons, then the last of the roamers. Once on the other side, the roamers would fan out and form their wide perimeter as usual.

The four front roamers comprised two Krijen from Flit's squad, plus Vulmin and Pago. Bish, Jokah, Darson, and another member of Flit's squad made up the back roamers. Meek now flanked the last wagon with Jin, who was glad to not be with Jokah this time. That left Flit and another one of her squad members on the front wagon, leaving the four from Myles' squad flanking the two middle wagons.

Not long after the front roamers jogged into the darkness of the Split,

212

the wagons followed suit. Without the moon to light their path, it was rather precarious underfoot. You had to be careful not to turn an ankle on loose stone.

Jin ran, pounding out the stiffness from the night before. The tension from being in the heart of the Split was probably the only thing keeping him awake in the blackness. He regretted not trying to sleep more. He needed to be sharper than this.

Fifteen minutes later, Jin could see the stars twinkling at the end. They exited the Split with a rush of air, the Deadlands expanding around them, flat and quiet. The dark cone of the mountain that held Valrue was visible in the distance.

The front roamers would already be well ahead of them, scoping out the route. Jin scanned the skies for flares. Nothing. Meek kept a great pace at the front of the wagon, spurring on the swiftrunners who were chatting to him. Somehow he was making jokes in between breaths.

Just as Jin felt himself relaxing, the earth exploded in front of them, and the front wagon flipped up towards the sky, chasing Flit's scream up to the moon.

CHAPTER 30:
AREN BHA

What did one wear to be a vigilante in the night? Surely black. But black was for Krijen, and Aren did not want to be Krijen. Also, Krijen were the only ones allowed black wraps. Aren was fairly certain it was a crime to be caught wearing them. Impersonating law enforcement, or something like that.

She dug through her closet, tossing wraps, dresses, trousers, skirts, and blouses aside. What a ridiculous amount of clothes she had. Yet lately, she couldn't decide on anything to wear. She felt as though she'd outgrown her once-favourite green wraps, even though they fitted fine.

At the very back of her wardrobe, there was some dark material of sorts. Aren tugged on it, pulling out long midnight-blue wraps. She'd almost forgotten about these. They were certainly the darkest thing she owned that wasn't black, hence why she'd stopped wearing them.

The temperatures were soaring in Valrue, so darker materials were very impractical. It suddenly made sense why the Squares wore the same black as the Krijen. They needed fifteen years to grow accustomed to it.

Aren had bought these wraps years ago when she was about fourteen or fifteen. Luckily, Aren thought bitterly, she hadn't grown an inch. She wrapped them around herself, then slid a dagger into the material by her thigh. Noel may have taken her favourite dagger, but he'd been silly to think she kept only one. Her father was the Weapons Master, for goodness' sake.

Aren tugged on her boots and dropped a little knife in there too. One more, perhaps? Jin always seemed to have an endless supply on him, even though you could never see them. Once she saw him pull a *spear* from behind his back. How he'd hidden that, she had no idea.

Aren had no more knives in her room. She could grab another one from the kitchen on her way out. Should she bring a backpack with a waterskin, perhaps? No, that would just slow her down. She hoped to be back in a few hours. It was cooler at night. She shouldn't get too thirsty.

Aren looked down at her hands. She'd left her lamps unlit to not arouse suspicion should anyone walk past her room, so she could see fairly well by the moonlight streaming in through her open windows. Her smudged white-ink pattern was visible just above her wrist wraps, and - as Maude had said - barely there against her skin. In fact, Aren's hands practically glowed in the dim, and she didn't have gloves to cover them. Gloves had gone out of fashion a while ago, and it was far too warm to consider wearing them, so her mother had given their pairs away. Aren's white, freckled face would be just as obvious.

An idea popped into her head. She dug back into her closet, hunting for that thing her mother had given her last year. Of course, it had fallen all the way to the back. After a minute of digging, Aren's fingers finally found it. She pulled out the little wooden box and flipped it open. Inside the lid was a mirror. Snuggled into the base was a charcoal-y substance.

Makeup. Finally, a decent use for it.

Aren tossed aside the tiny brush that came with it and stuck her finger in, wiping it across her cheek. She could hear Marigold's cry of dismay as she did so. Aren had once tried to wear it properly, around her eyes, but she'd felt so foolish she'd wiped it off on her sleeve and spent most of the day looking like she had bruises on her face. Jin's reaction when he'd seen her had been enough to put her off using it again. She'd felt bad about that.

Aren held the box to her face, looking in the mirror. There was a perfect black smudge across her freckles. Aren dug her fingers in and smeared her entire face and neck with it, then tied back her hair and smeared it over that too. She put some on the back of her hands, keeping her palms clean.

When that was done, Aren tossed the box aside and shoved her clothes back into the wardrobe. Then she arranged her blankets to make it look like she was in bed. She stepped back, admiring her work, before heading to the low window. She stepped over the wide sill and followed the wall to the gate, then slipped into the street.

Aren jogged through the shadows, her boots quiet on the cobblestones. She figured the most likely place for anything untoward to be happening would be in Rue. It was a long way to get there, so she needed to move quickly.

The streets were empty apart from beggars curled up in corners, the ones who hadn't been chased back across the bridge before night came. She slipped by them, leaving them squinting into the darkness wondering if they'd seen something.

Aren had never been out alone this late in Val before. In fact, she never went anywhere alone, save for a few errands at the marketplace when she briefly separated from her mother. She felt a thrill at the realisation, but the thought also bothered her. Why was that? She'd assumed no one in Valrue travelled alone if they could avoid it. But that wasn't right, because Jin did. Mae did. Even Maude had walked to her house alone the other day. Aren scowled. More of her family's coddling then.

Sometimes Aren couldn't decide if she was dumb or just ignorant. Or were they the same thing? Aren knew a lot of useless things, like how many Minders the Kahnen kept, and why water steamed when it boiled. What *not* to do when a baby mayj pulled on your hair. She frequently felt foolish when she was with Jin, or Marigold and Bish, because they knew so much more about the things that mattered. She felt a little resentful about that. It would be easy to blame her parents, saying they'd brought her up sheltered, living in a fantasy world, oblivious to the harsh truths of life. Wren certainly thought that. But Aren didn't think that was fair to her parents. Because really it was her fault for not doing something about it. Until now, that is.

She was halfway to the bridge before she realised she'd forgotten to grab another knife from the kitchen. *It's things like that*, Aren thought, kicking herself. Stupid, *basic* things like that.

The stone houses were growing taller, with lines of clothes strung between windows. It was spooky to look up and see headless dresses and shirts floating in the air, the lines invisible in the night. It was so quiet she could hear the river bubbling when she arrived at the bridge, even though the water was low for lack of rain. Tonight, there weren't any bodies strung up at the far end.

Unfortunately, the bridge was not empty. There were three men in the middle of it. They appeared drunk, pointing at things in the water and cackling to each other.

The moonlight was way too bright. With a sinking feeling, Aren realised that if she walked across the bridge as she was, the men would clearly see she was a young woman with makeup smeared all over her face. She should've brought a cloak, something with a hood that she could pull forward. Aren was annoyed at herself again. She hadn't even made it to Rue and she had made two mistakes.

She thought of the floating clothes strung between the houses. She could borrow something. She was coming back this way, so she could return it. Aren backtracked up the street and peered up at her options. No cloaks, of course. Did you normally wash your cloaks anyway? Probably not. Aren fidgeted, keeping one eye out for a suitable item while trying to keep the other on the street at the same time.

After fifteen minutes, Aren had grown frantic. She was wasting time. Should she take a chance and walk across the bridge, hoping the men wouldn't notice? No, too bold. Could she cause a distraction perhaps, then sprint across? Or maybe the men had moved on by now. She bit her lip. Should she go back to her room and try again tomorrow when she was more prepared?

No, she thought.

She would not be that pampered little rich girl that Wren thought she was. This was never going to be easy. It was okay to make mistakes, so long as she learned from them and did it right next time. It didn't have to be perfect. Just good enough.

There was something else that might work.

Aren broke into a run, ducking her head into alleyways and around corners, searching. Finally, she came across a beggar she had passed earlier. He had squeezed himself into an impossibly small space between two buildings. He wore rags and little else. His hair and beard were long enough to cover him, though made him indecent in a different way. On the ground in front of him was a floppy black hat with a wide brim. It held a small collection of coin, exposed for the world to see. Aren approached cautiously. It looked like he'd fallen asleep without hiding his stash.

'Um, excuse me. Sir?'

The beggar opened one beady eye. Okay, so not asleep after all.

'You're new to this, aren't ya?' the beggar said in a gravelly voice. From the way he spoke, Aren suspected he'd been on the streets for a long time. He certainly wasn't educated.

'I was wondering – wait. New to what?'

'New to stealing. No one ever tried to wake me *before* stealing from me,' the beggar sniffed. 'Not sure it'll work all that well.'

'I'm not trying to steal from you. I was hoping to borrow that,' Aren said, pointing to the hat. The beggar looked at her like she was crazy. 'You wanna borrow my coin? You taking me for some fool, kid.'

Kid? Was he calling her a young goat? It was odd to hear the animal's name in that context, but she supposed they still used the word, just in a different way.

Aren looked down at herself. She was small and covered in makeup. And it was dark. Fair enough.

'No, sir, I don't want your coin, just the hat. I promise I'll bring it back.'

The beggar rubbed his chin thoughtfully. 'What will you give me?'

'Um . . .' Aren had only her dagger, knife, and boots. She couldn't afford to give any of them up. 'How about I come back tomorrow, with some more coin?'

The beggar shook his head. 'Nope. I want paying up front.'

Aren could snatch the hat and run. The beggar didn't look like he could move that fast. But even if Aren did plan on returning it, she didn't think she could stoop that low.

'Sorry, I have nothing to offer you.' Aren turned and walked away, disappointed.

'Not so fast,' the beggar called after her.

Aren turned back around.

'I'll let you borrow my hat if you give me a kiss,' the beggar said sweetly.

Aren narrowed her eyes suspiciously. 'What kind of kiss?'

'Come on now, I'm no *sleaze*,' the beggar said, looking affronted. 'Just a nice peck on the cheek. Been so long since I had a nice peck on the cheek.'

The beggar sure used a lot of old words. Pecking was what birds did, but Aren knew what he meant. It wasn't the worst offer.

'All right then,' Aren said. 'But hat first.' She scooped up the hat and shook the coin into the beggar's hands. Then she bent down and gave him a small 'peck' on the dirty patch of skin that wasn't covered in beard. He chuckled, clearly pleased with himself. 'Lovely to meet you, little lady,' he said. 'Don't forget to bring back my hat!'

Aren tore down the street, far less careful. She pulled the hat onto her head, wrinkling her nose. It didn't smell the best. It was also too big, slipping low over her eyebrows. That was good, though. It hid her face.

She made it back to the bridge in no time at all. The men were still there, even more drunk than before. Two leant heavily against the walls of the bridge; the other sat at their feet.

Aren sped up, gathering momentum. She didn't want to give herself time to think. She stepped out into the moonlight and crossed the open square onto the bridge. How many steps to get across? She'd never counted. She started now. One, two, three . . .

She ducked her head low, the brim of her hat just high enough that she could see the men's feet ahead of her.

Eleven, twelve, thirteen . . .

She hugged the opposite wall, putting as much distance as she could between herself and the men. Their voices grew louder as she approached. Then they tapered off. She was walking right past them.

Twenty-two, twenty-three, twenty-four . . .

Their feet were gone from her vision. She was over the curve of the bridge, treading down the other side. She couldn't hear anything from behind her. They weren't following.

Forty-six, forty-seven, forty-eight . . .

She stepped off the bridge and hastened to the cover of the Rue towers. It did not escape her that this was where she was almost crushed to death. To her right, she could see the building she'd sheltered on with Wren. She wondered where he was now. If he were even alive.

She hunkered down along the walls, exhilarated that she'd made it this far. The streets of Rue were narrow, packed with abandoned carts and wheels that had lost their wagons. Unlike Val, Rue was awake. There were voices rumbling high above her in the towers. She even heard the fluttering notes of an instrument.

But while Rue was alive inside, the streets were empty of people. Aren had expected them to be haunted by sordid characters, sinister and seedy. She assumed finding trouble, like some citizen or mayj in distress, would be easy. But there were no screams of terror, no pleas for mercy. Aren told herself it would be very wrong to feel disappointed about that.

Mind you, Rue was immense, and she was only on the very edge of it. The streets bordering Val *would* be quieter.

Aren went deeper, trying to remember her route. It was hard when every single building staggered distantly into the sky, growing taller the further she crept. There weren't any decent landmarks to pick from.

There weren't even that many doors. Just huge stretches of blank wall, windowless until two or sometimes three storeys up. Most things on street level were made of stone, but as you looked up, wood took over. It was used to patch holes and put the finishing touches on the top storeys of the tallest towers, giving them a rickety look.

After a few minutes of coming across no one, Aren gave up on creeping and walked along quietly. There were many bizarre things scattered around which grabbed her interest. Aren picked up a long strip of metal with a bumpy design on one side. She recognised it as the city's insignia, stretched thin. This used to be a coin, now harnessed entirely out of shape. It wouldn't be usable anymore yet once would have bought a few meals. She turned it over in her hand as she walked. Who would risk majik for something so wasteful?

Aren was still musing over the coin when she turned a corner and something caught her foot. She gasped as she fell onto the cobblestones, the coin clattering away. She twisted around to see what she'd tripped over.

A pair of legs lay across the mouth of the alleyway. It was a woman, slumped against the wall. Aren scrambled over on her knees and reached out a trembling, makeup-smeared hand. She gave the woman's arm a single shake before snatching her hand back. The woman was stiff and cold.

Feeling light-headed, Aren rose to her feet, leaning on the wall of the alleyway. She took a few deep, calming breaths while she braced herself. Then she slowly bent back down to inspect the body.

How had the woman died? She didn't look injured. She didn't look that old either. Disease? But disease wasn't the problem it used to be in Valrue. Things that caused illness were natural too.

There was a crack behind Aren, so loud and so close she reacted instinctively, whirling around to the sound, pulling her dagger from her wraps and holding it in front of her. Her hand shook as she stared down the alleyway in horror.

She'd not noticed before.

Bodies scattered the length of it. But these bodies had their arms out, fingers twitching, foam frothing from their mouths, alive and convulsing.

Petrified, Aren raised a hand to her mouth so she wouldn't scream. She slowly backed into the wall behind her, right into something warm and soft, with a beating heart.

Aren couldn't help it. She screamed.

CHAPTER 31:
JIN KANJU

The swiftrunners yelled as the front wagon teetered on its back slat, their legs flailing uselessly in the air. The wagon spun and returned to the ground with a crash, splintering wood and snapping ropes, its contents spilling across the ground. From the earth burst a stream of bandits. They engulfed the wagon in seconds, swords flashing in the moonlight as they attacked.

By the Great *fucking* Kahn –

'Krijen, forward!' Jin shouted at the top of his lungs. He dumped his pack onto the ground and slid a dagger from the wraps at his wrist as he began to run. 'Flares!' he shouted.

Meek flung his pack from his shoulders, and within seconds, a burst of red exploded in the night sky above them.

Jin tore past the third and second wagons, the swiftrunners scrabbling at their straps to unbuckle themselves. 'No!' Jin yelled, 'do not abandon your wagons! Retreat to the Split! Meek, give them cover!' The back roamers would not see the flares if they were still in the Split.

Jin reached the edge of the frenzy. Two bandits came at him with their weapons, one a short sword and the other a double-headed axe topped with a long spike. Jin sidestepped a wild swing from the sword and stepped right into the arms of the axeman. He looked mildly surprised as Jin's dagger sank into his chest.

Jin snatched the axe from the dying man's hand, parried another amateur sword swing, and slid his bleeding dagger into the sinew between the swordsman's neck and shoulder. He quickly pulled his weapon free and vaulted over a wheel torn from the wagon. Somehow the next bandit he met was already so covered in gore Jin couldn't tell what the person looked like underneath it. Filip's face leapt into his mind, making him grimace. He cut the attacker down.

Jin reached the wagon and raced forward to free the trapped swiftrunners. Just as he raised his dagger, an invisible force wrenched both his dagger and the axe from his hands. Instantaneously, another axe head came down beside him, sending a burst of splinters into his face.

Jin threw himself away, rolling into a kneeling position, sliding a second dagger from his other wrist. The axe came down again, the shaft of it almost as long as his body.

Jin threw himself at the axeman's torso, taking advantage of the time needed to heave the massive weapon. The axeman doubled over with an 'oof'. Jin thrust his dagger upwards, intending to bury it in the man's side. Instead, the dagger wrenched itself free from his hand.

Fury surged within Jin, stoking the heat in his chest. It seared down his arms, threatening to burst from his fingertips, making him gasp in shock.

He *couldn't*.

Jin shoved it back down, and guilt rose instead. Bellowing in frustration, Jin threw himself into the axeman and heaved upwards, flipping him over his shoulder. There was a crunch as the bandit landed on the wooden shaft of his weapon, snapping it.

Jin lunged for the snapped-off axe head. The bandit flung up a leg and caught him across the jaw with his foot, sending a crack of pain up Jin's neck. He hit the ground.

Momentarily blinded, Jin scrabbled around in the dirt, somehow finding the splintered end of the axe head. He wrapped his hands around it and pushed himself to his feet just as something heavy crashed into him. Jin's stomach swooped as he soared through space before hitting the ground in a tangle of limbs, using the momentum to roll to his feet.

Disorientated, it took a moment to realise the heavy thing that had hit him was Arji. The Krijen lay on the ground at his feet, a broken wagon wheel underneath him. Jin grabbed Arji's arm and hauled him upright. Something dark was trickling down his face.

'Sir? What –'

'*Where's the mayj?*' The words bubbled in Jin's mouth. He'd bitten his tongue. He spat out a blob of blood and spun around.

The loose wagon wheel had flung them quite a distance from the fray, and Jin could see the scene in its entirety under the moonlight. A heaving mess of bodies struggled over the destroyed front wagon, the surrounding ground littered with Krijen daggers and broken weapons.

There were bandits *everywhere*. Twenty still standing, possibly another twenty dead or dying on the ground. They should have been easy prey for eight Krijen. They fought skillessly, using a random mess of styles that did not match the weapons they wielded. But there was a mayj somewhere, systematically disarming them.

'Where the fuck is he?' Jin yelled.

'Sir!'

Jin turned as Pago and Vulmin skidded to a stop next to them, having seen the flares and come running back. 'Sir,' Pago said, his eyes wide in the darkness as he drew his daggers. 'What are your orders?'

Vulmin looked equally shocked. 'They got around us,' he said in disbelief. 'How did they get around us?'

A group of bandits broke away and sprinted towards the Split after the retreating wagons.

No no no no!

Jin's power twinged so painfully in his forearms that he cried out. It was taunting him, he knew it. It was telling him that he could save them. But still he hesitated.

Suddenly, his father's voice was in his head. 'Why don't you fight back, boy?' his father asked, sounding repulsed, the way he always did when he spoke to Jin. 'Because you're a coward, that's why. I couldn't beat that out of you.'

His father's words hit hard. Jin *was* being a coward. He could use majik without them seeing, he just needed cover. He made up his mind.

'Go after them,' Jin said to the others. 'Protect the wagons, stay in your pairs, and keep hold of your weapons! I'll get the mayj!' He ignored their alarmed looks and charged back towards the fighting, knowing they would obey. He needed the Krijen as far away as possible.

As he ran, Jin tried to think, but the flames in his chest burned distractingly, making his arms ache. He'd never fought with majik before, and he had no idea what he was doing. He just knew he couldn't hold it in any longer. This was happening.

Jin splayed his fingers, his power responding immediately, yearning for release. Heat cascaded down his arms, bursting from his fingertips as he let it go.

Jin didn't really know what he did. He just snatched at the wind, the earth; and together they swirled into life around him, encasing him and the wagon ahead. He kept his hands moving, building on the whirlwind he had created. The world darkened, the moonlight almost completely obscured. Like always, it surprised him how *good* it felt to harness.

In the darkness, Jin could hear muffled shouting. He was worried about the next part; he needed his hands free if he were to defend himself. Tentatively, he let his power ease slightly. The whirlwind lost a bit of its force but – thankfully – continued spinning, trapped by its own momentum.

Jin allowed the air in front of him to still, unveiling two bandit shapes cowering above a body tangled in a harness. They'd killed the swiftrunner while he lay trapped. Jin felt a surge of anger, and he flung out a hand, sending a whip of dirt snapping out at the bandits, making them shriek. As Jin approached, their shapes held up quivering swords.

Murderers, Jin thought.

With a satisfying flick of his wrists, Jin wrenched their weapons away and drove them back into their owners' chests. It was so easy. The bandits fell.

The wind was calming around him, and Jin raised his hands to it again, letting his power flow once more. It only took a nudge and the whirlwind picked up, following his hands as he guided it around him.

Jin stepped over the bodies of the bandits and ran down the side of the wagon, taking the pocket of stillness with him as he moved. What he saw was devastating.

Two more swiftrunners lay unnaturally in their straps, black blood pooling on their clothing. The other straps were empty. Jin noticed a third body in grey clothing next to the wagon. He let go of the whirlwind again and knelt down, rolling the body gently over. It was the Krijen who'd been running with Flit. His face was a mess, a chunk of scalp missing above his eye. He was dead. Jin felt another surge of guilt. Maybe he could have saved him, had he harnessed sooner.

Jin raised his hands again and headed deeper.

From the first wagon, there were still five swiftrunners unaccounted for, as well as the Krijen who had rushed to help. Then there was Flit, who may not have survived being catapulted into the sky. Searching for them was slow work. His focus danced between his whirlwind and the ground, which was treacherous with dropped weapons, spikes of wood and metal, and slick with blood. He needed to find this mayj quickly but couldn't see anything beyond his whirlwind cover. Jin was wracked by indecision. Did he dare drop it? It was the only thing preventing anyone from seeing him harness.

A bandit staggered into his circle of calm, and Jin reacted instantly, letting his power go to grab the man's head in his bare hands and snap it around. Jin raised his hands again as the man flopped to the ground.

Fuck it, Jin thought. At this rate, he would not find the mayj unless he walked into him.

Just as he made to cut off his power, he froze, an awful realisation dawning on him. Wouldn't the mayj clear the whirlwind, if it was getting in the way? Could someone harness against something that was already being harnessed?

Jin cursed his inexperience with majik. He threw his arms down, sending his whirlwind gusting into the ground. It hit the earth and rippled away from him, dissipating into the night.

The moonlight was suddenly so bright, and Jin could see more clearly. There were three figures a short distance away. By their grey clothes, Jin knew they were Krijen, standing back to back and looking around frantically. They were from Myles' crew. One even still held his dagger.

Oh no, Jin thought, spinning around in a panic. The mayj wasn't here. The mayj was *there*. At the Split.

Jin ran as he'd never run in his life. He *poured* his power into his muscles, making his blood boil. It hurt.

Up ahead, Jin could see weapons flipping through the sky, the Krijen being disarmed just as easily as before. Without stopping, Jin thrust out his hands and grabbed hold of two of the daggers in the air, sending them back to their owners' hilt first, in case his aim was off. He hoped the Krijen wouldn't be too shocked to snatch them back.

Just then, Jin spotted the mayj. The man stood off to the left, out of the fight, tearing weapons from Krijen and lobbing chunks of earth. Jin was coming up on him. Fast.

The mayj spotted him too. A boulder of earth exploded out of the ground in front of Jin, who reacted instantly, raising his hands and ripping it in half with majik. He leapt through the gap, shaking the dirt from his eyes.

The mayj took a step back, startled. Then he harnessed a collection of Krijen daggers from the ground at his feet and hurled them, point first, towards Jin. His aim was terrible. Jin snatched the only blade that would have speared him from the air, leaving the rest to spike into the ground behind him.

Jin flung the dagger at the mayj, bolstering his throw with majik. The mayj threw up a hand just in time, sending the dagger off course before turning to the Split, twisting his arm to the side.

The second wagon – with all eight swiftrunners still strapped in at Jin's command – shot backwards from under the protective mouth of the Split and slammed into a row of Krijen. Jin watched in horror as his comrades disappeared beneath it, the sound of bones breaking echoing across the plains.

The wagon kept on coming, headed towards Jin. He flung out his arms and caught it with majik, bracing it until it skidded to a stop. The swiftrunners cried out, tossed around in their straps.

The mayj screamed something incoherent at the remaining bandits. They ran towards him, parallel to the jagged arms of the Split.

Jin fuelled his legs with power and leapt clear over the wagon and the astonished swiftrunners, angling towards the fleeing bandits and their mayj.

From the mouth of the Split burst Bish and Jokah, both of whom took off running after the bandits. Jokah leapt onto the closest man, and they fell together, rolling across the ground. Bish pulled out his dagger, preparing to throw it.

The mayj harnessed a wheel loose from the wagon nearest to him and flung it so fast it was invisible with speed, right until it collided with Bish with a sickening crack. Bish cartwheeled through the air and landed on his back. He didn't get up.

'BISH!'

Without thinking, Jin changed direction and raced towards his friend. *Please, please, please don't be dead*, Jin begged. *Don't be dead.*

Jin skidded in the dirt, throwing himself down beside Bish's limp form. Thankfully, Bish's eyes were open and looking at him, dazed.

'Bish!' Jin cried. 'Are you okay?'

'I can't feel anything,' Bish said. 'I'm okay. I can't feel anything.'

'Quickly, get up!' Jin grabbed his friend's arm, heaving on it. Bish's torso spun around, but his legs dragged in the dirt.

'I can't,' Bish said. 'I can't stand up.'

Jin was shaking. What was wrong with him? Was he in shock? 'You'll be okay,' Jin said. 'You'll be okay.'

Bish looked so pathetic lying on the ground, his legs splayed uselessly. Anger roared within Jin, and his power surged in response, singeing his arteries. That fucking mayj had hurt Bish. He'd nearly *killed* him. Jin couldn't stand it.

He forgot who was watching. He stood up and threw out an arm, blood on fire as he harnessed a jagged piece of wood from a ruined wagon ahead of him. He stared after the retreating backs of the bandits in the distance, eyes like slits. With as much power as he could muster, he sent the wood spearing towards the nearest bandit. It went right through him, leaving a hole so large that Jin could see the night sky through it, where the man's spine should have been.

Trailing blood and organs, Jin sent the wood tearing through each bandit, ripping holes through their backs so that they dropped to the ground. Finally, the mayj was the only one left. He was so very small now, so far away.

Jin gave chase. The mayj looked back in terror as Jin gained on him. He carelessly flung his splintered, sodden weapon at the mayj, hoping he would batter it away. Jin dared him to fight back.

The mayj threw back an arm and sent the wood snapping into the ground, stumbling under the weight of the majik. Jin felt only a gentle tug on his power, buried beneath his fury. *He'll Turn before I do*, Jin knew.

The mayj ran on, his majik-fuelled strides wide but weakening. He was running out of power. With a twisted smile, Jin flicked up a hand as he ran. A monolith of earth burst from the ground right in front of the mayj, who didn't have time to stop. He smacked into it, bouncing off and crashing to the ground.

Jin was suddenly upon him. He threw himself down onto the mayj and wrapped his hands around his neck, squeezing, driving his power down his arms and into his fingers. 'You murdering skahk!' he screamed. The mayj writhed beneath him, his fingers scrabbling uselessly at Jin's hands.

It took longer than Jin expected for the mayj to die. He held on, noticing a new weariness creeping around his navel. Maybe it was his power draining. But Jin felt alive. Like he could hold on forever.

Eventually, the mayj stopped moving and his body flopped in the dirt. Jin let him go, the man's ruined neck sagging. Jin stared down at him, hating him with every particle of his being. For all the damage he had done, the mayj was no one, just some middle-aged man, wearing nice clothes now stained with sweat and urine.

Still kneeling in the dirt, Jin leant his head back, face to the peaceful sky. The stars just twinkled above him, blissfully oblivious. *Maybe that's why the Bhouli want to go there*, Jin thought. Because it was the farthest possible place from here.

His ears were ringing a little, more obvious now that the fighting was done, and the Deadlands were quiet once more. When had his ears started ringing?

Jin heard quiet Krijen footsteps approaching. He brought his head forward too quickly, and it made him dizzy. He steadied himself with his hand on the ground, blinking away the stars that were burned into the back of his eyelids.

A group of six Krijen appeared in the darkness – Pago, Jokah, Arji, Darson, and two more that Jin still didn't know. Jin gave them a tired smile and raised an arm so they could help him up. Instead, Darson flung out a borrowed bandit sword and held it, point steady, to Jin's throat.

CHAPTER 32: AREN BHA

Strong, wiry arms wrapped around Aren from behind. She jerked back an elbow, aiming low, right for his groin. There was a satisfying grunt, and the arms released her.

Aren streaked back to the mouth of the alleyway, dashing past the dead woman and hurtling around the corner. She'd barely made it ten paces before she heard the rhythmic thud of footsteps ahead of her, out of time with her own. Someone was running this way.

Aren dug in her heels and spun around, taking off in the opposite direction. The street ahead of her was narrow and disappeared into darkness at the end. What if there wasn't an exit? Panicking, she skidded to a stop. She couldn't go back down the alleyway she'd come from, not towards the convulsing bodies.

The footsteps were way too close.

Next to her were some wooden planks tossed haphazardly over one another. Heart pounding, Aren dropped to her knees and crawled forward, pulling her hat from her head and squeezing into a gap between the planks, splinters catching at her wraps. She pressed in until her hands hit the street wall and she twisted around, tucking in her feet as best she could.

A thick loop of rope hung down by her head. It looked like a noose. Aren shuddered, realising she'd crawled beneath some old gallows. Hanging used to be common in Valrue, but now it was preferable to string criminals up and watch them suffer. Feeling slightly nauseated, Aren pulled the beggar's hat in front of her, hoping she wasn't visible from the street.

The footsteps slowed to a walk before stopping completely, outside the mouth of the alleyway. All was quiet, apart from the occasional groan or shriek from the bodies. A voice floated through the darkness, startling Aren. 'Oh, Kahlsi.'

The voice was unmistakable. It was Wren. He was alive.

There was a quiet shuffle, and the sound of something scraping across the ground. 'Breeve, are you all right? What's the matter?'

Aren smiled. So Wren hadn't walked off into the Deadlands, like she'd worried he would. What was he doing here, in this alleyway, of all places?

Wren spoke again. 'A girl? You're sure?'

He must be talking to the man in the alleyway, Aren thought. So other than her, someone was willing to speak to him, even though he was Lost. Aren was glad.

'Wearing a hat?'

Oh no. Aren waited, listening intently, but Wren didn't say anything more. Her breath was catching on her pounding heart.

Just then, a pair of boots stepped soundlessly into the gap in front of her. They were Squares' boots. Definitely Wren. So why, then, was she still hiding? Was she scared he would hurt her? No. It would just be terribly embarrassing to be found like this.

Aren imagined how the conversation would go. Entitled little rich girl snooping through Rue at night, thinking she's going to be some big heroine. That's when Wren would snort at her, because everything she said was laughable. Because he was a rude, know-it-all Square –

Aren stopped herself, realising how pathetic she sounded. If Wren said those things, he would be right. He'd risked his own life to save her not six months ago. If he caught her looking for trouble in the most dangerous part of the city, he would have every right to be furious.

Aren smothered a groan, astounded at her own arrogance. She really wanted to be useful, but she also needed to be realistic. Wren had been living on the streets of Valrue for months. Maybe talking to him would be the best way to help, instead of following this poorly thought-out plan of hers.

She opened her mouth to say his name, but a little voice in her head stopped her. She didn't actually *know* Wren. She'd spent a few hours with him one day, and that was all. There was a dead body out there too. How did she know he had nothing to do with it? He also knew the man out there by name, the one who had tried to grab her. Was Wren even a good person? He'd been so angry and bitter when they'd met. Yes, he'd saved her life, but there had also been something in it for him. Perhaps it had been foolish of her to trust him so readily.

Aren bit her lip. She waited.

Wren's boots were still there. Either he had fallen asleep standing upright or he was very patient. Aren tried not to squirm, but she was so incredibly uncomfortable.

Just when her whole body had begun to seize up and twitch like the people in the alleyway next door, Wren moved on. She could hear his quiet footfalls as they disappeared around the corner and down into the alleyway with the bodies.

Aren couldn't wait any longer. Carefully, she crawled out from her hiding spot. Her legs throbbed with pins and needles as she stood up and scurried to the mouth of the alleyway, hugging the wall, the beggar's hat clutched in her hand. She peeked around the corner.

The woman's body was gone and so was the man she'd backed into. Aren squinted into the darkness. She could just make out a silhouette in the middle of the alleyway, standing over one of the moving bodies.

Aren snatched her head back. Wren was doing something with those people. She had to know what. Aren took a breath, before peeking around the corner once more.

More silhouettes had gathered around Wren's. She could hear them murmuring quietly to each other, but she couldn't make out what they were saying.

A loud crack sounded from somewhere down the alleyway and travelled right up to where Aren stood. A little piece of stone wall popped under her fingers. All the silhouettes turned to her at once.

Run!

Aren bolted across the entrance of the alleyway and tore back up the street. She had never run so fast in her life, but she was terrified that it wasn't fast enough. She leapt over smashed barrels and shattered clay pots and other indiscernible objects which lay in her path. She pumped her arms madly, trying to get more momentum to drive herself forward. Thankfully, all the adrenaline had made her mind sharper, and she recognised every corner as she ran her route in reverse.

Raucous laughter bubbled from the roofs above her, and she had a sudden bizarre thought they were laughing at her as she sprinted down the streets of Rue, smeared with black makeup, borrowed beggar's hat flapping in her hand.

Before she knew it, the bridge was ahead of her, at the end of a street, across the open square. The sight of it sent a bolt of lightning through her, spurring her on –

For the second time that night, something caught her foot. She tripped spectacularly, skidding for ages on her stomach before she came to a stop, her front covered in grime. She was halfway to her feet when something heavy slammed between her shoulder blades, and she hit the ground again, the breath leaving her body with a whoosh.

Something hard pressed down on her head, grinding her forehead into the cobbles. At first, she thought it must be those men that she passed earlier on the bridge. She thrashed, a world of horrible imaginings flashing through her mind. What humiliating and degrading things would they do to her?

Then a child's voice spoke.

'Hey, hey, Juno, what've you caught this time?'

Aren stopped moving, breathing in the dirt of the street.

'Just another creeper,' said a deeper voice above her. Still young, though.

'They never learn,' the first voice said. It was high-pitched, that of a girl. 'Tongue first? Actually, no, let's do it afterwards, or she'll wriggle. We'll string her up at the border. They'll get a laugh out of that.'

Aren heard a click of something being notched, the sound which surely would mark the end of her life. It didn't even cross her mind to scream for help. The shock of what was happening had made her whole body seize up.

Then there was a clang accompanied by a curse, and her captor twisted above her. Moments later, a thick arrowhead buried itself into the stone right next to Aren's head, and whoever had been holding her down quickly let go.

'Oi!' the girl screeched. 'You –'

But Aren was up and running, not looking back, feeling a terror that she'd never felt before. She was across the square in twenty steps, then across the bridge in eighteen, then up into the streets of Val she sped, darting down every nook and side street she knew of in case she was being chased and she could throw them off –

The early risers were awake. The bakers and the beggars startled and leapt back as she ran past their doorways and crannies, and she ducked her head, forgetting she was smeared with makeup and muck and that they wouldn't have a chance of recognising her.

It wasn't until after she'd crawled through her bedroom window onto the floor, hugging her knees and tears rolling down her face, that she realised she'd left the beggar's hat behind.

CHAPTER 33:
JIN KANJU

Jin soon realised the Krijen didn't know what to do with him. It was a surreal experience, being an enemy behind ally lines. They walked him back to the Split encircled by their weapons. Their hands were steady, but their bodies shook. They looked scared, so he went quietly. The guilt would be too heavy to run with anyway.

He didn't try to give orders, assuming that privilege was stripped from him now. Luckily, they found Flit quickly, broken and bruised, but very much alive. Jin's squad gravitated to her, appearing relieved to have an untarnished chain of command to follow.

Although he would have allowed it, the Krijen did not restrain him. They just took his daggers. Jin assumed it was procedural, more than anything else. They let him see Bish, though whether that was a kindness or because they figured they couldn't stop him, Jin didn't know.

Bish was alive, but his legs hung limply from him in a way that left the others with shifting eyes, knowing it would be wrong to look at him for too long. Still in his daze, Bish insisted he couldn't feel anything other than the scrapes on his hands and face. They all knew what it meant, though no one said it to him.

Jin was fairly certain no one suspected Bish of having known he was a mayj. Jin wanted to sit with his friend and fuss over him, but he couldn't risk it. He wasn't even sure if Bish wanted to talk to him. The only person willing to speak to Jin was Jokah, but the older Krijen kept throwing him piteous looks, which was decidedly worse than the frank coldness of the others.

Because everyone was avoiding him, Jin wasn't sure of the extent of the losses they had suffered. He picked his way through their makeshift camp, finding missing faces and counting the survivors, tailed by whichever squad member was assigned to guard him. They followed Jin with a strained expression, as though they found it painful to be so close to him.

Jin's melancholy compounded when it was Meek's turn to watch him. Jin had never seen his face without a smile. Meek stood on edge, watching Jin as though he was about to smite them all. Jin couldn't believe he'd fucked up so profoundly.

At least there wasn't much time for wallowing. They had work to do. Condemned as he was, Jin was in better shape than most, even with the vague, hollowed-out feeling he felt around his midriff. When the Krijen began scavenging as much of the precious cargo as they could, Jin silently moved in to help. They didn't stop him; they just stayed out of his way.

Three of the four wagons had been reduced to splinters. They pulled the dead swiftrunners from their straps and laid them out. They would be left here; there was no point in moving them. Bodies were an inconvenience in Valrue and were sent to the Deadlands anyway. There were no animals to eat the corpses, so they would slowly dry in the sun.

One Krijen had died. It was such a rarity that no one knew what to do, even Jokah. They laid his body carefully at the end of the line of dead swiftrunners. Now and then Jin saw the other Krijen standing over the body, staring, as though they didn't quite believe what they were seeing. Jin had never learned his name.

The second convoy of Krijen, wagons, and swiftrunners caught up with them as the sun rose, their front roamers racing through the Split towards the flares that Flit sent up, timed with their expected arrival.

The roamers skidded to a stop in front of them, daggers at the ready. Flit called them over, away from Jin; and they walked to her, darting looks at him as she explained. He could see her pointing to the mutilated bodies of the bandits. Jin didn't feel a shred of regret for their deaths. The bandits hadn't tried to take the supplies; they'd just been in it for the killing. Jokah had been right, but no one understood why.

The squad leaders of the second convoy brought the wagons through the Split to rest up with them. In the evening, they spread the salvaged supplies across their three wagons and took off running as the sun set. They didn't have time to slow down.

The survivors of the first convoy solemnly loaded up the single-remaining wagon with their wounded, including Bish, whom they settled as comfortably as they could on top. Bish suffered the humiliation of them tying his legs down before he batted them away, sick of their fussing.

Jin felt immense respect for the eight swiftrunners who strapped themselves into the wagon and followed the front roamers on towards First Base East.

***

A day and a half later, the sun was up and blaring when they made their way across the last stretch of plain. Soon they spotted the walls of First Base East, accompanied by shouts from the scouting towers. They entered the gates, and a squad came up to meet them, surrounding the wounded. Jin watched from a distance as they carefully unstrapped Bish and took him into the barracks, leaving Jin alone with Jokah.

'Come on, son,' Jokah said, inclining his head towards the main hall after the others.

Jin didn't move. 'I'm not sure,' he said. He didn't think anyone would appreciate him being there.

'I've had no orders otherwise,' said Jokah.

Reluctantly, Jin went. The aging Base Master Durini was standing in the doorway and gave Jin a loathsome look when he entered. It said,

'Don't you dare make trouble or I'll take off your fucking head.' Durini was tall and willowy, but Jin knew looks were deceiving, especially when it came to the older Krijen. Durini wouldn't hesitate to cut him down.

There were several unfamiliar Krijen in the hall already, all of whom stared as Jin sat down. Word had spread.

The debrief was short and blunt. Flit soon dismissed them for the afternoon. Even with the other convoy having moved on already, there were far more Krijen and swiftrunners at the base than expected. Every barrack was full, so several of them slept on the floor, giving the bunks to the injured. That night Jin slept on the porch outside the barracks, under the stars. Pago joined him without complaint, but he laid his bedroll as far away as he reasonably could, while still being close enough to 'guard'.

Bish was in a different barrack to Jin. Krijen scurried back and forth with bandages and tonics, sewing kits, and boiled water. After two anxiety-filled days with nothing but the annoying ringing in Jin's ears to distract him, Jin made up his mind. He needed to speak to his friend.

After breakfast, Jin strode determinedly towards the barracks, daring someone to stop him. He leapt up the steps onto the porch and through the open door. Sleepy swiftrunners raised their heads as he passed.

'Where is he?' Jin asked. Of course, no one answered. Jin dashed from cubicle to cubicle, looking for Bish's blond head. He got to the end of the barracks only to find Arji sitting there having a deep cut re-dressed on his arm by a Krijen Jin didn't recognise. They both looked at him but said nothing.

Jin began to panic. Had Bish died and they'd not told him?

Jin turned to Vulmin. His latest guard had slipped into the barracks behind him and was watching him with a dark expression.

'Tell me where Bish is,' Jin demanded.

'He's been sent back to Valrue,' Vulmin said in a clipped tone, correctly assuming that Jin would not shut up until he got an answer.

'Alive?'

Vulmin nodded. Jin let out a sigh of relief. *Thank fuck.*

As much as Jin wished he could have seen Bish before he left, he knew it was better this way. He still didn't know what Bish thought about what he'd done, but he would have to live with that. Maybe Bish hated him now too. While the thought was gut-wrenching, Jin tried to let it go. Bish was going back to Marigold. She deserved him more than Jin did.

The days stretched on, and as the sun went down each night, Jin struggled to remember what he'd been doing to pass the time. No one gave him orders anymore. He just wandered around and did things where he thought he should. Squads, supplies, and swiftrunners came and went; but the squads that were a part of the bandit attack stayed. He didn't know what would happen to them now. If decisions were being made, they were kept from him.

Taunted by all the unknowns and with nothing anchoring him, Jin drifted, despondent, feeling Lost already. Not even Filip came to visit, which actually irked Jin. What was the point of seeing dead people if they didn't keep you company when no one else would?

Then again, maybe the dead were rejecting him now too.

Jin was barely hanging on when Flit broke the usual routine, coming up to him as he ate his breakfast on the steps of the barracks. Jokah was next to him, but he was quiet company.

'Jin,' Flit said. 'Come with me.'

Flit hadn't been as cold as the others, though he wouldn't describe her behaviour as friendly either. The fact she said his name showed a warmth that, until this point, Jin had been denied.

He put his empty bowl to the side – despite his misery, he'd been inexplicably ravenous for days – and followed her, leaving Jokah on the steps.

There had been a stirring at the base that morning. Something had happened that Jin was not privy to. Maybe he was about to find out what it was.

Flit walked gingerly ahead of him. He suspected she had broken ribs from the way she hunched to the side. 'I'm sorry, Flit,' Jin said to her back, knowing he might not get another chance to apologise. 'I'm sorry I led everyone into that attack.'

Flit glanced back at him but kept walking. They were heading towards the master's cabin. She was taking him to Durini.

Jin felt his fingers twitching, nerves feeding his power again. He remembered that indescribable feeling he'd felt on unleashing it on the bandits, unbridled for once. Not dissimilar to an orgasm, he mused grimly. How insane was he to be thinking about sex right now? Lottie would have found it amusing. For once, he didn't know what Aren would think. He'd not dared to talk about that with her. With a cold dread, Jin realised he might not see Aren again after today. Memories of her consumed him as he walked up the steps to the master's cabin.

Flit stopped in front of the door and turned to face Jin. 'Go in when you're ready,' she said, jerking her head to the door.

'You're not coming?' Jin asked.

'No, I'm not.'

'Why not? What does Durini want?'

Flit gave him a piteous look so reminiscent of Jokah it made Jin's stomach flip. What was waiting for him behind that door?

'Just do it. Please,' Flit said. She couldn't make him go, of course, but he felt compelled to turn the handle and step inside.

The room was well-lit, and modestly furnished with a bed, a wooden desk, and a small table and chairs off to the side.

Sitting at the table was FaKrijen Oji.

Instinctively, Jin brought his fist to his clavicle, bowing his head, though he could not take his eyes off the man. The FaKrijen's broad frame made him look too big for the chair he sat on. He'd grown a small beard since Jin had last seen him. This was a statement on its own, as Krijen were expected to be clean-shaven. Facial hair was unbecoming. But maybe the rules didn't apply to the FaKrijen.

The FaKrijen made a motion with his hand, and Jin closed the door. He turned back around to face him, trying to thumb his dagger hilts that weren't there.

FaKrijen Oji watched him with a reserved expression. Jin felt exposed and unclean. Traitorous, even.

'You have given everyone quite a turn, Jin,' the FaKrijen said. Jin jumped at the sound of his name. He wasn't expecting the FaKrijen to know it. Then he realised how stupid that was. Of course the FaKrijen would know his name. Jin was the dirty skahk in their midst.

'No one was quite sure what to do about you,' the FaKrijen said. 'That is why they sent for me.' Jin could hear the disappointment in his voice.

'Actually, I am rather surprised you are still here,' the FaKrijen continued. 'I am under no illusion we could stop you if you wanted to leave.'

Jin shifted, uncomfortable. It wasn't easy to meet the FaKrijen's eyes; his gaze was that intense. 'I didn't think it would be right, sir,' Jin said. 'I'm responsible for what happened.'

'Indeed, you are.'

Jin hung his head, exposing the back of his neck. Would he be cut down right here? Or should he expect a more public execution than a beheading in the master's cabin? At least being dead would be better than being Lost.

But the FaKrijen didn't seem to have any weapons on him. He wore the standard grey shirt and trousers like the rest of them, but no blades peeked out at his wrists. Knowing what Jin was, maybe he thought weapons would serve no purpose.

'Thank you,' FaKrijen Oji said gently.

Jin looked up.

'Thank you,' the FaKrijen repeated. 'I owe you the lives of every single man and woman who returned to First Base East a week ago. Not just those you travelled with, but the second convoy as well. They would certainly have fallen victim to the bandits too, had you not killed their mayj.'

Jin waited for the FaKrijen to finish. This was just the obligatory ramble at the start before they talked about the part where he'd broken the law. Then he would learn of his punishment.

'You have so much potential, Jin. You can still be a respected Krijen, and a leader.'

Jin frowned. That part was unexpected. 'Forgive me, sir, but that will never happen. The other Krijen hate me.'

'They do not hate you. You are simply a threat, for now.'

Jin didn't understand how that could be any better.

'The problem at hand,' the FaKrijen continued, 'is that you are now both Krijen and a criminal. Krijen must not take orders from, nor associate with, criminals. You can see why they do not know what to make of you. Do not worry. This is fixable.'

Jin shook his head. The FaKrijen didn't know the whole truth. 'Sir, there is something else.'

'What might that be?'

Jin steeled himself and squeezed his fists to stop his fingers twitching. 'It's my fault we walked into a trap. I suspected that the mayj might be more dangerous than everyone realised, but I said nothing.'

'It is not your fault. I do not blame you for protecting your secret, knowing what might happen if the Krijen discovered it.'

Jin said nothing. The FaKrijen could tell he wasn't convinced. 'Tell me, Jin, do you really think they would have done better without you? Do not make me suffer through any humility either. Tell me, honestly.' The FaKrijen trapped Jin with his piercing gaze.

'They . . . they would have done the supply run anyway,' Jin said. 'I was the only one who pushed back.'

The FaKrijen nodded. 'So I am told.' He inclined his head to the spare chair. Jin hesitated, then walked over and sat on the edge of it.

The FaKrijen cleared his throat. 'Jin Kanju. You are henceforth charged with deceitful and duplicitous behaviour, a charge extended only to Krijen. It is punishable by being stripped of your Krijen status and exiled for life. Furthermore, you are charged with illegal harnessing of the highest degree, given it was intentional, excessive, and also led to the deaths of at least ten citizens, whom we call bandits. The punishment is the removal of both of your hands and being strung up for no less than one month, in either case of survival or death.' The FaKrijen smiled at him. 'You do not do things halfway, son.'

Jin's mouth filled with bile. So what was it to be? Exile or having his hands cut off and being strung up on the bridge?

The FaKrijen was not finished. 'Before I left for the Deadlands, I had an audience with the Kahnen to receive their orders. Despite their eagerness to make an example of you, they were more reluctant to make you a martyr. Given you also saved the lives of other, rather less vulgar citizens by protecting the Krijen, swiftrunners, and ensuring the continuity of high-value supplies, they had justification enough to make an exception. That is why I am here with an official pardon for your second offense, granted by the Great Kahn himself. As for the first offense, that sits solely under my jurisdiction. I could not live with myself if I exiled a most exceptional young Krijen because he failed to mention he was a mayj.'

Jin was gripping the table so hard his fingers were white. 'I'm-I'm not . . . you're not going to . . ?'

'I believe you are one squad member down, is that correct?'

'Y-yes, sir.'

'As far as I am aware, your squad has yet to elect a new leader. If I remember correctly, Krijen procedure dictates that in this case, you are still squad leader. May I humbly ask your permission, Jin, to join your squad?'

Jin was at a loss for words. It hadn't yet sunk in that he wasn't going to be punished for what he'd done. As for the FaKrijen's request, first, Jin wasn't sure his squad would agree he was still leader. Second, Jin had never heard of a FaKrijen being part of a squad. They had more important things to do than roam the Deadlands or chase petty thieves through the streets of Valrue.

The FaKrijen was waiting politely for Jin to respond.

'It's-it's rather unprecedented, sir,' said Jin, unsure of how to question this deranged decision in a polite manner.

'It is, indeed. I rather like the idea of doing something that has never been done before.' FaKrijen Oji smiled at him again.

'Oh,' Jin said rather lamely. 'Okay then. How could I possibly –'

The FaKrijen stood up and bowed his head, raising his left hand to his right clavicle. 'Sir, I ask that you please call me Oji. FaKrijen Oji is a bit of a mouthful.'

Jin was still clinging to the table to stop himself from falling off his chair. He'd gone from staring down a death sentence to commanding the FaKrijen in the space of one conversation. Of all the Krijen, Jin felt he deserved it the least.

'Sir, I don't think I can do this –'

'Yes, you can. You are more than capable. Permission to leave, sir? We have a lot of work to do.'

Jin nodded, speechless.

FaKrijen Oji walked to the door and pulled it open. He took a single step onto the porch before he stopped in the doorway and turned back to Jin.

'One more thing. You did not cheat in your dance with Filip, did you?'

'No,' Jin said quickly, but truthfully. It didn't slip by him that the FaKrijen had used Filip's name. He did not seem beholden to any of the taboos so strongly enforced by his Krijen.

'Good. Now let us go tell the others they can follow your orders again. They have been denied a proper chain of command for too long.'

CHAPTER 34: AREN BHA

Aren slept with her daggers that night. She kept one under her pillow and another in the closet, on the other side of the room, just in case.

She'd woken up the next morning with black smudges all over her bedsheets, having forgotten to take off the makeup. She'd stripped her sheets and shoved them into her wardrobe, intending to wash them later when no one was looking. She'd locked the door to her room; she didn't want visitors, and her mother and Noel were gone for the day, sorting something for the children at Mama Hidel's while Sid was at the KahnenKeep. The maids wouldn't bother her.

Aren huddled in a corner of her room, wondering what had possessed her to venture into Rue last night. She'd thought she was untouchable. But she'd slunk through shadows, run from everything, and still almost died. Some heroine she was.

But it wasn't in Aren's nature to give up. Not just yet. It took a while, but eventually she got up to unlock her door. She stared out the window for a bit, watching as the clouds rolled by. Clouds were unusual nowadays. Perhaps a storm was coming.

Someone knocked quietly on her door. Aren looked suspiciously at it. Who was even home? She grabbed the dagger from under her pillow and edged towards the door, annoyed that she'd unlocked it.

'Who's there?'

'It's just me,' came her father's quiet voice. Aren opened the door, surprised to find her father standing there holding a tray with two bowls of soup and some bread.

'Why are you home so early?'

'I have news I thought you might want to hear. May I please come in?'

Aren stepped aside and let her father in, slipping her dagger into her wraps. If he noticed the stripped bed and the black smudges on her face, he didn't say anything. He set the tray down on the window ledge and patted the wide sill next to him. She sat down and smiled, just in case he wasn't sure if she was okay.

He'd never come to visit like this before. Sid was a good man, gentle and very kind, but he'd mostly left the fathering to Noel. Sid likely presumed he wasn't good at it, but Aren had never thought that.

Sid gestured to the soup between them. 'The maids said you hadn't left your room all day. I thought you might be hungry. Noel and your mother won't be back until late, so it is just us for the evening meal anyway.'

Aren hadn't realised she was hungry. She grabbed a spoon, digging in eagerly. 'What news do you have?'

'It's about Bish. And about Jin. I thought it best that you heard it from me, if word is getting around.' Sid looked rather sombre. So it wasn't good news.

Aren dropped her spoon and swallowed her mouthful. 'What's happened?'

'Oji came to speak to me a few days ago,' her father said. 'I would have said something sooner, but I wanted to be sure of what I'd heard. There was an incident on one of the Deadlands supply runs. Bandits attacked the wagons. Bish and Jin were both part of the convoy. Bish was injured, badly enough they sent him home. He'll live, but I don't know more than that. He'll be arriving shortly.'

Aren gasped, her hands flying to her mouth. 'Does Marigold know?'

Sid nodded. 'Yes, I spoke to her earlier. She was headed to his parents when I left. She misses you, you know,' he added. 'She says you haven't seen each other lately.'

Aren felt a pang of guilt. Her father was right. She'd been wrapped up in herself. She would fix that.

'What about Jin?'

'Well,' Sid said slowly, 'Jin helped to stop the attack, but in doing so, he was forced to harness. It's no secret that he is a mayj anymore.'

Aren's heart skipped a beat. 'Great Kahn save him,' she whispered. 'What will happen to him?'

'For once, it seems the Kahnen were merciful. They pardoned him. Oji has gone to the Deadlands to deliver the news himself. Jin is safe.'

Relief flooded Aren. She still regretted her last conversation with Jin. She needed to fix that too.

'Is Jin coming home?'

'I don't think so.'

Aren folded her hands in her lap and looked out at the sparring court. It had been so long since she'd sat with him under that stone tree, chatting about nothing together. She missed him so much.

They finished their soup in silence. The quiet didn't bother Aren when she was with her father. He seemed content to just spend time with her.

When they'd finished, her father stood up, rubbing his hands together. 'Aren, I want to give you something.'

Curious, Aren waited while he slipped out of the room for a few minutes. He came back holding a small, sheathed dagger. The sheath was black leather decorated with thin spirals of golden metal.

Sid sat down and held it out to her. 'I realised that in all my time as the Weapons Master, I've never made anything for you.'

Aren took it from him and slid the dagger from its sheath. The hilt and guard were black and gold, the same as the sheath. The blade was such a dark green it was almost black. It flashed when she turned it over.

'Given your love of sparring, I thought this would be a suitable gift,' her father said. 'It's made of cardonite. It's a substance crafted by mayjen, so it's very durable. I didn't make the blade itself but designed it with you in mind.'

Even to Aren's amateur eye, the dagger was stunning. She rolled her wrist, loving how it felt in her hand.

'I've noticed you've been putting in more effort with your training lately,' Sid continued. 'I'm proud of you for that, considering what happened to you earlier this year. I thought you deserved a blade that better matched your style and ability, rather than those old blades you carry around. I hope you like it.'

Sid seemed embarrassed by his short speech, but it meant the world to Aren. She sheathed the dagger and threw herself around her father's neck, giving him a kiss on the cheek. 'It's beautiful. Thank you.'

Sid hugged her back, then took one of her hands in his, his eyes running over the black smears on it. Sid turned her wrist gently, looking at the white ink on the inside of her arm. She wondered what he was thinking.

'Remember that Valrue is an unforgiving place, Aren. I know you must make your way in it like everyone else, but whatever you are doing, please be careful.'

Aren met her father's eyes and nodded. 'I promise I will.' She meant it too. Sid smiled at her, picked up the empty meal tray, and left.

***

A few nights later, Aren woke suddenly in the darkness. At first, she thought she'd had a nightmare, because her whole body was tense. Then she realised there was someone in her room.

Aren slipped her hand under her pillow and wrapped it tight about the hilt of her new dagger. She waited. Between the sound of her heartbeats, she could hear slow footfalls coming closer. She sensed the intruder edge up to the bed, then lean over her. Aren set her jaw. She would not be a victim this time.

In one smooth movement, she bolted upright and grabbed a fistful of the intruder's shirt in her free hand, sliding her dagger out from under her pillow and bringing it up to his exposed throat.

'Drop it,' she hissed.

'Aren, it's just me,' Wren said.

She didn't let go. '*Drop. It.*'

She wasn't even sure if Wren had a weapon in his hand, but she heard a satisfying whump as a dagger fell onto the blankets beside her.

'Happy?'

'What are you doing in my room?'

'I needed to ask you something.'

Aren didn't trust him. Wren was a stranger. Her dagger tip was pressing into his neck. If she pressed any harder, she might nick him.

But now that she had him, she didn't really know what to do. And it was likely that Wren was humouring her. He could probably disarm her in a second if he wanted to, even without a dagger.

Nervous about that, she pulled harder on his shirt, forcing his chest down farther, enough that he had to crane his head back to stop her dagger from digging in. 'I'll let go,' she said, 'if you promise to *get out.*'

'You were in Rue the other night.'

Oh. So he'd seen her after all, spying on him in the alleyway, catching him at something he shouldn't have been doing.

She pressed her dagger in a little harder.

Wren suddenly jerked back from her, but Aren was clinging on so tightly that he dragged her right out of bed. He grabbed her dagger arm, but she was ready, and she brought her knee up as hard as she could into his stomach. He made an 'oof' sound and doubled over, both of them falling awkwardly onto the floor. Her dagger slipped, leaving a thin red line across his neck.

Aren twisted away, rolling under the bed and out the other side. She leapt up and snatched his dagger off her blankets before backing away towards the window, holding both weapons in front of her.

Wren popped his head up above the bed. 'Aren, are you *mad?* What are you doing?' He stood up and walked around the bed, coming towards her.

Aren clenched her mouth shut, intending to keep as quiet as possible. She didn't need her family rushing in here, trying to save her. If she could get out of the window, perhaps she could draw him out to the street.

Wren was already far too close. Aren swiped at him with her daggers, and he stopped. 'Aren? What's wrong?'

'You said you wanted to ask me something,' she said. 'Is that going to be now, or should I wait until after you're done trying to kill me?'

'*What?*' Wren looked shocked. 'That's not why I'm here!'

'So why did you sneak in with a dagger in the middle of the night?'

'Force of habit. Sorry.'

But it was that hollow kind of sorry people use when they don't actually mean it.

'Get out of my house,' Aren demanded. 'Stay away from me and my family.'

Wren looked genuinely hurt this time. He even took a step back, chewing on his lip. 'This . . . this is because of the whole Lost thing, isn't it? You've come to your senses.'

Aren glowered at him. Did he really think she would stoop that low? 'No. It's nothing to do with that.' She would not feel bad for him. He was up to something, and she'd caught him at it.

Aren kept the daggers between them, tips pointed at Wren. His eyes flickered between her face and the daggers. Then, slowly, he sat down on the floor.

'What are you doing?' Aren asked.

Wren pulled off his boots, chucking them a short distance away. He rolled up his sleeves and did the same for his trousers. The six months on the streets were certainly showing. His clothes were filthy, riddled with holes.

Aren watched him, flummoxed.

Wren held up his hands. 'No weapons,' he announced. Aren wasn't sure what he was trying to achieve. He was a weapon all by himself. Wren obviously guessed what she was thinking, because he sat on his hands. 'I won't touch you, I promise.'

Was he playing some sort of trick on her?

'Look, you're armed. I'm not,' he said. 'I just want to talk.'

Wren looked rather innocent sitting on the ground with bare feet, gazing up at her hopefully. Quite different from the hardened criminal she'd recently painted him in her head. Maybe he hadn't come here to kill her after all. Aren almost put the daggers down. Almost.

Wren looked sideways at her. 'What were you doing at the Point?' His long-anticipated question made no sense to Aren.

'The – what?'

'That alleyway you were in. It's called Turning Point. It's where all the mayjen go who've given up.'

Aren blinked.

'They're Turning themselves,' Wren explained.

Aren was shocked. 'They're . . .' she hesitated, somewhat horrified by what she was about to ask. 'They're killing themselves?'

Wren shook his head. 'Not quite. Turned is when they die. Turn*ing* happens before that, when they start running out of power while they're harnessing. Apparently it's a really nice out-of-body experience, so some mayjen do it on purpose. I wish I could.' Wren grimaced. 'Gets addictive though, so, yeah, sometimes they take it too far. Like Kahlsi.'

Aren felt a shiver down her spine as she recalled the dead woman she found in the alleyway.

'That's terrible,' Aren said. 'If it's addictive, is that why they looked a little . . . crazed?'

Wren nodded. 'Yeah. Freaked me out when I first saw it. Well, it freaks a lot of people out. That's the problem. But they don't know themselves when they're doing it, and so they're really vulnerable. I caught a couple of streetlings there once just walking down the alleyway, slaughtering them. They didn't know what hit them until they were dead. I figured they didn't really deserve that. So I stayed around to keep the streetlings away. Now they know it's a safe place to go while they Turn, which is why there are so many of them.'

Aren was awestruck. She lowered the daggers, forgetting she wasn't supposed to believe or trust Wren. 'I want to help.'

Wren snorted. 'I'm sure you do.' His softened demeanour had not lasted long.

'What's that supposed to mean?'

Wren folded his arms and somehow looked down his nose at her, even though she stood above him. 'You're not meant for that sort of thing,' he said. 'It's too dangerous for you.'

'Too dangerous for me?' Aren had never met anyone who could make her so angry so fast. 'Do you get off on patronising me?'

Wren threw his hands wide. 'Prove me wrong, Aren! You're clearly lacking a normal sense of self-preservation. I've had to save your spoilt arse twice already. Let's not make it a third time. Why can't you just stay out of trouble like all the other precious little rich girls?'

He was so *nasty*.

Aren stormed towards him, waving the daggers in his face. 'You are beyond cruel!'

'Cruel? How do you figure that?'

'You criticise me for being so naïve and incapable, yet when I attempt to do anything to better myself, you try to stop me! Why do you condemn me to be this thing you find so insufferable?'

Wren didn't respond, probably distracted by the daggers that were almost touching his nose.

Aren dumped herself crossed-legged on the floor in front of him, daggers clenched in her fists. Wren's eyes latched onto hers. It was as though he was trying to stare the will out of her, but Aren would not back down. She was done with being treated like some breakable ornament. One that sat on the top shelf thinking itself important, earning glances of derision from the people beneath it because it was really just a waste of space.

'Why do you want to help so bad?' Wren asked. 'Helping mayjen isn't exactly a smart thing to do. You could end up in the KahnenKeep dungeons. Or dead. And these people won't thank you, you know. You won't get any recognition for this.'

'I don't need a thank you,' Aren said. 'I need a purpose. I sit about this house sulking all day, and people shut me out because they don't think I can handle it. I'm sick of it. But I can be useful, I swear. I'm resourceful, and people don't expect me to be good at anything, so they underestimate me. Please let me help. I'll go crazy otherwise.'

'Fine,' said Wren.

Aren blinked at him.

'Fine,' Wren said again. 'You want to help? We need food. And blankets.'

'Blankets? But-but it's not cold –' Aren stammered, stunned that he had given in so quickly.

Wren shook his head. 'They're to sit on to prevent sores. If you live on the street, you spend lots of time sitting on stone, and the residents are so malnourished they never heal up again.'

That made sense.

'I can find some spare blankets,' Aren said eagerly. 'And I've got old clothes, which would work.' She stood up and went to her closet, putting the daggers on her shelf. She began pulling out wads of clothing, mountains of useless fashion that people insisted on buying her over the years. She was glad it would not be wasted.

'Food will be harder because we –' she bit her lip, having nearly mentioned the children. 'We only buy exactly what we need for the house. But I can try to get some more.'

Wren was watching her, his expression unreadable.

Aren picked up a few pairs of shoes she hadn't worn in months and added them to the pile of clothing. 'I'm not sure how we are going to get everything to them –'

'Hold up,' Wren said. 'We? I said you could help. I didn't say you could come with me.'

Aren shot him an angry look. 'Because it's too dangerous for someone like me? You're going back on your word already?'

'No, that's not what I meant.' He didn't expound, but something in his tone struck a chord with her.

'You're worried about us being seen together?'

'I'm worried about *you* being seen with *me*. I'm Lost, Aren.'

'It's been six months. People forget.'

'Not something like this. Doesn't matter how long it's been.'

'I don't care –'

'I care,' Wren snapped at her.

She knew she should stop pushing him on this, but it was grating on her too much. 'If I get caught helping mayjen, I'll be shunned because of that, not because I'm running around with a Lost Square. You can't possibly carry all this stuff by yourself.'

Wren didn't reply, but his silence meant he was thinking about it.

'If you're that worried, then we can wear disguises,' Aren pressed. Wren looked pointedly at her ruined bedsheets, which had fallen out of her closet. She'd forgotten to wash them. 'Better ones than that,' Aren said.

'I should hope so,' Wren said. 'Black paint and a hat? You stood out worse than a horse in the square.'

'It was makeup. The hat I borrowed from a beggar.' Aren paused, frowning. She'd never got around to replacing it.

'A beggar? You *are* resourceful,' Wren said dryly.

'How did you know it was me anyway?'

'I wasn't sure it was you, not until I saw those sheets.'

'Oh.'

'Can I have my dagger back? Do you trust me now?'

Aren put her hands on her hips. 'Fine. And put your boots back on. Your feet stink.'

Wren scowled. 'It's hard to stay clean.'

His response made Aren feel a little guilty. He probably hadn't had a bath in months. Wren pulled his boots on, rolled down his trousers and sleeves, then stood up. He reached up a hand to his neck, wiping away a trickle of blood from the scratch that Aren had given him. He looked down at his wet fingers, surprise on his face. Then he turned whiter than a sheet and fell to the floor with a thud.

Aren ran over and crouched down by his head, pressing her ear to his chest. She could hear him breathing. Not dead, just passed out. Hopefully, no one had heard him hit the ground. She thanked the Great Kahn that the walls were thick stone. They hadn't been very quiet.

Wren groaned weakly.

'Are you okay?'

'Fuck. *Yes.*'

'You,' said Aren as it dawned on her, 'you faint at the sight of blood!'

Wren groaned again. He kept his eyes squeezed shut. 'Just my own,' he admitted through clenched teeth.

'How in the name of the Great Kahn did you make it to your Fifteenth year as a Square?'

Wren opened his eyes and slowly sat up, wincing. 'I learned not to look. It happened so rarely near the end anyway, it wasn't an issue.'

'You hypocrite! You say it's dangerous for me to go sneaking around Rue? What were you planning to do when someone scratched you? Collapse on them?'

'Shut up.'

Wren wiped his hands behind his knees, carefully not looking at the smears of blood he left. Aren was horrified. It was his only pair of trousers. 'Don't do that! Here, use this –' She ran to her closet and returned with an old shirt. She handed it to him, and he pressed it to his neck, keeping his eyes trained ahead of him.

'I can't believe you cut me,' he said.

Aren shrugged an apology. 'I thought you wanted to kill me. Or, you know, something else.'

Wren looked at her, disgusted. He knew what she meant. 'I would *never.*'

She crouched down in front of him. 'I know. Sorry.'

He still looked really pale. She held out her hand to take the shirt off him, but he shoved it into the back of his trousers. 'Nah, I'll keep it. Might come in handy.'

She kept her hand out to help him up, but he ignored it and pushed himself to his feet, only slightly unsteady. 'I'll take what I can now and come back tomorrow,' he said, avoiding looking at her. He's embarrassed, Aren realised.

'I'm coming with you tomorrow then,' Aren said forcefully, worried he would go back on their agreement.

Wren nodded. 'Try to get some sleep. I'll wake you.'

Aren twiddled her fingers nervously as he collected his dagger and grabbed a handful of folded blankets. He tucked them under his arm, then walked to the window and hopped up onto the sill.

Unable to stop herself, Aren dashed forward and caught him on the arm. 'You promise you'll come back?'

Wren turned to her, frowning. 'You really don't trust me, do you?'

'Sorry. I just worry I'll get left behind. Force of habit.' She smiled weakly.

'I won't leave you behind,' he said, before stepping off the windowsill. Aren watched him jog away, his silhouette disappearing into the backdrop of the moon.

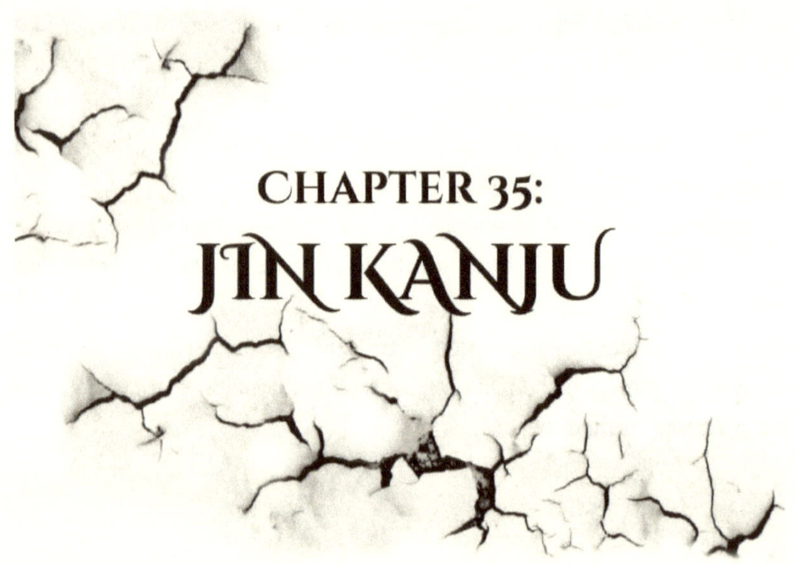

CHAPTER 35:
JIN KANJU

True to his word, Oji had announced Jin's pardon that same afternoon. Jin's squad had received the edict with blank stares that left Jin thumbing his freshly returned daggers. Their expressions had turned to shock when Oji mentioned his intention to join their squad, declining their immediate offer to make him squad leader. Although any other Krijen would have been obligated to accept, Oji could do what he wished. Pago took up the mantle instead.

As for the other Krijen, their hostility was gone, and they seemed content to talk and laugh with Jin again. The change was so sudden, he worried it wasn't genuine. His suspicions were confirmed when he was assigned to tend to the injured swiftrunners. After that, it was obvious the Krijen were just following orders.

Unlike the Krijen, the swiftrunners were not compelled to accept him. They looked frightened when he showed up at the first aid barracks. Jin walked from cubicle to cubicle, his offers of help rejected until he stood before the very last bunk. The occupant gave him a sceptical look, then, to Jin's surprise, nodded his consent.

Jin moved in to peel off the bloodied bandage around the swiftrunner's foot. The foot had been crushed so badly that the entire thing had lost its shape. There were still bits of debris and dirt in it that needed to be cleaned out, and the skin was discoloured. Jin pulled some tweezers from his first aid kit and carefully started plucking away. The man lay there stoically while Jin worked, eventually letting out an exaggerated sigh.

'Sorry,' Jin said, quickly pulling his hand back. 'Is this hurting?'

'Only a little,' the man said. 'But if I'm honest, I was hoping you would . . . you know.' The man wiggled his fingers at him.

Jin had no idea what he meant. 'Would what?'

'You know. Use a little majik.'

Jin froze, feeling the irony of the heat sputter in his chest.

'I mean, I heard a rumour that majik can heal people.' The man's face fell at Jin's expression. 'Oh, all right,' he said, even though Jin had said nothing. 'I know, I *know*. Majik doesn't work on people. Blast that Ret.' He folded his arms. 'You can at least clean it properly, right? Harness the dirt out of it?'

Jin looked nervously around the cubicle. Then he leant in towards the swiftrunner. 'I *can't*,' he said under his breath. It went unsaid that he should not, in any circumstances, harness ever again.

'What do you mean you can't?' The man was speaking far too loudly. The other swiftrunners in the cubicle glanced over at them. 'You've been pardoned, right?'

'Please,' said Jin, 'keep your voice down. I was pardoned for what I *did*, not for majik I use now. Not that I will,' he added hastily.

'Hey, I'm not judging,' the man said. 'I owe you my life. All I'm saying is what good is keeping a mayj like you from using your majik? Nothing is going to save Valrue at this point. We may as well not worry about it anymore.'

Jin was sweating from the heat building inside him. Everyone was watching them now. 'I'm sorry, I can't.'

The man seemed disappointed, but nodded. 'Yeah, yeah, all right. Seems a right shame, though.'

Jin worked silently on the man's foot, feeling decidedly worse than when he'd started. It wouldn't make a difference anyway. The man was almost certainly going to lose the foot.

'Look, can I give you a piece of advice?'

Jin looked up at the swiftrunner. 'Okay,' he said hesitantly.

'So about the other day with the mayj. You remember?'

Jin stifled a groan. He'd never met anyone so insistent on talking about majik.

'It's bad now, but it'll get better. We know where you went wrong, at least.'

Is he kidding? Jin thought.

'You came on too strong. You went and de-humanised yourself, ripping holes in the middle of those bandits, you see. Too much for us nomajik folk to handle.'

That wasn't what Jin expected. He had no idea how to respond.

'Now, I don't mean to sound ungrateful,' the swiftrunner went on. 'Really, I am. But next time just rein it in a bit, yeah? Less of the bloodthirsty stuff. Might be easier for us to get our delicate heads around.' He nodded around at the swiftrunners.

'Sorry,' Jin said. 'And thanks for the advice. But you forget I'm not harnessing again.' Jin gathered up his first aid kit, eager to get away.

'Hey, now,' the swiftrunner said. 'Don't sulk.' He leant out from under his bunk and called to the other swiftrunners in the cubicle. 'Come on, lads, let the man sort you out. He's not doing majik anymore, he says. Perfectly harmless.'

No one replied.

The swiftrunner huffed. 'Oh, come on, you sooks!'

Tentatively, one of the swiftrunners on the bottom bunk opposite them raised his hand. 'I pulled my stitches yesterday. I need those re-done.'

Feeling tense, Jin walked over and inspected his wound. The stitches had indeed torn all along his chest, and his skin was puckering. Jin settled down with some antiseptic, a needle, and thread. The swiftrunner craned his head forward to watch what Jin was doing.

'You need to put your head back,' Jin said. 'You're pulling the skin.' The swiftrunner did as he was told but kept his eyes on Jin.

Jin sewed quickly. He felt self-conscious under the swiftrunner's stern gaze, but appreciative all the same. Jin left Crushed Foot looking rather pleased with himself as he moved back through the same cubicles, every other person now letting him help.

Jin was tending to the final swiftrunner when Crushed Foot came hopping up the barracks. Jin watched him with horror, his hands too busy to help.

'What are you doing? Sit down!'

'I am, I am. Calm down.'

Crushed Foot lowered himself onto the end of the bunk. 'Ho, Catcher,' he said to the bunk's occupant, 'I didn't realise you were here. I thought they sent you back to Valrue!'

Catcher was lying on the bed grinning at Crushed Foot. 'I thought you'd been sent back too! Of course, that was before I heard your dulcet tones just now, pestering young Jin here.'

Jin stabbed himself with the needle, surprised as blood welled up on his finger. He would have to get used to people knowing his name.

'I'm waiting for the next supply run,' Crushed Foot said. 'I'll get a throne on top, I reckon. I've earned myself a nice hot bath and a kiss from Darli, my gorgeous girl. Boy, it'll be nice to see her again. Eighteen months it's been. Mind you, our livelihood is ruined,' he added with a frown, looking down at his foot.

'Say,' Catcher said to Jin, 'maybe a foot's a bit much, but how about this?' He held up two broken fingers that were strapped together.

'You moron,' Crushed Foot said. 'Majik doesn't work on people!'

'I knew it! That bloody Ret,' Catcher said.

Crushed Foot laughed, but the sound quickly died in his throat. He cocked his head at Jin. 'Hold on. I saw you out there. The way you were running, I mean. It was like you'd had a fire lit up under you. No one can run that fast, I swear it. And I should know, I'm a swiftrunner!'

Jin's fingers twitched so obviously holding the needle and thread that Catcher frowned, looking at Jin's hands. There was no point in trying to lie.

'I can use majik on myself,' Jin admitted quietly.

Crushed Foot cried out triumphantly. 'Ho! I knew it! Oh, son, why are you still sneaking around the Deadlands with us lot? You could be a KahnenMayj instead!' Crushed Foot chortled and smacked his thigh as the colour drained from Jin's face. 'Haha, I'm just messing with you. They'd be so shit scared they'd try to smite you where you stand. Not that they could.'

Jin looked up at the ceiling and counted down from ten in his head. As irritating as they were, these swiftrunners were the only people who seemed to like him.

'Hey, Jin.' Crushed Foot was waving at him, trying to get his attention. 'I've been thinking. I get that the Krijen are less forgiving than us folk, even if they don't act like it. Go ask them to play a game of cards.'

More great advice? 'I don't know how to play cards,' Jin said.

'Ah, but you see? That's perfect!' Crushed Foot leant forward eagerly. 'You've scared the living daylights out of everyone. What you need is bringing down a peg or two. Show them you can lose. Re-humanise yourself, you see?'

Jin screwed up his face. If that was the problem, he could see the logic in it. 'Sure. Thanks.'

A few minutes later, Jin stepped out into the sun. Filip fell in beside him. He hadn't seen Filip since his rather tense conversation with Jokah.

'You've been ignoring me,' the Filip said.

Jin hadn't been aware that Filip could talk. 'That's because you're dead,' Jin muttered, unable to stop himself.

'I know. You killed me.'

Jin dropped off the first aid supplies in his barracks, then headed towards the main gate on the hunt for Pago. Filip kept up next to him, his feet crunching on the dirt. It sounded disturbingly real.

'What do you want?' Jin asked. Filip didn't reply.

Pago wasn't at the gate. Jin looked up across the ramparts, using his hand to shade his eyes from the sun. Filip stood next to him, doing the same. 'He's there,' Filip said, pointing with a patterned hand.

Pago stood next to Flit and Oji on the ramparts, all three of them staring west towards Valrue.

Jin started up the wooden stairs, Filip in tow. Pago saw him coming and waved him over.

Flit turned her injured side away from Jin as he approached. 'She's scared of you,' said Filip. Jin shot him a dark look.

'I just finished in the first aid barracks,' said Jin.

Pago nodded. 'Good. I need someone to take over scouting for a while. Durini wants us to plan a roaming route to see if there are any more bandits camped nearby. It's best if we hit them now, while they are weak. Then we'll head to Fourth Base East.'

'Sir?'

'Oji wants to see the most remote bases, and they've been running short of Krijen for months now. They could do with another squad.'

Jin looked at Oji, who nodded, happy to let Pago speak for him as his leader. Jin turned to Flit. 'Are you coming too?'

'No. I'm going back to Valrue with my squad.'

The attack must have really spooked her, for her to return so quickly to the post she didn't like. Or maybe it was to get away from Jin.

'The city-based Krijen require more support,' Oji said. 'There have been several attacks on Krijen, like what happened with the bandits. We are redistributing Krijen where they are needed.' Jin frowned. The Deadlands bases didn't have enough Krijen, and the city didn't either?

Pago turned to Oji. 'Attacks from citizens?'

'Yes. The People are taking matters into their own hands. I've told the Krijen to stand down, at the command of the Kahnen.'

Flit looked shocked. 'The Kahnen *want* that? Doesn't that undermine their authority?'

'The Great Kahn has filled his house with Kahnen who share a particular hatred for the majikal community. They do not view these trial-by-neighbour executions as problematic. They are blind fools.'

A stunned silence followed Oji's words. His criticism of the Kahnen had been such that had he been anyone other than the FaKrijen, Pago would have been compelled to execute him on the spot.

Filip leant in towards Jin. 'Is he allowed to say that?'

Jin gave Filip an annoyed look. He didn't remember the Square being so talkative. Between Filip and the persistent ringing in his head, Jin could feel his temper rising. His fingers twitched endlessly these days.

Oji sighed. 'My sense of righteousness is getting the better of me lately. Please excuse me, I am neglecting my duties.' He headed back to his scout position farther down the ramparts.

Flit immediately turned on her heel and headed back down the stairs.

Pago looked out at the Deadlands. 'You're dismissed,' he said to Jin. 'Come find me again once you've eaten.'

'Sir, I thought you said you needed me to scout —'

Pago shook his head. 'No, go eat. Come back later.'

Jin was disappointed. He was hungry, but he would prefer to stay busy, and there were plenty of things that needed doing. But Jin was no longer squad leader, and it was no longer his decision.

He saluted Pago and started down the stairs, Filip half a step behind. 'I mean nothing by this,' Filip said as they descended, 'but if they are so intent on killing mayjen, why have the Kahnen pardoned you?'

Jin was listening, despite himself.

'It would have been easy. The Krijen would have killed you on command, and you would have let them,' Filip said matter-of-factly. 'From what Oji said just now, that's what the People want. But Oji also said they spared you to avoid making you a martyr. It's a contradiction.'

'Perhaps he meant a martyr for the mayjen sympathisers,' Jin suggested.

'Since when have the sympathisers been a threat?'

'Maybe they would be if the Kahnen killed me. Something to fight for.' Jin laughed at the absurdity of his own words. 'Actually, that's stupid. I'm not important.'

'And,' Filip continued, 'that's assuming the truth even got to Valrue about what happened. The Kahnen could have come up with any story they wanted. They could have told the People you'd gone rogue and attacked the Krijen.'

'Not with the number of survivors we had. We are sending too many swiftrunners back to the city.'

'It wouldn't take much to ensure their loyalty to the Kahnen. A bit of coin would do the trick.'

Jin didn't reply. He didn't want to think about what it might mean if Filip was right and Oji had lied. Oji had done so much for him that it felt wrong to question his honesty. Jin resolved to put it out of his mind, for now. He had enough of his own problems. His thoughts kept wandering back to Flit's reaction when he'd come up the stairs. Oji might have ordered their acceptance of him, but you couldn't order away fear.

Jin found himself standing outside the entrance of the dining hall. He listened to the laughter inside, feeling distinctly lonely. Bish, his one true friend in the Krijen, was gone. Even Filip had vanished again.

Maybe I should try Crushed Foot's suggestion, Jin thought grimly. Perhaps the Krijen would appreciate it if he made a fool of himself. Shocked by his own desperation, he jogged back to the barracks to see if he could find some cards.

The Thirty Eighth Letter

To You

Normally, I would not write again so soon after my last letter, but there is some urgency now. I am more certain than ever that what is happening in Valrue is because of you. I found something recently that made me question your reasons for leaving. It was disturbing enough to make me reconsider that the rumour I heard about you, so soon after you left, was true. Since then, I have questioned the truth behind why you came so often with me to the docks and – dare I say it – why you chose to approach me in the street on the day we met, to ask me something you already knew the answer to.

However, to be so calculating would require a particular kind of evil you do not possess. I am convinced that at the time, you did not fully understand what you were doing. Yet you have known my letters over many years (of this I am certain, as my letters have never been returned to me, which would be the case if the recipient is not found), and I have detailed many of the tragedies that have befallen Valrue.

As I write this, I hope you are making your way home, prepared to right this wrong. I grow excited at the thought of seeing you, though I must admit that I feel somewhat uncertain of our future together, considering it has taken this long for you to recognise responsibility. If I made the connection, I am in no doubt that you did so too, and well before me.

I know I promised to never doubt you, but something has stirred in me that I cannot explain. Perhaps my love for you is waning after all these years. Still, I am embarrassed to know, to the day, how long we have spent apart. It has been eighteen years, ten months, and twelve days Please come in haste, for I cannot bear one more day. I worry my love for you will not survive it.

From Yours,
Dijak

CHAPTER 36:
LORD LI

Twenty-six years ago

'It's despicable, the way they use their majik for entertainment. Making things fly to amuse children. It's demeaning to the art of majik!'

'Mav, come on now. They are nothing like you. Do not compare yourself to them.'

'Of course they aren't like me. No one is like me. But it's them the People see, sullying my reputation!'

Luka sighed. As much as he loved Mandavar's passion, this wasn't the work-up he'd had in mind. He desperately needed a release. The Kahnen had made a decision today, but Mandavar had yet to be told.

If Luka was being honest with himself, he was terrified of what was to come. But he was resolute too. If he were to become the Great Kahn one day, making decisions would be the easy part of the job. You had to be willing to get your hands dirty.

'Mav –'

'*Don't* call me that. I despise that nickname.'

'Mandavar –'

'They've asked me again to take on an apprentice. I've told them countless times, unless they find someone capable of atomik majik, I will not waste my time. The idiots have no idea what that even means.'

As if to prove his point, Mandavar slapped his hand against the bedroom wall and sank his fingers into it, gathering it up like silk. The wall was the darkest green, webbed with gold tendrils, a spectacular display of Mandavar's signature.

The wall surrendered under Mandavar's touch. He ripped part of it away, forming a ball in his hand. Then he splayed his other hand over it, stretching and pulling at threads until slowly it became a square of mesh in his palm. He turned and tossed it towards Luka's naked form.

Like a claw, it snatched itself around Luka's penis, who gasped as the cold metal melded around him, harder than diamond. The anticipation of what was to come was enough to make Luka hard, but Mandavar's prison made his desire excruciating. He moaned and bit his lip, nails digging into his palms.

'Is this what you wanted, Luka?'

Mandavar raised a hand, merciless. The cage grew hot, ice turning to fire. It was already too much, but Mandavar hadn't yet begun.

Mandavar strode over to where Luka lay quivering on the bed and leant over him. Mandavar breathed into the hollow of his neck. 'Tell me what you want. Talk to me.'

Luka whimpered, his teeth clenched, the cage still hot.

Mandavar was persistent. 'Come on, Luka. Don't make me wait. You know I don't like that.'

The cage cooled. Luka gasped and collapsed against the mattress, his body slick with sweat.

Mandavar lowered himself down onto the bed and trailed a hand down Luka's chest, easing along his midriff, finally tracing the little indentation that led to his groin. Mandavar splayed his hand, and Luka felt threatening, pulse-like vibrations roll down the length of the cage. Luka moaned again, eyes closed, his lips twitching.

'This is cardonite, you know,' Mandavar said quietly. 'I'm the only one who can work it like this. But even I get tired sometimes. There might come a time when I can't take it off you.' Even though it was a lie, Luka felt real fear. The cage was heating up again, and his penis strained against its prison. Everywhere it touched sent spoils of agony.

'Come on, Luka.'

Mandavar's voice was gentle in his ear. Luka was trying, but he couldn't pull a coherent thought together.

Mandavar grew tired of waiting. He stood up and, with a flick of his hand, flipped Luka onto his front. Mandavar grabbed him roughly around his waist and, with another flick of his wrist, slicked himself wet, drawing moisture from his skin with majik. Then he pushed himself into Luka, relentless as Luka bucked underneath him.

'I told you,' Mandavar whispered, grabbing fistfuls of Luka's hair. 'I told you I was going to do it. But you didn't listen.'

Mandavar rode him, ignoring Luka's pleadings until Mandavar came, lording his glory over his lover. Mandavar allowed the cage to cool, but he did not release Luka from it, his punishment not yet complete. Luka was weak with suppressed desire.

'You had a meeting with the Kahnen,' Mandavar said. 'What did they have to say?'

Luka trembled. It was now or never. 'The Kahnen have commanded the sterilisation of all KahnenMayjen,' he said, gasping. 'We have decided it is in the best interests of the city, in order to manage the natural balance.'

'They want to castrate me?'

Mandavar laughed, and he rose from the bed, semen dripping off the end of his penis. Even stark naked, he struck the most intimidating figure, having refused to allow his body to become soft and weak like the other KahnenMayjen.

'And you agreed to deliver the message? How sweet of you,' Mandavar mocked. 'So you're throwing me to the dogs?'

'It is not about you and me, Mandavar. It is about the People. We need to be able to guarantee their safety.'

'Lies!' Mandavar bellowed, suddenly furious. 'This is about control! The Kahnen fear me. This is just another poorly veiled attempt to tame me. And you,' Mandavar spat, 'they play you like a puppet. I've told you countless times to abandon this obsession you have with becoming the Great Kahn. You are enslaving yourself. What happened to you?'

To Luka, Mandavar's words were hollow. They had done this dance too often. A love like theirs prevailed against anything, and they thrived on the violence that came with it.

'You think *I* have changed?' Luka cried. 'Majik has ruined you. Your arrogance is unparalleled. I should never have vouched for you with the Kahnen –'

'Why? Am I ruining your chance to be called Great Lord?'

'Do not mock me! At least I made something of myself. You were born with this gift, yet you act like you earned it. The only reason you are here is because of me! You owe me this!' Luka scrambled off the bed and shoved Mandavar in the chest.

Angering Mandavar was a dangerous thing to do, but Luka's bottled frustration was over-riding his sense. 'What is it to you anyway, being sterilised? You have always made it clear you have no intention of having children, fearing that they might be greater mayjen than you!'

Mandavar looked thunderous. 'If you honestly believed that, then we wouldn't be having this conversation.'

Luka could tell that Mandavar was hurt, despite his rage. Mandavar's chest was heaving with exertion. He always felt emotions stronger than other men. His majik did that to him.

Luka breathed deeply to calm himself. 'Please. Listen to me. You are taking this too far. The Kahnen think you are becoming unpredictable, too selective about which orders you follow. If you continue like this, it will not end well. If not for you, then for me. Are you willing to risk my life, if they find out about us?'

Mandavar didn't reply.

'Are you willing to risk me?' Luka demanded again.

Mandavar met his eyes. Luka could see the fire there that he loved so much. But there was also something else there, a shadow lurking that had never been there before. What was going on in Mandavar's head?

'Please, Mandavar. You know I do not mean to control you.'

Mandavar blinked, then threw back his head and laughed. 'You can't even take control when we have sex, Luka. No, it's not about control for you. You want to be the Great Kahn. You think getting me to obey the Kahnen will get you there.' Mandavar scoffed at him. 'You think you've got what it takes to command Valrue? It's laughable. The only reason you're still in the Eighth House is because of me. Without me, they have no use for you. You are nothing.'

Luka felt like he'd been stabbed through the heart. His chest actually hurt, and he struggled to breathe. Mandavar turned away, walking towards the door.

'You are wrong. We are nothing without each other!' Luka yelled at Mandavar's back. 'Do not pretend like I am the only one who needs this relationship. I give you meaning, a soul. No one else understands you like me. You leave me, you will go back to being that miserable monstrosity you were before! No one else will have you!'

Mandavar's shoulders clenched, and he spun in a rage. Luka felt his body jerk across the room, and he smacked into the back wall, the cardonite cracking into his skull. He hung there helplessly, suspended by Mandavar's majik.

'You dare goad me?' Mandavar roared. 'You are weak and pathetic, and if it's the last thing I do, I will make sure that you never have your Valrue!'

Mandavar stormed from the room.

Released from his majik, Luka fell trembling to the floor, too weak to do anything but listen to the footsteps of the man he loved as they faded away.

CHAPTER 37: THE GREAT KAHN

A year after he was released from his cell, the boy finally came back to kill him. It was raining for the first time in months, a heavy downpour that drowned out the sound of anything else. The Great Kahn didn't know the boy was there until a white hand curled loosely around the stone columns on his mountain balcony. The Great Kahn had moved from the room he'd once shared with Mandavar, the green walls only stoking his bitterness towards his former lover. Even in his absence, Mandavar still made him feel inferior.

'I was wondering if you would come.'

The boy stepped out from behind the column. The Great Kahn sucked in a breath. It was like looking at Mandavar through a lens, one that left the image warped. Those blue, blue eyes.

'Incredible. I can see him.'

The boy said nothing.

'Your father, I mean. I know his face so well I could draw it from memory, every line of him. Well, what he used to look like anyway. I am not sure if I would know his face now. It has been twenty-six years after all.'

The boy's blank stare was disconcerting. Mandavar had never looked at him like that, too full of passion. It seemed ironic his son would be so lifeless.

'Tell me your name.'

'Drax.'

The voice was different, at least. Clear, but without his father's conviction.

'Unusual. Felle's work, I presume?'

If Drax wondered how the Great Kahn knew Felle, he said nothing.

The Great Kahn ran his eyes over the boy, being sure to take all of him in. He was rather marvellous, the Great Kahn decided. He'd only seen Drax a few times as a very young child. He'd quickly become deformed, starved of sunlight from a life in the cells. It was satisfying to see the scars peeking above the boy's collar, the raised purple rings visible on both wrists.

But underneath the baggy clothes, Drax looked less twisted than the Great Kahn remembered. The boy had reclaimed some of the bone structure of his father, probably under Felle's direction. The harnessing skill required to do that was extraordinary. But the boy still looked weak, which Mandavar would loathe. And his hands were limp, not moving as they should. Not that it mattered. The Great Kahn smiled. Not even Mandavar could harness without using his hands.

'I am listening, Drax. Explain why you are here.'

'Felle told me to come. You must do as she commands. If you don't, I am to kill you.'

There wasn't a lick of subtlety about him.

'An interesting dilemma for me, Drax. But I am curious. Let us say that I agree to do whatever Felle requests of me. There does not seem to be anything in it for you.'

Drax said nothing. The blank expression persisted.

'Now, I do not really want to do as Felle tells me,' the Great Kahn said, 'nor do I want to die. So let us make a deal. If you promise to let me live, I will tell you why you have those scars.'

Drax's face darkened, the first hint of emotion the Great Kahn had seen on the boy's face. *So he remembers.*

The Great Kahn waited. He wasn't sure if the boy could even indulge in independent thought. To refuse to carry out Felle's command might be too much to expect from him. But the boy was human, and all humans had desires. Surely it would be tempting.

'Take my offer back to Felle,' the Great Kahn said. 'I know she would want to help you.'

Drax stared at him for a long while. Then, without another word, he turned and slipped between the columns, back out into the rain.

CHAPTER 38:
AREN BHA

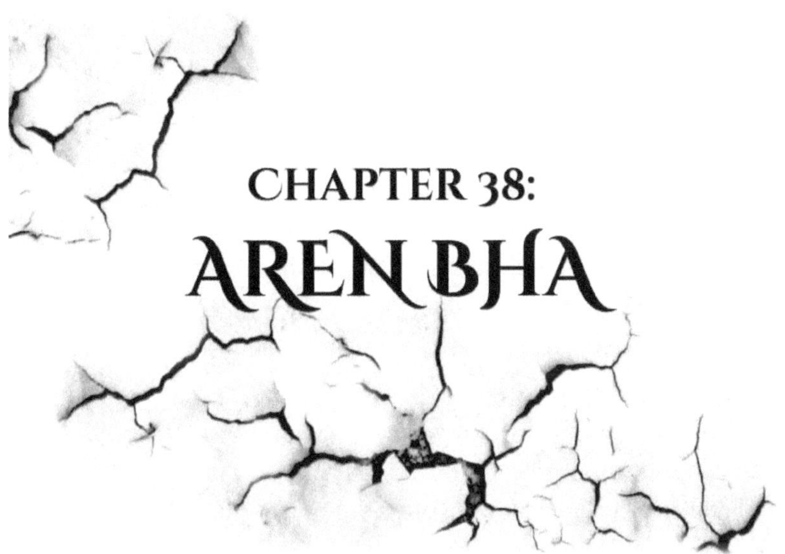

I t was late evening and the darkness was creeping in. Maude, Bish, and Marigold were in the sitting room, waiting for the rain to stop. At first, Aren found the rain terribly inconvenient. However, she quickly realised that it put the streetlings off, so the residents of Turning Point were actually safest when it was raining.

Aren joined Wren most evenings now to watch his back, stitch clothes, hand out food, and, when worst came to worst, help him move the dead bodies. It wasn't just the Turners they were helping, either. Word had got around, and all sorts of people now came to the Point.

Once, while Aren and Wren were in the alleyway looking at the growing line of desperate people, Wren commented that they only came because of Aren, insisting they wouldn't accept help from a Lost Square.

'But some people don't care,' Aren had argued. 'Breeve talks to you.'

Wren had snorted at that. 'Breeve doesn't know who *he* is, let alone what *I* am.'

After they'd bickered about it for a while, Wren had held some bread out to the starving people in the line. Proving his point, they'd all turned away from him. Aren hated it, but Wren didn't hold it against them, so she had to let it go.

When it rained, fewer people came to the Point for help, so Aren didn't always need to go. She relished the proper night's sleep, which was rare now.

When it rained, Wren would come to her bedroom a bit earlier, comfortable to leave the Turners without his protection for longer. So when it rained, Aren got more time with Wren, where she had *almost* his full attention, which was why she found it annoying that Maude, Bish, and Marigold wouldn't leave until the rain stopped.

Marigold was looking to make conversation. 'Sparring tomorrow, Aren?'

'Of course,' replied Aren. 'I should practise in the rain.' She was entirely serious.

'You're rather good now,' Bish said, smiling at her. 'I'm almost glad I've got an excuse not to challenge you to a duel.'

Marigold scowled, but Aren laughed. She couldn't deny Bish a bit of fun. He desperately needed it. 'Well, how about a dagger-throwing competition?' she suggested. 'You've got two perfectly good arms, I believe?'

'I do. But I only need one.'

Aren grinned at him. 'All right then. Marigold, are you in?'

Marigold rolled her eyes. 'As if, Aren. You know I can't throw a dagger.'

'Something else then? A stick of rouge?'

Marigold stuck out her tongue between her red lips. Marigold always made an effort to look nice. Aren wished Wren would allow himself the same decency. He stubbornly declined anything that might detract from the life he expected as a Lost Square. It took him two months from that first night he came to her room before he accepted a bath. Aren guiltlessly shamed him into it by lying, saying his smell preceded his appearance at her window. He'd finally agreed, and so she'd filled the bath late one night and snuck him there, waiting anxiously outside the room. She'd left a face razor out too, doubtful he would use it. To her surprise, he'd walked out clean-shaven. 'It was itchy,' he'd said in response to her questioning look. Aren hoped he was coming around to the idea of some self-reprieve. Now she kept a razor in her closet with a damp towel, which he used whenever he visited.

Aren realised her thoughts had drifted to Wren again, and she clamped down on them. She was seeing him later. She needed to concentrate on her friends.

Maude was curled up in an armchair across from her, fast asleep. Aren could see Mika's tail peeking out from under her collar. Noel still had not killed the mouse, for which Aren was grateful. Maude had been so happy lately. Aren's first ink pattern had rubbed off months ago, and she'd asked Maude to re-do it, which Maude had done with delight. Aren soon had as many beautiful white patterns as Maude. Maude was due to do her first permanent tattoo, and Aren had asked if she would do hers as well. It was going to hurt, but Aren didn't care.

Aren and Marigold continued to chat quietly. Bish was watching Mika's tail with a frown on his face. Perhaps he felt wrong not reporting it to the Krijen, but he had promised Noel he wouldn't.

Bish sat in a chair-like contraption with wheels that Sid had put together for him. Bish propelled himself around at speed, earning angry looks from Marigold, but she smiled when he wasn't looking. Even without the use of his legs, Bish was still wickedly dangerous. Aren knew she had no chance of winning their dagger-throwing competition. But it would be fun to try.

Finally, the rain stopped. Bish and Marigold woke Maude, waved goodbye to Aren, then set off into Val. Aren practically skipped to her room, knocking a little pattern on the door so that Wren would know it was her. When she opened it, he was by the window, wringing his shirt out. His hair was plastered to his face, so long now that it was in his eyes.

Aren's heart fluttered as she watched the muscles work in his arms and back. She knew he was strong, but he wore baggy clothes all the time, so she never got to see –

'What are you doing, Aren? Close the door.'

Aren quickly closed the door as he pulled his crinkled shirt back on. His boots were on the windowsill, dripping water down the wall. 'Shit, sorry,' Wren said, snatching them and tossing them outside.

'You don't have to do that!'

Wren shrugged. 'They wouldn't dry in time anyway. I've only got an hour.'

'You're going back out so soon?'

'Yeah. Breeve's not doing well. He's started seizing, and he's bitten off a chunk of his tongue. Do you have any alcohol?'

'Try the first aid box in my wardrobe. For the pain?'

'Antiseptic, really. He'll just Turn to get away from the pain.'

Aren winced. 'I didn't think infection was a problem in the city?'

Wren shrugged again. 'Who knows? I'm not taking any chances.'

As Wren started digging through the box, Aren noticed new tears in his shirt at his elbows. 'No fainting episodes lately?' she asked.

'No,' Wren grumbled back.

'The streetlings came back?'

'No.'

'Did you give away your bedroll again?'

'Might've done.'

That explained it. 'I'll need to patch your shirt again, then. Unless you'll take a new one?'

'No point. I'll just put holes in that too.'

Of course, he wouldn't accept a new shirt. Aren grabbed an empty satchel out from under her mattress and ducked underneath the bed. It had become a mess under there, between all the food and supplies she was hoarding. She'd been going through the unused rooms of the house and taking things her family had forgotten they owned. Mae and Sid wouldn't mind, not when everything was going to a good cause.

Aren grabbed a few wrapped chunks of dried meat she'd bought from the market and a waterskin she'd filled up earlier. She put them into the satchel and pulled the strings tight.

She sat down on the bed, watching Wren. He'd put the box back, his pockets bulging, then grabbed a little bottle of oil, the razor, and towel and came to sit cross-legged on the floor in front of her. There was just a light shadow around his chin because he'd only been gone a few days, but he oiled it up anyway and started shaving.

'So,' Wren said, 'are you going to the Celebrations?'

'Yes, and everyone else, it seems,' Aren replied. 'My father has to attend, of course.'

'Hm. Is Bish going?'

Aren snapped her wrist wraps. They hadn't talked about Bish since Wren had called him a cheat on the day of the rally. 'Um, I don't know,' Aren said.

Wren paused and looked up at her. 'It's okay. I don't mind talking about him.'

'You're not angry at Bish anymore?'

Wren put down his razor, half done. 'No, I'm not,' he said. 'I know I lost, fair and square. Besides, I always liked Bish. Jin, not so much. Kinda figures that he's a mayj.'

There was a bitterness in his tone that Aren didn't like. 'What do you mean by that?'

Wren studied her face for a moment. 'I don't know if you want to hear this.'

'I'm a big girl,' Aren said in a clipped tone.

'Fine then.' Wren leant back a little, looking up at her. 'There was always something off about Jin. He joked around a lot, but it was forced, you know? I'm amazed that he didn't let slip until now. He was always on edge. But despite that, he was better than everyone. He was the best fighter. He had the best luck with girls,' – Wren's eyes flickered away from Aren for a moment – 'he remembered every fucking sentence from all those dreary war books we had to read.'

'It sounds like you hated him.'

Wren looked horrified. 'No, *no*, Aren. I couldn't hate him. I'm ashamed to admit that we were all jealous, to start with. But it was impossible to keep that up after we found out what a piece of shit his father is.'

Everyone knew about Jin's father. Jin hadn't brought him up with Aren since the day they met. He didn't need to.

'You know, I found Jin once,' Wren said, 'just inside the entrance to the Squares' training grounds. I didn't recognise him, he'd been beaten so badly. His father had just dumped him there. I couldn't hate Jin after that, no matter what he did. And he looked out for everyone, especially Bish. Whenever we did training drills, everyone always wanted to be in his squad.'

Wren went silent and picked up his razor again. Aren sensed there was something more that he wasn't saying. 'What?'

Wren sighed. 'I'm not going to lie. It's hard knowing he didn't get kicked out of the Krijen, after what you said he did in the Deadlands. I mean, Prinn got his head chopped off for less than that.'

Aren shifted, uncomfortable. She struggled to hear any criticism of Jin. But that was irrational and unfair on Wren. She'd asked for honesty, and he'd given it to her.

'Aren?'

She looked up. Wren was watching her solemnly. 'Have I upset you?'

'No,' she replied.

By the look on his face, Wren didn't believe her. 'I shouldn't have said anything,' he said. 'I know that you and Jin were close . . .' He trailed off awkwardly.

'We were best friends. We *are* best friends,' Aren corrected herself, but with a frown. She hadn't intended to use the past tense, but she hadn't seen Jin in a year, and their last conversation was that stupid argument.

'You knew him as long as I did,' Aren realised. 'You just saw a different side of him.'

There was a palpable tension in the room. Aren rubbed at her wrist wraps, resisting the temptation to snap them again.

Wren quickly finished shaving, then got to his feet and picked up the satchel. 'I should go,' he said, heading towards the window.

'N-no,' Aren stammered, jumping to her feet. 'You said you had an hour!'

Wren turned back, one foot already on the sill. 'You want me to stay?'

'Yes!'

'I don't –' Wren's jaw dropped. 'Shit. Are you *crying?*'

'No,' Aren lied pathetically, wiping her eyes. She didn't know where it had come from. But she certainly didn't want Wren to leave.

Wren groaned. He dropped the satchel and took a few steps back towards her, waving his hands. 'Look, see? I'm staying. No need to cry.' He stopped in front of her, clearly at a loss for what to do. His hands kept moving to his daggers, but he didn't draw them, knowing he couldn't fight his way out of this problem.

His obvious distress at something as silly as her crying was enough to make Aren laugh through her tears. 'I'm guessing that comforting upset women was not something they taught the Squares?'

Wren gave her a wilted look, his restless hands dropping limply to his sides. 'No. It wasn't.'

Reassured that he would stay, Aren sat down on the bed again.

Wren slowly folded himself back onto the floor, looking relieved. Aren wiped her eyes again, hunting for a conversation topic to ride through the awkwardness.

'Are *you* coming to the Celebrations?'

'No,' Wren said. 'I don't trust Pyra's gang to not head to the Lower West Side while everyone is distracted. She's pissed off with me at the moment, not being able to have her usual fun at the Point.'

Pyra was the leader of the Upper West Side streetling gang. As it turned out, she'd been the girl with the red wrist ties at Lord Salli's rally. Pyra had a fearsome reputation, mostly because her favourite pastime was catching streetlings from surrounding gangs and removing their tongues. Rumour had it she ate them.

Aren thought it all so needlessly violent, but Wren disagreed. He said that as a streetling, you had to make your mark or die trying. Apparently, all the gang leaders had their own special thing. Pyra's was just the most revolting, which made it memorable. Wren said it wouldn't be long before someone trumped her. The streetlings treated it as a game, always trying to outdo each other.

Pyra was the person Wren had rescued Aren from that night in Rue. It made Aren feel sick just thinking of what the streetling girl had intended to do to her.

'I don't like the idea of you looking after the entire Lower West Side alone,' said Aren. 'I'll come with you.'

'Not a chance,' Wren said. 'First, you need to go to the Celebrations. It would look suspicious if you didn't. Second, I'm only staying in the Lower West Side as a precaution. Pyra loves crowds. She'll probably be smack in the middle of the Celebrations, soaking up the bedlam and inciting riots.' His face suddenly grew serious. 'Ah, fuck. Be careful tomorrow. Bring your daggers. Don't leave Noel.'

'I can look after myself now, you know.'

Wren made a dubious noise. 'Can you blame me for worrying, given how we met?'

Aren smiled. 'You worry about me?'

Wren gaped at her. 'I didn't mean it like that –'

'Well, you don't need to worry. I'm much less stupid than I was before, thanks to you.' Aren was being serious now too. 'But if it makes you feel better, I'll bring my daggers and stick close to Noel.'

Wren still looked rather grim.

'Lighten up,' Aren said. 'The place will be crawling with Krijen. And it's going to be fun! You know the meaning of the word fun, don't you?'

'Your idea of fun and my idea of fun are very different.'

That pulled Aren up short. She'd only ever known Wren to fight streetlings, rescue her from certain death, and come up with snarky comments. She was sure those weren't his first choice of hobbies.

'What do you do for fun then?'

Wren pushed his damp hair back out of his face. 'I like puzzles.'

'Puzzles?'

'What's wrong with puzzles?'

'Nothing! That's not what I meant. Anything else?'

Wren shook his head. His hair settled in front of his eyes again.

'Puzzles I can do. Come with me.'

Aren jumped up and pulled open her bedroom door, looking both ways. It was clear. She started down the moonlit corridor. The arches along the walls let in the hot night air, in the Valruean style.

Aren turned to make sure Wren was following her. He was startlingly close, stealthy as always. He'd become quite comfortable sneaking around her home. Aren assumed he'd not been spotted. At least, there had been no probing questions from her family, Noel, or the maids.

They came to a big wooden door. Aren pushed it open, leading them into the library. Rows of shelves stretched away from them, the far ends snuggled in shadow. It smelled dusty, but the air was dry despite the rain outside, which had started again, thrumming above them on the glass window in the ceiling. Moonlight from it bathed the centre of the room.

'Shit. This place is huge,' Wren breathed, looking up as they walked in.

'I spent a lot of time in here being tutored by Noel,' Aren said. 'It's been stripped of everything on majik of course, though there are books on just about every other topic you can think of. But,' Aren said, looking at Wren, 'we are here for *puzzles*.'

She headed to a massive wooden chest on the floor near the first row of books. She heaved it open and began pulling out stacks of wooden boxes. 'We've got quite a few games and logic puzzles,' she said. 'I like Bulbo, and Fickle and Foe. Noel's favourites are the older ones, because he said they are harder to cheat at and I have a tendency –'

'Aren,' Wren said from behind her.

'To do that, which I know is bad, but Noel is so wicked smart, and he always wins –'

'I'm sorry.'

Aren snapped upright, spinning around to face Wren. 'What?'

Wren was looking at his feet. 'When we first met, I was horrible. I called you some awful things.'

'Oh,' said Aren, grinning. 'You mean spoilt? Entitled? Pampered little rich girl?'

When Wren looked up at her, the anguish in his expression made her smile falter.

'Yes. All that. I want you to know that I don't actually think that. You aren't what I imagined you to be.'

'Don't worry about it,' Aren said. 'It comes with the "Bha", you know?'

'That's not right, though. It wasn't okay for me to say those things, especially when you had every right to judge *me*, and you didn't. I think that's why I was so mad, because you were just so much kinder than I wanted you to be. It's backwards, I know.'

'I get it, I do. I forgive you.'

Wren seemed to relax a bit. 'Thank you.'

Aren turned back to the chest. 'You're welcome to come to the library anytime, you know. I trust you can get around with no one seeing. Not that I care anyway. I still want to introduce you to everyone.'

'Not yet, Aren.'

It was worth a shot. At least it hadn't been a straight no, like before.

Aren smiled. *Ha*, she thought. *Progress*.

CHAPTER 39:
PAKKER

akker did not care for Felle's new face. At her direction, the boy had shattered her cheekbones and pulled them up at such an angle that she looked hollowed out. She liked it so much she asked the same of her jaw, softening its edges this time, making her chin more pointed.

Not long after this, she had demanded more mirrors, so the boy harnessed paper-thin slices off the one in her room and melted them onto every wall and ceiling so that no matter where she walked in Dijak's tower, she could see herself.

After that, she grew so sick of looking at the boy's twisted figure she commanded him to fix his legs, lengthening and straightening the bone until they looked right. Pakker had never seen anyone mutilate themselves so readily. He knew it hurt because the boy screamed in agony when he did it. It was only when Felle tried to get him to fix his scars that Pakker stepped in. 'It won't work,' he'd told a seething Felle. Few people understood that scar tissue was a byproduct of natural healing. Shearing it off with majik would only worsen the problem.

Felle was never satisfied. There was always something more she wanted or needed. It didn't matter that Felle had been unsuccessful in seducing Pakker after all, now that she had a new toy to play with. Pakker wondered if the boy thought of this as freedom, or if he knew he'd just found another prison without so many walls.

Felle wasn't just demanding of the boy either. She was furious at Pakker for refusing to continue with her standing order. He declined for two reasons, the first being that only an idiot would keep murdering people in the same place and not expect to get caught. The second was that while he needed to humour her to an extent, dumping more bodies in the lake was utterly pointless. Fifty-seven mayjen with their throats cut and she still wasn't satisfied. So Pakker stopped the killing, and no matter how many tantrums she threw, he wouldn't start again. She even threatened to set the boy on him, though prematurely. The boy wasn't ready for that just yet.

They'd spent months trying to coax him to do anything, which they had not foreseen would be so difficult. Like Pakker had told the Great Kahn, it had nearly brought the whole plan down around them.

Felle was entirely devoid of motherly instinct, so in order to groom the boy as required, Pakker found himself having to force a kindness that hadn't come naturally for a long time. To Pakker, it felt like walking a tightrope, with a fiery pit at the bottom. The boy had to be independent yet controlled, and it took a shockingly long time before he even fed himself without being prompted.

As soon as the boy showed a semblance of capability, Felle's arrogance grew exponentially. She indulged in his now limitless majikal capacity, dreaming of how she could use him to pursue her own selfish desires, exactly as the Great Kahn had expected. At first, it seemed the convoluted plan might actually work.

But when the boy came back one night, soaking wet from the rain and looking decidedly *emotional*, Pakker grew uncharacteristically tense. They were, of course, still balancing above the flames.

Felle straightened in her chair as Drax stepped into her bedroom. Pakker stood in the far corner and watched the boy amble over to her. No matter how straight his new bones were, he hadn't lost the hunched look as he moved about.

'Well?' Felle eyed Drax in the mirror. 'Tell me what happened.'

'He doesn't want to do what you tell him.'

Felle's eyes flashed, and she stood up, spinning to face the boy. 'You killed him?'

'No.'

'Why not?' Her tone was sharp, threatening.

Drax huddled on the floor at her feet. 'He knows about me.'

'So?'

'He knows why they hurt me.'

'Why who hurt you?'

Pakker stiffened. When Felle had eventually asked where Drax had come from, he'd told her a part truth – that he'd escaped from the KahnenKeep dungeon. Felle had taken great delight in possessing something of the Great Kahn's, the irony of which had prompted her to send the boy back to him with her demands.

'The people in the place I was before.'

Drax leant away from Felle as she swelled with rage.

'You let him live' – Felle's voice grew shrill – 'because he promised you some sort of *explanation?*'

Drax looked up at her, his blue eyes wide. 'He knows why they did it,' he repeated.

The boy had never seen the Great Kahn, that he would remember. He would know only the Krijen tasked with his 'taming', as the Great Kahn referred to it.

'*They?*' For a moment, Felle looked incredulous. Then she laughed. Her tinkling voice rang like bells off the mirrors and out through the open arches until it got caught in the rain. The tower was slowly filling with water, washing the bottom floor.

Drax seemed confused by her laughter. 'He said you would want to help me.'

'Did he now?' Felle looked over at Pakker and grinned, as though he would share her pleasure in the boy's humiliation. 'Can you believe it, Pakker? Duped at the first post.'

Felle leant down towards Drax as though explaining something to a child.

'You must know it was the Great Kahn himself who had you tortured. I thought that much would be obvious. You escaped from his dungeons, after all.

'As to why, I can tell you that. Because you are a mayj, and the Great Kahn *despises* mayjen. They've tarnished his rule. He does every hideosity possible to them in the name of saving his People. Torturing you was his way of exacting revenge. You're nothing special, just a means of sadistic release. So get back there *now*, and unless he agrees to do as I say, I order you to kill him.'

CHAPTER 40:
JIN KANJU

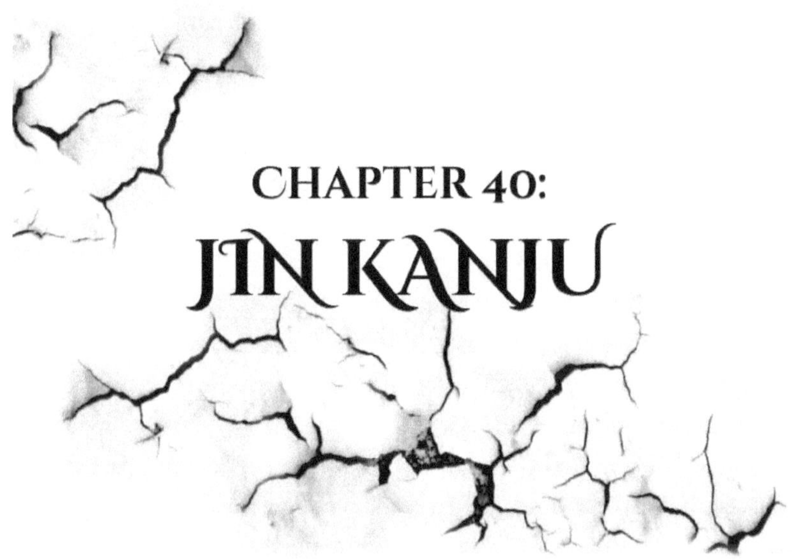

As it turned out, Jin was terrible at cards. It quickly became a regular evening activity for the Fourth Base East Krijen. After weeks of being shunned, Jin started to feel like he was one of them again. They stopped flinching when he moved too quickly and even dared to tease him. It made a difference that these Krijen hadn't seen Jin tear holes in people, which, as Crushed Foot said, wouldn't have helped.

But while they'd forgiven Jin, if only on the surface, the incident had not been forgotten. The story of the bandit attack had spread throughout the Deadlands. Newcomers to Fourth Base East felt it so over-embellished that on arrival to Fourth, they clamoured to hear the truth from Jin himself. Jin did not take to their requests with much enthusiasm, worried it might rock their tenuous new camaraderie. Meek even told him off once for giving 'a most embarrassingly boring rendition' of what had happened and had retold it himself, earning many 'oohs' and 'aahs' from the listening Krijen.

The other thing that was different about Fourth Base East was their proximity to the forest. Jin's squad never ventured to the farms like the other Krijen, but they could still see the trees of the forest from the ramparts, still feel the sticks crunch underfoot as they roamed the treeline. It was incredible. It smelled fresh and earthy, and it was strangely quiet. Jin didn't care that they never went into it. It was enough to be close to it.

As for Filip, he'd become Jin's constant companion, apparently having no greater purpose than following him around. Jin was so used to him that he had to remind himself not to talk to the dead Square when other people were within earshot.

But when Jin dared to embrace a semblance of happiness in his new life in the Deadlands, Aren popped into his head and made him long to return to Valrue. He wanted to see Bish too.

When Oji requested the squad return to the city for the upcoming Celebrations, Jin was glad that Pago agreed. The journey back to the mountain took over a month. They took a day here and there to help at the bases along the way, leaving a trail of supplies as they went. It was nice to see Kimjit again, even though she called him a 'fucking idiot' in front of the entirety of Second Base East when he walked through the gates. Just like everyone else, she seemed eager to hear the story of the bandit attack, which Meek took great delight in telling.

It was on the last night of their journey, with the mountain looming over them, that Oji took Jin aside. They walked far enough away from the squad that fear suddenly clawed at him again, terrified that Oji was going to take it all back and execute him on the spot. He'd not harnessed in the six months since the bandit attack, bottling his power up like he knew he shouldn't. It threatened to burst from him as they stopped.

'Calm yourself, Jin,' Oji said. 'You do not need to fear me.'

Jin's palms burned, but he held it in. He saw Filip place a hand on his dagger. Filip trusted no one. Jin had done that to him.

'I wanted to speak to you before we arrived in Valrue,' Oji said. 'There are things I want to say which would be very dangerous if the wrong people were listening in.

'I have been FaKrijen for thirty years. Over this time, I have learned that we Krijen are our own worst enemy. Our system is fatally flawed, creating men and women incapable of any action that would endanger their place in our ranks, no matter the cost.

'And in exiling the Lost Squares, we allow the crippling of our numbers, ensuring a stranglehold over us by the Kahnen and the People. It is senseless but makes becoming one of us seem more unobtainable, more desirable to the families of aspiring young boys and girls, who choose to send their children to the Squares. The constant threat of failure reinforces our vulnerability, in so many ways.' Oji paused, looking older than Jin had ever seen him. His hulking shoulders were rounded, drooping under some invisible weight.

'Why are you telling me this, sir? What's happened?'

'I need you to understand me and what I am about to ask of you. I once was young and impressionable. I did terrible things in the name of the Kahnen. I searched for solace in the lie that I did not have a choice. It was my duty, therefore, it was justified. Now I am older, wiser, and I daresay a better man, but I still cannot escape from the choices I made. My debt to morality is due.'

He spoke as though awaiting some impending doom, such that Jin caught himself moving into a defensive stance, hands on his dagger hilts, even though they were surrounded only by the dirt of the Deadlands.

'And so, Jin, I need you to be ready to lead again. Critique the orders given to you. Be courageous, be daring, be disruptive. I learned the hard way about what it means to be Krijen. Do not lose your humanity, as I did, for the sake of remaining one of us.'

Jin wasn't sure what Oji was asking of him. It sounded mutinous. He mustn't have understood. 'You need me to be ready to lead again? But Pago is squad leader, sir. Is he in danger?'

'No, son. I am asking you to lead the Krijen. All of us.'

'But . . . that's not how it works, sir,' Jin said, wondering why he needed to explain this to Oji, of all people. 'The Kahnen pick the FaKrijen –'

'Yes, they do. And that scares me. They will choose someone who they can control. But I am not asking you to be FaKrijen. I am asking you to be something else entirely. You need to be the voice of reason, the light in the dark. You need to save us.'

Save them? Like Jin saved them in the bandit attack? Fuck. The man had gone senile.

'You've got the wrong person, sir. I can't lead anyone anymore. The Krijen only tolerate me because of you.'

'It is *you* the Krijen need. I have never been more sure of anything.'

'But there are so many others!' Jin pointed back to where the squad was resting in the distance. 'Look at Jokah! He's said similar things to me about the Krijen. Or Flit! She is a born leader. Everyone looks up to her.'

Oji shook his head. 'By his own admission, Jokah does not have what it takes. Like me, he is growing old and weary. I cannot ask him to forgo the peace he has found after the life he has had. Flit is respected, yes, but she runs from the things that scare her. But you, you run towards them.

'When I first met you as a Fifteenth, I sensed a strength of spirit that is lost, beaten from most Squares. In spite of what you think, everyone looks up to you not because they are ordered to, but because you have a presence that commands it. You are a better man to lead the Krijen than I ever was. I know you will do right by them.'

Jin's hands were clenched, his jaw shaking with the effort of keeping his power inside. 'You're making it sound like I don't have a choice.'

'You have a choice. I just hope you make the one that will allow you to look back on your life without regret. Despite what people think, my life was nothing to be envied, I assure you.'

'You speak as if you are about to die.'

'We all die, Jin.'

'That's not what I meant –'

'I will hear no more of this. I have said my piece. Take a few minutes. Calm yourself. Then we must leave for Valrue.' With that, Oji headed back to camp, leaving Jin alone with Filip.

Jin felt like he was about to explode. He dug his nails into his palms, his nerves screaming at him. He needed to harness. He turned and ran, releasing the heat that had condensed inside his chest and using it to bolster his muscles. Power surged through him, and it felt so good; better than he remembered.

'Jin,' Filip called after him. 'Where are you going?'

Jin ignored him. He picked up speed so fast that his eyes watered as he tore into the wind. He ran and ran, unhindered by fatigue, even though it was what he wanted. He ran with such ease that he felt weightless, as though he was flying, like the birds he read about when he was younger.

Could he do that too? Could he hold himself up in the air, like they did? The idea was so absurd that Jin laughed and threw it aside before he'd really even considered it, and it looped back to him as he ran. He knew so little about his majik. Who was to say he couldn't do it?

'You can't do it,' Filip said as he ran alongside Jin, somehow keeping up. 'It's a dumb idea.'

Jin skidded to a stop, sending a strip of dirt clouding up behind him. It disappeared quickly into the light breeze. 'I want to try,' Jin said. It sounded difficult, *effortful*, which made it appealing. He had so much energy bubbling inside, and running wasn't enough to get rid of it, not right now. He needed something more, especially if he was going back to Valrue. He couldn't accidentally harness in the city. The thought was unimaginable.

Jin looked down at his boots, both firmly on the ground. He wasn't exactly sure where to start. He thought about how he used his power to fuel his muscles.

Filip sighed, sounding resigned to Jin's determined rebellion. 'Start there then.'

Experimenting, Jin bent his knees and released a stream of power down into his legs, pushing off from the ground. He shot into the air, high enough to make himself balk at how far away the ground suddenly was.

Unfortunately, the power surging through him did not keep him airborne. As he reached the crest of his jump, he found a brief moment of weightlessness just before he began falling. A sickening sensation took hold of him as he dropped like a stone, the ground hurtling up to meet him.

'Oh, *shit –*'

Jin teetered and flailed his arms uselessly in the air before hitting the ground so hard he was forced to roll across the dirt to prevent the bones in his legs from shattering.

Even so, his feet smarted as he groaned and sat up, spitting out dirt. Filip stood next to him, his arms folded. 'What the fuck was that?'

Jin hauled himself to his feet. That had not gone the way he'd hoped.

'Of course it didn't,' Filip said in a patronising tone. 'Think about it. How do you use majik on other things? Whatever it is, just do that to yourself.'

'Easy for you to say,' Jin grumbled, but he could see what Filip meant. When he harnessed things, he picked them up and held them in the air. He didn't toss them upwards and then let go, expecting them to stay there.

Jin looked down at himself again.

'This is going to be weird,' Filip said.

Tentatively, Jin reached his hands down by his sides, splayed his fingers, and grabbed onto his torso with majik. He couldn't feel anything in his hands other than the power burning his fingertips, waiting on the precipice. He curled his fingers in a little, unsure of how tightly he had to hold on. Feeling anything but ready, he slowly raised his hands half an inch.

Jin gasped as he felt the resistance of his own weight, his heels pulling ever so slightly off the ground. 'Shit,' he breathed. 'I am *heavy*.' He could feel the tug on his power now, strong enough that if he held on, it might eventually tire him out. More quickly than running anyway. But it wasn't Jin's muscles that were taking the strain. It was his power. It was the most peculiar sensation. It felt *wonderful*.

'Go on then,' Filip said. 'You haven't left the ground yet.'

A little nervous, Jin carefully raised his hands higher. He felt himself rise onto his tiptoes, then eventually his feet came off the ground.

'Ha,' Jin said, as he hovered a foot in the air. He let the stream of heat continue to roll from his chest and down his arms, into his hands. He was steadier than he expected.

'Of course you're steady. You're holding on to your middle,' Filip said. 'You're balancing yourself that way.'

Jin held himself where he was, adjusting to the sensation.

'Go higher,' Filip commanded, suddenly impatient.

It didn't seem that scary an idea. Jin obliged and delicately raised his hands, his stomach lurching as the ground slipped away from him.

'Keep going,' Filip urged.

Jin's hands were already at shoulder height and angled awkwardly downwards, still holding on to his torso. Jin could see an issue even before he got there.

'What happens when my arms can't go up any farther?'

'Give it a try.'

Feeling rather stupid, Jin stretched his hands carefully above his head. He rose higher, coming to a halt when his elbows locked out. He looked down. Filip stood on the ground below him, looking up.

It was only a little disconcerting to see his feet dangling above nothing, but not as bad as he'd expected. Probably because he knew he wasn't going to drop himself. He guessed he was thirty feet or so off the ground.

'Well, I guess that's it,' Filip called. 'This seems to be your limit.'

Jin was disappointed. He looked up at his hands, twisted awkwardly down to his torso. It was rather uncomfortable. Jin lowered his hands, bringing himself down halfway into a more comfortable position.

Curious, he rolled his wrists gently forward. As he did so, he felt himself tilt towards the ground. 'Ah. This is weird,' he said. He rolled his wrists back, righting himself.

'It's nothing like flying though,' Filip said from the ground. 'Not like what the birds did. You're just lifting yourself. Can you even go sideways?'

'Hold on.' Jin slowly shifted his hands to the right. His body moved with them.

'Okay, fine,' Filip said.

Keeping a grip on himself, his hands steady, Jin carefully rotated his arms in a circle, his body following.

'It's fun,' Filip said, 'but it's not exactly helpful, is it? You're too restricted to do anything. You need longer arms.'

Jin's hands were growing sweaty with the heat, but his chest was cooling down. Between that and the gentle breeze, Jin felt almost comfortable. The heat in his hands gave him a thought. 'Let me try something.'

Feeling eager, Jin lowered his arms and brought himself steadily back to the ground. He shook his hands out, his capillaries tingling from having heat pulsing through them for so long.

Jin checked in with himself. He felt a little tired, but not the regular kind of tired. Just more relaxed than before, like he'd loosened up his muscles, but not his muscles.

'Stop thinking in loops,' Filip said. 'You're driving me crazy.'

'How hypocritical of you,' Jin said, rolling his shoulders. 'Okay, let's try this.'

Jin wondered if this would be like when he'd harnessed that circle of shard from the Split. If he pushed out more power when he lifted his hands, would he go higher, with the same movement?

Jin flexed his fingers, brought his hands to his sides, and grabbed a hold of his torso again, feeling his weight once more. He took a deep breath, then let a burst of power explode down his arms as he lifted his hands just an inch.

Jin yelled out as he shot into the air, streaking well beyond where he'd been before. The wind battered him, his face turned upwards towards the sky. He kept lifting his arms, enjoying the rush. His eyes were watering again by the time he brought his hands up to chest height. He slowed, then came to a stop in the air, his breath catching at the sudden drag on his power. But it wasn't enough to scare him.

'This is *amazing*,' Jin muttered to no one as he looked out across the Deadlands. He could see the jagged hills of the west to his left, the black slash of the Crevasse to his right, the shadowed ring of the treeline impossibly far in every direction. He could see the circle of death around Valrue. He couldn't see the city itself, not quite high enough to look inside the mountain crater.

He looked down again, seeing his feet hanging over nothingness.

But when he looked up, it was like he was lost in the stars. Jin wished Filip could be up here with him. Maybe Jin could tempt the dead Bhouli to stay here and leave him alone.

It wasn't long before Jin needed to go down. His fatigue was growing, something different that went deeper than a muscle ache. It would be moronic to die by falling out of the sky.

Jin descended slowly at first, lowering his hands. But there was another way to come down, Jin realised. Keeping his hands where they were, he doused some of the flames in his chest, expecting to sink downwards. He didn't move at all. Jin pulled back a bit more on his majik, until only a trickle of heat was running down his arms. Slowly, he began to drift downwards, his hands in the same place.

Good to know, Jin thought. Of course, he could just let go and fall down. But something told him it wouldn't be so easy to catch himself.

Filip was waiting for him on the ground.

When he got close, Jin cut off his power and dropped lightly to his feet. He'd expected to feel jittery with adrenaline, but he was calm, for once. Tired even, though not in the usual way. The heat in his chest was gone. He felt pleasantly cold. Normal again, he realised.

'That was incredible,' Jin said.

'It's not an achievement,' Filip snapped, sounding a lot like Jin's father. 'It's useless. You can't do anything else if you're lifting yourself. You need your hands.'

It was a rather anticlimactic truth.

'Go back to the others,' Filip said. 'They'll be waiting for you.'

Feeling familiarly reprimanded, but lighter for his efforts, Jin took off running towards the camp. He wasn't sure how long he'd been gone.

Everyone was standing in a circle when Jin arrived, loaded packs at their feet. Everyone but Oji anyway. Jin wondered if he'd even come back after their conversation earlier.

Pago stared as Jin jogged slowly up to them. 'Jin? What have you been doing?'

Vulmin, Jokah, and Meek all turned to face Jin. He hesitated on the edge of the circle as Vulmin scowled. Meek, however, looked positively gleeful. 'Shit,' he said, 'you look like you've gone a hundred rounds with Mama Hidel's best whore!'

Jin froze. 'Excuse me?'

'You're looking rather dishevelled, son,' Jokah said kindly.

Jin looked down at himself.

Meek was cackling. 'Your hair is sticking up, your clothes are torn, and look at the face on him! Rather glorious, if you ask me.'

Jin felt himself redden, trying to flatten his hair.

'No one did ask you, Meek,' Pago said. 'What have you been doing, Jin?'

Jin's hands twitched guilty, incriminating him.

'You've been harnessing,' said Vulmin, his voice tight. The smile slid off Meek's face.

Jin tensed with fear as he looked around at the dark faces of his squad. So quick they were to turn on him.

'I gave him permission,' said a stern voice behind Jin. He spun around.

Oji stood there, looking enraged, his stance akin to the mountain above them. 'Jin has my trust,' the FaKrijen said loudly. 'He saved your lives. The Kahnen chose to pardon him. What more could you possibly need?'

Oji's massive body exuded power, a very different kind to Jin's. Everyone but Jokah ducked their heads, ashamed, but this only seemed to further anger their FaKrijen.

'Look at me!'

All their eyes turned upwards, compelled to obey.

'I will not tolerate this disgracefulness any longer,' Oji bellowed. 'Jin is a mayj, and he is Krijen. He has more than earned your loyalty, and you *will* accept him!'

Jin's squad cowered into the ground, as though the force of Oji's will was crushing them.

'Krijen,' Oji thundered, 'am I understood?'

'Yes, sir,' Pago said at once, raising his hand to his clavicle. The rest of the squad followed suit. They wouldn't dare disappoint the FaKrijen.

'Good,' Oji growled. He looked to Pago. 'Let us go then. The city awaits.'

CHAPTER 41: THE GREAT KAHN

The Great Kahn woke because he couldn't breathe. His lungs wouldn't expand, as though someone had woven them into cardonite.

Above him floated a face framed with curling black hair and blue eyes. It drove a flash of panic into him, mingled with desire, as his mind went to Mandavar. Then he noticed the pale skin, the deadness of the eyes, the scars tickling the boy's chin. Drax was suffocating him.

Unable to speak, the Great Kahn threw back his bedcovers and sat up, holding up a hand that said, '*Wait.*'

One second passed. Then another. His vision was blackening when suddenly he could breathe again. The Great Kahn sucked in glorious air so fast he almost choked on it.

'It was you,' Drax said. He stood by the edge of the bed. 'You did this to me. Felle said so. You lied to me.' He didn't look angry. Just empty.

The Great Kahn shook his head, his throat burning. 'No,' he rasped. 'I never told you it was not to do with me. I said I would explain why you have those scars.'

Drax's face changed, but to what, the Great Kahn did not know.

Usually, this would anger him, but the boy's barren expression unnerved the Great Kahn. He looked too similar to Mandavar.

'I will explain,' the Great Kahn said. 'But first, tell me what Felle had to say.'

Drax's face returned to its usual vacant mask. 'Felle wasn't happy,' he said simply.

'She does not care about your scars then.'

Drax just stared at him.

'You remember I said how much you look like your father?'

Drax blinked.

'His name was Mandavar, and he was a mayj, like you. He was very dangerous. At the time, majikal abilities like his were unheard of. We were lucky he agreed to be a KahnenMayj. I was not the Great Kahn then, just a member of the Eighth House. As time went on, Mandavar became increasingly difficult to work with. The Kahnen recognised the threat he posed, and we could not risk someone like Mandavar being born outside of our control. So we passed a law requiring all KahnenMayjen to be sterilised.'

The Great Kahn looked Drax dead in the eye.

'Mandavar was furious when he heard, and given what he could do, we were entirely at his mercy. So when he simply walked away, the Kahnen were shocked. Shortly after that, I became the Great Kahn. For the first few years of my reign, the city thrived. Then something happened. The beginning of the Unsettlement, as we call it now.

'I suspected it had something to do with Mandavar. After a few months of searching for him, I heard an intriguing rumour: a young woman in Rue claiming to be pregnant with Mandavar's child. While it seemed unlikely, there was enough reason to believe her. I did not know what to do, so I asked our FaKrijen what he thought. The FaKrijen was adamant the child would be a threat. The woman had to be killed. So I gave the order.

'There was a KahnenMinder in the room for our conversation. As chance would have it, she knew the mother of the pregnant girl. The mother came to the Keep and begged us to spare her daughter's life. The

FaKrijen reluctantly agreed to take the baby after it was born.

'And so your grandmother handed you to the Krijen. But once I had you, I struggled to justify killing you. You were just like any other baby. As much as I wanted to believe it, I knew your existence alone would not cause the Unsettlement. You were also born too late, after the signs of an imbalance were visible.

'So we arranged for a wet nurse and saw that you lived. When you started harnessing, the Krijen ensured you would use majik only when commanded. I regret to say the methods used were unkind. I did not hear the details of what was being done until much later. I wanted you released, but the FaKrijen pushed back. He said you were too dangerous to simply set free. That is when the Krijen cut off your hands.'

The Great Kahn watched the boy's face for a reaction. There was none. He looked down at the boy's hands, limp below the raised purple scars encircling each wrist, marking the path of the cleaver.

'I was told it had no effect on your majik,' the Great Kahn continued. 'You were gifted beyond any mayj I had ever heard of. Even Mandavar himself could only dream of your abilities. But it meant we could not let you go. So you lived on in our dungeons, until one day, you escaped.'

Drax stared at the Great Kahn for what seemed an endless time.

'Drax, I know you are angry. You deserve vengeance. But I am not the one you are looking for. The FaKrijen is the man who condemned you, forced your grandmother to give you up to save her daughter's life, and ordered your torture. He is the man you want to kill.'

'Who is he?'

The question came without hesitation. The Great Kahn hid a smile.

'In just a few days, there will be a citywide celebration. At first, I found the idea proposed by my Kahnen ugly and indulgent, and so I denied them. But they insisted the People would love it. A few days of games and entertainment following on from the Dancing Ceremony to improve everyone's spirits. How could I refuse my citizens something that could bring them relief, albeit temporary, from their pain and suffering? I conceded.

'I am telling you this because the person you want to kill will be there.

At the opening ceremony, he will be standing on the stage with me and my Kahnen, and I will call him forward. It will be easiest to kill him when everyone is watching because no one will suspect it. His name is Oji Mimundmen. He is the FaKrijen of Valrue.'

The Great Kahn felt a sense of accomplishment as the boy left. There was no guilt. He did not owe Drax anything, not after what his father had done. But he hadn't told the whole truth. It had not been the Great Kahn who had wanted to release the boy.

It had been Oji.

The FaKrijen had fought hard against the boy's continued imprisonment after he'd seen the disfigured child sitting in a cell one day and had asked who he was. And that was why, when Drax's cell was discovered empty after his 'escape', the Krijen on duty had done nothing, and told no one, undoubtably at Oji's command.

But Drax didn't need to know that.

The Great Kahn was going to get what he wanted after all these years. Oji, troublesome as he had become, was going to die. Using the boy, Pakker would see the Unsettlement end, with Felle to take the fall. And from Mandavar's stranglehold, Lord Luka Li would finally be free.

CHAPTER 42:
SID BHA

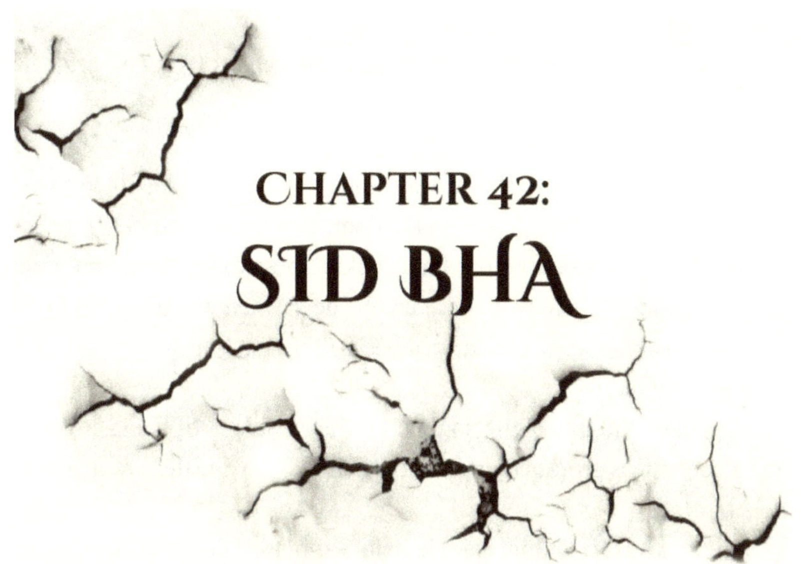

Sid hid in Night before the Celebrations. Eden had visited yesterday with a design request, the explanation sickening. After Eden had left, Sid had thrown up all over his drawing desk. Eden had said he would return the morning of the Celebrations to review the first draft. Sid, to his own disgust, had completed it. He'd rolled it up, tucked it under his arm, then locked himself in the dark room, hoping Eden wouldn't come.

Sid had spent months dreading the moment when Eden came up with a further use for the cardonite. Given Sid had no way to destroy it himself, he had toyed with the idea of 'losing' the final piece of armour. Unfortunately, no one would believe him to be that careless. He also couldn't accidentally use it for something else – he couldn't manipulate it on his own. While Stolt had agreed to help him create the dagger for Aren, it had at least been a weapon, and Stolt had asked for no explanation of why it was commissioned.

Sid huddled in the darkness, watching the slit of light under the door that led to Day. He heard a door hinge creak, and footsteps echoed through Day towards him. A shadow blocked the light under the door, which crunched loudly as someone walked into it, as though expecting it to be open.

Sid closed his eyes, the scroll clasped between his fists. *Go away*, he pleaded. *I'm not here . . .*

'Sid? Sid, are you there?'

Sid opened his eyes. That wasn't Eden's voice. He scrambled to his feet and pulled up the iron bar on the door, heaving it open. 'Oji?'

The FaKrijen stood before him, looking perplexed. 'What on earth are you doing? You know not to lock the door when the furnace is lit.'

'Oh, thank goodness,' Sid breathed. 'I thought you were Eden. It's great to see you –'

Oji pulled Sid into a hug so tight he was in danger of being crushed. Sid's very bones protested, unable to do anything while the stronger man held him.

Eventually, Oji let him go. He held Sid out by the arms, looking at him endearingly.

'Oh my,' Sid stammered, 'that was . . . unexpected –'

'How are you? Why did you think I was Eden? Where is that twisted little shit anyway?'

Oji was even less reserved than before, if that were possible. He had clearly not taken heed of Sid's warning. That had been a year ago, though. Maybe he had forgotten.

'I'm doing okay, but I'd be lying if I said any better than that,' Sid admitted. 'Eden was coming to speak to me about something today, and I'm afraid I was rather dreading it.'

'Oh yes? What was it?'

'I'll-I'll show you.'

Sid gestured to his desk, and Oji followed him over, wrinkling his nose. Maybe Sid hadn't cleaned up the vomit as well as he'd thought.

Sid unrolled the design and placed some weights on the corners. Oji stared at it for a full minute before looking at Sid. 'It is for mayjen prisoners?'

Sid nodded.

'I do not understand how it works.'

Sid reluctantly pointed to the drawing. 'It's a simple concept, with a rather horrific effect. You restrain the mayj using the cardonite arms here and across the chest, here. Then this lever is pulled. It first sends a blade across the wrists, removing the hands.' Sid could taste something foul in his mouth. 'Then this bit here is a cardonite shaving. It pierces the chest cavity half a second later. The aim is not to kill, however. Correct placement is important, hence why it needs to be adjustable.'

Oji rubbed his chin, his eyes still on the drawing. 'Knowing Eden, I assume there is some additional cruel significance to this technique?'

'Eden believes that majik originates in the chest,' Sid said. 'Not in the heart, but near the heart, somehow interacting with the nervous system. Once a mayj has consciously drawn on their power, it needs to go somewhere. It is channelled out through the fingertips, where the most nerves are situated. If a mayj harnesses just as their hands are removed, the power becomes trapped in the chest cavity. Instinctively, the mayj stops harnessing. With their hands gone and the nerve channel interrupted, they lose their ability to harness from that point onward. However, if something artificially forces the flow of power after their hands are removed, it continues to build within the chest cavity.

'Taking care to avoid major organs, cardonite pierced through the chest in the correct place triggers the point of origin of the power. As cardonite is sturdy enough to withstand a flow of power running through it, the sensation, however excruciating, must be endured until either the cardonite shaving is ruined or is removed.'

'Or until the mayj Turns,' Oji added bitterly. 'How grotesque. I am so sorry, Sid.'

Sid wiped his brow, feeling rather light-headed. 'Only mayjen committing the most heinous crimes will be subject to this treatment. Even so, I'm finding it difficult to allow my skills to be used this way.' Sid cringed at his own words. How gutless they sounded. Stolt was right.

But Oji gave him a sympathetic look, then removed the paper weights and allowed the scroll to curl up. 'Never mind all that now. Today is a day of Celebration!' Oji threw his hands up and beamed.

Sid smiled weakly. Something jogged his memory. 'How is young Jin? You remember he is a friend of my daughter? She worries about him, though tries not to let on. Another friend who was injured in the attack returned home, but he is unwilling to speak on the matter.'

'Ah yes,' said Oji. 'I remember the young Krijen who broke his back. Did he ever regain the use of his legs?'

'I'm afraid not. I designed him a wheeling chair so he could get around independently. He is adjusting well.'

'I am glad. I have seen that kind of injury before. It is often harder on the mind than anything else.'

'Yes, especially for someone as capable as Bish. And Jin?' Sid prompted.

'Yes. Jin. An incredible young Krijen with a terrible burden, having to hide such a secret. Considering that, I found it strange he chose the career he did, one that invites scrutiny. I expected him to have deserted before I arrived at First Base East, but when I told him so, he said he had not even considered leaving. I thought at first it was because of his training – you know how mindlessly obedient Krijen can be – but perhaps there was something else stopping him . . .'

Oji trailed off, looking distractedly into space before finding himself again. 'All things considered, Jin is doing well now. I suspect he is looking forward to seeing your daughter. He has been rather preoccupied since we arrived in Valrue.' Oji winked.

Sid almost missed Oji's quip, distracted by how taken the FaKrijen was by Jin. It was hardly surprising, though. Everyone liked Jin.

'Jin is in Valrue? Aren will be delighted,' Sid commented. 'She might see him at the Celebrations, then. Knowing her, she'll want to head in early to get a good spot. She amazes me sometimes. If you recall, Aren got caught in that crush at Lord Salli's rally a while back, yet she seems no less eager to be in the middle of a crowd.'

'Ah, the invincibility of youth,' said Oji with a reminiscent look in his eye. 'I remember that feeling. Every day that passes, I grow more aware of my mortality. Such a cumbersome thing is time.

'Speaking of, we should go. It is one of the irritating things about doing what we do. Everyone notices if you are late. Also,' – he winked again – 'it will be *much* harder for Eden to find us if we leave this room.'

CHAPTER 43:
AREN BHA

Maude was unimpressed to hear she couldn't go to the centre stage. 'The Eighth House will be protected by KahnenMayjen,' Aren explained. 'If something happens and you're too close, they won't be able to help.'

After this, in a very unlike-Maude fashion, Maude sulked the whole way into Rue. However, once they crossed into the Squares' training grounds where the Celebrations were being held, she quickly became entranced by a young entertainer holding an enormous ornamented pole, which he offered to the crowd. Moping forgotten, Maude leapt forward and grabbed one end of it while another young girl grabbed the other, holding it horizontally between them. Noel, Mae, Aren, and Marigold all stopped to watch.

'A little higher,' directed the entertainer. Maude and the other girl pulled the pole to waist height. The crowd parted for the entertainer as he took a few steps back, then, with a running leap, he cleared the pole.

The crowd fussed; a few clapped weakly. 'Bah,' someone jeered. '*I* could do better than that.' The entertainer shrugged before motioning for the pole to be lifted higher.

Maude and the girl obliged, lifting the pole to shoulder height. The entertainer cracked his neck and fingers, then splayed his hands dramatically behind him. He ran and jumped so high his knees tapped his chin, clearing the pole. More people cheered, encouraging a round of clapping. The entertainer bowed.

'Higher!' the crowd chorused.

Maude's eyes grew wide with excitement as the entertainer nodded. They hefted the pole to the top of Maude's headscarf.

The entertainer laughed. He waved his hands, motioning for it to go even higher. Looking incredulous, Maude pushed the pole up over her head, her arm straight up towards the sky.

'Oh my, it's rather high, isn't it?' The entertainer knelt down to speak to a little boy who was watching with his mouth open. 'Do you think I can do it?'

The little boy nodded. With a wink, the entertainer stood up and rubbed his hands together. He took an additional step back this time, then with a bounding leap and a tight little flip, he spun right over the pole. The crowd bellowed and whistled as the entertainer gave a sweeping bow, grinning from ear to ear as he came to collect the pole. Maude clapped madly.

An angry yell erupted from the crowd. 'He's a fraud! He's using majik!' A few people stopped clapping, suddenly unsure. The accuser was a grumpy-looking man, standing with his arms folded, his upper lip pulled back.

Maude turned to him, eyes flashing. 'No, he isn't! He's amazing!'

Aren stopped her clapping, suddenly nervous. Maude wouldn't be so naïve. Surely.

The grumpy man scoffed. 'You can't prove it, little girl.'

'Yes, I can,' Maude snapped back. 'I can stop people from –'

Noel lunged forward and grabbed Maude by her arm, tugging her roughly back into the crowd. Aren and the others raced after them.

Noel didn't stop until they had cleared the exit to the training grounds and were back in one of Rue's busy streets. 'Maude!' he cried. 'Have you gone mad? What were you thinking?'

Maude pulled her arm out of Noel's grip and turned her face away.

Aren suspected no one from the crowd could have guessed what Maude had been about to say, let alone believe her. But they were lucky Noel had stopped her when he did.

Aren glanced nervously around. Noel was pale and clammy from holding on to Maude. Mae was red in the face, angry. Marigold just looked frightened.

Maude turned back to them, her eyes wet. 'I hate this! He wasn't cheating!'

'No, he wasn't,' said Noel exasperatedly, 'but is proving it to that horrid man worth telling the world about *how* you know that?'

'Yes, it is!' Maude yelled, clearly not caring who heard. 'What is the point in having this stupid ability if I can't do any good with it?' She turned and ran.

'Maude!' Noel closed his eyes and pinched his nose, as though trying to fend off a headache. 'Why did she decide to become a teenager today? Can someone please get her? I can't.'

'I'll find her,' said Aren. 'Wait here.'

She wove through the crowd, searching for Maude's white headscarf. It didn't take long to find her. Maude had stopped not far up the street and was leaning against a wall, patting the little lump tucked in by her collarbone. She clearly felt bad to go farther, mature even in her rebellion.

As Aren approached, Maude wiped her eyes. 'I'm sorry,' she said. 'Noel is right. I don't want to upset anyone. That was silly of me.'

Aren gathered her into a hug, being careful not to squash Mika. 'You are allowed to be silly sometimes,' Aren said. 'You're fourteen! The Great Kahn knows I was silly at fourteen. *Much* more silly than you.'

Aren leant back a little to look up at her. Maude was so tall it hurt Aren's neck. She hated what she was about to say because she could see the irony of it, but it needed to be said. 'But, Maude, please don't do that again. I know you feel you miss out on things, but you need to keep yourself safe.'

Maude sniffed. 'I don't care about being safe. No one can hurt me.'

Concerned, Aren leant forward again and dropped her voice lower.

'Mayjen aren't the only danger out there.'

'No, that's not what I meant. I have chosen my purpose, and I am ready for whatever comes with it.'

Aren didn't like the sound of that. 'What do you mean your purpose?'

'It's the reason we don't do tattoos until we are sure,' Maude explained. 'Tattoos are permanent, and we must choose wisely. We can't change them once they are under our skin.'

'But . . . but you inked "saviour" under your skin.'

Aren felt a chill. She'd let Maude permanently ink 'happiness' onto her wrist, but somehow that didn't seem so ominous.

'Exactly,' Maude said.

Aren quietly cursed her poor understanding of the Bhouli. 'This is about more than saving Mika, isn't it?'

Peals of laughter started up right behind them, and Aren jumped, spinning around. This wasn't the time or place for this conversation. They would be lucky if they got back into the training grounds with this many people. Maybe a seat on the rooftops? Aren smiled, thinking of Wren. 'Okay, we need to – Maude!'

The mouse had shuffled half of her little body out of Maude's wraps, her tail curling over Maude's hand. Aren darted forward and covered the mouse with her hand, stepping in close to obscure what she was doing. 'Great Kahn save me,' Aren hissed. 'What are you *doing?*'

'I'm sorry, Aren –'

'Your aunt was kind enough to let you come today! Are you trying to make her regret it?'

Maude hung her head. Mika had dived back to safety, a quivering lump once more.

That stupid mouse will be the death of her, thought Aren. She was beginning to understand Noel's inclination to kill it.

'Let's go,' Aren said sharply, falling in behind Maude as they headed back to where the others were waiting.

CHAPTER 44:
PAKKER

It didn't bother Pakker, being the boy's minder. He was curious to follow, behaving like no target Pakker had followed before. It wasn't easy, though. Drax ran from things like streamers and the jingle of bells but got too close to people whom Pakker would rather give a wide berth. He also never stood upright, which made keeping sight of him in a crowd particularly difficult.

Pakker wasn't certain if the boy would kill the FaKrijen or not. He wondered which would dominate: the boy's fear of Felle or his growing sense of self-preservation. The two strongly contradicted each other. Felle certainly had a cruel way of showing her displeasure. But perhaps compared to what he'd endured before, Felle wasn't all that bad. The boy was tough, despite his feeble manner.

As he pondered this, Pakker realised he had developed a soft spot for Drax. The thought was so distracting, he nearly missed what was right in front of him.

Pakker did a double take.

It was that auburn-haired girl. She wasn't in her fashionable green wraps, and her hair was longer and up in a bun, but Pakker never forgot a face. But what stood out even more was the mouse that her tall Bhouli companion was cradling against her chest.

Pakker reacted on instinct, ducking into an open doorway on his left. It was a little shop full of shoes, busy with Celebration-goers. Pakker slipped to the dirty window, looking out. The auburn-haired girl had been facing the other way, but now she'd turned around and moved closer to the Bhouli girl, blocking Pakker's view. Their hands were folded between them. The Bhouli girl looked down, as though guilty. Finally, they both headed towards the gates to the Squares' training grounds.

Unlike most people, Pakker trusted his eyes. That mouse had been real.

It didn't matter that he'd lost Drax. Pakker knew where he would be. Pakker would rather not be in the middle of the training grounds if the boy went through with it anyway. He would climb up onto the wall when the Celebrations started, to watch.

For now, he had someone much more interesting to follow.

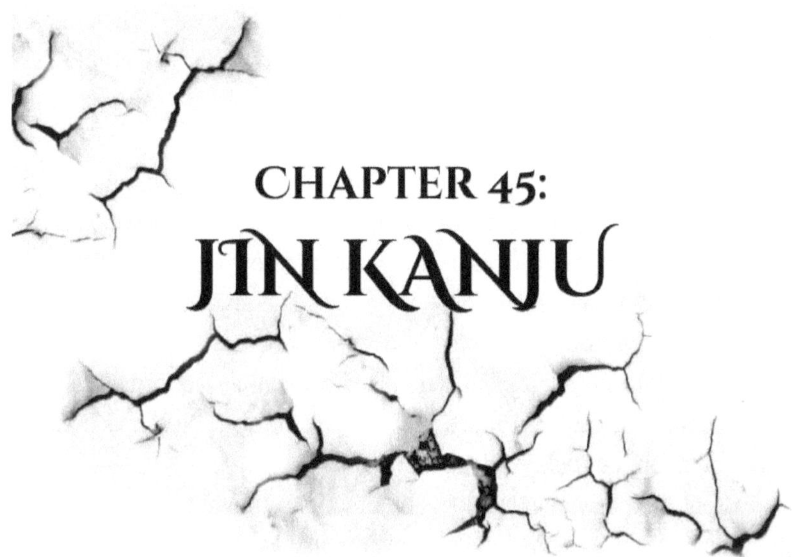

CHAPTER 45:
JIN KANJU

It was both exciting and overwhelming to be back in the city. Exciting to think that he would see Aren again. Overwhelming, because of all the *people*. That, and a strange trepidation had settled over him that he'd never noticed before, like he wanted to escape but didn't know why. It had started as they climbed the mountain, worsening as they walked through the city gates. But it was easy to brush aside, right now.

The Squares' training grounds were unrecognizable, bursting with colour and noise. Jin wondered which brave soul had convinced the Geni to allow it. The wooden barracks had disappeared, replaced by an enormous stage on the eighth square, right in the middle of the massive rectangle.

Jin was posted back from the stage at an intersection set up to enable people to walk up and down the row of squares. With the exception of Oji, Jin's squad and another larger squad of nine were posted in concentric circles back from it, making up the protective detail for the Eighth House.

The grounds were packed with people, entertainers, and roaming Krijen. They'd not been out in this much force in all of Jin's memory.

Despite their numbers, Jin twitched with nerves, as always. The more he learned about his majik, the more he understood how vulnerable they were. An attack could come from the ground, the sky, *anyone* in the crowd.

Jin assumed there would be KahnenMayjen hidden among the people, but he didn't want to rely on them. He couldn't wait for the opening ceremony to be over. It frustrated him how little he could see of the stage. As tall as he was, he was on the same level as the crowd and quite a distance from where his protectees would be.

Some of the entertainment was raised on smaller platforms scattered throughout the training grounds. Jin walked to the one closest to him and jumped up onto it, taking in the view.

A sea of heads expanded in every direction, streamers of every colour popping into the air. Jin could see several black-wrapped figures leaping onto other platforms about the crowd, doing the same as him. Filip stood next to him, scanning the people below, looking like the Filip that Jin remembered from when they were Squares. Serious, calm. Quiet.

The People were behaving themselves so far. Not even the constant jostling and shoving could dissuade them from merriment today.

Even better again, the performers whose platform Jin shared were rather good and didn't seem bothered by his presence. It was a trio of women in colourful dresses who would each sing, dance, and play a flute to a jolly tune that became faster and faster and faster until it reached a crescendo. While the crowd cheered, the women switched positions, passed the instrument along, and began again at a lazier pace. Jin even found himself tapping his feet along to the music. He smiled at the women, who laughed in delight at his attention, earning enthusiastic whistles from the crowd at his feet.

After watching a few rounds of this, he turned his back to the performers. The Eighth House had not arrived yet, but he was eager to spot Aren, or any familiar face in the crowd. It had been so long since he'd seen Bish or Noel or even Mama Hidel and her women.

Closer to the central stage, the crowd was less dense. Coloured sunshades were slung between wooden posts over large areas cordoned off for high-ranking citizens. It would mainly be for Kahnen of the other houses and their families, and the wealthy North Val inhabitants. *Aren might be under there*, Jin thought. Then again, she had a habit of being in places she shouldn't, blissfully defiant of her own status. But he kept a keen eye on the area, just in case.

There was a commotion at the edge of the training grounds, signalling the arrival of the Eighth House. Two rigid rows of Krijen marched down the main strip, protecting the line of Kahnen who walked between them. It was painfully slow, but the Eighth House were obviously enjoying the attention of the People.

It was easy to spot the blood-red cloak of the Great Kahn at the front, followed by the seven other members of his house. They were dressed so ostentatiously that their sparkling gowns made Jin's eyes water, even from where he stood. A tall man with a distinctly arrogant air attended them, whom Jin didn't recognise.

The crowd screamed and clapped as the Eighth House made it to the stage and climbed the wide steps, sending a wave of movement through the training grounds as everyone turned inwards. Ribbons, trinkets, and jewellery soon covered the Krijen surrounding the stage as they knocked the thrown objects of affection from the air before they reached the Kahnen. There was every chance they could be a disguised weapon.

Following the Eighth House, Oji walked up the wide steps to a roar of noise. He waved away his Krijen guards and allowed the gifts to shower him. Jin smirked as a pair of what looked like women's undergarments landed on his arm. The Eighth House did not look impressed, but Oji laughed, and the crowd laughed with him, his joy infectious.

Sid Bha followed Oji up onstage, making Jin's palms tingle. He did not get his own cheer but walked in the echo of Oji's. As Weapons Master, Sid sat just under the Kahnen in terms of status, becoming part of whichever house had the seat in government, and so was obligated to join the Eighth House for the Celebrations. He looked like he wanted to be anywhere else. Once he got to the top of the steps he hurried off to the side and looked down at his feet, a weak attempt at hiding. His elegant slim-fitting robes made him look tiny next to the Eighth House in all their grandeur.

The Great Kahn stepped forward into the middle of the stage. The tall, unfamiliar man was half a step behind him. *He must be a KahnenMayj*, Jin thought. He couldn't think of who else the man might be. The Kahnen would not take any chances while being so surrounded by the People. The People who apparently loved them.

The Great Kahn raised his hands, and a hush rolled over the grounds. 'People of Valrue,' he called, his quiet voice echoed by a number of KahnenSpeakers spaced about the crowd.

'Welcome to the first day of the Celebrations. We are here to honour your strength, your endurance, your dedication to us, the Eighth House. Today marks my twenty-sixth year as Great Kahn. This privilege is all that matters to me. I will slave to your desires. I will rip the throats from anyone who dares to harm you. I will gut those who take from you. I will fight eternally for you, my People of Valrue.'

The People became frenzied, spittle flying and eyes rolling as they howled their approval at his words, the thought of their great leader spilling blood beckoning the beasts from them. The platform jerked under Jin's feet, and the performers next to him cried out and clutched at each other.

The Great Kahn raised his hands again, and silence fell once more, even more absolute than the last.

'Our brave new Krijen walk with us today, victorious from yesterday's dances. They have joined the ranks of the most formidable warriors, the ones amongst you in black. Right now, we stand on the very squares they sweated on, paying with their blood and grit, to bring you protection and peace. Their honourable leader is here today to start the Celebrations. Come join me, my friend, Oji Mimundmen, FaKrijen of Valrue.'

CHAPTER 46:
SID BHA

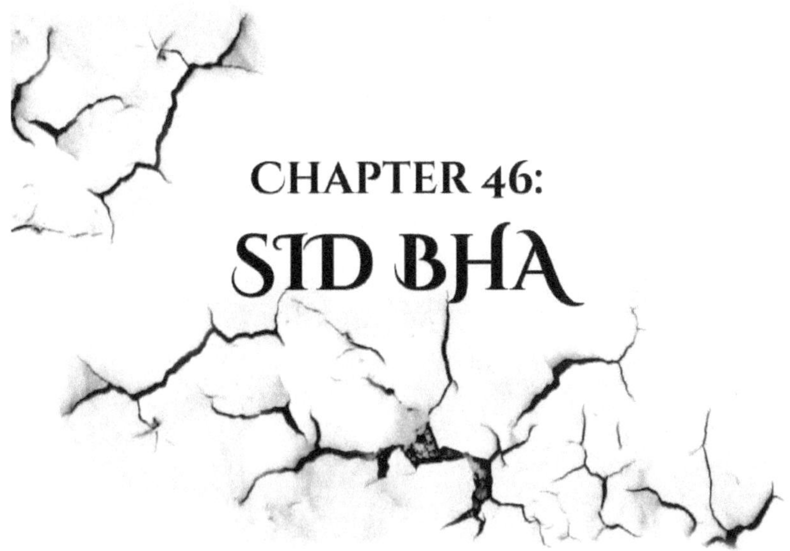

From where Sid stood raised above the crowd, the People looked like the animals he remembered from his younger days. They were heaving, wild creatures that pawed at the ground and threw back their heads, froth dripping from their mouths. People swelled around the stage, kept back only by the threat of the Krijen blades. Sid didn't understand the Kahnen, their lips wet with their cravings for the attention of the crowd.

As the Great Kahn called Oji's name and the FaKrijen stepped forward, something distracted Sid. In front of the stage, the People were parting in the most unnatural way, as though something of great momentum was bowling through at waist height.

A boy appeared at the front, unfurling from a crouched position at the base of the steps. There was something wrong with him. No youth should have that look in his eyes. The eyes were looking at Oji.

The boy placed a foot on the steps. Immediately the Krijen reacted, krije tips held up to him. The people nearest screamed and shoved backwards, unsteadying the crowd.

'Stand down,' Oji commanded.

The Krijen lowered their weapons.

The boy continued up the steps. He moved with a curious gait, as though he wasn't used to being on two feet. Oji stepped forward to meet him, his arms hanging limp by his sides, weaponless. He opened his mouth to speak.

Then there was a crack like a bone snapping, and Oji was gone, and in his place, there was nothing but a haze of red that gently settled over Sid and the Kahnen beside him.

CHAPTER 47: JIN KANJU

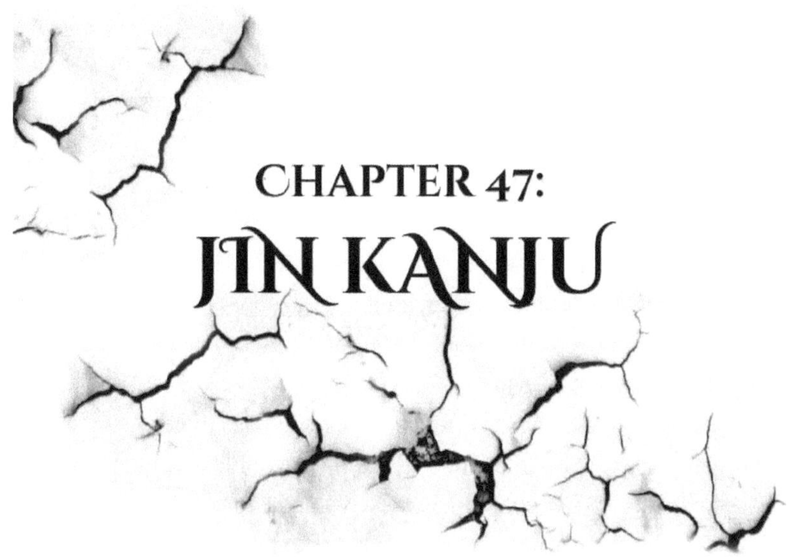

Jin couldn't hear much other than the cheering of the crowd when Oji walked towards the Great Kahn.

Suddenly, the Krijen on stage surged forwards with their krije held before them, surrounding what looked like a streetling attempting to walk up the steps. Jin's own hands shot to hover above the daggers at his thighs.

Tense, he watched, eyes narrowed at the streetling. After a pause, the Krijen inexplicably lowered their weapons. Then Oji disappeared, his body replaced by a clap of red cloud which hung suspended in the air for a few breaths before fading into the wind.

'Jin,' Filip said in his ear. 'That streetling is a mayj! He just killed Oji!'

No. Not possible. Oji wouldn't go down without a fight. It was simply a trick of the light. Jin blinked rapidly, searching for Oji.

Then the chaos started.

People surged back from the central stage, creating a tidal wave of bodies. Within moments, it crashed into the platform Jin stood on. A jagged crack appeared in the wood beneath his feet a second before it exploded, sending Jin, Filip, and the performers tumbling into its splintery mouth.

One of the performers screamed as a large piece of wood pierced her shoulder. Simultaneously, a small ball of fire soared over Jin's head, through the floating debris, showering him with flecks of oil that reeked of shit. The air above him ignited for a moment, and people shrieked and covered their heads, diving blindly into the masses.

Jin could feel his power surging in his chest as he dragged himself from the wreckage, splinters snatching at his wraps. Once free, he leant back in and grabbed hold of one of the performers' hands, tugging her free from the ruined platform.

The one with the chunk of wood in her shoulder didn't even see his hand when he reached in for her. Instead, she clutched at the wood, her fingers slipping on her own blood, clearly unable to believe her eyes. Jin wrapped a hand under her arm, pulling her out and setting her on her feet. She looked at him, still dazed, then her gaze drifted up above his head. Her face changed from disbelief to horror.

'Wait!' Jin cried out, wanting to help her, but she'd already shoved backwards from him and was quickly carried away by the crowd.

Jin looked up. The flaming ball that had passed above them had apparently flown rogue. There were many more in the air now, all arching towards the central stage, coming from where the seventh square would be marked on the ground. Jin could try to pluck them from the air with majik, but the Kahnen might see.

He had to get to them.

Jin began to shove through the crowd towards the stage, Filip right behind him. Above the cordoned-off area where Jin had been searching for Aren, the sunshades were on fire.

'No, Jin,' Filip warned. 'You have to get to the Eighth House. She might not even be there, and then you'll have wasted time!'

Filip was right.

Jin gritted his teeth and pressed against the flow of the crowd, continuing towards the central stage. It was a painfully slow process. He couldn't lift himself there. Great Kahn only knew what the Kahnen would think if they saw him do that.

There was an endless crush of people. Most were screaming and running in all directions, battering others out of the way, though there were a few standing still, open-mouthed, shock overriding sense as they stared into the sky while flames rained down.

Jin picked up countless people from the sand as he wrestled onwards, shoving them back at their tearful companions. As he went, he realised it was going to be immensely difficult to get the Kahnen out. Whose arrogance was to blame for putting the main stage in the *middle?*

Jin could hear the Kahnen screaming. He looked up at the stage, still quite a distance away. The Krijen were pressing against the Eighth House, trying to force them down off the platform, out of harm's way, while leaving their own bodies terribly exposed. Jin couldn't fathom why the Kahnen resisted.

The Great Kahn was in the centre, the KahnenMayj at his side. But the KahnenMayj was doing nothing. He stood still, his eyes darting overhead, watching the flaming balls and blatantly ignoring what was happening before him on the stage.

Jin felt a bolt of anger strike through him, making his fingers sting. 'Why isn't he doing anything? What's he waiting for?'

'I don't know,' Filip replied, 'but they're standing on a perfectly good shield.' It was true. The stage was enormous and solid. It would burn slowly. But Jin didn't want the Kahnen to see.

He pressed harder into the crowd, refraining from bolstering himself with power. The Kahnen wouldn't see that, but he was worried that if he overdid it, he might hurt people. He was infuriatingly far away still.

A Krijen on the stage was suddenly alight with flame. The Kahn nearest to him shrieked and shoved him away from her. He toppled into the crowd.

'You need to do something!' Filip yelled at Jin.

It was the bandit attack all over again. Jin felt trapped, hating the weight of his useless daggers strapped at his thighs. His chest hurt as his power reared its head, awakened at the prospect of release. His recent efforts to burn himself out had been in vain.

'I *can't!* What if the Kahnen see?'

'Just harness, Jin!' Filip yelled. 'It doesn't matter if the Kahnen see. You answer to the FaKrijen!'

'Oji is dead –'

'So? The Kahnen can't do shit to you without a FaKrijen. You're untouchable unless your squad leader commands it now. Pago was there when Oji give you permission to harness. He won't go back on it.'

'But what if –'

'All I'm hearing is that you're a coward, Jin!'

Filip spoke them, but they were his father's words. Jin couldn't disappoint him, not now, after everything he'd made it through.

Here we go again then.

As Jin ran, he threw out a hand and sank his fingers into the air, grasping the edge of the stage ahead of him with majik. Allowing his power to burst from him, he pulled hard, tilting the entire thing onto its side, without breaking stride. The Kahnen and Krijen slid down its length, toppling over the steps at the front. The Great Kahn leapt off gracefully, the KahnenMayj just behind him.

As Jin hoped, the stage was high enough that the flaming balls thudded into it and rolled down, leaving lines of fire, but the Kahnen beneath it untouched. Satisfied, Jin let go of his majik. Thankfully, the stage stayed upright on its own.

Having finally arrived, Jin raced around the back of the stage towards the Krijen who had been hit by one of the balls of flame. The Krijen was screaming, contorting on the ground as his wraps melted onto him, while people swatted desperately at him, trying to douse the flames.

Jin elbowed through and fell to his knees beside the Krijen. He reached out with majik, trying to snatch at the flames, but they slipped through his fingers.

'It's not working!'

'Grab the oil,' Filip said. Jin did as he was told, and to his relief, the oil came free. Bit by bit he pulled it from the Krijen, smearing it onto the ground, ignoring the crowd behind him who were retching on the smell of burning flesh. Eventually, the Krijen stopped screaming and lay shivering, smoke rising off him.

Jin looked at two bystanders who were staring down at him in horror. 'Don't let people step on him,' Jin said. 'Move him if you can.' They nodded, their faces scared. Jin hoped it wasn't because of him.

As Jin stood up, Vulmin and Pago burst out of the crowd ahead of him, racing around the stage towards the Eighth House. Jin sprinted to catch up, almost colliding with Pago when his squad leader suddenly pulled up short.

Pago was looking astonishedly at the Kahnen, who were all extravagantly dishevelled, some still picking themselves up off the ground. Pago gazed up the length of the stage towering above them. Then he turned to Jin.

'Did you do this?'

'Yes,' Jin replied, feeling a spike of fear when Pago stiffened. Jin hoped that Oji's recent outburst was still fresh in Pago's mind. It was a lot to accept that one of his squad members was harnessing in the middle of the city.

'Orders?' Jin prompted, hoping that their current state of peril would distract Pago from his shock. To Jin's relief, Pago turned to the Krijen. 'Get them up!' he commanded, indicating to the Eighth House. 'We'll move them through the back exit as planned!'

Jin moved forward to pull the Kahnen up off the ground. The Krijen formed a protective circle around them, facing outwards. Jin reached a hand behind his back and grabbed the hilt of his krije, pulling it from his wraps.

'Send the signal!' Pago yelled. 'Is the exit clear?'

A blue flare went up overhead as Pago leant over to Jin. 'Have you seen Meek or Jokah?'

Jin shook his head.

'Is-is Oji dead?' Pago looked so young all of a sudden, his eyes pleading. Jin felt sorry for the word that came out of his mouth. 'Yes.'

Pago raised a trembling hand to his head. 'Shit.'

Despite everything that was happening, Jin felt strangely calm about the FaKrijen. Numb even, apart from the twitch in his fingers, the raging heat in his chest, the ringing in his ears. Which was numb for him.

Meek burst through the crowd and spotted the circle of Krijen. He dashed to Pago.

'Sir, the exit is blocked. The area has been overwhelmed by streetlings. I think they planned it.'

The colour drained from Pago's face. 'And the Krijen posted there?'

'Dead, sir. The streetlings had mayjen. I-I couldn't help.' Meek looked at Jin, his expression devastating.

Again, Jin felt that gut-wrenching guilt he'd experienced in the Deadlands. He should have been there to fight against those streetlings. He could have helped. But he'd been too busy worrying about himself.

As Meek joined the circle on his other side, Jin looked around at the Krijen, stoically holding their positions despite the fire, the surges of the crowd, and the gross lack of faith from the Kahnen. Their faces were set, and their heads kept turning to Pago, waiting for orders. Jin realised then that the Krijen he'd rescued from the flames must have been their squad leader. They needed a new one to turn to.

Glancing over his shoulder, Jin could see Vulmin on the other side of the circle, his red hair visible above the Kahnen. Just as Jin was wondering where the oldest squad member was, Jokah burst from the crowd, having finally fought his way through. He quickly slid in next to Vulmin.

Within their circle, the Kahnen had squashed themselves together in terror. The Great Kahn was visible in the centre, his red cloak too bright a target. Jin wished he would take it off. Next to the Great Kahn was the KahnenMayj, looking up at the stage as though someone had just eaten his dinner. From what Jin had seen, he had yet to make any effort to protect the Kahnen at all, content to let the Krijen make the sacrifices. Jin couldn't put into words how much he already hated the man.

'Jin? What should I do?'

Jin turned his head to Pago, hearing a note of fear in his voice. His squad leader was breathing rapidly, his fists white on his krije hilt. Meek was watching Pago too, a small frown line between his eyes.

'You're squad leader,' Jin said. 'It's your call.'

Pago's jaw clenched, and he nodded but gave no commands. The circle of Kahnen heaved, as though sensing something was wrong.

'Pago,' Jin said. 'Take a breath. We need to get the Kahnen out. Think it through.'

Pago took a deep breath, as advised.

'He's freaking out,' Filip said loudly to Jin. Jin bit his tongue to stop himself from snarling at Filip. It was true, but Pago just needed some time. They had a little to spare. Just a little.

Flames were growing threateningly close. Having consumed the sunshades nearby, they now licked at the wooden platforms on either side of the main stage. The air was hot around them, the stage burning above. But the sandy ground shouldn't allow the fire to cross to their feet.

Meek opened his mouth, but Jin held up his hand. *Wait.*

Eventually, Pago spoke. 'We'll have to get out through the main exit,' he said, his voice small. 'The back exit is blocked.'

Jin nodded as his squad leader looked up at him, terror now stark on his face.

'What do we do if the streetling mayj comes back?' Pago asked. Jin felt Meek shudder at the question. The bandit attack was obviously still raw for them both.

The image of the boy on the stage flashed into Jin's mind. Heat rampaged through his blood vessels, so intense it hurt. His rage at the FaKrijen's death had finally found him, through the numbness. What he wouldn't give to know where that murderous mayj was right now. Jin would strangle him like he did the last one.

'Just let him try,' Jin spat.

'Hey, Jin,' Filip said, distracting him. 'Where is Sid?'

CHAPTER 48:
SID BHA

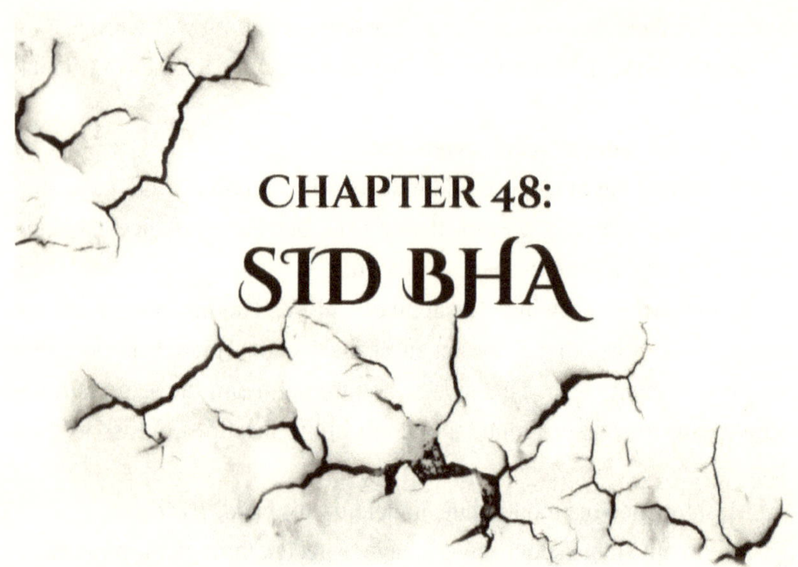

Sid blinked, hardly believing his eyes. He blinked again and wiped his face. The backs of his hands were wet with red. Vaguely, he was aware of shouting around him.

In quick succession he was jostled, grabbed by the arms, then hauled right off the front edge of the stage. Sid came to his senses when his knees hit wood, because it hurt more than he could have imagined.

He was on the bottom steps of the stage. People were running in all directions, just a series of legs flashing endlessly past him. A Krijen appeared by his side and pressed him down into the crook of the stairs. 'Keep your head down!' the Krijen yelled. 'They're firing at us!' Sid did not know what he meant.

Something hot grazed his cheek and landed, spitting fire, next to his hand. It looked like a little ball of flame, dripping oil and reeking of human excrement.

The screaming was so loud that Sid couldn't think straight. He huddled down as another Krijen landed on his other side, flashing krije in hand, swatting away balls of flame.

'The KahnenMayjen! Where are the KahnenMayjen?'

Sid looked up at the angry voice. Lord Salli stood at the top of the stairs, wrestling with a Krijen who was trying to protect him from the missiles.

'Get *off* me!' Lord Oman yelled, slapping away another Krijen who was trying to pull him down the steps after Sid. The Krijen let go but shadowed him closely, unwilling to leave his side.

A red figure drew Sid's stare. The Great Kahn stood erect in the middle of the stage, Stolt next to him, along with three Krijen, pressed in close. Whether he was in shock or if it were on purpose, the Great Kahn clearly did not intend to move. The Krijen did not seem willing to force him either, unlike the other Kahnen.

Sid could sense the Krijen's frustration. Of the Kahnen, only Lord Flynn and Lord Reider crouched on the steps with Sid, allowing the Krijen to stand guard over them. The other Kahnen resisted all efforts to get them off the stage, instead clawing their way back towards the middle.

Towards Stolt, Sid realised. The only KahnenMayj in sight. The Kahnen didn't care for Krijen protection, not after what had just happened to Oji. They wanted majik.

'*Where are the other KahnenMayjen?*' Lord Oman yelled, repeating Lord Salli's question as he pushed against his Krijen protector.

'There are no others,' the Great Kahn replied blandly. He could have been standing in an empty square, counting the grains of sand, he appeared so unfazed by his surroundings.

'What did you say, my Great Lord?' Lady Macey asked, looking mortified. 'There are *no other* KahnenMayjen?'

Lady Hia clutched at the Krijen standing next to her, grabbing fistfuls of his wraps. 'We're going to die here!'

'We can protect you,' the Krijen said, grabbing her wrists, 'but you have to listen to us!'

'Protect us?' Lord Salli sneered at the Krijen. 'Did you not see what that skahk did? He turned the FaKrijen into *nothing!* You cannot help us!'

At his words, the Kahnen all began yelling over each other.

'We're going to die here!' Lady Hia screamed again, tears streaming down her face.

There were so many balls of flame coming at them now that the air was hot. Sid watched in horror as one of the Krijen caught fire, his sleeve suddenly wet with oil spatters. Lady Elira, who stood on the other side of the man, screamed and pushed the Krijen away from her. He fell off the steps into the crowd.

The world tilted.

Sid saw blue sky below his feet, then crashed into a wall of legs, finally coming to a jarring stop face-first on the ground. Dirt sprayed into his eyes, and he accidentally breathed it in, sending him into a coughing fit.

Terrified of being trampled, Sid tried to stand up, but the ground bucked beneath him, and he fell again, landing on his bruised knees.

Eyes watering, he crawled, moving forward because he didn't know where else to go until suddenly he found himself blinking at a pair of icy blue eyes framed by curling black hair. Sid froze, not quite believing what he was seeing.

It was the mayj who had obliterated Oji.

The boy was hunched into a ball, his limp fingers curled strangely across his face as though playing a poor version of peek-a-boo. Sid stared at the boy, who stared back through his fingers.

Legs cascaded past them, completely unaware that Oji's murderer cowered in their midst. Sid was certain he would feel a boot to his head soon, or someone would surely trip over them and fall. But not a single person touched either of them.

This close, Sid could see that the boy was older than he'd first appeared, despite being barely larger than a child. Sid began to doubt himself. Maybe he'd misremembered the boy's face. This petrified creature didn't seem like a killer.

Sid wasn't sure how long they stayed there, staring at each other, until suddenly the boy's eyes flicked up, and he scrambled away, leaving Sid alone in the sand.

Something powerful gripped Sid by the back of his robes and wrenched him upright with such force his feet briefly left the ground.

'Sid! Are you okay?'

It took a moment for Sid to recognise who had picked him up. The young man looked older, his jaw more angular. His hair was shaved around his ears in the Krijen style; the rest had grown longer and blonder, bleached by the sun.

'Jin!'

Jin put an arm around Sid and practically carried him back to the Eighth House, who now stood huddled in a circle of Krijen.

'Jin! I-I think I just saw the boy –'

'Take this, Sid!' Jin pressed a knife into his hand. 'Go with Vulmin! That Krijen there – go!' Jin shoved him towards a gruff-looking older Krijen.

'Wait! Jin!'

But Jin was gone. Sid hesitated, but the Krijen who was called Vulmin growled, and Sid hurried to his side, allowing himself to be dragged into the inner circle with the Eighth House. They were all in shadow.

Sid looked up. The stage which they had stood on now lay on its edge, towering above them. Sid shivered. Had the boy who'd killed Oji done that?

Sid tugged on Vulmin's arm. 'Excuse me, the mayj –'

Silence crashed down around them. Sid stopped talking, conscious of how loud his voice suddenly was. Vulmin and the other Krijen shifted, stepping together and tightening the gaps in their protective circle. Sid ducked down, peering past Vulmin's waist. His stomach dropped out beneath him at what he saw.

They were surrounded by a wall of filthy, stick-thin youths armed with nails, belts with sharp buckles, and old horseshoes, their tips filed to points. Their eyes were keen, and they licked their lips wickedly. It was an army of streetlings, thirsting for Kahnen blood.

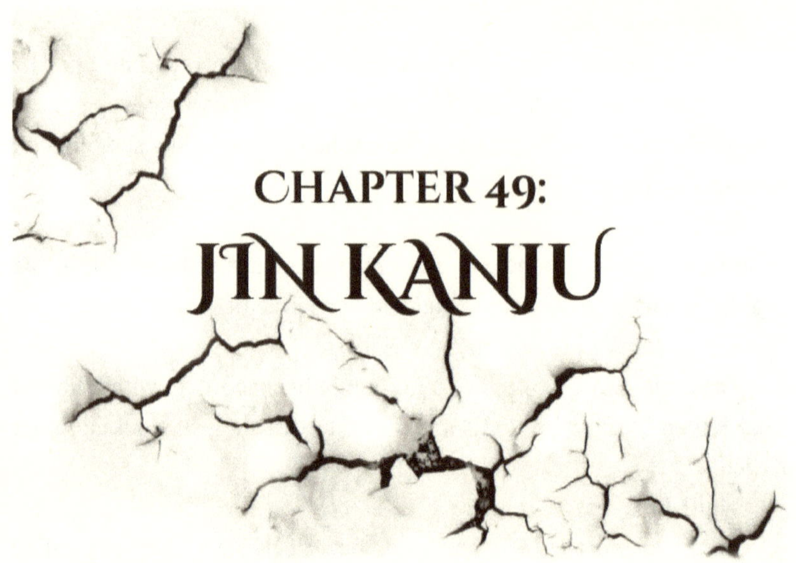

CHAPTER 49:
JIN KANJU

Jin was facing a wall of savage-looking youths.

Although the flames around them had subsided, trapped by the sand, he was sweating from the fire raging in his chest. It was so high in his throat that he was almost choking on it.

'Calm down, Jin,' Filip said quietly. 'Don't give us away just yet.'

There was a fuss in the streetlings nearest to them, and they parted, a streetling girl stepping through. She had on a wide-brimmed floppy black hat and red ties around her wrists. From the way the streetlings looked at her, they held her in reverence, an odd contrast to their rabid appearances.

Jin glanced at Pago. He looked like he was about to vomit.

The girl with the red wrist ties grinned wickedly, baring her teeth. 'Welcome to the prelude to your Reckonings,' she said. Her voice was high and sweet. Jin couldn't understand why this surprised him. She was little more than a child, after all.

'Thank you for setting this up today. What a wonderful opportunity for us to have that chat that I've *so* been wanting.' The streetlings around her cackled. The girl smiled around at them all until they quietened. Then she threw her arms wide.

'Kahnen! You have done nothing but prove that you are not fit to govern. Look at us! Do we look like satisfied citizens to you?'

The streetlings jeered this time, shaking their fists at the Eighth House and their Krijen protectors. Jin wished he could turn to see the reactions of the Kahnen behind him, but he didn't dare take his eyes off the girl. In the corners of his vision, the streetlings pulled vulgar faces at him, trying to goad a response.

'To make this much easier on us all, I have a simple request for you.' The girl clasped her hands behind her back and began to stroll up and down, her steps wide and slow, throwing the Kahnen mocking smiles at every turn. She paced for so long that the streetlings began to hoot softly in anticipation.

Jin's hand ached from the prolonged stranglehold on his krije, the hilt so hot from his bridled power that it was burning him. He quickly slid his krije behind his back, instead pulling a dagger from his thigh wraps. He preferred his dagger anyway. He would keep a hand free for harnessing. The streetlings closest to him pointed and jumped up and down, excited by his movement.

'Listen to me!' The girl stopped mid-stride and turned to the Kahnen again. 'There are those among you who are worse than the worst of us! And that's pretty bad.'

The hooting grew louder.

'You know who you are,' the girl continued. 'I won't drone on. My request is simple. You will stand down from the Eighth House.'

The hooting grew to an unbearable volume. It even drowned out the ringing in Jin's ears.

'I'll give you until sundown, I think!' the girl bellowed over the sound of the streetlings. 'Meet me at the bridge. You know the one. It's your favourite place to string us up.' She winked at them. 'And if you plead innocent, if you try to blame someone else, make sorry excuses for your indiscretions – as I'm sure you like to call them – I will make you swallow your lies.' She made a strange gesture, running her finger across her chin, tongue lolling to the side.

The streetlings screamed in delight, shaking each other. It made Jin feel sick.

He felt movement behind him, and Pago stepped away from his side. Jin glanced back, unexpectedly finding himself looking down into the eyes of the Great Kahn.

Jin hadn't seen him up close until now. The Great Kahn had deep-set eyes above high cheekbones and a jaw that was beyond smooth, highlighting the flawless rich brown of his skin. His black hair was straight and pulled back, not a streak of grey. Had Jin not been standing so close, he might have missed that despite his calm outwards demeanour, the Great Kahn's eyes blazed.

The KahnenMayj came up behind him. Jin almost hissed; he was so angry with the man. But there was something else there too, something prodding his nerves, making him want to step away.

The KahnenMayj's eyes snapped to Jin's, narrowing to slits.

'He doesn't like you either,' said Filip.

'Move aside,' the Great Kahn said in his quiet voice, recapturing Jin's attention.

Jin fell into position on the Great Kahn's exposed side. He would not leave the Great Kahn with no protection other than that useless KahnenMayj.

When she saw who was coming to greet her, the streetling girl folded her arms and smiled widely, looking rather pleased with herself.

'I have a question,' the Great Kahn said softly, stopping in the gap between the Krijen and the streetlings. Everyone leant forwards to hear him better.

To Jin's surprise, the Great Kahn pulled a sword from beneath his gown. The blade was dark green with golden webbing across its surface. He held it slightly away from his body, point towards the ground.

The streetlings stilled, no longer hooting, all eyes on his sword.

'You come here to threaten us,' the Great Kahn said to the streetling girl. 'You terrify my citizens. You ruin their day of Celebration. You set fire to the streets they call home. Yet you stand before me, claiming there are Kahnen in my house who are *worse* than you?'

The Kahnen shuffled uncomfortably behind Jin. One woman was

trembling so much that Jin could hear the golden drops on her gown rattling.

The Great Kahn lifted his blade, inspecting the edge, as though he thought it more interesting than the streetling girl's accusations. 'Would you care to enlighten me as to the nature of these . . . indiscretions?'

He puts on a great show, Jin thought. Only he could see the gentle shake of the Great Kahn's hand, clenched on the hilt of his sword. The man was furious.

The streetling girl's smile stretched further. Jin was sure her lips must split soon.

'Oh no,' she said. 'That would ruin all the fun now, wouldn't it?'

The Great Kahn slowly lowered his sword. 'A shame. Nonetheless, colour me intrigued. Let us say your claims are true and the rightfully accused Kahnen step down. Who did you have in mind to replace them? My citizens would be interested to know.'

'Oh, don't stress about having to organise another vote,' the girl said sweetly. 'We will pick the replacements.'

'You think yourselves above the vote?'

'I would say above, but it could be below. I never know what all the little black lines on the paper mean, you know?'

The streetlings loved this, hooting their approval. The Great Kahn's composure seemed to fracture, cracks splitting across its surface. All it would take was the tap of a fingernail to shatter it.

'Unfortunately,' the Great Kahn said, 'that is not how we do things in Valrue. You are not above the People. You will vote like everyone else.'

'Like everyone else?' the girl replied, raising an eyebrow. 'Okay then, can you please explain to me what cronyism means? I feel like it's important, but –'

The Great Kahn took a lunging step closer to the girl. Alarmed, Jin matched him. The Great Kahn's anger was clear now, a tempest beneath the fragile surface.

'Since you clearly have no interest in our democracy,' the Great Kahn growled, 'my Kahnen and I will not entertain this request of yours. Let us pass, or I will have the Krijen execute you for insurrection.'

The smile slid off the streetling girl's face. 'You're in no position to make threats,' she said. 'You have, by my count, fifteen Krijen and one KahnenMayj. I have the might of all the streetling gangs and *countless* mayjen. You can't risk it. You don't have as much control as you think you do.'

The Great Kahn's facade ruptured as he swung his blade at her.

CHAPTER 50:
SID BHA

Sid did not see what happened, but he knew it was bad, because the wall of streetlings was coming up to meet them. Metal clanged, and children yelled, and Sid put his hands over his head so all he could see was Vulmin's back as it twisted and tensed with exertion.

He was gripping the knife that Jin had given him, wishing the young Krijen had kept it. Sid might be trained to fight, but in a carefully controlled setting with a single opponent and rules. Not like this.

Streetlings were scratching, biting, gouging at any flesh in reach while Krijen slit throats, caved in tiny chests, and hurled the youths into the air to protect their crop of Kahnen, ripe for picking.

There were so many streetlings. Bold hands breached Krijen walls, snatching at the gold adornments on the clothes of the Kahnen. The Krijen sliced at little fingers and cracked heads, tossing bodies aside.

'No,' Sid gasped. 'Stop, *please*, they just want our finery!' He pulled weakly on the back of Vulmin's wraps, but the Krijen shoved him back, out of the way.

'They aren't attacking to kill!' Sid cried. No one was listening.

Sid pulled his robe over his head, leaving him in his undergarments

– a plain shirt and trousers – and held it out in front of himself, his eyes squeezed shut. Immediately, Sid felt a forceful tug on the end of it, and he was ripped from the circle of Krijen into a swarm of streetlings. They clawed at his hands, and he released the robe quickly, watching in horror as they tore it every which way. He backed away.

A yell went up ahead. The streetlings froze, then dove to the side, clearing a space. From their midst strode a boy, remarkably solid for a streetling, a strange patchwork of leather covering his shoulders. Behind him was the streetling girl with the red wrist ties who'd spoken to the Great Kahn.

The streetling boy stopped in front of her and knelt on the ground, hands pressed into the sand. He tucked his head down, as though he was about to start a running race. Sid watched in disbelief as the girl swung an enormous loaded crossbow up and onto his shoulders. She took aim.

Sid turned and ran, hearing the sickening twang as the girl fired upon the circle of Kahnen.

CHAPTER 51:
PAKKER

Pakker was crouched atop the training grounds wall thinking about the Bhouli girl when Oji became nothing but red in the wind.

Pakker blinked. If he wasn't mistaken, he'd seen the boy walking up the steps of the stage just before it happened. So he'd done it, after all.

Then the chaos began.

Spectators close to the stage threw themselves backwards as black-wrapped Krijen dove forwards. At the same time, balls of flame burst into the air, the crowd below them screaming in terror.

The entirety of the seventh square was filled with streetlings. Something was going down in the gangs. Pakker had not been into Rue for so long he'd missed out on the whispers of it.

He watched as the streetlings hurled another round of homemade missiles towards the stage. He noted with interest that few of them reached it. Others were overshooting. Either the streetlings had terrible aim, or they were missing on purpose. The first seemed much more likely, given Pakker had never known streetlings to show any kind of restraint, but he'd learned long ago not to make assumptions. Surprises did not bode well for mercenaries.

High-pitched screams to Pakker's right dragged his attention to the distant end of the grounds. The crowd there was a mess of citizens, black-wrapped figures, and belt-slung bodies of streetlings. Pakker imagined blades flashing and gore flying.

He leant forward as he watched. There were hundreds of streetlings by that exit alone, and the Krijen were heavily outnumbered. Not that it should have mattered, but the streetlings were not falling back as they should. In fact, it was the Krijen who were falling. Pakker knew his eyes were not deceiving him. He could only assume the streetlings had mayjen.

Pakker looked back to the central stage. The blood-red cloak of the Great Kahn was in the centre. He had not moved since the FaKrijen had been killed. Pakker could not see the Great Kahn's face from here, but he seemed calm, despite the bedlam. Either that, or the Great Kahn was just panicking on the inside. The Great Kahn knew he need not fear Drax, though Pakker was unsure about the streetlings, unexpected as they were. Perhaps there was something that Pakker did not know.

The KahnenMayj Stolt had taken a few steps closer to the Great Kahn and was looking up at the flaming missiles. Of course, Stolt wouldn't do anything unless absolutely necessary. Pakker could see the logic in that, given how apparently useless he was, and it was better to look lazy than inadequate. It was one of the many reasons why the Great Kahn always spoke so derisively of him. Pakker had assumed that 'useless' meant he was lacking in power, yet the Great Kahn seemed content to keep Stolt by his side today. Maybe not so powerless after all.

To Pakker's amusement, it looked like the rest of the Eighth House had completely lost their minds. He watched as they fought their Krijen guards, desperately trying to shove their way towards Stolt. The Kahnen thought the KahnenMayj was going to save them, faithless that the Krijen could protect them from Drax. Pakker could understand that, given what they'd seen the boy do to the FaKrijen.

What Pakker did not understand was why the stage they stood on suddenly tilted, dumping Kahnen and Krijen alike into the masses. Black-wrapped Krijen converged around the sprawled Kahnen, the red cloak in the middle.

Drax would not have done it. Had it been Stolt who tipped the stage? Surely not. The Great Kahn had been in no immediate danger. It would have been wasteful. Perhaps there was an unknown mayj in the midst, other than Stolt and Drax.

Pakker realised he'd grown distracted, and silently berated himself. He had to find the boy.

It took a while in the chaos, but eventually Pakker spotted the telltale pockets of crowd bulging around something at waist height, not far from the stage.

Pakker turned his eyes briefly back to the stage, watching as the surrounding crowd changed. Streetlings converged from every side, weaving their way towards the upturned stage, passing spectators running in the opposite direction.

Pakker checked in on the boy. He couldn't see him. Perhaps he'd stopped moving. Pakker's eyes turned back to the Kahnen.

In the seconds he had looked away, the Kahnen had become completely surrounded. A lanky figure in a hat stepped forward, tiny spots of red at her wrists. Pakker knew who she was. Pyra. She was one of the streetling gang leaders.

Pyra was speaking; the commotion settling around her. The streetlings began hooting, a dull throb that grew into a jarring roar, echoing around the training grounds and sending the still fleeing crowd into new peals of terror.

Pakker quickly searched for the boy again, but he still couldn't spot him. Either Pakker had lost him, or the boy remained stationary in the crowd. The later was more likely. Pakker's eyes darted back to the middle.

The Great Kahn's red cloak pushed forwards to meet Pyra. Pakker didn't know what was going on, which was rare for him. He didn't like it. He still couldn't see the Great Kahn's face as he spoke to Pyra.

The Great Kahn pulled out his sword, an obvious threat. *Surely not,* Pakker thought. What would possess the Great Kahn to do such a thing? Even from here, Pakker could sense the unease rolling off Stolt.

Pakker did not mind if the Great Kahn lived or died; he cared nothing for the sordid man. But surely the Great Kahn would not risk losing everything, just when he thought he'd got it all, by attacking a streetling gang leader.

The Great Kahn swung his sword.

Cursing, Pakker leapt to his feet and ran along the section of wall just above the main exit, searching for the boy. Finally, he spotted him. The boy's movements were odd, broken by sudden pauses, before backtracking, then changing direction. It took a moment for Pakker to realise that Drax was following something. Or someone.

Pakker leapt nimbly down into the crowd, careful to keep Drax in sight but struggling to concentrate, stuck on the Great Kahn's mindless attack. He followed the boy out of the grounds, and they were almost at the bridge when Pakker figured out who he was trailing. It was Sid Bha, the Weapons Master. He had slipped away from the Kahnen and shaken off his riches. *What a smart man*, Pakker thought. Sid Bha was almost unrecognizable in his plain undergarments that were dyed a faint red at the wrists, matching his face. It was probably the FaKrijen's blood.

As the rushing crowd thinned, Pakker could see Drax following the Weapons Master with a hint of desperation, tripping over his own legs to stay close to Sid Bha, panicking when people stepped in his way.

The boy glanced behind him and spotted Pakker. They locked eyes.

Pakker stopped mid-stride, causing people to shout as they bumped into him, hurrying to escape from the Celebrations. The boy turned and scurried up into the streets of Val.

Pakker, for once, was torn. The Great Kahn's plan crumbled further with every step the boy took, though it was still salvageable. It wouldn't take much to remind Drax who his master was.

But the Great Kahn might not survive his own madness today. Even if he did, there might be another way, one that didn't involve the boy. One that wasn't dependent on letting Felle get her way. There would be more coin in it too.

Pakker stood and watched the boy disappear into Val, then turned on his heel and headed back the way he'd come.

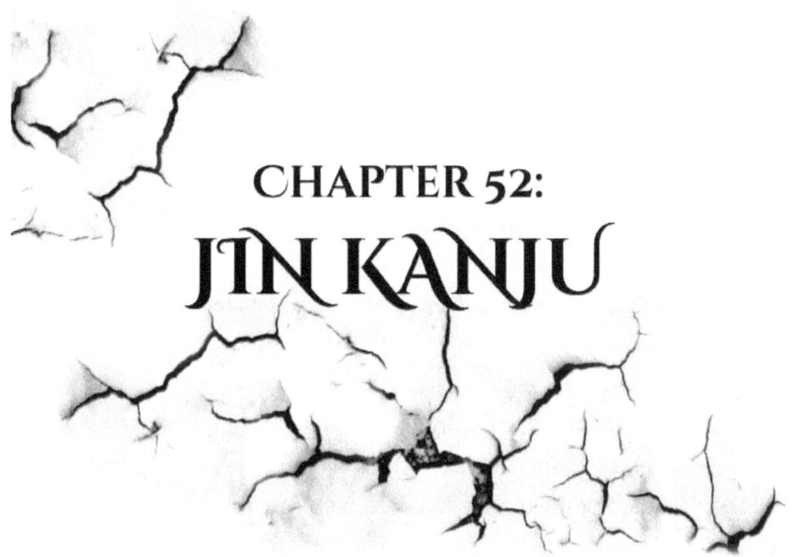

CHAPTER 52:
JIN KANJU

The streetling girl ducked not a second too late, the green blade whizzing over the top of her hat. The streetlings charged with their weapons in the air, hollering at the top of their lungs.

It was something else, Jin thought, to have children running at you, full of bloodlust. Jin couldn't deny that he hesitated.

A streetling leapt at the Great Kahn, and Jin stepped forward, cracking the youth on the head with his dagger.

'You have to kill them,' Filip said.

'But they are children!' Jin protested.

'They're streetlings,' Filip spat. 'They're not innocent. Their mayj murdered Oji.'

Jin hugged the Great Kahn's side, punching and elbowing with as much strength as he dared. The streetling skulls cracked more easily than those of adults.

The Great Kahn was swinging his sword, sharing none of Jin's sentiment, though the weapon was too long to be used properly in such close quarters.

'My Great Lord!' Jin yelled at him, the title sounding ridiculous on his tongue. 'Get behind me!'

The Great Kahn completely ignored him.

Fuck, these Kahnen are arrogant, Jin thought. He flung the closest streetling into the air by the scruff of his neck, sparing them a second or two. He pulled a second dagger from his wraps and pressed it to the Great Kahn's chest. 'Use this!' Jin yelled.

The Great Kahn sheathed his sword and took the weapon wordlessly, immediately slashing at his closest assailant.

As shockingly *reckless* as it was to attack the streetling girl, Jin felt an unexpected surge of respect for the Great Kahn. At least he wasn't cowering behind the warm body of a Krijen.

The KahnenMayj was finally doing something. Makeshift weapons flew away from them as he tore them from streetlings hands, much like the mayj had done during the bandit attack. Even though Jin knew the KahnenMayj was on their side, the reminder made his blood boil.

Suddenly, Jin was wrestling with a little streetling who had leapt clean of the crowd and landed on him, repeatedly hitting him on the head with something heavy. Jin reached up with his free hand and dragged the boy off, slamming him into the sand and holding him down. The streetling slashed at his arm with a glove spiked with nails, leaving long deep cuts through Jin's wraps into his skin. Jin dropped his dagger and punched the streetling hard in the head, and he flopped back, unconscious.

Filip was suddenly in Jin's face, screaming at him. 'Why aren't you killing them, Jin? You killed me! Why is it so hard for you to do the same to these murderous little streetlings?'

Jin looked up in shock at Filip, completely distracted. 'Killing you was an accident –'

'No, it wasn't! You can't lie to me, Jin. Now do what I say, or you're going to end up regretting it!'

Jin clenched his teeth and looked down at the streetling boy, whose eyes were closed, his mouth open, a lump already swelling on his head. Jin picked up his dagger from the dirt and hovered it above the boy's throat, hesitating, hating himself.

'On your left!' Filip yelled.

Jin spun to his feet, thrusting out his empty hand and grabbing hold of a thick arrowhead with majik, making it lurch to a halt just in front of his stomach. Had he not stood up, it would have hit him in the head. Jin released his majik, and the arrow clattered to the ground at his feet.

He looked up to see where it had come from. Ahead of him was a huge crossbow, wielded by the streetling girl, the weapon balanced on the leather-clad shoulders of another youth. Of all the horrors of this world –

Without thinking, Jin focused on the crossbow and squeezed his outstretched hand into a fist. The entire thing crunched, splinters popping away into the air.

The streetling girl screeched, and a dozen rusty knives shot at him at once. Too many. He stopped one in the air with majik and knocked another away with his dagger, but the rest he could only twist away from, and they sliced at him, leaving more cuts along his arms and shoulders, the material of his wraps bursting around him.

Jin turned back to the streetling girl, enraged, only to find her gone. In her place was a willowy boy with a belt strapped over his bare torso. The streetling reached back and pulled out an enormous blade from behind his back, swinging it in one hand.

'You made yourself a target,' Filip said.

'Shut up!' Jin snapped back. The stupid Square enjoyed the luxury of already being dead.

The streetling swung at Jin, who reassessed quickly. Keeping his dagger in one hand, with the other he pulled his krije out from behind his back and bolstered it with a touch of power, bringing it up to greet the streetling's sword. The streetling twisted his blade at the last second so that Jin's krije glanced off it, wasting the force of the blow.

The streetling duelled with a style unknown to Jin, but one that was fuelled with passion. He cared about what he fought for.

'Stop fucking around!' Filip cried. 'Your squad needs you! Finish him!'

Filip was right, again. Jin was holding back, desperate to delay the inevitable slaughter. It felt hideously wrong, but Jin gritted his teeth and obeyed. He pressed forward, swatting the streetling's sword away with his krije, then sliding his dagger across the streetling's throat to make it quick. The streetling dropped.

'Jin!'

Jin spun to see Pago behind him.

'We need to round up the Kahnen!'

Jin nodded. With Pago at his back, he quickly surveyed the scene. Not too far from him, the Great Kahn was still on his feet and fighting furiously, the KahnenMayj at his side. As for the rest of the Eighth House, the streetlings had breached the Krijen's protective circle, and the Kahnen had scattered. The streetling girl had boasted that they had mayjen in their numbers. Meek had said the same.

Jin whipped around, searching for signs of majik. Vulmin was close by, sparring with the same streetling boy who had avoided having his throat cut by Jin earlier, now wielding a thin metal pole with a sharpened end. Two Kahnen huddled on the ground at Vulmin's feet.

The streetling boy moved like a whip, lunging with wicked speed before retreating with a flourish, spinning around in a showy style that Jin normally would have attributed to an amateur fighter, apart from the fact Vulmin couldn't get a mark on him.

Jin snapped his bloodied dagger into the air towards the streetling. The boy saw it coming, and with a small flick of his wrist, the dagger jerked off course and went spinning into the fray.

'He's a mayj,' said Filip.

Master of the fucking obvious, thought Jin.

He started towards Vulmin, sliding his krije behind his back to have two hands free for harnessing. The boy spun like a top with his pole, the tip whizzing so fast it blurred. Suddenly, the boy lashed out, his weapon spearing straight into Vulmin's chest. The Krijen's eyes widened in shock.

Jin roared, bowling streetlings aside. The boy spun in a circle, ripped out the pole, and in the next turn stabbed Vulmin through his gut once more, before wrenching it free.

Vulmin fell to his knees.

Jin crossed the distance in a single majikal bound. He grabbed the slick end of the weapon, ripping it from the boy's grasp. Jin spun it in his hand and rammed the pointy end back down towards the streetling.

The boy grinned and raised his hand to harness the pole aside, but he didn't account for the amount of power Jin poured into his attack. The pole pierced the streetling's cheek and sprouted out the back of his head. Jin felt no mercy for him. He tossed the streetling's body aside, the pole with it.

Jin was raging with power now, his lungs snagging on it. He turned to the two cowering Kahnen, one of whom looked like she was about to faint.

'Get behind me!'

They ran to him, ducking under his arms.

Dagger-less, Jin pulled out his krije once more and sliced a space through the streetlings in front of him. Jokah barrelled through to join them, another Kahn in tow. The terrified man had a gash on his head, and the streetlings had stripped him down to his undergarments, but at least he was alive.

Three Kahnen were up ahead, protected by only two Krijen, struggling under the sheer volume of streetlings. Jin shouldered through, cutting down the youths as he went. It was easy. His fire-fuelled muscles lifted his krije as though it weighed nothing.

As he approached, the Krijen turned towards him in shock, daggers raised, the Kahnen quivering behind them.

Just then, Jin remembered Sid. He paused, his krije held in front of him. 'Where is the Weapons Master?' he asked. No one answered.

Pago appeared to the side, mercilessly dragging another Kahn behind him. He'd clearly given up on being polite. 'Jin, you have to do something,' he said. 'We can't keep this up.'

'Do something? With majik, you mean?'

'Yes!'

'Do what?'

'I don't know, anything! You did it before with the stage, right?'

'Yes, but –'

'Then do it again! Oji said it was okay!'

Jin looked to Jokah, who nodded grimly. Jin slid his krije behind him, palms burning in anticipation. This time, everyone was watching. Waiting.

Filip leant in. 'What are you going to do?'

'I'll use the stage again,' Jin replied. 'I'll get everyone onto it. If that KahnenMayj sorts his shit out and helps to keep the streetling mayjen off our backs, I can lift us out of the training grounds and take us to the Keep.' *It will be like when I lifted myself*, Jin thought. *I'll just have to get the power right.*

'You are a mayj?'

Jin turned to see the pale faces of the Kahnen staring back at him. The one who had spoken had the biggest eyebrows Jin had ever seen.

Before Jin could reply, Pago grabbed Jin's shoulder and pulled him around to face him.

Pago's face was red; his forehead and upper lip shone with sweat. 'If you see the mayj who killed Oji,' he said, 'you have my permission to rip a hole in him too.'

Filip laughed. 'He means like the bandits.'

'With pleasure,' Jin breathed.

He looked up. The stage was close by, towering into the sky. It was smouldering but still whole, the flames struggling to consume its massive surface.

'Cover me.'

Pago and Jokah stepped forward, weapons out. Jin squared his feet, the hair on the back of his neck standing up. He felt dangerously exposed, the eyes of the Kahnen needling into his back. He raised steady hands towards the stage and released a blast of power from his chest.

CHAPTER 53: THE GREAT KAHN

When the Great Kahn saw the stage soaring towards him, loaded with Kahnen and Krijen, he took a step back from the bleeding body of his latest foe, incredulous. Streetlings fled from beneath it, revealing the body of Lord Oman, sprawled on the blood-wet sand, stripped of its riches.

Two Krijen jumped from the stage and grabbed the Great Kahn, steering him towards it. The Great Kahn wanted to scream at them, loath to walk up the wooden steps that reeked so strongly of majik. But that simply wouldn't do.

The Great Kahn stepped up onto the platform, smothering his rage. Before him knelt the blond Krijen who had fought beside him earlier, his hands hovering just above the blackened wood of the stage.

The blond Krijen looked up as the Great Kahn stopped above him. The Great Kahn noticed the heat pulsing from him, the veins standing out in his neck, so exposed.

With a jolt, the Great Kahn realised who he must be. He was the mayj from the Deadlands. The one that the Great Kahn had ordered Oji to kill, when news of the bandit attack reached them. Even in death, the man was still rorting him. Another heinous surprise today.

The Great Kahn tightened his grip on his sword. It would be immensely satisfying if this mayj were to die by Mandavar's blade –

Stolt cried out in protest as the Krijen dragged him up onto the stage. 'This is insanity!' Stolt yelled. 'They will bring us down in an instant!'

'Not if you *help*,' the blond Krijen snarled.

Stolt stared down at the Krijen. His expression would melt cardonite. 'You conceited little –'

'Stolt,' the Great Kahn warned. He would not deal with the man's inferiority complex right now.

Stolt cursed and pushed the other Krijen off, striding over to stand next to the Great Kahn.

The blond Krijen's face changed, suddenly anxious as two other Krijen dragged Lord Oman's body onstage. 'Is it the Weapons Master?' he asked.

'No,' one of them replied. 'We've got all the Kahnen. We have to go, Jin.'

'But –'

'That's an order!'

The Great Kahn watched the exchange with cynical interest. It confirmed only what he'd suspected. This blond Krijen was the spawn of Oji. Questioning orders, outrageously cavalier, blatantly *harnessing*. He was a waking nightmare. But the Great Kahn could not kill him right now. He would have to wait.

The stage rose into the air at speed, and the Great Kahn knelt down to steady himself, almost face-to-face with the blond Krijen. The one they'd called Jin.

The *skahk*, the Great Kahn corrected. Despite his hatred of them, he'd so rarely entertained that word, but he couldn't think of a more suitable label. To use his name would be to humanise him, and skahks like him deserved nothing of the sort.

The Great Kahn watched as a bead of sweat dripped off the end of the skahk's nose, concentrating as his hands drifted ever so slightly in the direction they were going. Despite himself, the Great Kahn acknowledged it was impressive, what the skahk was doing. He must be powerful.

The stage soared over the city. They quickly left the bridge behind as they crossed over Val.

The Great Kahn could hear faint cries from his citizens below. He imagined them pointing up at the stage, in awe of the might of the Eighth House. Either that or disgusted by their flagrant use of majik. He gripped his sword tighter.

The Great Kahn looked around at the faces of his Kahnen, all various shades of white or green. Even the Krijen, usually utterly composed, looked uneasy. Everyone was crouched or sitting down, clinging on to the wood as best they could.

It wasn't long before the KahnenKeep courtyard appeared below them, a stone mouth surrounded by columns of teeth, beckoning them down. The stage landed with a gentle thud in the centre, causing nearby KahnenMinders to fall over themselves in astonishment.

The Great Kahn led the way off the stage, followed by the weak-kneed Kahnen. The Krijen carried off Lord Oman's body. Just as they placed it gently at their feet, Stolt pushed past the Kahnen and pointed a ring-laden finger at the skahk.

'Arrest him! What a disgraceful show of illegal majik!'

The skahk stiffened, but three Krijen stepped in around him.

They must be his squad, the Great Kahn thought.

The other Krijen quickly did the same. 'We do not answer to you,' one of them said.

Stolt staggered back, as though the Krijen had struck him. 'You-you don't answer to me?'

The Kahnen were muttering between themselves, eyes flickering between Stolt and the Krijen.

Stolt turned red, apoplecticity brewing. 'You're *Krijen*,' he spat. 'You're nothing more than well-trained *dogs!*' Stolt was showing his age. It was possible that half the Krijen standing before them didn't know what he meant, as young as they were. They looked at Stolt, stone-faced.

Lady Macey hurried forward, sending a reproachful glance in Stolt's direction. 'It is neither the time nor the place for this,' she said. 'Our government is under threat. The FaKrijen and a member of the Eighth House are dead, and I am under no illusions about what might have happened had this Krijen not been there.' She pointed at the skahk. 'You will not touch him.'

Some of the Kahnen gasped.

Lord Salli stepped forward. 'You cannot be serious? You want to spare him? He is an abomination! A mockery of our laws!'

The oldest-looking Krijen moved to stand directly in front of the skahk, his long white braid swinging. 'You would go back on your word?' he asked.

Lord Salli bristled. 'What are you talking about?'

'You pardoned him after what happened in the Deadlands,' the older Krijen said. 'He harnesses now under the command of the late FaKrijen, and his squad leader. As Lady Macey said, he is the reason you survived today.'

There was another outbreak of muttering among the Kahnen. Lord Salli looked outraged. 'Pardoned, for *majik?* We did no such thing –'

The Great Kahn let out a guttural sound, making everyone turn to him. He refused to be outplayed by Oji.

'I sent the late FaKrijen to pardon this mayj,' the Great Kahn lied. 'He saved a valuable supply run in the Deadlands. I was merciful on that occasion. That is why he lives.'

Lord Salli stared at him, mouth agape. The other Kahnen were likewise rendered speechless. No one would dare contradict him.

'In that case, it seems we owe this Krijen another debt,' Lady Macey said, meeting the Great Kahn's eyes with unabashed audacity, her detestable colours finally showing.

Lord Reider, who had been quietly observing until this point, moved to stand next to Lady Macey. 'I agree,' he said. 'We owe him our lives. We can spare him his.'

Lord Flynn also walked over to join them. 'I think we can all agree that his harnessing was well justified.' He nodded to the skahk.

Lady Elira swept over. 'Agreed as well,' she said, shameless.

'In fact,' said Lord Flynn, speaking to the Kahnen, 'we seem to be in greater need of majikal protection than ever before. Surely you can see the value in having a Krijen who is also a mayj in our employ?'

That opinionated little –

'You fools!'

Everyone turned to Stolt, who stood with his feet apart, fists clenched, eyes fixated on the skahk. His posturing was so transparent. The skahk scared him.

'You want this bloodthirsty lunatic to protect you?' Stolt cried. 'He doesn't know what he is doing! He harnessed pointlessly, right in front of your citizens. He is exactly the type of mayj you want to eradicate!'

At this, the skahk pushed past his squad and strode towards Stolt. As he came closer, the Great Kahn noticed his black wraps were spattered with gore. Most worrisome were his twitching fingers. He wasn't even close to running out of power, despite the majikal spectacle he'd just put on. The Kahnen backed away from him.

'Pointless? You think I did all that for fun?'

The skahk was breathing heavily. The Great Kahn remembered when Mandavar used to do the same, his power pressing on his emotions, making him angrier, meaner, more impulsive. More dangerous.

'You did *nothing*,' the skahk spat. 'You were supposed to be protecting the Kahnen, but you just stood there and watched while the streetlings attacked us!'

'You dare insult my judgement?' Stolt stepped forward to meet the skahk. 'You *imbecile*. Having restraint with majik is important to protect this city! Or have you forgotten about the Unsettlement, having spent so long hiding in the Deadlands?'

'It's convenient that sitting on your lazy arse is your way of doing something,' the skahk retorted. 'If you won't harness, then pick up a fucking sword!'

'Oh yes, because stabbing people *clearly* works,' Stolt said, his voice dripping with sarcasm. 'Thanks to the incompetence of the Krijen we lost a member of the Eighth House today. Your own FaKrijen couldn't even stop himself from being killed –'

There was a flash of metal as the skahk drew his krije, holding it up to Stolt's enraged face. The other Krijen tensed, instinctively placing hands on their own weapons.

'Say that again,' the skahk said quietly.

Stolt laughed, throwing back his head, his shoulders shaking. 'You think pointing something sharp in my direction will scare me? You are nothing more than an ignorant *barbarian*.'

'YOU –'

'Enough!' The Great Kahn stepped forward, pointing his own sword at Stolt. 'You, leave. *Now*.'

Stolt eyed the sword. He knew exactly what it was made of. This sharp object *did* scare him a little.

Stolt stared down its length for a moment longer, then threw a filthy look towards the skahk. 'I see you,' Stolt hissed as he shouldered past him, loud enough for everyone to hear. 'The only thing you're good for is destruction. Maniacal savage.'

'Sanctimonious prick,' the skahk shot back.

Stolt stalked off, disappearing between the stone columns. The Kahnen watched him go, some in disbelief and others shaking their heads. They'd not yet seen that side of Stolt.

The Great Kahn slowly lowered his sword. He kept his face straight as he turned to the skahk. 'It seems you are to be pardoned, yet again. I hope we are not setting precedent.'

'Thank you, my Great Lord,' came the strained reply.

The skahk slid his krije behind him once more. He was able to keep a lid on his majik, for now, but the Great Kahn could tell it was difficult for him. Even the Kahnen were wearily eyeing up the flexing of the skahk's hands, his shoulders and arms twitching.

Lady Macey was not deterred by the tension. 'Without a FaKrijen, to whom do you defer?' She looked around at the Krijen, waiting for an answer.

Of course. None of the Eighth House had even seen a new FaKrijen. Neither had the Great Kahn, but he'd waited a year for this day. He knew exactly what to expect.

Lord Flynn cleared his throat. 'They defer to their squad leaders,' he said in his usual scholarly tone. 'The Kahnen have three days to elect a successor. Beyond that, it falls to the Krijen themselves.'

It went unsaid that must never be allowed to happen.

They were in a perilous juxtaposition, designed that way by the founders of Valrue to force cooperation in tenuous times. Kahnen authority was compromised without a FaKrijen, although they had all the power of electing a new one. A historical blunder in the Great Kahn's opinion. One that he must navigate carefully.

'Kahnen, convene to the Red Room,' he ordered.

The Kahnen slowly headed between the columns towards the KahnenKeep, some sparing a backward glance at the skahk, some to the body of Lord Oman. A smattering of KahnenMinders hurried after them.

'I expect you will hunt the mayj who killed the FaKrijen,' the Great Kahn said, turning to the Krijen. One of the younger Krijen who'd given commands earlier stepped forward. He must be the squad leader. 'Yes, my Great Lord,' he said, 'while we await your decision.'

The Great Kahn nodded and turned to follow his Kahnen.

'My Great Lord?'

The skahk had spoken. The Great Kahn turned back, his jaw clenched, trying to keep his fury hidden.

'You'll allow me to harness to catch the FaKrijen's killer?'

It came out like a question, with the inflection at the end, but the Great Kahn knew it wasn't. The skahk was testing him. They'd just confirmed that the Kahnen provided empty authority without a FaKrijen.

That, and the Eighth House should demand vengeance for the murder of the FaKrijen no matter the cost. Under the circumstances, denying him the use of his majik would be suspicious, regardless of the impact on the Unsettlement.

The Great Kahn would *not* be played.

'If you must,' the Great Kahn gritted out, before heading into the KahnenKeep after his house.

CHAPTER 54: AREN BHA

After the Celebrations, Aren, Noel, and Mae waited in the entrance to the house. Aren snapped her wrist wraps incessantly, tense with worry. The thought of what might have happened to her father chilled her to her bones. He could be lying on the ground somewhere, trampled and hurt, like how she had been at the rally. Before Wren had saved her.

'We've got to go find him!' she cried, after too long a silence.

'No one is going anywhere,' Noel said sharply. He stood with his arms folded in front of the door, creating a blockade as though he expected Aren to charge. She was considering it. But even if she got past him, she figured Noel could probably run faster than her.

'Your father was with the Kahnen, surrounded by Krijen and undoubtedly KahnenMayjen as well,' Noel reassured her. 'He is in the safest hands. We will wait for him here.'

Aren folded her arms and glared at Noel. Stupid, logical, always-right Noel.

Mae chewed her lip, shifting her weight from side to side.

'It's okay, Mae,' Noel said. 'He will be safe. I mean it.'

Mae nodded, eyes brimming with tears. Aren reached out and took her mother in her arms. If Aren was to be forced to stay, the least she could do was offer some comfort.

On the way home, they'd dropped Maude at the brothel. Mama Hidel had greeted her niece with a vice-like hug, yelling her appreciation back to them as she hurried Maude inside. Marigold had gone home to Bish, who, if he'd heard, would be waiting for her anxiously.

Noel had even sent the maids home to their families. Tonight would be a night of mourning. They'd seen little of what had actually happened in the middle of the Squares' training grounds, but they'd heard the rumour echoing through the crowd as they fled. The FaKrijen was dead. Killed by a streetling mayj.

Aren thanked the Great Kahn that Wren had not attended the Celebrations. He would have only put himself in harm's way trying to be the hero. Maybe against the streetlings he could hold his own, but against a mayj? It was too much to think about.

Tonight she would go help Wren at the Point. People would already be making their way there, likely wounded needing medical attention and scared mayjen seeking protection.

Just then, the front door creaked open behind Noel, and Sid sidled into the house.

'Thank the Great Kahn!' Mae pushed Noel out of the way and pulled Sid into a tight embrace, tears streaming down her face.

Sid wrapped his arm around Aren's mother and gently kissed the top of her head. 'I'm okay,' he said quietly. Aren moved forward and hugged them both, then stepped back. Her father was in his undergarments, his face stained with a dusting of something that looked suspiciously like dried blood.

'What happened?' Aren asked. 'Are you hurt?'

Noel snatched his first aid bag off the floor and hurried towards Sid, who waved him away with a tired hand. 'I'm not hurt. Did everyone get home safely?'

They walked into the sitting room and settled onto the chairs while Sid explained what he'd seen.

'So the FaKrijen really is dead?' Aren asked, struggling to believe it.

Sid nodded, looking strained. 'Killed by a young mayj boy, I think.'

'A streetling, we heard,' Noel said.

Sid frowned. 'Maybe.'

'I'm so sorry, Sid,' Mae said gently.

Sid nodded, his eyes shining. He looked over at Aren. 'I saw Jin,' he said with a small smile.

Aren leapt off her chair. '*What?* Where? Is he okay?'

'He was on the protective detail for the Eighth House. He pulled me out of the crowd. I didn't see what happened, but I trust the Krijen had the situation under control.'

Aren sank back into her seat, holding on to the arms of the chair to steady herself. It was *wrong* that Jin was back in Valrue and she hadn't yet seen him.

'How do I find him? Where do the Krijen go when they're in the city?'

'Aren, just wait,' Noel shushed, leaning in towards Sid. 'You said you didn't see what happened to the Eighth House? Why not? And why are you here without a Krijen escort?'

'I was with the Eighth House when we found ourselves surrounded by streetlings,' Sid began. 'They had a leader, a girl who made threats against the Kahnen. I fear they have been coordinating an uprising of sorts. I didn't see what happened, but they attacked us. I got separated, my robes taken.' Sid was not one to add unpleasant details. Aren knew it would have been ugly.

'So what happens now?' Mae asked.

'They'll arrange a Remembrance for Oji tonight,' Sid replied. 'Tomorrow, we will hear from the Speaker of the Eighth House.' Sid looked to Aren once more, his face full of concern. 'The Krijen will start hunting for Oji's killer. I suspect Jin will be in the thick of it because it is a mayj they are chasing. That, and I think Jin knew Oji fairly well.' Sid wrung his hands, looking wretched.

'Poor Jin,' whispered Aren. 'When can I see him?'

'I'm not sure,' Sid said. 'It will be a tumultuous time for the Krijen right now, especially until a new FaKrijen is elected.'

'Let him come to you, Aren,' Noel advised. Aren didn't like it, but she nodded. She would wait.

It was dark by the time Aren made her way back to her room. She walked quickly, aware she still needed to gather supplies and put on a disguise before she left. Even then, it was a long run to Turning Point.

Lost in thought, she pushed open her bedroom door and immediately walked into something solid.

'Aren!'

Wren's strong arms folded around her, crushing her into his chest. He must have been right behind the door, waiting for her.

Suddenly wobbly with excitement, she wrapped her arms around his waist, squeezing back. It felt *amazing*. Aren could feel his chin on the top of her head, hear his heart beating. Heat was radiating off him, as though he'd run here –

Wren gently pushed her away. Then he stepped around her and closed the door quietly. 'Sorry,' he muttered. 'I didn't mean to do that.'

Aren swayed on the spot. She felt light-headed, her mind sluggish, trying to catch up. 'That's okay,' she said. It sounded very inadequate, considering how she was feeling. 'I-I wasn't expecting you to be here.'

'Well,' Wren began slowly, 'I knew you were going to the Celebrations today. When I heard what happened, I –' he paused. 'I thought I should come grab some more supplies. For the Point.' He stood a short distance away with his hands awkwardly by his sides, looking everywhere but at her.

Just as Aren reached out a hand towards him, he turned away and picked up his satchel from where he'd dropped it on the floor. Then he dove under her bed and began pulling out tonics and bandages.

Aren stood there watching, doing nothing helpful. Her mind was stuck on his answer, which didn't sound right. She couldn't figure out why. 'It was a mayj who killed Oji,' Aren said carefully.

'Yes, I heard,' Wren said, his voice muffled.

'But you left Turning Point. The residents would be targets for the Krijen. But you left there, to come here.'

Wren didn't respond. He dug further under the bed.

'But you know I would have come with supplies,' Aren said. 'I was just bringing some now. You didn't need to leave.'

'I know, I know,' Wren said tersely. He stood up and buckled the satchel shut.

'Hold on.' Aren pinched the bridge of her nose like Noel did when he was trying to think. Wren wasn't making sense. Wren always did things that made sense. He was logically infallible, which was part of the reason why Aren annoyed him so much.

'Do you mean to say,' Aren said, 'that you just spent all this time getting here to get supplies that I would have brought anyway, leaving everyone at Turning Point unprotected –'

'I *know*.' Wren looked angry now. He swung the satchel onto his back and stalked towards the window.

'So if you knew that, why did you come?'

Wren stopped, one foot on the windowsill, still not looking at her. His refusal to meet her eyes was stoking Aren's anger. He was lying to her, and she thought she knew why, but she also didn't dare to believe it. She wanted to hear it from his mouth.

'Tell me why, Wren.'

'You know why –'

'No, I don't!' Aren knew she shouldn't yell in case her family heard, but she didn't care. Months of pent-up frustration had suddenly bubbled up inside of her, and she couldn't keep it in any longer.

'You can be so difficult, Wren! And mean, and distant! I don't know what you want. I can't tell what you're thinking half the time. Sometimes I even think you hate me, and that's fine. I can deal with that so long as I know I'm being helpful. But when I came in just now you acted like you were glad to see me – for, like, half a second – and now you've made me think I have it all wrong again –'

Wren spun around to face her. 'For fuck's sake, Aren. I couldn't just sit there, waiting at the Point. I needed to see if you were okay.'

Aren blinked at him. Was he saying what she thought he was saying? It was hardly a groundbreaking confession. She took a step towards him.

'But *why?*'

'Stop pushing me. You never know what's good for you.'

Aren narrowed her eyes at him. 'You're saying you're not good for me?'

Wren said nothing for a moment. Then –

'That's *exactly* what I'm saying.'

Aren felt a surge of triumph. They were getting somewhere.

'Well, I think you're wrong.' She took another step towards him. They were close, not touching, but almost. She longed for him to wrap his arms around her like he had before.

'Wren, listen to me. I've spent my whole life around people who tell me what's good for me, and keep me away from the bad. You're the one person who never smothered me with silk cushions. Don't start now.'

Wren's eyes were boring into hers, so bright, even though they were the darkest brown. Aren's heart couldn't beat any faster. If it did, she might die. She wanted to kiss him so badly. Aren steeled herself, then stretched up on her toes –

Wren stepped away. 'I have to go,' he said. 'I need to get back to the Point.'

Aren shot him the ugliest look she could muster. He knew she couldn't ask him to stay, not for the selfish reasons she had in mind. But he wouldn't shake her off that easily.

'Fine. Just give me a minute –'

Wren shook his head. 'You need to stay here.'

'NO!'

Aren let the fury flare inside her because it drowned out the feeling of rejection, which was going to be far worse when it eventually sank in.

'Don't you *dare* start coddling me –'

'Calm down! I promise that's not what I'm doing.' Wren held up his hands. 'It's not that I don't think you can look after yourself. You've more than proven that' – Aren felt a touch of pride at his words – 'but tonight is going to be so bad that I . . . I don't even know how to say it.' Wren pushed his hair off his face, clearly frustrated. It fell straight back down into his eyes again.

'Look. The streetlings are in an uproar, and the Krijen will go after them, hunting the FaKrijen's killer. They'll come to the Point looking for him. I haven't figured out how I'm going to deal with that, and I just . . .' He growled at the look on Aren's face. 'All right, I'll say it! No matter how good you are at keeping yourself safe, if you're there when the fight comes, I'll be too distracted. I meant it before when I said I worry about you. I need you to be here when it's over.'

Aren huffed outwardly, but inside she felt radiant. It was probably the closest to a declaration of his feelings that she was ever going to get. She had to fight to keep the smile off her face. But it was still a double standard.

'So you think it's fair to refuse my help and leave me to worry about *you*?'

'Aren, please. For once in your life, can you do as I ask?'

Wow, Aren thought. He'd said please. 'Fine,' Aren said, her mouth twitching. 'I'll stay. You'll come back as soon as you're done, right?'

Wren gave her the rarest of smiles. It made her heart dance. 'You know I will,' he said. 'But I might be a few days. Is that okay?'

It wasn't. Not now that he'd admitted, ever so reluctantly, that there was something happening between them. But Aren was getting better at being patient. 'That's okay,' she gritted out.

With that, Wren turned and slipped out the window. Aren tucked her hands into her armpits so she wouldn't snatch him back. *He better not cut himself*, she thought. That nearly prompted her to go after him, but for once, she stopped herself. Wren was definitely at his limit for how much of her persistence he could tolerate. For tonight anyway.

As she prepared for bed, flares burst into the night sky, raining gold onto the city. They must be in Remembrance for Oji. Aren watched them for a while from her bed, thinking how pretty they were. As she drifted off to sleep, she wondered if it made her a bad person to fall asleep feeling this happy, considering the horrors of the day.

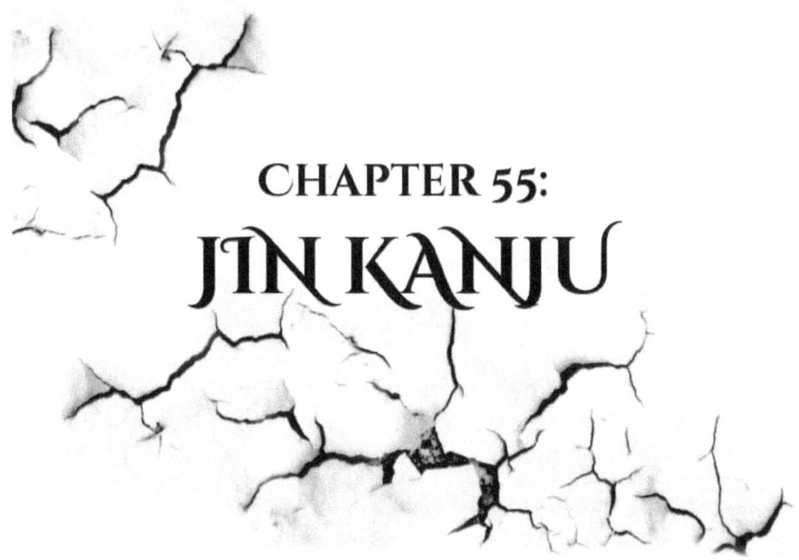

CHAPTER 55:
JIN KANJU

The sun was coming up when they returned to the Krijen barracks in the Left South Side of Rue. It had been a long night and Jin's squad – or what remained of it, now having lost Bish, Oji, and Vulmin – were sitting forlornly around the fountain outside.

The Sparks of Remembrance had stopped now, but Jin could still hear them popping in his head, in among the ringing. It seemed the ringing was here to stay. As were a few other annoying things.

'I'm sorry about Oji,' Filip said.

Jin glanced at the dead Square sitting by his side. 'Don't worry,' Jin said to him. 'I'll find his killer.'

Jokah looked up at Jin. 'Did you say something?'

'No. Sorry. I'm just tired.'

'We should all get some rest,' Jokah said, but he didn't move. Instead, he put his head in his hands, elbows propped against his knees. Other Krijen squads were shuffling about, also having just returned. The streetlings had been in an uproar. It had taken a long time to subdue them.

'Hey!'

Jin's head snapped up. He knew that voice.

It was Bish, seated in a wooden contraption that he wheeled towards them. Jin hadn't seen Bish since he'd left him in the Deadlands, back when he was still a criminal. Jin's throat tightened with fear. He'd never found out what Bish thought about him doing majik during the bandit attack.

That's why it was an enormous relief when Bish smiled at him from across the courtyard. Sorrow and exhaustion forgotten, Jin ran over and threw his arms around Bish, hauling him up out of his chair into a hug.

'Jin! Jin, *stop*. You're squishing me –'

'It's so good to see you!'

Jin settled him back down into his chair, trying to ignore the way Bish's legs just fell to the side, the muscles now having wasted away.

With cries of delight, Pago, Meek, and Jokah jogged over to join them, slapping Bish on the shoulders and wringing his hands. The other Krijen squads watched them fondly, happy to see some joy after all the abhorrence.

'I thought now would be a good time to catch you,' Bish said. 'I figured you would've been out all night. We're all okay in Val. We were worried for Sid, but Noel sent a message to say he came back unharmed.'

Jin nodded, grateful for the news.

'So it's true then?' Bish asked. 'About the FaKrijen? I saw the Remembrance, but I also heard Lord Oman died, so I wasn't sure . . .'

'It's true,' Jin said. It made him angry to think about it again. 'The streetlings got Lord Oman. And some fucking *skahk* got Oji.'

Bish frowned up at Jin. He'd probably never heard him use that word before.

'And you? Do the Kahnen know about you?'

Meek slapped Jin on the back, laughing. 'They sure do! Mighty impressed them, he did! "We can all agree that his harnessing was well justified,"' Meek said, sounding eerily similar to Lord Flynn.

'The Kahnen admitted that they owed him,' Pago agreed with a smile.

Bish's jaw dropped. 'Shit. That's –'

'Staggering?' Meek offered. 'Impossible? Downright fucking insane?'

'All of the above,' Bish said weakly. 'So . . . can you tell me what happened?' He looked nervous. Bish knew it would be hard for them to relive the things that they saw. As expected, the faces of the Krijen darkened.

'Come on,' Jin said, inclining his head towards the fountain. The others quickly wandered off to the barracks, and the courtyard emptied, leaving Bish and Jin alone.

Jin sat down next to Filip on the low fountain wall, watching as Bish manoeuvred himself smoothly into place. 'Where did you get that?' Jin asked, indicating to the wheeling chair. He hoped it wouldn't be too obvious that he was delaying the conversation.

'Sid made it for me,' Bish said. 'Don't know what I'd do without it.'

'Have you seen Aren?'

Bish looked Jin in the eye. Jin didn't look away. He wasn't ashamed to admit he missed her desperately. Bish would know that.

'Yes, plenty,' Bish replied. 'She's doing well. You wouldn't know her to spar against anymore. She'd actually give you a run for your coin.'

'Seriously?' Jin was impressed. 'But she was never that bad.'

'She was pretty bad,' Bish said, sounding exasperated. 'You just needed the excuse.'

Jin didn't deny it.

'Are you going to see her?' Bish asked.

Jin ducked his head and ran his hands through his hair. 'As soon as I get a minute to myself,' he said. 'I'd go now but –' He glanced at Bish, feeling guilty. He didn't want Bish to think that he'd got in the way. It wasn't true.

Bish shook his head. 'I'll not stay long. But you look like shit, Jin. Maybe you should get some sleep before you see Aren. You might never see her again, otherwise.'

Jin laughed. He loved it when Bish made jokes. Then again, he was still stained with blood from the night before. Perhaps not a joke, after all.

'So.' Bish's expression was serious again. He never could keep a conversation lighthearted for long. 'The Kahnen pardoned you. The others seem to have accepted it pretty quickly. They're acting a lot different from when I left.'

'Yeah, I can't quite believe it either,' Jin said truthfully. 'You can't tell me off for harnessing anymore,' he added, giving Bish a gentle nudge. More gently than before anyway. Bish was more delicate now.

Bish frowned. 'What? You've been told you can keep harnessing?'

'That's right.'

'By who?'

'Well, Oji, for starters,' Jin replied. 'And the Great Kahn himself.'

'The Great Kahn?' Bish shook his head, looking astounded. 'Be careful, Jin,' he warned. 'I don't think the Kahnen want you to throw majik about.'

Jin made a face. 'You sound like Stolt.'

'Who is Stolt?'

'One of the KahnenMayjen.'

'Oh. Wow, I missed out on a lot, didn't I?'

Jin didn't reply. It was true, but that didn't mean he needed to say it.

'Well, it sounds like Stolt is right,' Bish continued. 'Majik is still damaging, remember?'

At this, Filip leant back and stretched, yawning loudly. 'Was Bish always this determined to spoil the fun?'

Jin scowled, but at Bish, not at Filip. 'I'm not going to "throw majik about". I'm going to use it to catch Oji's murderer.'

Bish had on his usual concerned expression, the one he reserved just for Jin. 'You know this isn't all on you? Have you forgotten all of our training? Krijen are supposed to work together.'

'You weren't there. You didn't see what that skahk did to Oji. Then he disappeared under our noses. No Krijen dagger is going to get near him.'

Bish leant forward in his chair. 'Look. I can tell you don't want to talk about it, and that's fine. I'm not going to ask again. But swear to me that you'll be careful on this hunt. Only use your majik if you need to, especially if you're going up against a mayj who knows what he's doing.'

'I'm telling you now, normal weapons won't be enough,' Jin insisted.

'If we are going to have a shot at this, we need to take him on with majik.'

'Krijen have gotten by without majik for years. I don't think it's a good idea to start relying on it.'

Bish's reply pissed Jin off. Bish would be Lost if it weren't for majik. 'You don't even realise what you're saying,' Jin shot back.

The second the words were out of his mouth, he regretted them. He tried to keep talking, but Bish cut him off.

'What did you say?'

'Nothing. I didn't mean –'

'What did you mean I don't realise what I'm saying?'

Jin's palms were burning. He kept his hands perfectly still, knowing he didn't have any daggers left to thumb anyway. That, and Bish would know his tells.

'Ooh, you've done it now,' Filip said with a smirk. Jin wished he could punch him.

'All I meant is that I've been using some majik here and there,' Jin said carefully. 'You know that.'

'Yes, I know that,' Bish said slowly, looking sideways at him. 'But you never used it for anything other than silly little things, like that nail in the bunk. You meant something else.'

Jin could feel his chest tightening, his adrenaline messing with him.

Bish was quickly starting to look angry. 'What did you mean, Jin?'

'It's nothing.'

'Great Kahn help me if you don't *explain* yourself –'

'Okay, okay!' Jin held up his hands. He couldn't believe he'd been so stupid as to have let it slip. But he was sleep-deprived, and sick of Bish's needling. Of course, trying to lie had been dumb; he never got away with it. And although the truth was scary, Bish would understand, given what Jin had saved him from. Telling him would be okay. Even so, Jin took a few deep breaths, trying to stay calm.

'I used majik during the Dancing Ceremony.'

Bish was silent. Jin bit his lip, waiting, listening to the water bubbling in the fountain. He could feel beads of sweat gathering on his forehead as the heat grew inside him. He felt alive, taut like a spring, his fatigue suddenly buried deep, lost beneath his power.

Bish's expression had grown ice cold.

'I did it because you weren't going to win,' Jin said, before Bish could speak. It sounded pathetic when he said it out loud.

'I – wait,' Bish said. 'You did it during *my* dance?'

Jin hated the way Bish was looking at him. Shock mingled with a touch of revulsion.

Jin panicked. 'Everyone could see what was going to happen!' he cried. 'You weren't walking straight. Your skull was bashed in. You were blind in one eye! I couldn't let you throw away your victory for the sake of your pride.'

'My *pride?*' Bish reeled backwards in his chair, his hands gripping the armrests tightly.

'Careful, Jin,' said Filip. 'Don't speak now.'

Jin got off the fountain wall and crouched down in front of Bish. 'I'm sorry –'

'How did you do it?'

'What?'

'How did you do it?'

'You mean the dance –'

'Don't you dare play coy with me!'

Bish looked a little crazed. His eyes were too wide, his upper lip quivering. Jin stood up again and took a step back. He'd never seen Bish lose control like this before. 'Bish –'

Bish pulled out a dagger from his wraps and flung it at Jin's face. Without thinking, Jin flicked his hand, harnessing the knife off its trajectory. It clattered to the ground behind them.

Filip sighed. 'Really?'

Bish was straining out of his chair, his arms holding up the weight of his body while his legs splayed awkwardly from the knees. He looked so helpless.

Jin felt guilt wallop him in the face. *He* had done that to Bish. He was the reason that Bish had won that dance. He was the reason that Bish had become Krijen, been sent to the Deadlands, been at the mercy of the bandit mayj, had his back broken –

'So that's how you did it then,' Bish said, staring after the dagger he'd thrown.

'I didn't mean for you to get hurt.'

'You're worried about *me?* What about Wren? You rigged the dance! You used majik on his krije!'

Jin cringed at the sound of the Lost Square's name. 'No, no, I didn't –'

'You stole his future from him! Or have you forgotten what happens to Squares who lose their dance?' Bish was trembling. Jin was shocked to see tears dripping down his face.

'But,' Jin said, 'it would have been *you* –'

'I don't give a fuck about me! Look at what you did to *Wren!*'

Jin flinched away from the malice in Bish's voice. This wasn't fair. Bish wasn't getting it.

'You've got to tell him the whole truth,' Filip said quietly. Jin shook his head, but Filip wasn't having it. He stood up and moved to Jin's side, glaring at him. 'You need to tell him now. He's going to work it out eventually when he hears the details of what happened to Oji.' Jin hated that Filip was right. It was best that Bish heard it from him firsthand.

'I didn't move Wren's blade.'

Bish glowered at him. 'So what then? You moved *my* krije? You can't have. I would have felt it.'

'No, Bish,' Jin said. 'I moved *you.*'

Bish stared at him. 'No. You can't do that. Majik doesn't work on people.'

'Yes, it does.'

'No! You couldn't have moved me. It's not possible.'

'It is possible. I didn't know about it until then. And it's how Oji died,' he added quietly. 'The streetling mayj tore him apart. Turned him into nothing.'

'But-but,' Bish stammered, clearly thrown by this information, 'then you would have done it in the Deadlands! Why didn't you do it in the Deadlands, with the bandit mayj?'

'I was scared,' Jin admitted. It was enough to be able to control things. But to control people? To force them against their will? It was too much. Jin felt ashamed that he'd done it to Bish.

'When did you do it?' Bish asked. He meant during his dance.

'A few times,' Jin admitted. 'I just gave you a bit of strength, that's all. Helped you move faster when you needed it.'

'But I would have known –'

'No.' Jin shook his head. 'No, I was careful not to push too hard. It wasn't easy. I'd never done it before. I figured if I tried to move your krije, then you would definitely notice, because it wouldn't feel right in your hands. But if I moved you –'

Jin withered at Bish's thunderous expression. 'You made me a *cheater*,' he spat.

'No, listen to me,' Jin pleaded. 'You have to understand why I did it. You'd already won your first dance. To lose your second, after that –'

'Then I would have deserved it!'

Jin stared at him in shock. 'But you would have been Lost –

'I'm Lost anyway!' Bish shouted so loudly his voice cracked on the words. 'Look at me! I lasted six months as a Krijen. I can't even walk. I didn't go to the Celebrations yesterday because I was too ashamed of this!' He grabbed his wraps above his knees and shook his legs. They flopped around uselessly.

'There is no point to anything I do anymore! My life is over. And now you've told me that I'm responsible for the same thing happening to Wren?' Bish wiped his eyes. 'Fuck, Jin, what is *wrong* with you?'

Jin reached out towards Bish, but his friend smacked his hand away.

'No, don't touch me!' Bish's face twisted, unrecognisable. 'It's no wonder your father hit you,' he said.

Jin slowly sank to his knees, the weight of the truth pulling him down. His hands hit the ground, his face inches from the cobbles.

Filip knelt next to him. 'You kind of deserved that,' he said.

Jin knew he deserved the beatings from his father. He could have fought back, but he never did. He accepted them as a punishment for who he was, for never being good enough. He could live with that. But he couldn't live without Bish as his friend, to temper him, to help get him through it all.

'Bish, I'm sorry –'

'Fuck off, Jin. Don't you dare come near me again. Stay away from Aren too. You're poison.'

Bish spun his chair around and wheeled away, leaving Jin on the ground by the fountain.

CHAPTER 56:
AREN BHA

Aren slept terribly that night, for all the right reasons. Wren's smile was etched into her brain, and she couldn't stop thinking about his warm arms wrapped around her.

It was barely dawn when she stepped out into the sparring court the next morning, yawning and stretching her arms. However, she wasn't the only one there. There was a boy crouched under the stone tree, watching her with a blank expression.

'Hello,' she said. She rested her hand lightly on her cardonite dagger hilt as she wandered over to him. 'Who are you? Do you need help?'

He looked kind of like a streetling. He had that underfed look, but he didn't reach for any weapons as she approached. So probably not a streetling. They wouldn't be caught dead without at least a rusty nail to stab you with.

The boy was also whiter than the stone tree above him. Definitely not a streetling, who were normally tanned, or burnt, living their days under the hot Valrue sun.

The boy's eyes widened as she grew closer. 'It's you,' he said.

That was not what Aren expected. She stopped a short distance from him and squatted down to get a better view of his face behind his black hair. It was so long it touched his shoulders, curling a little.

'Have we met?'

'Yes.'

Aren waited. No explanation was forthcoming. His stare was so familiar, the unusual blue eyes niggling at a memory buried in the back of her mind.

'No, Aren!'

Noel came sprinting out of the house, followed closely by her father. To Aren's bemusement, they stopped halfway across the sparring court. She stood up. 'What's wrong?'

'Come here, please,' Noel pleaded, motioning with his hand.

Aren walked over to them, glancing back at the boy under the tree. The second she was in reach, Noel grabbed her by the arm and steered her underneath the covered stone columns and into the dining room. The bowls were laid out for breakfast, the table laden with uneaten food. Sid looked incredibly pale; his hands shook as he rested them on the back of a chair.

'What's going on?'

Noel and Sid glanced at each other. 'That boy out there is the one who killed the FaKrijen,' Noel said.

Aren's jaw dropped. '*What?*' She whipped back around to stare at the figure in the sparring court. He hadn't moved from underneath the stone tree. 'How do you know?'

'Because I saw him,' Sid said. 'I saw him yesterday, right after the attack.'

'Really? Why is he here?'

Sid raised a hand to his clammy forehead. 'I think he followed me. But for the life of me, I don't know why.'

Just then, Mae wandered into the dining room, humming to herself and straightening her dress. She stopped when she saw them all standing there. 'Good morning. What are you all doing?' She frowned as she noticed their expressions. 'What's wrong?'

'The person sitting in our sparring court killed the FaKrijen,' Aren said.

Mae blinked at her. 'The – what?'

Noel pointed. Mae walked over to the open window. She stared at the boy outside for a moment, before making a tiny 'oh!' sound and raising a hand to her mouth. 'Oh, Great Kahn save us! What do we do?'

'We must send a runner for the Krijen,' Noel said. 'They'll come to arrest him.'

Mae turned to him in horror. 'And risk him killing us all when we bring his executioners over?'

Noel threw up his hands. 'What else can we do?'

Aren looked back out at the boy, pondering his strange demeanour, the way he crouched. 'I think I know him from somewhere,' she said.

Noel looked over at her. 'What? From where?'

'I'm not sure. But he said he knows me too.'

'You spoke to him?' Mae sounded horrified.

'Only briefly,' Aren mumbled. Suddenly it came flooding back to her. The pale face, the black hair, the blue eyes of death. 'It's the beggar!'

'What?'

'He's a beggar! Or he used to be anyway. I saw him in the street once, about a year ago.'

'A beggar? Are you sure?' Noel strode over to join Mae by the window. 'A mayj like him would not be a beggar.'

Aren turned to her father. 'Are you certain he's the one who killed the FaKrijen?'

Sid had a pained expression on his face. 'I could be wrong. His hands didn't move when Oji . . . disappeared.' Sid glanced at Noel, who frowned. 'Not possible,' Noel said. 'Mayjen must use their hands to direct their majik.'

'With no exceptions?'

'None at all. If you say he didn't move them, then he's not the killer.'

Everyone looked around at each other, Aren battling the urge to flick her wrist wraps.

Her newfound patience did not last long. 'All right, she said. 'Let's go ask him, shall we?' She turned and strolled back out the door.

'Aren, come back here!' her mother cried, but Aren did not turn around. She stopped just underneath the shade of the stone columns. The beggar was looking at her.

'Can I come talk?' she called to him. His head tilted slightly to the side, but he said nothing.

Aren stepped onto the sparring court and walked to where she had before. She stopped and crouched down again. He was definitely the beggar. He wasn't as skinny, nor as dirty, but his eyes still had that dead look about them.

'My name is Aren,' she said slowly.

'You gave me a piece of dried apple,' the beggar said.

Aren blinked, surprised. 'I tried. You didn't take it.'

The beggar said nothing back, even though she waited. It seemed awkward to just launch into it, but she didn't think he'd be one for small talk.

'I have to ask you something really important. Did you kill the FaKrijen?'

The beggar recoiled. 'Yes,' he said.

Aren's blood ran cold. She didn't reach for her dagger; it would be useless against majik. Instead, she remained as she was, trying to think of what to do next, without panicking.

'Please, I don't want to do it again,' said the beggar. His face might not show it, but his voice was fearful.

It distracted Aren. When she didn't respond, the beggar started to tremble. 'Please,' he repeated, 'I don't want to do it again. I don't want to do it again –'

Flustered, Aren held up her hands. 'Okay – it's okay!' she said. 'I-I won't make you do it again!'

The beggar relaxed instantly, his whole body sagging back against the stone tree. As shocked as she was by his confession of killing the FaKrijen, she was more disturbed by his reaction. He was clearly terrified.

Aren glanced back at her family and Noel who watched from under the columns, before turning back to the beggar. Hardly believing what she was doing, she sat down on the ground and folded her legs.

'What's your name?'

'Drax.'

That wasn't a Valruean name. 'Where did you come from?'

'I don't understand.' He stiffened, stressed again.

'It's okay, it's okay,' Aren said gently. 'Too many questions, right?'

He shifted a little but didn't reply.

'Okay. One more, I promise. Why are you here?'

'I wanted to get away from Felle.'

His answer made no sense to her. 'Who is –' Aren caught herself. She'd promised only one more question. 'Okay. Um, thank you. I'll be back.'

She stood up, dusted herself off, and headed to the shade of the columns. Noel grabbed her and steered her back inside, everyone anxiously following. 'Well?'

'He said he did it,' Aren replied. 'He killed Oji.'

Noel looked like he'd been hit over the head with something very heavy. 'It . . . it can't be,' he said. 'I don't understand.'

'Great Kahn, have mercy,' Mae breathed. 'What do we do?'

Everyone was silent. Aren's mind was jammed with thoughts, bothered by her interaction with Drax.

Noel began to pace up and down the room, muttering to himself. After a few turns he stopped, and faced them, shaking a little. 'We *must* call the Krijen,' he repeated. 'And leave here immediately.'

'You said he followed Sid here,' Mae said. 'Won't he follow if we leave?'

Noel bit his lip. 'Possibly.'

More silence.

Aren looked at her father. He was leaning heavily against Mae, looking distraught. They wouldn't dream of leaving him behind.

'Are we sure the Krijen could even do anything?' Mae asked.

'They'll come with KahnenMayjen,' Noel replied. 'They'll know what to do.'

'KahnenMayj,' Sid corrected.

'What?

'There is only one left.'

Noel seemed to stagger under the weight of this news. 'What? What happened to them?'

Sid shook his head. 'I don't know. But the Great Kahn himself said it.'

'Great Kahn, have mercy . . .' Noel placed his hands on the back of the chair nearest to him. 'One KahnenMayj cannot take this boy down.'

'How do you know?'

'Because of what he did to the FaKrijen!'

Mae and Sid just looked at him with blank expressions.

Aren frowned. 'You mean because he used majik on a person?'

'That is not what I am referring to,' Noel said. 'It's part of it, but . . . I cannot even begin to explain the kind of majikal abilities he must have.'

'He is clearly himajik,' Mae said. 'But does it matter, if the KahnenMayj is himajik too?'

'That preposterous word has never been more inadequate!'

Aren didn't know what Noel meant by that. 'Look,' she said, interjecting, 'I know Drax said he killed the FaKrijen, but he doesn't seem all that dangerous.'

'Drax?' Mae asked. 'That's his name?'

Noel made an indignant noise. 'That mayj might not look like much, but I can assure you, he is very dangerous.'

'I don't think he's going to hurt us,' Aren replied stubbornly. 'It sounds like someone made him kill Oji.'

'It doesn't matter if he was coerced, Aren. He murdered someone!'

'I think we should hear his side of the story.'

'"His side of the story"?' Noel looked flabbergasted. 'That boy tore the FaKrijen into the very atoms of his being. Do you realise what that *means?*'

'No, I don't,' Aren snapped back, 'because you never taught me!'

'Excuse me?'

'You refused to teach me about majik. So no, I don't know what that means.' Aren folded her arms. 'And so what? It doesn't mean Drax wants to hurt us. Just because I could stab you with my dagger right now it doesn't mean I'm going to.'

'Aren,' Noel said in a carefully controlled voice. 'That boy is covered in scars. We have no idea what he's been through. We can't predict what he'll do.'

Aren was quiet. She hadn't noticed the scars.

Mae was still looking out the window at Drax, her face uncertain. 'It's certainly hard to believe he's a killer. He just looks so young–'

'He's older than he looks,' Sid said quietly.

Noel sat down at the table, spreading his hands on the tablecloth in front of him. 'I don't think we should take any risks,' he said. 'I understand why we shouldn't call the Krijen, so I won't, for now. But can we please all keep our distance, at least until we figure out what he wants? *Please*,' he repeated to Aren. After a brief hesitation, she nodded reluctantly.

Mae heaved a sigh and sat down too. 'Okay,' she said, looking around at them all. 'What do we do now?'

CHAPTER 57:
JIN KANJU

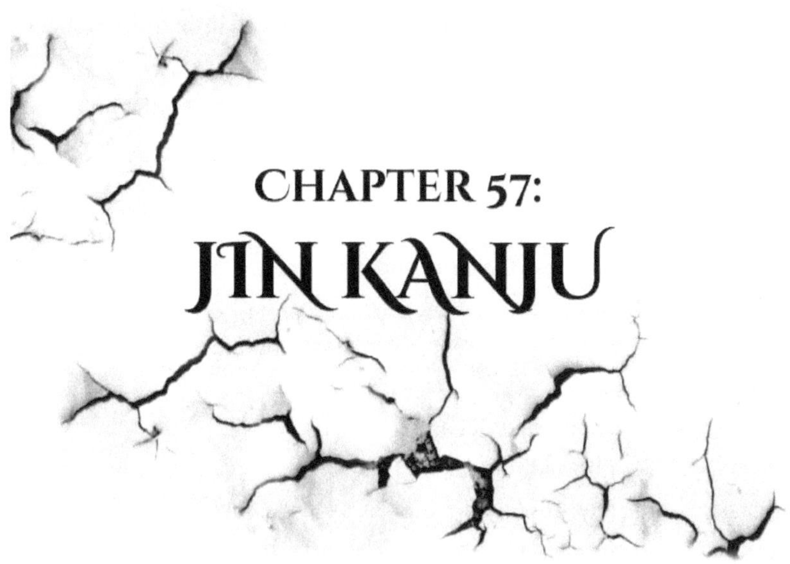

'Jin. Jin, get up.'

Shit. Geni Igna was going to kill him. If you slept late as a Square, you got beaten. Simple as that.

'Jin, what are you playing at?'

His bed was much harder than he remembered it being. Everything hurt. The ringing in his ears, especially. He stretched out a hand, feeling for a pillow or blankets or something to throw over his head to drown out the noise.

'Jin!'

Jin's eyes snapped open. He was lying on the ground next to the fountain surrounded by the dregs of his squad, and a few other curious Krijen.

Filip squatted beside him, looking rather unsympathetic. 'They've been trying to wake you for ages, you know,' he said.

Jin quickly pushed himself to his feet, staggering a little. He flicked his hair back from his face, bits of blond stuck to his cheek. 'Sorry,' he said, bleary-eyed. 'What did I miss?'

'Did you sleep out here?' Meek asked, looking baffled.

'I think I dozed off.'

Meek made a noise that Jin couldn't interpret in his current stupor.

'We heard shouting after we left,' Jokah said. 'Is everything okay?'

Oh no. Had they heard his confession to Bish about what he'd done at the Dancing Ceremony? The heat in his chest started creeping down his arms.

'What did you hear?'

Jokah took him by the arm and led him away from the others. 'Honestly, we didn't hear much. But you sounded . . .' Jokah trailed off, looking uncomfortable. He cleared his throat. 'Well, you seemed to be talking to yourself.'

Oh. 'So you didn't hear me talking to Bish?'

'What? No, I don't think so –'

A wave of relief rolled over Jin. Jokah was looking at him intently, waiting for an answer.

'I'm okay,' Jin reassured him. 'I guess I just haven't had much sleep.'

Jokah raised an eyebrow. 'I'm not surprised. You slept on the ground.'

'Yeah. I probably shouldn't have done that.' Jin flushed under Jokah's piercing gaze.

'You would let us know if this is all a bit much for you, right? You've gone through a lot lately.'

'I'm fine. Honestly.'

Jokah shook his head. 'Has anyone ever told you that you're a bad liar?'

Jin forced out a laugh. 'You certainly aren't the first.'

'Well, if you won't talk to me, please talk to someone. I worry about you. With Oji gone, we have to be careful. I don't trust the Kahnen,' Jokah said, so quietly that Jin almost missed it. 'They are about to announce the new FaKrijen. We are expected at the KahnenKeep.'

'What, *now?* Why didn't you say?'

Jin spun and made to follow the rest of the Krijen as they headed into the main street, but Jokah grabbed the back of his wraps. 'Son, you need to change.'

Jin looked down at himself. He was still covered in dried blood, and his wraps hung loose from his arms where the rusty streetling knives had sliced through them.

He raced to the barracks and donned a new set of wraps, sliding fresh daggers into them. He stepped outside to where Meek, Pago, and Jokah were waiting; and together they joined the throngs of Krijen making their way up to the KahnenKeep.

The citizens of Rue lined the streets to watch, old women hanging out of windows and children scurrying across washing lines slung between towers. Everyone looked so thin. It had been a long time since Jin had been in the Left South Side of Rue. It was even drearier than he remembered it.

Every now and then a streetling would step forward from the crowd, a shadow on their face, their skinny frame decorated with homemade weapons. Their eyes would roll over the Krijen, teeth bared, remembering yesterday. But they did not attack, and so the Krijen continued up the street, murmuring quietly to each other.

Jokah was the only one who'd seen the announcement of a new FaKrijen before. 'Oji and I were Squares together,' he told them as they walked. 'I remember when he was chosen. Everyone knew it would be him.'

'Did he suspect it?' Pago asked.

'Oh yes, he knew. He was a different man back then. Oji and I only became friends about a decade or so ago. You youngsters need to remember that I've known him for over fifty years.'

'But you weren't friends as Squares?' Meek asked.

'No. We were not.'

Jokah alluded to an Oji that Jin had never known. The one that Oji himself had told Jin about.

Jin shivered in spite of the heat in his body, the heat from the beating sun, the heat reflecting back up at them off the street. Somehow Oji had known he was going to die at the Celebrations. That's why he'd said all those things the night before they arrived in the city, Jin realised. But why? Oji had more than made up for his mistakes, and now he'd paid with his life.

Jin squeezed his hands into fists, his power mounting again. Filip glanced at him sideways. 'You should really look into that. No one else looks ready to explode at any moment.'

The comment annoyed Jin. How would Filip even know who was a mayj and who wasn't? But Jin couldn't deny he'd been struggling to stay on top of his nerves lately. Being back in Valrue was harder than he'd realised, and he didn't know why. He was constantly fighting the urge to run. But if he ran, it would make him a coward. And a coward he would not be.

'Do they normally pick a new FaKrijen this quickly?' Jin asked, seeking distraction. 'It seems rushed.'

'I suspect the Kahnen already had someone in mind,' Jokah said. 'Any idea who it could be?'

They all shook their heads.

Hours later, they reached the KahnenKeep, the high gates thrown open to a massive black stone courtyard, different from the one Jin had lowered the stage into. Jagged peaks loomed above them, the white stone of the Keep jutting forward from the mountain face, an iridescent facade that contrasted with the black ground. There was a webbed pattern across its surface, like the Split. Despite this, Jin felt no revulsion towards it, or an urge to flee.

He remembered the Great Kahn's gold-webbed sword too. He wasn't sure if he'd noticed anything off-putting about it. He'd been a mess of nerves that day. More than usual anyway.

There was a podium set up directly in front of the KahnenKeep. Krijen filed around it into perfectly curved rows. Jin had never seen so many Krijen at once, even at the Celebrations. They would not all fit inside the courtyard.

Jin and his squad got inside the gates, just barely. Jin spotted a few familiar faces in the crowd, including Nommo, whom he'd been a Square with, and Flit, who smiled at him. Her acknowledgement was nice. Maybe she wasn't scared of him after all.

The courtyard of Krijen stilled as Teal, the KahnenSpeaker, led the Kahnen out of the Keep. He looked barely an inch tall from where Jin stood.

All eight houses were in attendance today, sixty-three Kahnen in total, having yet to replace Lord Oman. The Great Kahn came last, though without his usual blood-red cloak. Instead, he wore white, ironically blending in with the stone behind him, when he'd been so stark at the Celebrations.

Teal walked up to the podium and cleared his throat. A large bronze dish was stuck to the top of it, which he spoke into, making his voice boom.

'Welcome, Krijen of Valrue, to the KahnenKeep. While this is a day of sorrow as we mourn the loss of our great FaKrijen, Oji Mimundmen, it is also a momentous day, for the Kahnen have chosen his successor. First, let us say farewell to the late FaKrijen.'

As one, every Krijen in attendance raised their hands to their clavicles in salute. Jin thought he saw a tear shining on Flit's cheek. The Kahnen did not salute, but they bowed their heads respectfully, as did the Great Kahn.

A minute of silence passed. Teal continued. 'Lord Reider, of the Eighth House, will announce your new FaKrijen.'

Lord Reider strode forward. He looked far more regal than when Jin had seen him yesterday, pale and shaking with fear. But Lord Reider had vouched for him. Jin would remember that.

'Krijen, I cannot express in words the pain that we have suffered since yesterday. Not only did we lose the late FaKrijen, we lost Lord Oman, of the Eighth House. Many of your comrades, your friends, died in defence of their city, and in protection of the People. A terrible shame on those responsible. It is this loss that drove our decision in electing your new leader. We need a FaKrijen who will reassert strength and demand justice. We need a FaKrijen who has already proven to us they are ready to do right by Valrue and make the necessary sacrifices to keep her safe.' Lord Reider paused, turning to look behind him at the Great Kahn, who nodded.

'Krijen,' Lord Reider continued, 'we found that someone. Please step forward, Eden Lavu.'

Flit's face paled as Eden waded through the rows of Krijen and climbed the podium. The Great Kahn swept forward to greet him, grasping their hands together. The new FaKrijen turned to face them, his pride blinding as he stepped up to speak.

'I am most honoured, my Kahnen, by your decision. I will be what Valrue needs, I swear to you. And to you, my Krijen. Let justice not wait another day. We will continue the hunt for the mayj who killed the late FaKrijen. Squad leaders, come with me! Krijen, you will have your orders in an hour. Prepare yourselves to roam.'

A united cheer went up from the hundreds of Krijen in the square, Jin included. He had not forgotten what Flit had said about the man, but Eden also wanted to avenge Oji's murder. If Eden was as vile as Flit had made him out to be, maybe he was just the person they needed to catch this skahk.

As one, the Krijen saluted their new FaKrijen.

An hour later, Pago returned looking grim. Meek stepped forward to meet him. 'What's wrong? What are the orders?'

'It's not the orders,' Pago said. 'The Speaker approached me at the end.' Pago looked over at Jin. 'The Eighth House has requested an immediate audience with you.'

CHAPTER 58:
PAKKER

Felle had lost her mind when the boy hadn't returned. She'd ripped her mirrors from the walls, leaving bloody streaks. Then she'd disembowelled her pillows so that feathers were floating gently down from the ceiling when Pakker stepped into her bedroom.

'Where is he? How can you have lost him?'

'I know exactly where he is,' said Pakker, feeling a touch of annoyance at her assumption. 'That is not the problem. He won't come back.'

Felle convulsed as she spun to face him, her muscles spasming as she lost control. 'THEN MAKE HIM!'

'Listen to me,' Pakker said calmly, staring her down. 'Even if I made him come back, you would not have the same control over him. He would not stay long. I told you. You needed to be kinder.'

'Kinder?' Felle laughed, bells tinkling. 'Kinder? *This*, from a mercenary? And a useless one at that!' She threw a piece of broken mirror at him, which he sidestepped.

Pakker hated this woman. The strength of this emotion surprised him. He'd been surprising himself a lot lately. That wasn't a good thing.

'So,' Felle hissed, 'you're telling me I can't have him?'

'Not in the way that you want.'

'Then kill him.'

Felle did not look beautiful right now. Her angular face was frenzied, and her chest heaved from throwing around her belongings. Her long dark hair was in disarray, her rouge smudged.

'No,' said Pakker.

'No? What do you mean no? You want more coin, is that it?'

'This is not about coin,' Pakker said. He could hardly believe those words came out of his mouth.

'Then tell me what you want!'

'I am not yours to order around,' Pakker said to her, composed. 'Neither is the boy. Go find a new toy.'

Pakker turned and walked away. He even allowed himself a small smile as he listened to Felle's screams, echoing up through the tower.

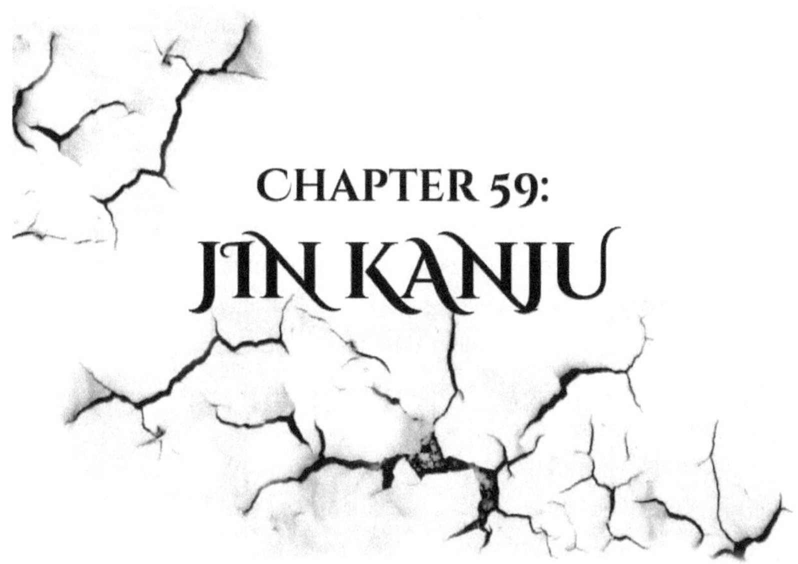

CHAPTER 59:
JIN KANJU

The Red Room was the creepiest thing Jin had ever seen. The velvet on the walls, the long slab of a table, all the way down to the empty throne at the top of the dais, gave him the shivers. And he had plenty of those already.

What made it even worse was that Stolt himself slipped in the door, just before it closed. Jin felt all his muscles knot together around his spine. Stolt made him want to snap his teeth at him, the way Jin remembered the dogs doing when he was little. Maybe he should. It would be rather amusing in the circumstances, Stolt having called him a dog the last time he saw him.

'Jin Kanju,' one of the Kahnen said from behind him. Jin slowly turned around, reluctant to put his back to Stolt. It was hard not to feel trapped, surrounded as he was by Kahnen and padded walls.

'Easy now,' Filip said. Jin carefully unfurled his fists. 'Be polite, at the very least.'

'We wanted to speak with you,' the Kahn said again. Jin didn't know her name. 'Thank you for coming.'

They all looked very stern. Jin's thoughts raced, suddenly convinced they were about to take it all back. They were going to tell him they'd changed their minds and that he was a smear on Valrue and they would string him up like they did all the other skahks –

'I must apologise,' the Kahn continued. 'I failed to introduce myself the other day, as did we all.' She gestured around at the others. The Great Kahn was not there. Jin wasn't sure what that meant.

'That's okay, my lady,' Jin gritted out. 'It was a stressful day.'

The woman tittered, even though Jin hadn't meant it to be amusing. 'My name is Lady Macey,' she said. 'Here you have Lady Elira, Lady Hia, Lord Reider, Lord Salli, and Lord Flynn. Lord Oman, as you know, was sadly taken from us.' She pointed to the empty seat at the end of the cold slab. 'Please sit.'

Jin opened his mouth to decline – he'd much rather stay on his feet – but Filip hissed at him. 'Do it!'

Jin sat, feeling the point of his krije spearing into the chair beneath him. This is why Krijen did not sit on plush cushions. They sat on hard wooden benches and seats without backs.

'You are the mayj from the Deadlands,' said Lady Macey.

Jin couldn't tell if it was a statement or a question, so he said nothing. He didn't like that everyone in the room was looking at him. It made it almost impossible for him not to twitch.

'Your squad leader briefly filled us in on what happened. It sounds rather incredible, if you ask me. And terrifying. You must have been very brave.'

Jin frowned. Was she belittling him? Or was she flirting? It seemed wrong that he couldn't tell.

'After yesterday, it being the *second* time you have showed your loyalty to the Kahnen at great risk to your own life, we felt that a more significant display of our appreciation was in order.'

Filip laughed softly next to Jin, who almost looked at him, before he caught himself. 'She failed to mention the risk to your life was an execution order from *them*,' Filip said.

'It has recently come to our attention that our numbers of KahnenMayjen have diminished significantly. We are in a difficult position. Whilst the Eighth House condemns the use of majik for the greater good, yesterday's devastation proved to us that there are still dangerous himajik individuals at large who pose a threat to our safety, who do not care for our laws. It is essential that we have adequate protection. Fight fire with fire, if you will.' She looked down the table at Jin, who still wasn't sure if he was supposed to reply. He waited.

Eventually, Lady Macey continued. 'It is clear you are himajik yourself. You have the potential to be an asset to both the Kahnen and Krijen. We want you to feel assured that you can harness in the course of your duties, without fear of retribution. We wish to extend an honour title, to reflect this. We would like to make you our first-ever KrijenMayj.'

The Kahnen leant forward towards Jin at this announcement. Clearly, he was supposed to answer now. 'Think before you speak,' Filip warned. Jin took a moment, as advised.

'Thank you,' he said slowly. 'But I'm not sure what that means.'

Lord Flynn smiled at him. 'What it means is that you remain Krijen, under the command of the FaKrijen, but we Kahnen acknowledge that you will use majik to defend against majikal adversaries in the course of your duties.'

'You will harness with great discretion, of course,' Lord Reider added.

Lord Flynn nodded. 'The title is important to distinguish between you and a KahnenMayj, having both a different chain of command and a broader set of skills.'

Jin could feel Stolt seething behind him. Filip snickered.

'What about my squad?'

Lord Flynn frowned. 'What about them?'

'Will I still have one, I mean?'

The lords and ladies looked around at each other. 'KahnenMayjen tend to work alone,' Lady Macey said. 'Working in squads is specific to Krijen because the nature of the job demands it. If it is something that you want . . ?' She turned her head to the side, questioning.

'They really want you to do this,' Filip said. 'They'll give you what you ask for.'

Jin mused on that for a moment. 'I am still Krijen, so I'll remain part of a squad,' he said clearly.

'Of course,' Lady Macey nodded.

'Wait,' said Lord Flynn. 'Authority in the squad rotates. This could be problematic if he is not squad leader. This is why I wanted him as a KahnenMayj,' he said to the other Kahnen. 'He would defer to our command, not to the FaKrijen or whichever Krijen is his squad leader at the time.'

'We do not have the authority to annex Jin from the Krijen,' Lord Reider said.

One of the female Kahnen – Lady Elira, Jin remembered – spoke for the first time. 'Surely Eden would consider it?'

'Even FaKrijen are bound by their own laws. They cannot simply expel Krijen from their numbers without good cause.'

'He has harnessed illegally. Surely that is reason enough –'

'He has since been pardoned by us,' Lord Reider reminded her. 'If we do not pardon Jin, we must execute him. You cannot have it both ways.'

Filip folded his arms. 'I think they've forgotten that you're here,' he muttered. Jin nodded briefly, then stopped, realising what he was doing. No one had noticed.

'All we need to do is ensure that Jin's squad receives the appropriate training and understand our expectations,' Lady Macey said. 'I am aware that this has never been done before, but FaKrijen Eden is open to change. He will support this, I know it.'

Everyone looked expectantly at Jin. He had a question ready. 'Will there be other KrijenMayjen?'

The Kahnen all exchanged glances. Lord Salli frowned deeply.

He looks pretty mad, Jin thought.

'Yeah,' Filip agreed. 'But I've no idea why.'

'This is a very delicate situation,' explained Lady Macey. 'There are almost certainly more Krijen like yourself who it would be in our interest to recruit. However, I am sure you can appreciate that there are challenges we face, given the Eighth House still actively condemn the use of majik. We hope to keep this development discreet. The Krijen are to be informed, of course, but we will not be making an announcement to the People about you just yet.'

'Consider this a trial of sorts,' Lord Reider said. 'There are several of us who need a little more persuading, but I am confident you will do well.'

Filip leant in towards Jin. 'Should we be worried that the Great Kahn isn't here then?'

'I'm not sure what you're all expecting of me,' Jin said, thumbing his daggers under the table. 'I really don't know much about majik. I'm still figuring it out.'

'Do not worry, Jin,' Lady Macey said to him. 'We expected that. That is why we have arranged for you to receive some majikal instruction.'

'From who?' He had a sinking feeling he already knew the answer.

'From me,' Stolt said from behind him.

'Great,' said Filip. 'This is going to be fun.'

CHAPTER 60:
AREN BHA

They hadn't left the dining room all day. For the first time in as long as Aren could remember, there had been no visitors to the house. It seemed the whole city had locked themselves away in fear of falling victim to Oji's killer. If only Aren could reassure them that they were all perfectly safe, because the killer in question was still sitting in her sparring court.

Drax stayed under the tree all day, shuffling only to move himself into the shade which had all but disappeared with the late-afternoon sun. He must be so hot. And hungry.

Sid's face had been a dull mask for the last hour. Aren had no idea what he was thinking. Mae appeared to be struggling against her motherly instincts, on both counts – wanting to protect her family but also feeling guilty for leaving Drax outside, alone. After all, she'd spent years caring for mistreated mayjen children. This must be killing her.

Noel, however, was adamant they would not go near him. Aren knew it was because there were things he understood about majik that they didn't. But given Noel wasn't willing to explain himself, Aren was going with what she knew. And she knew Drax didn't want to kill again. He'd made that much very clear.

Aren's chair scraped the floor as she stood up from the table. 'This is ridiculous,' she said. 'If he's going to hurt us, then we are just dragging out the inevitable.'

Before anyone could object, she headed into the kitchen, grabbing a chunk of cheese, some dried meat, and a waterskin. When she turned around, Sid was in the doorway. 'Aren, please don't,' he said.

'I'll be careful,' she reassured him. 'I'm sick of waiting for something to happen. Surely, no harm can come from offering him food?'

'You have no idea what that boy has been through. You heard what Noel said. We just can't predict what he'll do.'

'So what, you're okay to have him suffer some more? Watch as he starves in our sparring court, or dies from heatstroke?'

'You think we are being cruel?' Her father's tone made Aren hesitate. She focused on him properly, trying to understand. His face was all scrunched up in worry. And hurt. He was struggling with this as well.

'I'm sorry, Pa, that's not what I meant. I know you're scared. I'm scared. But to be honest, Drax seems scared too. I think we might make it worse by leaving him out there. He said he came here to get away from someone. He needs help. So I'm going to help him.'

Aren started towards the door, but Sid held his hands up, pleading. 'Aren, listen to me,' he began in a trembling voice. 'He followed me home. I brought him to us. This is my fault. Just give me some more time to figure it out –'

Aren reached out and touched her father's cheek. He stopped speaking, his wide eyes boring into hers. 'You can't stop me, Pa,' Aren said.

'No – wait!'

Aren gently pushed past her father. If something went wrong, it would be on her, not on him. But Aren knew that Drax wasn't the cold-blooded murderer everyone thought he was. She could feel it in her bones.

Aren slipped straight out under the columns, avoiding the dining room so that Noel wouldn't have another chance to stop her.

Drax watched with dead eyes as she approached. This time, she didn't stop until her shadow covered his face. This close, she could see the white scars up his neck and on the backs of his hands that Sid had mentioned.

Great Kahn save me, Aren thought. What had happened to him?

She settled down in front of Drax. 'I thought you might want some food,' she said, holding out the cheese and dried meat. 'Sorry, I didn't bring a napkin.'

Drax held out his hands, cupped together. She tipped the food into them. He stared down at the meat and cheese for a moment before his eyes flickered to the waterskin. 'Have it, please,' Aren said, holding it out.

Drax dropped the cheese and meat in his lap and gently grasped the waterskin with both hands. His fingers didn't seem to work properly, and he fumbled with the lid.

'Here,' Aren said, taking the waterskin back off him and unscrewing the cap, before giving it back to him. His sleeve slipped down as he tipped the waterskin towards his mouth. Those awful scars went as far up his arms as she could see. He had two distinctive lines around his wrists, the skin raised and discoloured.

Oblivious to her gaze, Drax sculled the whole waterskin and placed it by his side, empty. He looked down at the food in his lap, then back up at Aren, apparently with an unspoken question. 'Yes, you can eat it,' Aren said, frowning. 'You've not seen that sort of food before?'

'Once,' he said. 'Pakker brought it.'

Drax grabbed the whole chunk of cheese and held it up to his mouth, taking a bite. Aren eyed the thick scars around his wrists once more. It looked like someone had tried to cut his hands off, which sort of explained why he couldn't move them properly. Even so, Aren didn't understand why he wouldn't just harness his hands to move the way he wanted. It was perhaps too probing a question, so soon. Instead, she went with another.

'Who is Pakker?'

Drax froze mid-chew. He began to shake, like when he'd begged her not to make him kill again.

Aren backtracked quickly. 'It's okay! Don't tell me. I don't need to know.'

Drax relaxed. He swallowed, then ducked his head into his neck in a strangely defensive pose.

'You can trust me,' Aren said. 'I won't hurt you.'

A tiny frown line appeared between his eyes. 'You won't hurt me,' he repeated.

'No, I won't. You thought I would?'

Drax glanced up at her but did not reply. If Aren wasn't wrong, his expression was vaguely accusatory. He took another bite of the cheese.

'Did you follow my father home? That man in there?'

'Yes.'

'Why?'

Drax cocked his head. 'To get away from Felle.'

'You said that before. But why did you follow my *father?*'

Drax blinked. His mouth fell open a little. He looked over at the dining room and kept his gaze there for the longest time. Then he slowly looked back at Aren. 'He looked kind.'

'Kind?'

'Yes.'

Aren could have laughed. Of all the terrifying reasons they had postulated why Drax had followed Sid home, looking 'kind' was not one of them.

'So you said you're here to get away from Felle. You can't tell me about Pakker, but can you tell me about Felle?'

Drax froze again. 'No.'

'So why mention them if you can't talk about them?'

'Because I want to tell you,' he said. 'But I can't. I'm sorry, I'm sorry, I'm sorry –'

'Shh, it's okay,' Aren said gently. Noel was right, in one way. Drax was rather unpredictable. Aren had no idea why he reacted the way he did to some questions, but not to others. But his behaviour wasn't threatening by any means. It was deferential. But perhaps it was still best to avoid stressing him unnecessarily. She tried a different strategy.

'Do you have anything you want to ask me?'

Drax returned her question with his lifeless stare. His attention on her was so prolonged she felt her cheeks reddening. 'What? What's wrong?'

'No one has asked me that before.'

Aren frowned. She wasn't sure if she was getting anywhere or not. Drax seemed as puzzled by her as she was by him. He was even stranger than Maude. In saying that, Maude would probably know exactly what to ask him, not that she would ever go close enough to do so, as kind as she was. Noel and her parents had briefly discussed it, but none of them could bear the thought of using Maude as an instrument like that. Not unless they had no other choice.

And right now, Aren trusted Drax would not hurt them. She just needed to convince the others. She sat with him in silence while he ate his food, then stood and walked back into her mother's waiting arms, repeating word for word what Drax had said. Noel scowled the entire time, but Aren could see Mae's face lighting up.

'He's not coming in the house, Aren,' Noel said. 'With any luck, he'll be gone in the morning. And if that's the case, I'll submit a report to the Krijen.'

But after the sun had set, Mae helped Aren gather some blankets, which they placed next to an expressionless Drax. Later, when Aren crept back to check on him, she was glad to see he'd curled up on the blankets, sleeping peacefully beneath the stars.

CHAPTER 61:
SID BHA

In spite of Noel's misgivings, Sid agreed with Aren. He did not think the boy – the beggar – whatever he was, was going to hurt them.

But that did not take away from the fact that he'd killed Oji. Sid tossed and turned the whole night, seeing it all over again every time he closed his eyes. Drax would walk up the steps. Oji would step forward as if to welcome him, before he vanished into blood. No one should be able to do that to a person. It was *wrong*.

And if the Krijen came, Drax would likely go quietly. Everyone would suspect that Noel had called them, of course.

The only thing that made Sid hesitate was that Oji had obviously known what was coming. He'd recognised Drax, which was why he'd told the Krijen to stand down. Sid was sure of it. But was that because Oji hadn't realised what Drax was about to do? Possibly. Or was it to spare the Krijen? *That* sounded like something Oji would do.

The sun wasn't quite up as Sid peered out from behind the columns into the sparring court. Of course, Aren was already there, cross-legged in front of Drax, a napkin of food between them. He was sitting on blankets, watching her with a blank expression. Even so, Sid could tell the boy was hanging on her every word. Aren did that to people. Her enthusiasm was entrancing, the way she could stare down every setback with a smile. Sid wished he could be more like his daughter.

Sid's stomach churned with indecision.

In the distance, he heard a knock at the main door. He didn't have the faintest idea who would visit at this early hour. He made his way there, the knocking growing more frantic as he approached.

Sid opened the main door to a whole squad of Krijen with their hands hovering over the hilts of their weapons. Sid's heart skipped a beat. Had Noel called them?

The squad leader stepped forward. 'Sir, we apologise for the intrusion. The FaKrijen has commanded a search of every property in Valrue.'

'The-the FaKrijen?'

'Yes, sir, FaKrijen Eden was elected yesterday.'

Sid's knees became weak. Eden. No, it couldn't be. FaKrijen Eden. How could the Kahnen choose that sadistic man?

'Sir, we wish to enter the property.'

'What . . . what are you searching for?'

'Mayjen youths, sir. Do not fear. We will catch the late FaKrijen's killer.' The squad all saluted at the mention of Oji.

Here was Sid's opportunity to hand over Oji's killer. The Krijen had come of their own accord. He would not have to live with the guilt of calling them after all, or blaming Noel.

But Sid hesitated. He could feel nausea rising up inside of him. If the Krijen took Drax, he would be turned over to Eden. Eden, whose favourite pastime was torture.

Sid couldn't do it. He couldn't hand Drax over to Eden. If Oji were here now, Sid was sure that Oji wouldn't want him to hand Drax over either.

Noel joined Sid in the doorway. 'What is going on?'

'They're searching for Oji's killer,' Sid said quietly.

Noel took one look at Sid's face, then turned to the Krijen. 'I have been doing sweeps since yesterday. No skahk is on this property, I can assure you.'

The squad leader frowned. 'Our orders are to search every property.'

'I heard the murderer was a streetling. What business would a streetling possibly have in our home? It's Rue you should be searching. Not wasting your time here.'

The squad leader met Noel's fierce gaze with his own. 'Sir, we are leaving no stone unturned. I have orders –'

'You do,' said Noel, 'and I know you intend to see them through. But this is the home of the Bha family, Sid Bha being a highly respected member of the Eighth House. The implication of you wanting to search this home astounds me. You will not enter. If the FaKrijen takes issue with this, he can discuss it with the Great Kahn.'

The squad leader looked to Sid, who hoped that no one could tell he was only clinging to the door to stop himself from collapsing in a heap. Krijen could surely smell deception. Sid had no evidence to the contrary.

Blessedly, the squad leader nodded. 'As you wish. Sir, do not fear,' he said to Sid. 'We will catch the mayj responsible.' The Krijen turned and marched back down the path.

Noel prised Sid from the door and closed it behind them.

'Thank you,' Sid whispered to him. 'Eden is the new FaKrijen. I couldn't give Drax to Eden. You *know* what he would do.'

'Sid. The children.'

Sid didn't know what Noel meant.

'The mayjen children,' Noel repeated. 'At Mama Hidel's?'

Realisation smacked into Sid. 'Oh, Great Kahn help us! We must warn them!'

'We would never get them out without being seen.' Noel pinched the bridge of his nose, his eyes squeezed shut. 'And our being there would arouse suspicion right now. We can only hope that the Krijen don't find them.'

Noel lead the way into the sitting room. Sid sat down in a chair, head in his hands. 'Please don't tell Aren,' he said. 'You know she would go.'

'I know.'

Noel sat down too. Normally calm and controlled, Noel was visibly shaking. Sid dreaded having to tell Mae. All they could do was wait.

CHAPTER 62:
PAKKER

Just over one year ago

Pakker was already at the top of the ramparts when the Great Kahn came. He knew the man didn't trust him. And so he shouldn't. Considering that, Pakker couldn't believe what he'd been privy to. In all his time as a mercenary, Pakker had never come across a secret so rich as this.

The Great Kahn was right to be suspicious when the letters from Dijak stopped. He'd shown Pakker the collection he'd intercepted from Dijak's tower for twenty years, a stack of yellowing envelopes that were oily with fingerprints and worn with having been read and folded and read and folded and in some cases, in obvious fits of frustration, torn right down the middle. The Great Kahn had clearly been desperate. That's why he'd hired Pakker and told him truths that would shock even the most hardened of mercenaries.

Pakker had not found it difficult to convince Felle of his value. It had been obvious that she was looking for someone like him, so he'd just put himself in the right place, at the right time, and she'd fallen for it. She'd not been able to seduce him, as she'd so clearly wanted, but upon discovering he had a certain skill set, she was eager to keep him around. Almost immediately, she had let Pakker in on her plan.

The Great Kahn strode towards Pakker across the ramparts, his mouth already open to demand answers. Before he could speak, Pakker held up the letter. 'You will want to read this,' he said. The Great Kahn snatched it from him.

Pakker watched the Great Kahn's expression change from indignation to astonishment. He was surprised the man didn't collapse, shaking, on the ground before him. He did, however, reach out a hand and steady himself on the ramparts.

'This is the latest letter?'

'It's the final letter. Dijak is gone. I don't know where, but he left recently. His things are not dusty. Felle gave me this letter, and I'll need to give it back, so she doesn't grow suspicious,' Pakker said.

'You read this?'

'Naturally.'

The Great Kahn stood up off the ramparts, collecting himself.

'I am old enough to know who Luka is,' Pakker said quietly. 'Felle, it seems, is not. I will need more coin.'

The Great Kahn had the audacity to look angry for a moment. Then he nodded. 'Very well. But you must see that I did not know –'

'I don't care.' Pakker held up the torn-out page. 'Felle gave this to me too. You may read it, but I'll keep it. It would be suspicious if I didn't have it if she asks for it back.'

The Great Kahn took the torn-out page from him. This time, the Great Kahn did stumble back as his eyes danced over the words, his breath catching in gasps. The torn-out page shook in his hand.

'Do . . . do you realise what this means?' The Great Kahn looked up at Pakker. 'Do you realise what this *means?*'

'I do,' Pakker said. 'But our hands are tied. Even I can't find Mandavar.'

'We do not need him,' the Great Kahn said. 'Because I have his son.'

Pakker could count on his hand the number of times he'd been speechless. This was one of them, though he managed to keep himself carefully guarded.

The Great Kahn licked his lips. 'Is Felle aware that Mandavar has a child?'

'She is aware,' Pakker replied. 'Dijak did a poor job of keeping secrets.' Pakker imagined that was how the Great Kahn had found Dijak in the first place. 'Felle asked me to start killing mayjen, to bolster the power,' Pakker said.

'She does not understand how it works?'

'It appears not.'

The Great Kahn nodded. 'So she is not so smart. We can use her.' The Great Kahn looked out over the city, down towards the lake and its empty depths. 'Let me think about this. I will call for you soon.'

Pakker held his hands out to take back the final letter and the torn-out page. For a moment, the Great Kahn looked like he wouldn't relinquish either of them. But he did.

Pakker tucked both into the pocket of his sleeve. He turned to leave, just as the Great Kahn spoke once more.

'If you are going to kill mayjen to placate Felle, feel free to kill the KahnenMayjen. I need only one to keep up appearances. The one called Stolton Ono will do.'

Pakker nodded. The Great Kahn had lost a little of his sanity in all of this. But it did not matter to Pakker. He was getting paid far too much coin. If this was to be the last job he did as a mercenary, it would be a good one indeed.

The Final Letter

I know now why you did what you did. While it pains me greatly to write this truth, I know that you never truly loved me. I was merely a tool for you to exact your revenge. My love for you blinded me to the depths of your despair in losing Him.

It is not out of spite that I have decided to reveal your secret, but out of a sense of duty to the People and – I would be lying to omit it – for my own sanity. I have long suspected you to be a monster, but I did nothing about it. Countless people have since died because I did not act sooner.

But I am not so noble as to take full responsibility for their suffering. You deceived me, cruelly I might add, and for this I despise you. You have warped me so entirely from the person I wished to be.

This hate has given me purpose, which I have not felt for a long time. I will go now, to Him, as I should have done a year ago. I hope desperately that He will know what to do.

As I write this, I grow so angry that I will now make clear this 'thing' that you did. If someone comes upon this letter, I shall rest easier knowing your depravity was wholly unveiled.

You, Mandavar, caused the Unsettlement.

Twenty years ago, back when Valrue was flourishing, the mountain holding her surrounded by lush forests and nothing but prosperity in sight, you discovered a way to lock a segment of your power into the Lake of Valrue.

Over the years, this power segment grew and began to throttle nature. The animals fled or died in their stables, and the trees died back from the base of the mountain, leaving a barren ring that became known as the Deadlands. To this day, the Deadlands continue to grow; there is no end in sight, and the city is turning on itself.

For the longest time I did not know what you had done, not until I came across a torn-out page from a book in my home. I can only assume you stole it from the KahnenLibrary and left it here to prevent anyone from finding it and realising what you had done.

I struggled for a long time with the reason for it all. I tried to justify it, thinking you had made a mistake, that you did not know what you were doing, despite all the clues that kept me up at night.

Thankfully, I have since opened my eyes to the truth.

You forged the Unsettlement as a nonsensical act of malice towards a single individual – Him. You knew it would destroy Valrue and in essence, the man you called Luka. Considering my own disgraceful actions in realising I suffered a similar, poisonous romance, you may think it unfair for me to blame you for acting as you did. But I will take responsibility for doing nothing. I will accept whatever consequences I am due, for foolishly trying to protect you.

You never did. For this reason, I know I am different from you. That is all I need.

Dijak

CHAPTER 63:
PAKKER

The Great Kahn was muttering to himself when Pakker arrived on the ramparts overlooking the city, his impeccable masquerade cracking.

'It is madness to think that just because he is Krijen he will bow to every whim! Has Oji's insurrectious legacy already been forgotten?'

Pakker leant against the stone wall, his arms folded. He waited until the Great Kahn saw him and swept over, his robes blustering about his feet. 'What is it? Why did you call this meeting?'

Pakker stood up off the wall. It was notable that the Great Kahn had survived the Celebrations, though it was obvious how. It had been impossible to miss the stage flying across the city. It had not been Stolt, Pakker knew that much. He would find out, but first, he needed to deal with the priorities.

'The streetlings,' Pakker said. 'Were they part of some plan?'

The Great Kahn sneered at him. 'No.'

So it was that simple, Pakker thought. The Great Kahn hadn't seen their attack coming. That alone would have been enough to infuriate the man. His obsession with control was unparalleled by anyone other than

Felle. But the Great Kahn was not so stupid as her. Something else must have tipped him over the edge.

'Why did you attack the streetling girl?'

'You dare criticise my decisions?'

'I do when they have questionable sense. You and your Kahnen were in the *middle*.'

The Great Kahn growled and looked away. 'She threatened my democracy.'

Pakker couldn't believe what he was hearing. 'You attacked a streetling gang leader because you heard something you didn't like?'

'She made accusations about my Kahnen.'

That gave Pakker pause. It sounded as though the Great Kahn actually thought them unfounded. Pakker understood then just how unhinged the Great Kahn had become.

'I assumed,' Pakker said slowly, 'that you were making it look like you sought vengeance for Oji, to cover your tracks. The boy looked like a streetling from afar. You attacking the girl would have made more sense had you suspected her of working with Drax.'

The Great Kahn said nothing. The thought hadn't even crossed his mind, Pakker realised.

'I have a plan,' the Great Kahn said. 'Why would I complicate it?'

Pakker scowled. He would be upfront about it. 'Your plan isn't going to work. Our hold on the boy is gone.'

'What? How is that possible?'

'Felle has been just as cruel as you were. She has driven him away.'

'Too cruel?' The Great Kahn swelled quickly, his face reddening. 'The word is meaningless to that boy!'

'Apparently not.'

'How could you allow Felle to ruin this? You said she would be easy to manipulate!' The Great Kahn sprayed Pakker with spit as he spoke. Pakker resisted the urge to wipe it off his face.

'I said she was predictable. And she is. She made herself his master, the perfect person to blame, as you wanted. But she did not give the boy what he needed, and I have no more control over Felle than you do.'

'Felle was only ever a prop!' the Great Kahn screamed, his quiet voice straining. 'You were supposed to ensure the power stored in the lake was harnessed! And do not dare lie to me again and tell me he could not do it. I know better than anyone what that boy is capable of!'

'We tried. It wasn't enough.'

'You tried? You *tried?*' The Great Kahn's eyes were popping out of his head. In one swift movement, he swung out his green-and-gold blade and held its point toward Pakker. 'The existence of my city depends on this!'

'Enough,' Pakker snapped, swatting the sword down. 'I'm sick of this puppet show of yours. The strings are broken. It makes no sense to me why you didn't just order the boy to do it yourself from the start.'

'No! No, do you not see?' The Great Kahn's eyes were rolling. 'This is what Mandavar does. He plays games with people. He chose a spell to destroy Valrue because it could only be fixed with majik. He wanted to force my hand, make me use majik in desperation, because he knows how much I hate it!'

'You're insane,' Pakker said.

'If I used the boy, then I would be bending to Mandavar's will! That is why you had to command him, so I was free from Mandavar's game!' The Great Kahn's voice became soft again. 'It goes so much deeper than you realise. The endless depravity of his plan . . . Do you not see it?'

'No, I don't. And I don't understand your logic. You used the boy to kill the FaKrijen. You haven't distanced yourself at all.' It was true, and Pakker relished saying it. Normally he wouldn't get so involved in the twisted delusions of his employers, but he wanted to watch the Great Kahn squirm.

'I did not order him to do it,' the Great Kahn snapped. 'He did it of his own accord. And that was part of *my* plan. Not some sick, manipulative plan of Mandavar's. It was not part of our game!'

Pakker smirked and shook his head. 'No. You can't have it both ways. Drax was a temptation that Mandavar left behind, and you used him, no matter how you look at it.'

The Great Kahn raised his sword again, murder in his eyes. Pakker smacked the sword aside for the second time. Clearly, the Great Kahn didn't see the irony in wielding Mandavar's weapon either.

'Listen to me! I have a new plan, one that doesn't require using majik. Do you want to hear it?'

The Great Kahn shuddered, as though suppressing a violent response. His voice was flat as he replied. 'Go on.'

'In Val, there is a girl who carries a mouse on her person. A living, breathing creature. I've spent a long time thinking about how that's even possible. Perhaps, just maybe, nature has found its own way to correct this majikal perversion. I think the girl can inhibit majik.'

The Great Kahn thought on it for a moment before he scowled. 'An interesting theory, but meaningless. If she was going to make a difference to the Unsettlement, we would have seen it already. This girl is useless to me.'

'Not necessarily. My question,' Pakker continued, 'is what happens if we throw her into the lake?'

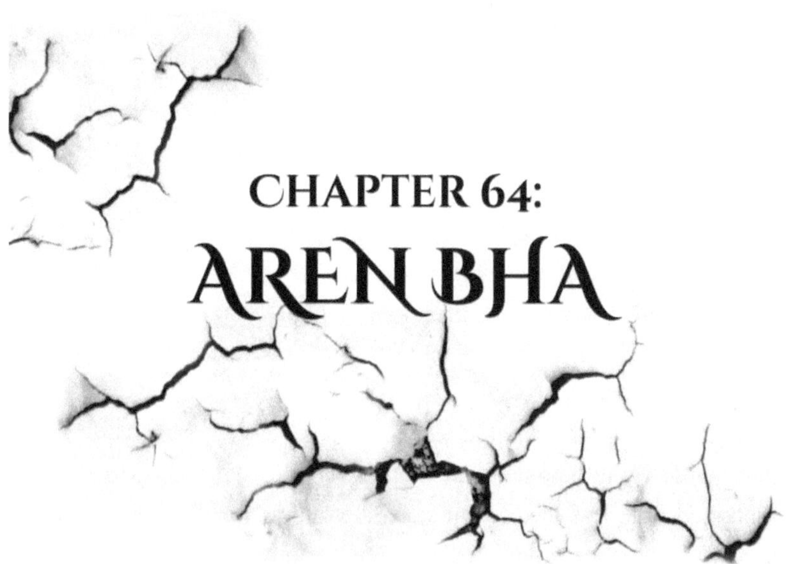

CHAPTER 64:
AREN BHA

The persistent, haunted look on Sid's face scared Aren. At first, she thought it was because of Drax. Knowing her father and his tendency for self-reproach, she resolved to speak to him again about it not being his fault that Drax followed him home.

The very next morning she'd woken to see Sid sitting in the sparring court with Drax who watched him blankly, unafraid. Sid was gesticulating, clearly telling him a story, oblivious to the wonderment of his daughter.

So it wasn't Drax that was bothering him.

Mae had also taken to Drax, her motherly instincts quickly overriding her reservations. She'd even begun making the boy come inside for mealtimes. Drax obeyed, despite an obvious reluctance. He consistently declined to sit in a proffered chair, instead huddling on the wide windowsill with his plate. He'd become unreasonably distressed when Mae had first offered him a knife and fork, so she'd begun cutting up his food for him, watching with a pained expression as he struggled to eat with his mangled hands.

Unlike Mae and Sid, Noel had shown Drax no warmth of any kind. Aren knew she should be grateful he hadn't called the Krijen, but his stubborn insistence that Drax was dangerous was really getting on her nerves. How Noel could reconcile the FaKrijen's brutal murder with Drax, as gentle as he was, was a mystery to her. Most tellingly, Drax had yet to do any majik at all. Aren suspected this, more than anything else, was unnerving Noel.

But despite everything, Noel was willing to keep Drax a secret. He'd turned the maids away again when they'd shown up one morning, pressing a week's pay into their hands. Lana and Tilina left looking slightly baffled, but without complaint. So Aren wasn't ready to give up on convincing Noel just yet.

Even so, it was hard not to feel tense as the days stretched on, unsure about what would happen with Drax. Aren had stopped asking him so many questions and instead had taken her father's lead, sitting with him and chattering about nothing. He listened quietly, but she couldn't tell if he was interested or not. He was incredibly difficult to read. The only frank emotion Drax ever showed was fear, and from seemingly insignificant things.

So the Bha family and Noel all carried on about their day as normally as they could, under Drax's unobtrusive eye. Aren sparred in the morning. Noel baked in the kitchen. Mae even ventured to the markets, and Sid came and went from the KahnenKeep so as to not arouse suspicion.

But after three days, Aren was itching to leave the house. More than anything, she wanted to see Wren. He'd said he would be awhile, but Aren couldn't sleep at night, waiting for him to come through her window. It was torturous.

But Aren also wanted to see Marigold and Bish, and she wanted to see Maude. It was strange that Maude had not shown up on their doorstep already. So one morning when Aren announced at breakfast that she was going to visit the brothel, it came as a great shock when Noel stood up so fast his chair clattered to the floor.

'No! Aren, you will *not!*'

Something shattered by the window. Drax appeared next to Aren's chair, his blue eyes on Noel. They had a curious spark in them. Aren glanced distractedly at Drax before looking back to Noel. 'What's wrong?'

'Sorry, I'm sorry,' Noel said, righting his chair and slowly sitting back down. 'You have such a knack for . . . well . . .' Noel rubbed his temples. Aren had rarely seen Noel look this uncomfortable. 'Look. We will tell you why, but promise you'll stay here.'

'We?'

Mae and Sid were watching her with guarded expressions. So. They'd all been keeping something from her.

'What is it?'

'A few days ago, some Krijen came to the house. They're systematically searching Valrue for him.' Noel's eyes flickered to Drax. 'We sent them away. But from what Sid has heard at the KahnenKeep, they've raided other homes.'

'Oh no,' Aren whispered. 'They discovered the children.'

'Yes.'

Aren was already halfway out of her seat. 'Why didn't you tell me?' she cried. 'Where are they? We have to go help them!'

'Sit down, Aren!' Noel snapped. 'You wonder why we didn't tell you? Because you don't think about consequences!'

Aren paused. 'What?'

'You dive headfirst into everything without thinking about what it might mean, if not for you, then for others!' Noel's words rang about the dining room. He'd never been so harsh with her. But Aren recognised the truth when she heard it.

She lowered herself back into her chair.

'Mama Hidel and her women are in the KahnenKeep dungeons,' Mae said. 'We need time to figure out what is going to be done with them.'

'And the children?'

Noel looked at Aren sadly. Mae leant forward and grabbed Aren's hand, her eyes brimming with tears. 'They killed them, Aren.'

Great Kahn save me, Aren thought. She closed her eyes. How could this have happened?

'We are responsible for this,' Mae said. 'We will do what we can to help Mama and the women. But we mustn't make it worse.'

'Sid has offered to speak to the Great Kahn,' Noel said to Aren. 'But remember, we aren't supposed to know about the children. It makes sense that Sid would seek reprieve on behalf of Mama Hidel, given that their friendship is common knowledge. But we must be careful how we handle this.'

Aren opened her eyes. Drax was watching her face. 'You'll leave Drax out of this?' she asked. Noel, Sid, and Mae all looked at each other.

'You would use him as a bargaining chip?' Aren asked, horrified.

Noel shook his head. 'No. Presenting him to the Kahnen now would incriminate us, and any association with Drax would make it worse for the women. He will remain a secret, for the time being. But I won't make any promises. There is too much at stake.'

Aren turned to her father. 'When are you going to speak with the Great Kahn?'

Sid shifted in his seat. 'Tomorrow.'

Mae gave him a frightened look.

'I can't put it off any longer,' Sid said to her. He looked terribly pale.

Aren felt for her poor, wretched father. She knew he wished that someone else could do this for him. But for once, it had to be him.

'Consequences,' Aren said quietly.

Noel looked up, clearly startled at the bitterness in her voice.

Aren stood up and walked outside into the sunshine. She needed to breathe. Drax ambled along behind her. She walked right out to the stone tree and looked down into the deep pond at her reflection. She was disappointed it had changed so little since a year ago. Her jaw was a little sharper, her arms a little more muscled. Her hair was longer. But that was it.

'Aren,' Drax said. It was the first time he'd said her name. She turned to meet his blank stare.

'Do you understand what's happened, Drax?'

'Something bad.'

'Yes,' Aren said, even though 'bad' was so outrageously lacking. 'Look, Drax. I'm going to be straight with you.'

Drax cocked his head to the side. He didn't understand what she meant.

'I'm going to tell you the truth,' she said clearly. 'But you have to do the same for me.'

Drax pulled his head in a touch, sinking into his shoulders. Fear.

'*Nothing* you say will make me hurt you,' Aren said to him. 'I promise I won't ever hurt you. But you have to be honest with me. Can you do that?'

Drax nodded.

'Why did you kill the FaKrijen?'

'Because he hurt me.'

'FaKrijen Oji hurt you?' The answer had thrown her. 'How?'

Drax tugged his collar down, revealing his scars, layers and layers of cruelty stretched across his chest. There wasn't an inch of unblemished skin.

'FaKrijen Oji did that to you?'

'His Krijen did.'

Aren shook her head, struggling to believe it. Jin was Krijen, as was Bish. Wren had wanted to *be* one. The thought made her shudder. It was definitely better that Wren was Lost.

'How do you know?

'Because the Great Kahn told me.'

'What? When did you meet the Great Kahn?'

'I don't know exactly. Not long ago?' Drax looked frightened. He couldn't answer her question.

'It doesn't matter. Do you know why they hurt you?'

'I didn't really understand it. Something to do with Mandavar.'

'Who is Mandavar?'

'My father.'

Aren made little sense of his answers. But he was being honest, which is what she had asked for.

'I'm sorry I killed the FaKrijen,' Drax said.

Aren gave him a sad smile. 'It's okay. I understand.'

'So you will help me?'

Aren hesitated. 'I'm not sure how,' she admitted. 'But I'll try.'

'If you want me to, I can do majik for you. That's what everyone wants.'

'That's a kind offer, Drax. But right now, I don't need anything.'

'You . . . you don't want it?' Drax was shifting again, his distress now obvious to Aren.

'What's the matter?'

'If you don't want anything, what do I do?'

Aren had no idea what Drax meant by that. 'Um . . . anything you want, I guess. But please don't leave the mansion. You're safe here.'

'So I can stay?'

Aren looked at him, confused. 'Of course you can stay. Do you want to?'

Drax nodded. 'Yes,' he said.

'Okay,' said Aren. Drax had on another vague expression that she couldn't quite figure out. It was almost . . . happy. As happy as anyone could appear, without a smile anyway.

'But if you're going to stay,' Aren said, 'you can't sleep outside anymore.' Drax's face became the unreadable mask again. *Hm, maybe it's defensive,* Aren thought. But she couldn't understand why what she'd said would upset him.

'Okay,' Drax said, his tone defeated. 'I'll sleep with you.'

Aren reeled. '*What?* No, that's not what I meant! I meant we will get you your own room!'

'You . . . you don't want me to sleep with you?'

'By the Great Kahn, no, I don't,' Aren said. 'Sorry,' she added quickly. If anything, Drax looked relieved. Aren didn't know if she should feel offended or not.

'If you don't want me to sleep with you, can I stay outside?'

'Um, sure! I guess. But we have lots of rooms, you know. With beds. Wouldn't you be more comfortable inside?'

'I like the outside.'

Aren looked at his scars again, his shirt still gaping open. It dawned on her that he'd probably spent years of his life locked up. 'Okay,' she said. 'Outside it is.'

Drax stared at her for a moment. 'Thank you,' he said slowly, as though trying the words for the first time. It made Aren sad to think that he was grateful to be allowed to sleep on the ground outside, under a stone tree. What had his life been like?

'Drax, if you need anything at all, you'll tell me, won't you?'

Drax turned his blue, blue eyes on her. 'Okay, Aren,' he said.

CHAPTER 65:
JIN KANJU

Jin returned to the Krijen barracks in a daze, exhausted from sleep deprivation. But even after three days, the entire city searched and every suspect slain, Jin was suffering a restlessness which denied him sleep. Now he had nothing to distract him from Bish's angry words, which echoed over and over and over in his head.

"'Stay away from Aren,'" Filip repeated. "'You're poison.'"

Jin stared up at the slats of the bunk above his head, so very much like the ones in the Squares' barracks. It had been over a year since Jin had harnessed that irritating little nail back into place, for the last time.

'You know, you're lucky Bish hasn't told anyone about what you did at the Dancing Ceremony,' Filip said. 'Can you imagine how bad that would be?'

Jin hadn't harnessed since his meeting with the Kahnen, which should have been fine, but he was twitching all over. After an hour of lying in bed, staring up at the perfectly screwed-in nails, he couldn't bear it any longer.

Jin left the compound and began to run, without majik, up the streets. He couldn't even lift himself to burn off some power because now that he was a KrijenMayj, the Kahnen had made it clear he should refrain from harnessing until told otherwise. The irony of it all.

He also didn't want people watching him. But it was still light outside, and despite his wishes, the streets were full of people who stared as he passed. The Krijen had violated the city, torn through people's homes, ripped screaming children from their parents to see if they would harness under the stress of it all.

He guessed they also stared because it was odd to see a Krijen out alone.

Jin could have got there faster, had he bolstered his muscles – not enough to be noticeable to bystanders, of course – but he tempered himself. Like Bish said, majik was just as damaging as it had always been. Jin shouldn't contribute to the Unsettlement more than necessary. And maybe Jin needed to burn off some physical energy, from his actual muscles. Whatever that meant. He suspected his majik was making it difficult for him to tire his body out, even if his brain was spent. Maybe if he exhausted himself properly, he would sleep better.

Before he knew it, he came upon the bridge. It was a horror to behold. It was lined with strung-up children of every age and inclination. There were children of Val in shined shoes and streetlings in stolen finery and beggars in rags.

They had no hands.

Jin ran on.

Mama Hidel's was a welcome sight as he crossed the darkening street. Jin raced up the steps, stopping dead on the threshold.

It was clear that a struggle had taken place. The lounging chairs were overturned. Shattered glass covered the floor. The whole place reeked of alcohol. The rooms upstairs were dark and empty, some doors ripped from their hinges.

'Shit!'

Jin ran back down the staircase and tossed a chair aside in anger. Could Mama Hidel and Mae have been that stupid? To have continued to harbour those mayjen children, even after majik was declared illegal? Of course they had. Their arrogance on this matter had always been obscene. And Aren couldn't stay out of it, always in over her head, trying to do things she shouldn't.

Jin ran back up the stairs again, going from room to room, checking, double-checking. There was no one.

He burst through the swinging doors of the brothel and ran back to the bridge, scanning the bodies as the sun faded down them. There were only a few of adult size.

Jin hurried over. *No Lottie. No Sari, no Josefina, no Dhuna –*

He reached the end of the row and stopped, shaking his hands out in relief. *No Eliza.*

Jin looked up towards the peak of the mountain in the distance, the KahnenKeep nestled in for the night. The FaKrijen was taking prisoners.

'So much for tempering yourself,' Filip muttered, as Jin poured fire into his legs and began running up the slope into Val, not caring who saw.

CHAPTER 66: AREN BHA

Wren slipped through her window that evening, looking exhausted. It took all of Aren's self-control not to run over and wrap her arms around him. Instead, she stayed back, knowing he was more edgy when he was tired. Wren's long hair was rumpled, and he was filthy. There was dried blood on his clothes, but he didn't seem hurt. It wasn't his.

'What do you need?'

'Food.'

Aren chucked a bread roll at him. He caught it and took a bite.

'What happened out there?'

'Carnage,' Wren replied. 'The Krijen are done.'

'The residents at Turning Point?'

'They're okay. But it wasn't easy.'

'You didn't fight the Krijen, did you?'

Wren shook his head. 'Not much. Luckily, there aren't any mayjen children at the Point right now. But there were a few streetlings who came looking for trouble. The Krijen went after them.' Wren looked wretched. 'I couldn't let the Krijen catch them.'

'You-you saved the streetlings? From the Krijen?'

'I had to. They were just being dumb. They didn't deserve to die for that.'

'Did you know any of the Krijen?'

Wren shook his head. 'No. But they knew what I was. They didn't like it.'

Aren frowned. 'What does that mean?'

Wren shrugged. 'I don't know. We'll wait and see.'

Aren didn't like the sound of that.

'I'm going to wash,' Wren said. Aren nodded towards the door. It was dark inside the house. Everyone was asleep.

While Wren was gone, Aren sat picking at her wrist wraps. She thought about Maude and the women from the brothel, probably lying cold and scared in a dungeon somewhere. And the children. Strung up on the bridge, no doubt. Mae had said that little Clara had been walking, saying her name. Aren wiped her tears. Tears weren't helpful.

When Wren came back, her eyes were dry again. He was clean-shaven, and his hair was wet. Aren watched him contentedly as he settled down on the floor in front of her bed, another bread roll in hand.

'Who is sleeping in your sparring court?'

Oh, right. She'd forgotten Wren would see Drax on his walk through the house. She hesitated. She wanted to tell him; she did. But she honestly didn't know how he would react.

'His name is Drax,' she said slowly.

'Okay. Who is he?'

Best to be cautious, Aren decided. 'Do you trust me, Wren?'

Wren stopped chewing, suddenly suspicious. He forced his mouthful down. 'Why?'

'Do you trust me?'

Wren glowered at her. 'Is that contingent on you telling me more?'

'Yes, it is.'

'Fuck, Aren. You've got me worried now.'

Aren folded her arms, resolute.

Wren knew he had no choice but to back down. 'Fine. Yes,' he conceded, rolling his eyes. 'I trust you.'

'Drax is the mayj that the Krijen are looking for.'

Wren dropped his bread roll. '*What? Aren!*'

'He's not dangerous. He's just scared –'

Wren was already on his feet, daggers in his hands. Aren dashed to stand in front of the door, her hands held up. 'Don't you dare hurt him!'

Wren stared so intently at the door it was as though he was trying to bore a hole in the wood. 'What is he doing here?' Wren hissed. 'What the fuck happened while I was gone?'

'Put your daggers down and I'll tell you.'

Wren did no such thing. Aren stepped forward and prised them from his hands. Wren folded his arms, fuming.

'Drax won't hurt me, or anyone, anymore,' Aren said. 'He needs a safe place, so he is here.'

'You've got to be joking,' said Wren. 'Do your parents know about this? Does Noel?'

Aren nodded. 'Everyone knows.'

'But it's so reckless to have him here! What if the Krijen come?'

'They have done. It was fine. We are the Bha family,' Aren said. 'No one is coming back to check on us.'

'Shit.' Wren shook his head in disbelief. 'Your family is insane.'

'But you won't hurt him?'

'I have no reason to,' Wren said, looking rather annoyed by it. 'But he better not give me one. I suppose there is no point in me asking you to stay away from him?'

'None at all.'

Wren stared at her. Even though he looked angry, Aren felt her heart flutter again. She was so distracted by his attention that she accidentally dropped his daggers. They landed on the floor with a cringe-worthy clatter. Wren's eyes flickered down to them, then back up to her face.

Aren took a step forward. 'Do you know how hard the last three days were?'

Wren didn't reply.

'Do you know how many times I nearly came running out there after you, worried you might be hurt? That you'd scratched yourself and I wasn't there to have your back?'

Wren rolled his eyes. 'Aren, it's not that dire –'

'Never again,' Aren said through clenched teeth. 'Either we go together or not at all.'

'Fine. *Okay*.'

He seemed unusually agreeable tonight. It was tempting. Aren stepped in closer, her eyes lingering on his lips. Maybe –

'Woah,' Wren said, putting a hand to her ribs, locking a gap between them. 'What are you doing?'

'What do you think?'

'You must be joking. You know we can't.'

'I think *won't* is actually your problem.'

'For good reason too.' Wren dropped his arm and took a step back.

Aren made a frustrated noise. 'Have I got this all wrong, again? Am I just making a fool of myself?'

'You're not wrong,' Wren said darkly.

'Then this isn't fair!'

'Of course it's not fucking *fair!* That's the way the fucking world works! People don't always get what they want. Get used to it.'

Aren stared down Wren's furious expression until he turned away, rubbing his temples. But she wasn't giving up. Wren was only denying them this because he thought it was what he was expected to do.

'It's the whole Lost thing, isn't it?' Aren asked. 'Something about Lost Squares not deserving to be happy? Because you're not beholden to that anymore!'

'Yes, I am,' Wren said, turning back to her. 'And if you don't get that by now, then you won't ever get it. But it's not just that. It's also me not wanting to be some sort of replacement for Jin.'

It took a moment for Aren to process what he'd said. '*Huh?*'

'Come on. You must see where I'm coming from.'

'No, I don't.'

'Okay. Here it is then. Everyone knows Jin is in love with you.' Wren paused, waiting to see if Aren was going to say something.

She didn't.

'Back when we were Squares, the whole fifteen fucking years, everything he did revolved around you. And look, I don't know if anything happened between you –'

'It didn't,' Aren said.

'And if it didn't, then you must be crazy. I'm not blind. All of us noticed how the girls looked at him, because he was tall and handsome or whatever. Jin even had that dark, brooding thing going on that you all seem to love.'

Aren smirked. 'Then he's got nothing on you.'

Wren gave her an exasperated look. 'See? You're even making jokes like he did, avoiding the truth. There is something between you, and I'm not getting in the way of that.'

Aren bit her lip. Unfortunately, what Wren said was true, at least the part about how Jin felt about her. Until recently, she'd been oblivious, brushing her family's comments aside as empty teasings, laughing at the insinuation that they would ever be more than friends. She'd assumed she and Jin had never spoken about it because it wasn't worth mentioning.

But now she understood Jin's devotion to their friendship for what it was. She had realised the truth when she began to fall in love herself. With someone else, entirely.

'Whatever Jin feels for me, I'm never going to feel the same.'

'Does he know that?'

'I don't know. But if I ever speak to him again, I'll tell him.'

'What if you change your mind?'

'Do I seem fickle to you?'

'No,' Wren admitted. 'I've never known anyone to be so sure of themselves.' This thought seemed to amuse him, even though he didn't smile. 'But that doesn't negate the other thing,' Wren said quickly. 'The Lost thing.'

'You said you wouldn't coddle me!'

Wren looked taken aback. 'That's not what I'm doing –'

'Yes, it is! We both know that the only person who is going to get hurt if this goes wrong is *me*,' Aren snapped. 'And you think by denying yourself this next part, you're doing what a Lost Square should do; but if you actually intended to do it right, then you would have killed yourself after your Dancing Ceremony!'

Aren gasped, suddenly terrified by the words that had tumbled from her mouth. Surely, this time, she'd pushed too far. Wren would walk out, and she would never see him again.

Wren narrowed his eyes at her. But he didn't move. 'No one else will ever have you,' he said quietly. 'Not if they know you've been with me.'

'I don't care. I don't want anyone else.'

'Right now,' Wren challenged. 'I'll only end up being something you regret.'

'*Enough*,' Aren said vehemently. 'There is nothing you can say to make me change my mind. I want you, Wren, and you seem to want me too, so either act like you mean it or stop pretending because I'm sick to death of trying and getting nowhere!'

Wren was silent.

Not quite believing her own boldness, Aren went to him and stepped heavily into his chest, grabbing fistfuls of his shirt to steady herself. She looked up at him, daring him to push her away.

He didn't. Instead, Wren brought his arms around her, finally holding her the way she'd wanted for so long. Aren closed her eyes and rested her head against his chest because she wanted to feel this moment, the sensation of having him this close.

Slowly, carefully, she ran a hand across his torso and slipped it beneath his shirt, her palm splayed across his bare skin. He felt hot underneath her fingers.

After his heart beat once, Wren's hands moved too, running down her waist until they stopped at the knot that kept her wraps in place. Wren lingered there. Aren couldn't tell if he'd chosen that spot intentionally or if he didn't realise he was taunting her.

Aren breathed in, then out, still listening to his heart as it thrummed just above hers.

'Wren?'

He said nothing.

Done waiting, Aren opened her eyes and lifted her head to see his face. 'Wren! Do you want me or not?'

Wren was already looking at her. 'Fuck yes,' he whispered.

Then he lifted her up, and their lips met, and Aren breathed him in, ripping at his shirt while he tore at her wraps, cursing endlessly at how hard they were to take off.

They fell onto the bed, trailing material and boots. Wren's touch was unreal. The thrill of it crashed into Aren, her skin tingling as his fingers found her nipples, her ribs, the crease atop her thighs.

'Have you done this before?' Aren gasped.

Wren paused, his lips on her collarbone. 'Yes,' he said. He pulled back to look at her. 'You haven't?'

'Is that going to be a problem?'

Wren raised an eyebrow. 'So you were being serious about Jin?'

'Are you kidding me right now?'

Wren gave her another one of his glorious smiles. 'If it's fine by you, it's fine by me.'

Aren pulled his face down to hers.

CHAPTER 67:
JIN KANJU

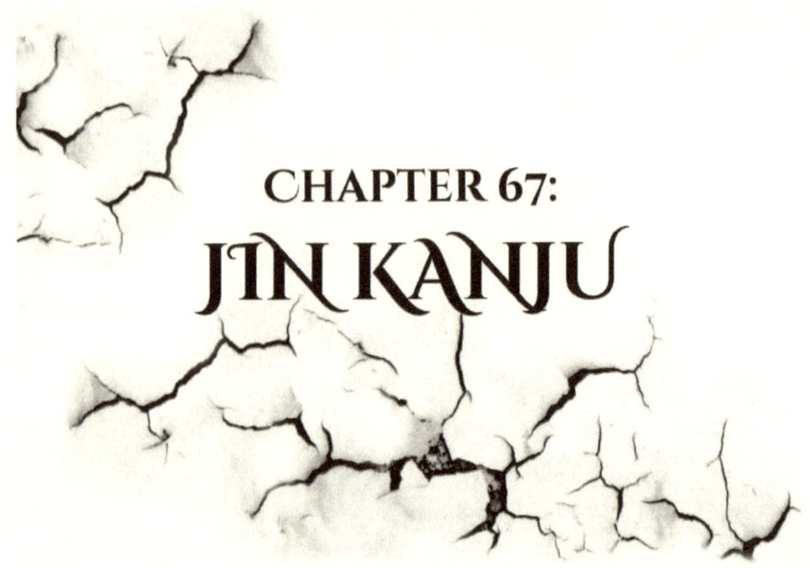

Jin expected to have to force his way into the KahnenKeep dungeons, but the Krijen guards simply stepped aside.

He sprinted up the rows of cells. They were packed full. Some prisoners huddled by the cold walls, their eyes touching on him fleetingly as he passed. Others seemed desperate to press their whole bodies through the bars, their arms hanging through, snatching at anyone who got too close. Some called out to him, but their voices weren't familiar, and he didn't stop for them.

'Lottie? Lottie, where are you? Eliza?'

His yelling roused more prisoners, who yelled back, adding to the cacophony. The dungeons were a maze of endless intersections. He couldn't believe how many cells there were. Surely not all of them were occupied? Jin rounded another corner, panic setting in.

'The Krijen might've strung them up,' Filip said as he followed. 'They might've just put them somewhere else, not on the bridge.'

'Only Lottie can harness,' Jin said, hissing as his blood burned him. 'Eliza isn't a threat anymore, and the others are nomajik. They can't have strung them up –'

'They were hiding mayjen children in the cellar,' Filip said. 'If that doesn't deserve a stringing up, I don't know what does.'

Jin pulled back his fist to punch the dead Square.

'Jin!'

He spun on the spot. Mama Hidel was pressed up against the bars of a cell ahead of him, the terrified faces of her women peering out from behind her. Jin raced towards them.

Eliza was crouched at the back with someone. Jin's gut wrenched as he saw Lottie, both her hands enclosed in a solid iron ball in front of her, manacled to the wall. She wouldn't have a chance of escape. She swayed where she sat, her eyes unfocused, her long blonde hair in matted ribbons. Jin felt a surge of anger. What had they done to her?

'I'm getting you out of here –'

Jin didn't have a key. Not that he needed it. He grabbed the bars of the cell door in his hands, ready to wrench it off its hinges with majik.

'Stop. Wait.' Mama leant through the bars and swatted at his hands. 'You can't let us out.'

'Yes, I can!'

'No. We aren't worth you getting into trouble.'

'But you don't deserve to be here!'

'We knew exactly what we were doing, Jin. Don't you dare open that door! Remember, you're a Krijen now. You can't help us. We broke the law!'

Jin froze. He slowly let go of the bars.

Mama Hidel reached through and grabbed his arm, tugging him towards her. Her eyes shone with fear in the dim. 'Do you know why they took Maude?'

'She was with you?'

'Yes! I'll never forgive myself. She was with us in this cell until a man came and took her, not long ago. Please,' Mama Hidel begged, 'please, find her. I couldn't bear it if anything were to happen to her.'

'Who was the man? Was he Krijen?'

'I don't know. I don't think so. He took her that way –' Mama Hidel pointed down the row of cells that headed deeper into the mountain.

'Going after her will be dangerous,' Filip warned quietly. 'You don't have a clue who took her. You won't be able to harness. You'll feel weak. You might not be able to fight.'

'Don't worry, I'll get her,' Jin promised, squeezing Mama Hidel's hand. 'I'll bring her back.'

Jin pushed off from the bars and headed deeper into the mountain.

CHAPTER 68:
PAKKER

'Who are you?'

The girl was going to die anyway. She deserved the truth.

'My name is Pakker.'

'Pakker,' the girl tried it out on her tongue. It echoed a little way down the dark tunnel ahead of them. The metal lamp squeaked in Pakker's hand as they walked.

'What do you want with me?'

'I'm going to kill you.'

'Why?'

The girl could have been asking how far away the stars were, a mild curiosity with a difficult answer. 'That depends on who you ask.'

She was quiet as she mulled over his response. 'Who should I ask?'

Pakker wondered if he was going to regret killing this girl.

'Me. And the Great Kahn.' Pakker had really come to despise the man, which was why Pakker had kept a trick up his sleeve. Just in case.

'Okay. You first then,' the girl said.

'I want you dead because I get paid for it.'

'Hm.' The girl scratched her head, just below the white headscarf she wore. 'And how much am I worth?'

Pakker made sure to meet her eyes. 'More than what I'm getting,' he said.

They continued down the tunnel, their footsteps now in rhythm with the squeaky lamp. The girl seemed content to walk ahead of him, strolling towards her death.

'Why does the Great Kahn want to kill me?'

'Because he thinks you can save Valrue.'

The girl's eyes grew wide. 'Really? Is it because of my ability?'

So. She knew. 'Yes.'

'I knew it.' The girl rubbed an ink pattern on her chest, just visible above her wraps. Unlike the other patterns on her body, this one was not smudging.

'You're certain I can fix it?'

'Not at all.'

'Oh. Well, do you want to know what I can do? To be sure?'

Pakker stopped walking. The girl clasped her hands together and looked at him expectantly. She was almost the same height as him.

'Tell me.'

'I take away people's majik,' she said, bouncing on the balls of her feet. 'At first, I thought people just didn't like me because I'm Bhouli. But then I realised that most of the people who didn't like me were mayjen. It was hard to figure it out at first because everyone is so secretive, you know?' The girl was breathless, excited.

'What happens when mayjen get close to you?'

'They get all woozy. Some more than others. I reckon it's the himajik ones that feel the worst.'

'You're sure they can't harness around you?'

'I'm sure. When I was with my father in Rue, we were attacked by a streetling mayj. He tried to harness, and I didn't mean to stop us from dying, but his majik didn't work. After that, my mother didn't think I would be safe in Rue anymore, so she sent me to Val.'

'What do you feel when you are near mayjen?'

'Nothing. I can't feel a thing.'

'Even the himajik ones?'

'Nothing.'

'And if they touch you?'

'It feels awful. But not for me, for them. I don't really feel anything at all.'

'That's good.'

'Why?'

Pakker thought about that before answering. 'You are a void of sorts. I think you absorb power from the world around you. Limitlessly, I hope. There is a lot of power in the lake, and we will only have one shot at it.'

'The lake?'

'Yes. A mayj used a spell to trap power in the lake. It grew over time and got out of control. That's what caused the Unsettlement.'

'Wow.'

Pakker had known for just over a year now. It had been a lot to take in, even for him. They walked a little further before the girl spoke again.

'So why do you think we have one shot? You think it will kill me?'

'Probably.'

She nodded. 'I think you're right. So how will it work? The lake is the other way, you know.'

Pakker stopped walking again. He knew he should feel disturbed. The girl had such an unnatural willingness to discuss her own death. She was really quite pleasant to talk to.

'If we go by the lakeside, someone might see. This tunnel opens out to a viewing point that looks out over the lake.'

'You're going to push me off a cliff?'

Pakker nodded, then started walking again. She skipped along behind him. 'That's cold.'

Pakker couldn't help it. He laughed. 'You're not bothered by us talking about this?'

'No. Death is inevitable.'

'Doesn't mean you jump when it comes calling.'

The girl gave him a twisted smile. 'I think Aren would agree with you.'

'Who is Aren?'

'My best friend. She is scared of death.'

'So are most people.'

'Are you?'

Pakker had to think about it for a minute. 'Yes, I guess I am.'

'Why?'

Another difficult question. 'Because there are things I want to do before I die, and I don't know if I'll get to do them.'

The girl clapped her hands. 'Oh, tell me! What are they?'

Pakker had not spoken to anyone like this for the longest time. It was rather cathartic. 'I want to see something more than the inside of this mountain.'

'Do you mean inside of this mountain or *inside* of this mountain?'

'What's the difference?'

The girl was quiet for so long that Pakker wondered if she had finally grown scared, which was why what came out of her mouth next shocked him.

'The Bhouli live inside the mountain, beneath Valrue. We don't tell other people about it, but we welcome them if they come.'

'They live inside the mountain?'

'In tunnels like this. They go all the way under the lake. Other people, the ones who aren't Bhouli, prefer to live on the surface, closer to the sky. I prefer it too. But that's too tempting for most of the Bhouli, you see.'

'If you don't tell people about it, why did you tell me?'

'It's where we went to save us from ourselves. You should go there, because you seem like you need to be saved too.'

Pakker didn't know what to say to that.

CHAPTER 69:
JIN KANJU

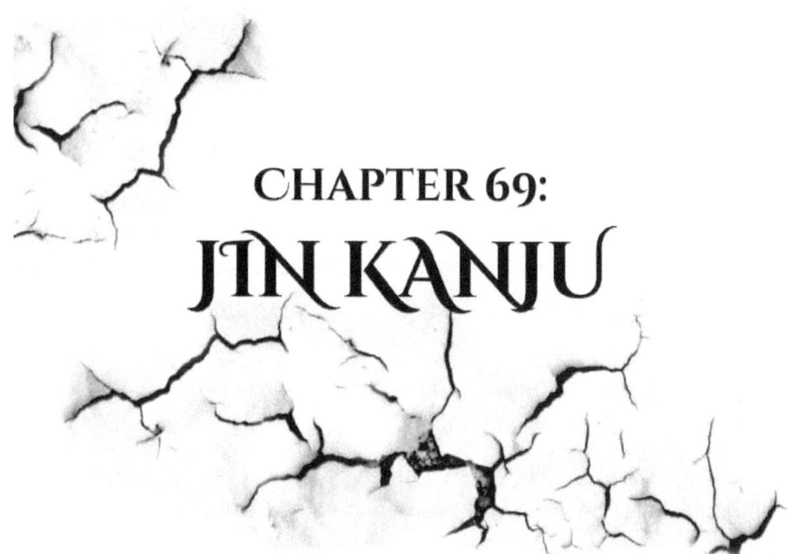

Jin felt Maude before he saw her. For the first time, the sickening, hideous drain on him was a relief. It meant Maude was alive. That, and he thought he might lose himself in these tunnels. At least now he had something to follow.

Against every instinct and Filip's incessant rebukes, he sprinted towards the sensation. A deep ache was corrupting his muscles, accompanied by a coldness in his chest that alarmed him after so many months consumed by fire.

He could see light ahead, the outline of two figures around the same height, one springing along and the other taking careful steps. Jin's fingers were no longer twitching, his nerves all but dead. He did not feel good.

'At least we know that man isn't a mayj,' Filip said, not at all affected by Maude's proximity.

Jin struggled to maintain his pace as stomach acid climbed up his throat. He slowed as much as he dared, a hand slipping to the hilt of one of his daggers. He didn't pull it out. He could barely see straight. If he were to throw it, he had every chance of hitting Maude.

'If you are going to do this,' Filip said, 'remember that above everything else, you're a Krijen. No man in their right mind would fuck with a Krijen. So be sure to act like one.'

As the figures turned towards Jin's staggering footsteps, he pulled out his dagger and threw himself at the man who walked next to Maude.

The man grunted as he crunched sideways into the tunnel wall under Jin's weight, bringing up a hand to deflect Jin's dagger. The sharp tip of it barely missed the man's nose. The lamp the man had been holding clattered to the ground and rolled away, leaving a trail of burning oil.

With shaking muscles, Jin struggled against him. Swallowing the hot saliva that had pooled in his mouth, Jin took a deep breath.

'RUN, MAUDE!'

Jin's cry was so loud in the tunnel that it sent a shock wave right through his weary body. There was a moment of nothing before footsteps began pounding away from them.

With monstrous effort, Jin brought his dagger around and slashed it down towards his adversary's neck. The man grabbed Jin's wrist and pushed his dagger off course, their combined strength embedding it into the wall of the tunnel. The man twisted under Jin and clapped him hard across the ear with his free hand.

Usually, Jin would have seen it coming, but Maude was too close. His eardrum screamed as it burst.

Staggering, Jin left his dagger in the wall and snatched a fistful of the man's clothes, tugging him forward and punching him hard in the face. The man's nose broke under his knuckles, but he still managed to duck under Jin's next swing.

Jin saw the flash of a knife, the sharp chill of it making him gag as it sank between his ribs. The man held onto it, and pressed it in, twisting the blade.

Jin wrapped the man's fist in his own to steady the knife and grabbed him by his hair. He pulled the man's head down and brought his knee up to meet it.

There was a satisfying crack, and Jin set his teeth against the pain as the knife buried deeper between his ribs. It cut a momentary touch of clarity through his fatigue.

Luckily, the knife had a short blade.

Maude was still too close.

Filip stood back, stepping around the pair as they fought, running an antagonising commentary that Jin had no ability to snap back at. 'He's no novice,' Filip said. 'He knows what he's doing. But he's not as strong as you. You'll have him soon, when Maude gets far enough away –'

Jin kicked the man away from him, hissing as the tip of the knife slid free from his flesh, the hilt still clutched in the assailant's hand. Jin snatched another dagger from his wraps and drove forward again, even though he wasn't ready, terrified to give the man a moment of reprieve.

But Jin could feel the nausea subsiding, a subtle warmth in his chest. Or was that just the blood running down his front? The echoing in the tunnel was disorientating him, along with the pain in his ear, the ringing in his head, Filip's nattering –

Jin swung his dagger just as the man threw himself backwards, leaving nothing but a long graze across the man's chest. The man fell back a few extra steps, putting distance between them.

'You've got him now,' Filip said. 'You've got him. He knows it. Look at him –'

A tiny spark fluttered in Jin's chest, then with a sudden roar the heat was back, searing through his veins, branding him from the inside out. Jin raised his empty hand.

This was what the man had been waiting for. Before Jin could harness, the man crossed the distance between them, wrapped both hands tight about Jin's outstretched arm and placed a foot squarely in the middle of his chest, wrenching backwards with all his might.

Jin's shoulder made a loud popping sound, and his power boiled to agony inside him, trapped in the joint of his dislocated arm.

He hit the ground, screaming.

Jin clenched his fist, instinctively trying to stem the majik, his vision blurring. Delirious, he held on as he drowned in the excess of his own power. It spilled over and seeped from his lips, making them burn.

When it died down enough that he could breathe again, Jin found himself on his back, the man straddling his chest. He'd trapped Jin's twisted arm beneath one of his boots and pierced a knife through the palm of Jin's other hand, skewering it to the floor of the tunnel. The man held onto the hilt, keeping it there. Jin hadn't even felt it.

'You,' the man puffed, 'are the Bhouli killer.'

Jin didn't really hear him. He was twitching uncontrollably, fighting against every instinct to harness, because he knew it would only hurt more. Jin slowly lowered his head to the floor, not taking his eyes off the man, who was calmly searching his face for answers.

'Who sent you to kill me?'

When Jin didn't reply, the man spoke again. 'Look, don't make me torture it out of you. It's not something I enjoy doing.'

'No one sent me,' Jin said. It wasn't even a lie. But the man sighed and nudged Jin's arm with his boot. Jin swallowed his scream as best he could, but an awful, strangled sound still came out of his throat and echoed down the tunnel.

'No one sent me!' Jin didn't know how to make the man believe him. 'Who are you? Where were you taking Maude?'

The man gave him a peculiar look. The light from the flames flickered, losing its energy source. They would be plunged into darkness soon.

'That doesn't matter,' the man said. Then, for reasons unknown, he reached out and pressed his hand against Jin's chest. Jin tried to squirm away from his touch, which made the heat flare inside him again, sending him gasping into another wave of pain.

'Shit, son. You're the KrijenMayj too, aren't you? No wonder he wanted the gloves on you.'

Jin's sudden hatred for the word overrode everything else. 'Don't call me son!'

Filip sniffed as he leant over them both. 'What is everyone's obsession with being your father? Don't they know?'

Maude's kidnapper had on the smallest of frowns. 'Did you catch the FaKrijen's killer?'

'What?'

'Did you catch him? You strung up enough children.' The man

sounded strangely bitter.

'You're worried about us hurting streetlings?' Jin gasped. 'That's rich coming from you, isn't it? What were you doing with Maude?'

'Something more useful than what you Krijen were doing. You didn't catch him, did you?'

What was that skahk to this man? 'No,' Jin breathed, hating the truth. 'We didn't.'

The corners of the man's mouth pulled up. 'I'm sorry to hear that.' He didn't sound sorry at all. 'Now, look. It's no bother for me to let you live. But I can't let you keep your majik.'

The man started patting down Jin's wraps. Jin winced as rough hands moved across his ribs. He'd momentarily forgotten he'd been stabbed. It hurt less than everything else.

'But would you rather die, perhaps?' the man asked him. 'A Krijen without hands is like a mayj without hands. Worse than a Bhouli without a purpose.'

The man found the edge of Jin's cleaver, tucked into the wraps on his side. 'I bet you would've cut these off a long time ago if you weren't Krijen,' he said, inclining his head to Jin's hand, the knife still sticking out of his palm. 'That power of yours must be killing you.'

The man started to ease Jin's cleaver from his wraps.

Jin closed his eyes to block out the little stars that were darting around his head. His breath was coming in short, sharp gasps, made harder by the man sitting on his chest, and his power, crushing him.

'This is it, Jin,' Filip said. 'He's given you two shitty choices. Are you going to pick one?'

Jin couldn't remember the choices. He couldn't think straight.

'Are you going to beg for an easy way out, like you did when you were a little boy?'

The man pulled Jin's cleaver free and held it above Jin's skewered hand.

'Or are you going to fight back, for once?'

Jin couldn't stand it any longer. His eyes flew open. 'SHUT UP, FILIP!'

The man leapt to his feet with the cleaver in hand, spinning to face whoever Jin was screaming at. Jin saw his opening.

With cosmic effort, Jin wrenched his skewered hand from the ground and bit down on the hilt of the knife, tearing it loose from his palm as the man turned back to him, surprise on his face.

Jin didn't think. He thrust out his bleeding hand, and with a blast of power that ignited his nerves, he grabbed the man's body with majik and jerked him up into the air, his head cracking into the ceiling of the tunnel.

Jin *felt* the weight of him, and the release of his restless power was solace. The man crashed back down to the floor.

Jin was on his feet, harnessing his shoulder back into place with a flick of his wrist, the relief indescribable.

The man was getting up.

Immediately, Jin harnessed him back up off the floor, lifting the man into the air and holding him suspended there, feeling the wonderful drain of it. The man's eyes went wide, blood trickling from the top of his head.

Raising his other hand, Jin tore the man's heart out with majik. Jin knew it was too much. That swiftrunner had told him so. But he *needed* it.

The forceful tug on his power left him with a void-like furore in his chest that made Jin feel weightless, like he was up by the stars again. For a second, Filip was gone, the ringing was gone, the pain was gone. Then, as Jin let go and the man's heart and body hit the ground, it all came flooding back.

The flames on the floor went out, plunging Jin into darkness. He sagged to the ground, finally feeling the tangible weariness he'd been seeking.

Filip's voice floated over to him. 'First, you kill me, and now I've saved your life. How is that fair?'

Jin sat in the blackness, listening to the sound of air as it flowed in and out of his lungs. Breathing hurt. But it felt good.

'Jin,' Filip said. 'You can't stop now. Go find Maude.'

There was a tiny light at the end of the tunnel. Jin dragged himself to his feet and moved towards it.

CHAPTER 70: MAUDE

The tunnel ended at the lake. It bulged outwards right at the edge, like a little viewing room before the fall. And how far it fell.

If Maude had to guess, she was almost as close to the lake as she was to the stars. If she leant out onto the edge of the cliff, she could see them up above, twinkling at her.

She heard a noise in the tunnel at her back, and she turned to see Jin's tall figure stumbling towards her.

'Maude! It's okay,' Jin called out. 'He's dead now.'

Jin looked terrible. He was all shiny, and even from here, Maude could see veins standing out along his neck and around his temples. One of his hands was bleeding. His black wraps looked wet too. Oh, Jin. What had he done, thinking it was for her?

'Maude, come away from the edge! Aren will have my head if you fall.' Jin fell onto his hands and knees, coughing.

'Don't worry,' Maude reassured him. 'I'll be okay. I don't think I'll feel it from this height.'

Maude looked down at the water. She expected it to be glassy, but it wasn't. It churned, as if it contained a beast that was trying to get free. It was a funny thought, because beasts wouldn't go where there was so much majik.

'What did you say?'

Jin raised his head, squinting up at her. A dark trickle stained one side of his face, coming out of his ear. 'What did you say, Maude? Get away from the edge!'

'Stay back!' Maude called. 'I know I make you feel all wrong.'

As if on cue, Jin vomited all over his hands. Maude felt bad; she did. But it would be over soon, and he would forgive her. Jin, of all people, would get it, because it wouldn't matter to people that he was a mayj anymore. It was almost nice that he was up here with her, to watch it happen.

'It's okay, Jin. I'm doing it for a good reason.'

'Get away from the edge!' Jin sounded scared. He was worried about her dying, of course.

Speaking of, Maude reached inside her wraps and pulled out Mika. The little mouse had been sleeping soundly against her chest. Maude placed her on the ground at her feet. Mika looked up at her with bleary eyes. Mika didn't need to die right now. She had more time in this world.

Maude turned back to Jin. 'The Unsettlement is because of the lake,' she explained. 'There is power locked inside it, and it's poisoning the city. I'm going to release it.'

Silence. Then –

'What? Did that man tell you that?'

'He said I can save Valrue. I'll absorb the power from the lake.'

'What the actual *fuck?*'

Jin must be really upset to be swearing like that. He kept dragging himself towards her.

Maude reached up and unwrapped her headscarf, dropping it on the ground. The warm breeze felt strangely cold against her bare scalp.

'Maude,' Jin cried, 'don't believe what he said! He knew about your ability. He wanted to kill you!'

'Yes.' Maude smiled. 'That's exactly what he told me.' She stepped up to the edge. 'You'll see soon enough.'

'NO!' Jin's voice broke a little. 'Get back!'

'It's okay, Jin, I promise. I'll see you in the stars.'

Maude turned to the lake, putting her toes right up to the edge. Then she closed her eyes, threw her arms wide, and leapt into the ether.

439

CHAPTER 71:
AREN BHA

'It's time to go.'

'You can stay, you know. This bed is big enough for both of us.'

Wren laughed, but he got out of the bed anyway, leaving her twisted in her sheets. 'Too many things to do,' he said.

Well, Aren thought with a sad smile, she could forgive him for that. He had people to protect, after all. There were Turners and streetlings and other criminals to save.

Wren dressed quickly, pulling on his trousers, dragging his shirt over his head. In no time at all, he had his boots tied. He wanted to escape.

Aren suddenly felt very alone. The bed was too big and empty without him. She gathered the sheets around herself and stood up, wandering over to the window so that she wouldn't have to watch as he gathered his things. She was upset with herself, more upset than she knew how to explain, because she couldn't really blame him for wanting to leave. Aren knew she was pushy, and she'd pushed too hard this time. She was kidding herself to think that Wren had time for her, along with everything else.

'Are you coming?'

Aren spun around to face Wren. 'What? You want me to come?'

Wren gave her a strange look. 'Didn't you just say that you'd never let me leave without you again?'

'Oh. Well . . . yes.' Suddenly she felt very self-conscious. To her immense horror, Aren found herself blushing.

'What? What's wrong?'

She hid her face, pulling the sheets up over it. 'Ugh. It's just some silly little rich girl thing,' she said into them.

'Aren,' Wren said.

Aren peeked over the top of the sheets.

'You have never yet failed to tell me' – Wren scooped her wraps up from the floor – 'what's going on inside your head. I rather like it. So don't start now.' He reached out a hand and tugged her towards him.

Wren looked at her so earnestly. Aren wasn't used to him looking at her like that. Mostly he'd stared at the floor or the ceiling or anywhere but at her face when they spoke like this. She kind of wished he would look away, for once. She didn't need to feel any more exposed. It was especially unfair because he was fully dressed, and all she had was a sheet.

Aren was also mortally embarrassed by her thoughts. She wasn't sure if she wanted to share them with Wren.

She hesitated long enough that Wren let her go and took a step back. 'For fuck's sake, what did I do?'

He was upset now. She had to tell him.

'So . . . you've done all that before,' Aren said, waving a hand at the bed, feeling herself blush again.

'You mean sex?'

'Yes. And, I dunno, it's new to me. But I hoped you'd want to stay longer afterwards. You know?'

Aren picked nervously at the sheets scrunched in her hands as she watched Wren's face. He looked confused, his brow crinkling a little. 'You thought I was making a run for it?'

Aren nodded.

Wren let out a breath, that gorgeous smile back on his face. 'You can't be serious. Are you actually accusing me of being opportunistic after I've spent months fending off *your* seductions?'

Aren's knees wobbled in relief. She threw her arms around Wren's neck, dropping the bedsheet she had wrapped around herself. 'And I finally succeeded.' She grinned at him.

'You were very persistent.'

'No regrets about besmirching my honour?'

'*Don't* say that –'

'Sorry, sorry. You're just so fun to tease.'

Wren gently pushed her away and held out her wraps. 'Put these on,' he said. 'Please.'

Aren took her wraps from him and slowly dressed, holding out the loose ends to him. He took them wordlessly, wrapping her up in the same style that the Squares wore. She wondered if he realised there was another way to do it. He looked so different to a Square now. She was sure he'd done that on purpose.

Wren finished tying the knots and scooped his satchel up off the floor. They would pull together a proper disguise for her as they ran. Not that she cared for one anymore.

'Let's go,' Wren said.

Just as Aren stepped onto the windowsill, the stone beneath her feet began to shake. Before she knew what was happening, Wren grabbed her around the waist and pushed her into the corner of the window, steadying himself above her. Her mind flashed back to when he'd saved her at the rally all those months ago.

Suddenly, there was a boom so loud that Aren screamed and covered her ears. Heavy water droplets pelted down upon them, for the briefest of moments, stopping as quickly as they had started. Everything was still.

Wren shook water from his hair, looking startled. 'What the fuck was that?'

'I-I have no idea.'

They both looked up at the sky, but the stars did nothing but twinkle mischievously back. Aren faintly heard her mother calling her name.

'I'll need to speak with them,' Aren said. She looked expectantly up at Wren. 'You'll come with me?'

Wren groaned and shook his head. '*No*, Aren. Have mercy on me. One thing at a time.'

Well, it was worth a shot.

Aren's mother called again, almost right outside her door. Wren slipped around the corner of the window, just out of sight. 'Be quick. I'll wait for you,' came his voice.

Aren fought to keep the smile off her face as she dashed to her door. She knew Wren would wait for her. For now, that was all she needed.

CHAPTER 72: JIN KANJU

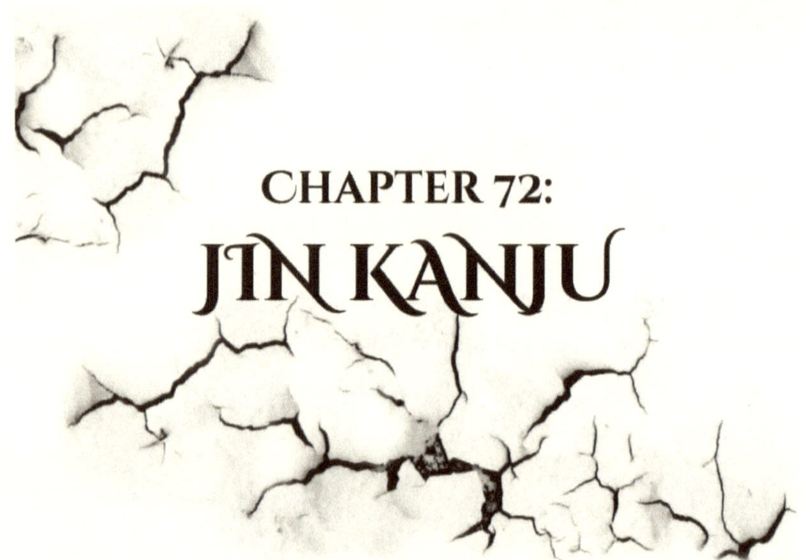

Jin woke to the glare of the dawn, his fingertips cold, for once. He was damp everywhere, as though he'd gone swimming and then lain down to dry. He sat up slowly, every nerve ending protesting against the movement.

Filip stood by the cliff's edge, looking down. 'Something's different.' That was all he said.

Pain bit at Jin's chest, his hand, his head. Always his head. He staggered upright, his fingers to his temples, his mind fuzzy.

Then it all came back to him. The man who took Maude. Maude jumping into oblivion.

Jin howled into his hands, and the sound reverberated across every facet of the mountain crater, crashing right back to him. He'd never felt such a failure in all his life. Even with a father like his, the futile shittiness of this feeling was entirely new.

'Get a grip,' Filip said. 'This wasn't your fault. She jumped all on her own.'

Jin clenched his fists, itching to shove Filip off the cliff after Maude. 'I was so close to her!' he cried. 'All I needed to do was get there –'

'You couldn't have done it. You know you couldn't have touched her. So stop whining. We need to move.' Filip retreated into the tunnel. He stopped and called back when he noticed Jin wasn't following. 'Don't you want to know if it worked?'

Hating himself, Jin started after Filip. It wasn't long before they came across the man's body. There was a bloody hole in his chest. His heart lay a short distance away.

'Overkill,' Filip said, laughing. 'No point wasting perfectly good weapons. Search him.'

Jin knelt down, unable to pull his eyes away from the hole where the man's heart should have been. Not that he'd deserved one. He'd *wanted* to murder a child.

'That's right, don't feel sorry for him,' Filip agreed. 'He's sick in the head for what he tried to do.'

Other than the knife he'd pressed through Jin's palm – which lay a short distance away – the man didn't have any other weapons of his own. Jin felt around the man's arm, finding a strange ridge in his shirt material. He pulled up the man's stiff wrist to get a better look. Something was stitched into a pocket inside the sleeve.

With his dagger that he wrenched from the tunnel wall, Jin slit the stitches and pulled out a square of thick, folded paper. Jin opened it up.

The paper was yellowing, quite old. On it were scrawled words splotched with ink. One edge of the paper was a little rough under the pads of his fingers, as though it had been torn from a book.

Jin began to read.

The Du Bellor Spell

The Du Bellor Spell is unique from the other Spells of Weaving in that it remains purely theoretical. The Du Bellor Spell allows the Weaver to store large amounts of power outside the body for later use. Whilst the spell has great potential, its bonds do not trap power so efficiently as the other spells. Hence, it is described as 'leaky' and burdensome. This feature is a necessary fail-safe to prevent the stored power from becoming devastating.

The spell was theorised by Lili Du Bellor, a female scholar of the Breaker expression, one of the most prominent names in theoretical majik.

I consider the Du Bellor the most intriguing of the spells. Whilst theoretically sound, it has several challenging practicalities:

Firstly, this 'leaky' fail-safe exponentially increases the risk of rapid Turning and subsequent death. In order to maintain the spell, the Weaver must be extraordinarily powerful. Given this combination of both harnessing ability and power has yet to be expressed in a single individual, scholars believe the spell will never go beyond the theoretical stage. Notably, it is hypothesised that if the stored power reaches a certain 'mass' (for lack of a better word), it will become self-sustaining.

Secondly, given the amount of power required in order to become self-sustaining as described above (which would be inadvisable considering the obvious risks), I would think it wise to choose a malleable vessel in which to store the power. If a vessel is exceedingly rigid, such as stone, it is more likely to fracture, wasting the stored power. The trouble is in procuring such a vessel, as it must also be of considerable size for the required 'mass' to be achieved.

Thirdly, it is not clear who could extract the stored power. As powerful mayjen often react poorly to one another in close quarters, it is possible only the caster themselves could extract power from the spell. However, given that mayjen within the same family are majikally compatible and do not experience this 'repulsion', I think it plausible that mayjen who share genetic similarities could extract power from another's spell.

Alas, these questions torment me. There is so much we have yet to learn about majik that for now, I can only dream of all the possibilities. I hope that one day, I will know the answers.

447

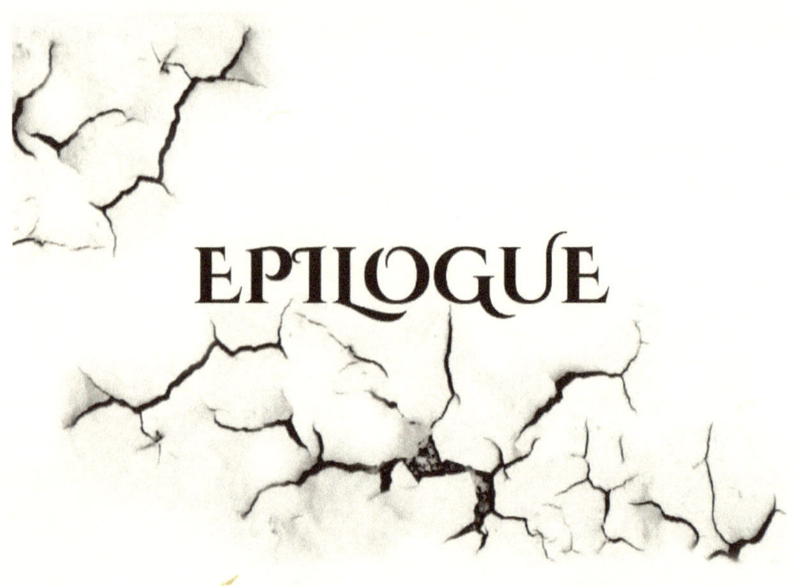

EPILOGUE

A month later, Ruha knew it was the end. She could tell by the way she looked up at the dark roof of the tunnel when her lights were out and the glowworms winked to life, as though the stars themselves were twinkling back at her, tempting her to go. Ruha stared up at them for a moment, letting the feeling sink in. 'Maude, you are wonderful,' she said.

Ruha relit her lights, then reached inside her wraps and pulled out her white headscarf, which she wound around and around her bald head, before tucking the end neatly into place.

It was always hard going up to the city, but Ruha had a purpose, and she would fulfil it because the world depended on it. Or, at least, until she was ready for the next one, beyond the stars.

But not yet, she told herself. It was not her time, though she had to admit she felt a little jealous of Maude, for being able to go so quickly, with such meaning. Ruha could provoke her own death, of course, but her purpose was incomplete enough that she knew she would not deserve it, even if she went to the stars. That was the only thing stopping her.

Ruha shook herself to be rid of those thoughts, then began the long walk upwards. It would take her hours, but it was worth it. As she walked, she pondered on other things. For one, she thought it silly that the people in the city above them believed they lived without a purpose.

Jakki, especially, insisted she did not need one; and she refused to put patterns on her skin. Ruha found it almost laughable because of all the people who were not Bhouli, Jakki was the most driven, the most purpose-filled person Ruha had ever met.

Never mind, Ruha thought. Jakki knew it to be true, deep down. And at least Ruha need not worry about Jakki keeping her chest unblemished. She was a mayj, after all.

Ruha's thoughts kept her busy until she reached the base of the stone steps, indicating the final stretch of her journey up past the lake. She began to climb, stepping on the moisture that collected on the steps.

Soon the glowworms were gone from above her. Ruha was sad to see them go, but it would not be long before she was back. The city was rather foul, and she would spend only what time was needed in the KahnenKeep before returning. She knew exactly where to go, to make sure she would not be seen. She'd done it a hundred times before. It was appalling how blind the people in the city were sometimes. But that was a good thing, for Ruha did not particularly want them to come anymore.

Ruha stopped. She was at the top of the stairs. There was a black stone wall in front of her, blocking the landing. The end.

She reached out her hands towards a round flat stone, almost invisible against the walls, feeling a vague disturbance as she touched it. Despite the majik, the Lockstone still took effort to twist, the wall of rock so thick and heavy. As she heaved, Ruha hoped it would not take long for the sentiment towards majik to change. Change had been what the Bhouli needed, and it was what Valrue needed too.

Slowly, a crack of light appeared as the mountain stone shifted to the side. It was not all that bright, but enough to sting Ruha's eyes, after so long in the dark.

Blinking, Ruha dropped her hands to her sides. She took a deep breath, steeling herself, then stepped out beyond the tunnel. As she turned and twisted the matching Lockstone, heaving the wall back into place, she was already wishing herself back in the dark, where the glowworms winked from above, away from the condemnatory whispers of the People of Valrue who would watch with wary eyes as she passed them.

Death could not come soon enough.

About the Author

Nicole (Coley) Taylor was born in Perth, Western Australia. When she was one year old, her family immigrated to Tāmaki Makaurau, Aotearoa (Auckland, New Zealand), where she grew up as a 'Kiwi'.

Nicole is a Registered Dietitian and practices in both public and private healthcare sectors. She holds a Bachelor of Science (BSc) majoring in Human Nutrition, and a Master of Science in Nutrition and Dietetics from Massey University. Her love of all things edible (particularly salmon) has governed her life, for better or worse.

Over the COVID-19 lockdowns, Nicole started planning her first book (which you now hold in your hand), as well as starting her own nutrition business alongside her work for Te Whatu Ora. She remains happily busy writing, consulting, and eating, and still lives in beautiful Aotearoa with her husband, Sean.

CHARACTER MAP

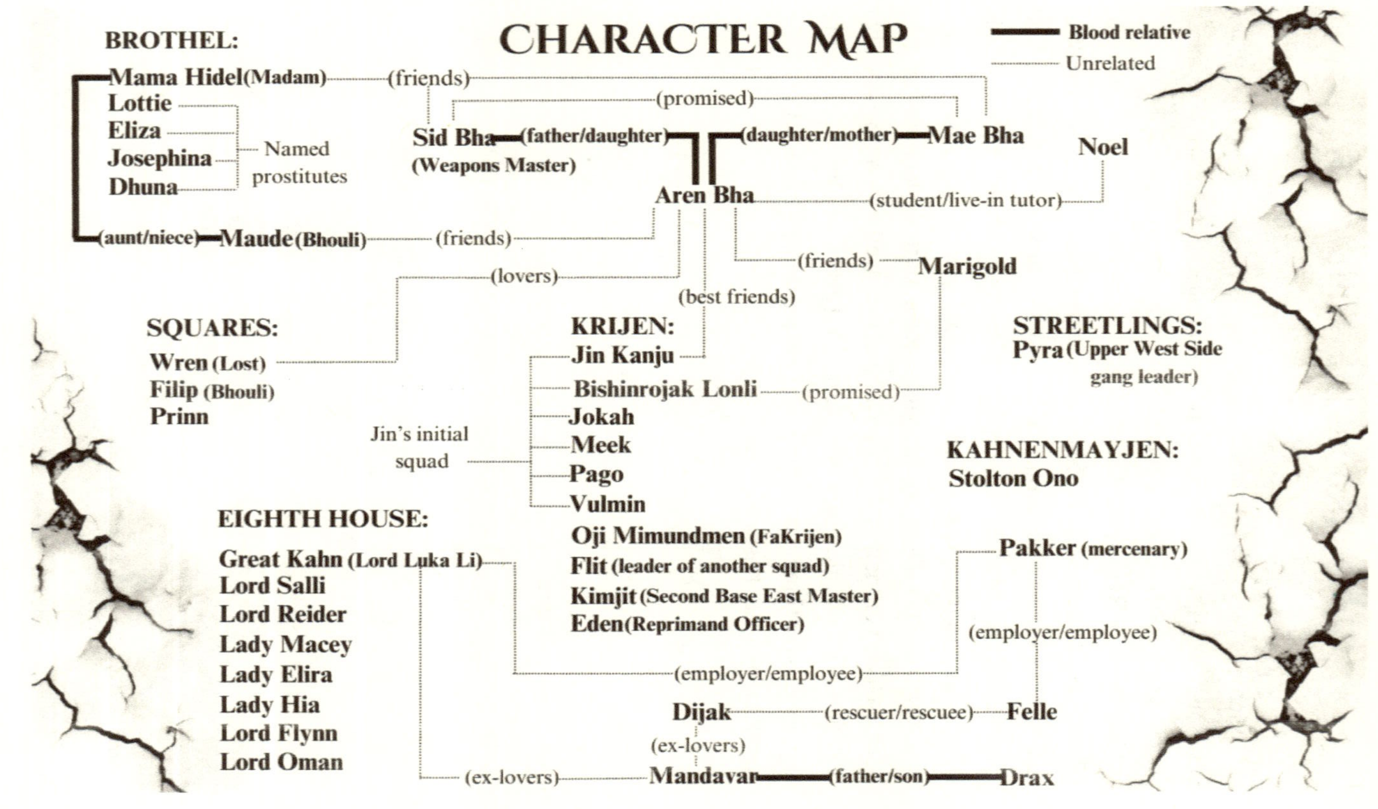